I0599761

A REIGN OF BLOOD

THE SONGS OF BEASTS
BOOK ONE

SAMANTHA GONDA

CONTENTS

The Gods & Goddesses of the Arkts

Amia	Goddess of the Arts
Baldrei	God of the Sun
D'Ak	God of the Harvest
Freyite	Goddess of Love, Beauty & Birth
Kel	God of Death, Darkness & Destruction
Loor	Goddess of the Moon & Wild Things
Rahn	God of the Seas
Svati	Goddess of Kindness
Tsu	God of the Skies and Keeper of Paradise
Voskulle	God of War

A Guide to Lithen Magic

Blooded Lithe	To increase ruthlessness, strength, and speed
Bronze Lithe	To increase strength
Cobalt Lithe	A sleeping aid
Crystal Lithe	To give oxygen
Cyan Lithe	Treats anxiety and calms
Emerald Lithe	To calm, induces euphoria
Fuschia Lithe	To cause euphoria and hallucinations
Plum Lithe	To slow signs of aging on the skin
Silver Lithe	To control the winds
Tawny Lithe	To give energy
Twilight Lithe	Treats pain and numbs
White Lithe	Raw power

CHAPTER I
ARIA

With a gasp of air filling her aching lungs, Aria dug her claws deep into the sand and began to crawl. Inch by inch, she kept moving forward.

Each crawl, each reach of the hand, felt like needles under her nails. The sharp pinch of the crabs beneath her. The razor-like spikes of the sand-dwellers. Her raw limbs. It all hurt, but Aria's life had always been filled with pain. These little scrapes and pinches were nothing more than a match in an inferno. They centered her. Pushed her.

She had to keep going. Forward. Always forward.

She was almost there. Almost out and away from the horrifying black waters filled with the never-ending sounds of spines snapping and claws scraping. The home to the songs of the beasts. They called it the Dahs. The thick, black waters to the southwest of Skierka. And she had to get away, put it behind her. She had to move forward.

An uneasy hunk of oxygen made its way down her throat and into her lungs. Her frantic eyes, used to being filled with salted water, attempted to take in her surroundings as she continued crawling up the black sands of the shore.

From far away, Aria was vaguely aware of this strange land. She forced herself to look, to pay attention. *Be smart. This was important.* She had to do this right if she wanted to survive. But it felt nearly impossible to think, as her body was assaulted by the sudden stillness of the land. The wrongness of it all, the black sand and the harsh, dry air, it hurt.

Disoriented, Aria looked up, shoving her wild hair out of her eyes. Immediately, she noted the riches. The stoned streets. The grandeur of the city lit with fires upon each corner and glossy stone buildings. It had to be Etra. No other land nor city could afford to dress their guards so finely with lush furs and jeweled swords.

Through her blurred vision she saw a golden-haired man standing with a woman in front of a dimly lit tavern. The smell of lust and ale wafted into her nose, mixing with the blood and salt that had been all she'd known.

She could not make out if the couple was able to see her. And Gods, she needed them to see her.

With no other option, Aria's scream pierced through the night. Red-cloaked men ran to her aid. Not far behind them was the golden-haired one, so bright against the black skies like some sort of beacon in her tunnel vision.

"What were you doing in there?" A red-cloaked man cried as he picked her up, taking her away from the black waters.

"You poor creature." He whispered. The man with the hair of the sun had suddenly come crashing into Aria's view. "What's going on, Gustav? Is she okay?" He asked the guard carrying her.

Still gasping for oxygen, Aria found herself unable to form any sort of words or language. And with her adrenaline leaving, the cold was beginning to settle into her bones, making it impossible to form a thought outside of how cold she was. The rush of the pain was ebbing, and Aria knew well enough that soon she would lose consciousness.

"She needs to get to a healer," the man who carried her reported to the man of the sun.

"Is she okay? Where did she come from?" The light-haired one frantically continued.

"My prince, please. Where is your carriage?" The man carrying her asked, as if he sensed the thoughts in her head. So lost in the chaos of it all, it took longer than it usually would for the words to settle on Aria.

Finally snapping to attention, the prince led the one carrying her to his carriage around the corner, where his driver was drinking a pint of ambrosia.

"Cristo, quick! We need to get this girl to the medics." With one look at her dangling in the arms of Gustav, Cristo rushed back into his riding position within seconds. "The infirmary at the palace will be the quickest to treat her, my prince. Is she of trust?"

Prince again.

And with hair of the sun, not black as the Dahs . . . This must be the crown prince then. Raask.

"Yes, just take her now." The prince snapped at Gustav, who laid Aria onto the stiff bench within the carriage, then inspected her once more before laying his cloak against her too cold body. She instantly held onto the warmth and wrapped it around herself in a sort of cocoon.

She didn't miss the look of concern the man gave to the prince as he whispered something that she couldn't quite hear over the loud beating of her own heart. She watched as the prince's lips tightened and he gave a shallow nod, clearly not happy with whatever the other man had said. Whatever was agreed upon, he came closer to her, hand reaching into his pocket to pull out a dark blue powder. Aria immediately understood what was to happen next.

The man quietly apologized before forcing the cobalt lithe up her nose and down her throat, drugging her unconscious. How stupid were these Skierkans? The fools only had to wait a few moments longer before she would have passed out. But go ahead and let them waste the lithe on her, what did she care? As long as she was warm.

When Aria awoke, she immediately knew where she was.

Although she had never entered the Bleached Palace, the stronghold of the Kingdom of Skierka, she could recognize it immediately.

Across the Arkts, everyone had heard tales of the Bleached Palace, forever stained by the infusion of the rawest and most powerful substance in the Arkts: white lithe. All the power built into the very stone of the Palace and the constant buzzing that came with the unholy amount of magic, overpowered every other sensation. Aria threw up almost immediately upon waking. A middle-aged human woman with long, blonde braids and kind eyes had anticipated it, and had a bucket at the ready. She wore a long white skirt and blouse that draped over her body, with a blue band around her right bicep.

"I'm Selby, I'm the lead medic here at the palace." The blonde woman introduced herself as she rubbed circles on Aria's back. "Would you like some cyan?" Selby didn't wait for Aria to verbally accept as she packed the cyan lithe into a pipe. "It helps for getting used to the ... the strength of the Palace."

Aria nodded, she had never used cyan lithe before, but recognized it as an anxiety treatment. Selby lit the pipe with a match before handing it to Aria—who took a deep pull from the vibrant powder. "And what is your name?" Selby asked, still rubbing a hand on Aria's back.

It was a comforting physical sensation, but also alarming. Aria had never enjoyed being touched, especially not by strangers. And she knew from her nearly three decades of life that the injuries she sustained should still be raw and bleeding. But there was no blood dripping down her back. And Selby's warm hand didn't snag against any torn skin either.

They must have mended her.

Did the mending fix the old wounds, too? Would she still bear the scars of her years on her back? Or would it all be gone now that the House of Morlok had intervened?

She should be happy that the pain was gone and that she was healed. But to Aria, it was only another thing to add to the list of grievances against the Morloks, the royal family that ruled the Skierkan Kingdom.

What a shame it was that she needed to be here, among the house that she hated most. Needing their medicine, needing their shelter. She felt disgusted by herself. But what was she to do? Die out there? Maybe it would have been better.

Feeling the effects of the cyan already trickling down her body like a warm oil, she finally answered Selby's question and introduced herself. "I'm Aria."

Selby kept a patient smile and nodded encouragingly at the few words that she spoke. "It's nice to meet you, Aria. Can you tell me what happened to you?"

She wanted to ask Selby the same question.

What *had* happened to her?

What a question to ask someone mere moments after they had clearly lived through a trauma and then ingested a relaxant. Tricky, tricky Morloks. She was about to answer back when she noticed hair of sunlight in the corner of the room. The buzz of the lithe had stopped her from taking in her surroundings when she immediately awoke. It was unlike her, but this was all unlike her anyways.

Aria took one look at the prince and shut her mouth. She continued her gaze across the room, noting the tall ceilings and dozens of colorful potions all neatly organized onto the open shelves behind her. They must not be worried about thieves here at the Palace.

Her gaze landed back onto the prince's even though she fought against it. It was hard not to look at him. He was as handsome as they had said — tall with a fine layer of muscle on his frame. His skin was tanned with undertones of the same gold and bronze that coursed through his hair.

Aria had known beauty; her people were known for it. Beauty among her kind was about as noticeable as wings were among birds. But on the prince, Aria couldn't help but notice his striking features. Full lips. Chiseled jaw. With the calming properties of the cyan fully integrated into her bloodstream now, Aria did not feel self-conscious at all to be staring at the prince.

She only wondered, with his deep blue eyes, what he was seeing when he studied her back. Like most predators, Aria loved to observe, but hated to be watched herself.

"Your highness, if you are going to keep distracting Aria, I am going to have to ask you to leave," Selby said while motioning to the door.

"Excuse me?" The prince asked, obviously not accustomed to being told he was not welcome. "I'm the one who saved her."

His voice was stern and ungiving. It did not match the playful messiness of his hair, nor the ostentatious jewels on his hands.

"He can stay, Selby." Aria ordered, mirroring the same ungiving tone that the prince had used.

His tight face turned smug and slightly amused as Selby's eyes narrowed. "What happened to you, Aria? It will help us plan the best course of action for your recovery if you are honest with us."

More medics entered the room then, all wearing blue ribbons across their arms like Selby. They rushed over to Aria, grabbing at her body like she was a fowl to be prepared for dinner. Selby gave a few of them reprimanding looks as they inspected the stitches that littered various parts of her body and sprayed some kind of black mist onto them that settled onto the skin leaving nothing but a sheen.

Prince Raask grunted in disapproval, "Must she answer these tedious questions just now? Hasn't she been through enough today?" He looked back to her, his gaze warming and gentle as his eyes rested on her. When they moved back towards Selby, they immediately hardened. "The girl is clearly afraid. Let her rest."

Aria went from stricken by the prince's brief kindness to annoyance. "I am not afraid; I am only cold."

Selby nodded, clearly holding back some words, before instructing some of the medics to fetch more blankets and a towel for Aria's hair. "You're going to need to get some rest, Aria. I'm going to mix a dose of cobalt lithe into some tea to help you sleep. You can take it up to your chambers. Cristo, the one who drove your carriage, will take you," Selby told her as she mixed the cobalt lithe into a cup of hot water that one of the younger medics had brought in.

"I can take you," The prince offered.

Aria didn't miss the quick look of surprise that crossed Selby's face. She nodded in answer. If the prince wanted to escort her in his own palace, it wasn't her place to deny him.

One of the younger medics, a young dwarf, brought in a black blanket with the red Morlok crest stitched on it. Aria accepted the blanket, trying not to think of the damned crest she now wrapped tightly around herself before finally getting onto her own two feet. She fought the blush that rushed to her cheeks as she had to place a hand back on the bed to steady herself. It had been ages since she had used her own two legs.

Once she was balanced enough, and the cyan had worked away any embarrassment, Aria quickly gulped down the cobalt tea and handed the mug back to Selby before following the prince out.

Aria did the best she could to take in her surroundings and memorize each pathway and room as she passed through the medical chambers with the prince. Although the medical chambers looked as if they were built to treat an army, it seemed as if she was the only patient.

She watched, with critical eyes, as the medics choked down gallons of hot, tawny lithe for boosts of energy. There was lithe everywhere, they used it for everything. Even the prince himself had the tiniest smudge of fuschia lithe powder underneath his nose, although Aria wasn't certain if others noticed such a detail. Or perhaps they were simply too polite to share that they did in fact see such things. Maybe even too scared to point it out, depending on his temperament, which she had yet to decipher.

She couldn't even begin to understand how they had all grown accustomed to the constant buzzing of the white, lithe bleached walls. The palace was a weapon in itself. A source of power for the

Morloks who supposedly grew a powerful connection to the white lithe upon ascension to the throne. The gift of the Morlok Crown. To anyone else who couldn't tap into its raw power, it was a nasty headache.

Heavy torches ran along the hall, each emblazoned with the Morlok family crest in case anyone were to somehow forget which castle they were in, and which family remained master of the land. She did her best to memorize the route from the medical chamber to her own chamber. But after several flights of stairs, Aria's breathing became heavy, and she was too dizzy to properly assess her surroundings. She'd grown so weak in the past week. Years of muscle packed on from mining the white lithe that the palace used so freely, torturing her body, watching her family and friends die in pursuit of it, what did she have to show for it?

She did her best to hide her obvious panting and wobbly legs, but even a drunken prince could spot her weakness.

"I'm sorry it's such a hike, but you'll see why soon. And trust me, you'll be glad I chose this wing for you." He looked back at Aria to give her a cheeky wink, and his eyes lingered, drifting down. Down. Down. Down. And too slowly, his eyes finally went back up. Meeting her gaze but not with the hunger she expected from a prince, but a look of pity. "Hop on my back," he commanded.

She wanted to spit on him for the insult. But thought better when she remembered that he was a prince of Skierka, the most powerful empire in the entire Arkts and they were in the Morlok's keep.

"Don't be shy," he laughed as he kneeled, exposing his back to her. He must have mistaken her refusal to hop on his back as a coy act of shyness—interesting that he couldn't assess when he had offended a woman. When Aria still didn't jump onto the prince's back, he sent her an impatient look over his shoulder. "Come on. It'll be quicker this way."

With a loud overexaggerated and exasperated sigh, Aria looped her legs one by one around the prince's torso. "Good girl," Raask quipped. She didn't know if she wanted to slap him across the face or laugh. Instead, she settled on digging her heels into his sides.

"Ouch!" He mocked a dramatic injury from her heels in his side.

This time Aria didn't bother biting back her laugh. It hurt coming out, as if her muscles had forgotten how to do such a thing.

After several more flights, the bleached stone turned to some kind of hard, transparent, glass-like material that hummed in a way that told Aria it was also lithe-infused. She had never been so high up before, and for the first time in her life, she was able to look down upon the city of Etra, the capital of Skierka.

It was beautiful in the same way a child with missing teeth was when it smiled, innocent and damaged, and it hurt her chest to look at for too long. From this high tower, the people of Etra seemed so small and so far away, and far more beautiful than they must be up close. How beautiful the world must be from this palace.

"Are you from Etra?" Raask asked, still climbing the stairs at a steady pace.

"I am from the countryside," Aria answered.

Raask whistled, "There's nothing quite like it." The pair finally reached the top of the stairs and stood in front of a heavily-guarded door. The guards of the palace bowed to the prince as Raask strode past without even a look. "You forgot to dismiss them," Aria reminded Raask.

"I've found that eventually they realize that they're dismissed all on their own." Raask continued to carry Aria to the end of the corridor past dozens of other rooms. She carefully scanned the massive stone doors, her eyes hesitating on the locking mechanism above the handles on each door.

"Am I to be a prisoner?" She asked.

"No."

"Will I be locked into my chambers?"

"Yes."

Aria's eyes widened, before Raask erupted into laughter. Apparently locking women in a room was hilarious to him.

"Don't worry. It's only a precaution since you have not been vetted. Tomorrow morning you'll have to answer a few questions, and once you are confirmed to not be a wicked assassin you will be free to roam the palace."

He stopped in front of the room at the end of the hall, he crouched down low and helped her get off his back in a surprisingly gentle manner. His body heat radiated against her like a hot spring, staying close to her as he placed a lithe-tattooed thumb over the locking sphere. The door swung open on its own after only a few moments and Aria couldn't help but gasp at the sight of her rooms.

The chamber was immaculate. The white stone within the room was similar to those in the hallways, but far more polished, sleeker. An oversized down-filled cream couch lay in the center of the room, across from a fire that was already being tended to by human servants.

There was an eating table suitable for an entire family and cupboards filled with food her family would ration out for months. As Aria took in the room, she thought of the sheer number of rooms and halls she had passed on the way to this random chamber so high up. She walked around the room, letting her hand run across the plush furs and cold decorative stones. Aria had only walked past a small portion of the castle, and that had contained dozens of chambers. From the looks of it, the pantry held approximately fifteen jars each of pickled fish, beets, vegetables, even fish eggs. Did they all contain these goods?

Aria's eyes shot to the window on instinct, remembering briefly the too-skinny beggars that had gawked at her when she had first crawled into Etra. How many Skierkan beggars did she see? How many children? Was she only not among them because she had caught the prince's eye?

"Your bed is in the room back there. I had the servants bring up more blankets for you. I hope it is suitable," Raask said. Then, he walked over to the birch table in the center of the room and ripped a piece of bread off of the loaf that lay in the center. "Don't mind me, I am starving after all that ale."

Within the bedroom, the mattress lay on a gigantic marble rock that seemed to come out of the wall somehow. The polish on the stone caught the light, and from any angle of the room the reflection of the light somehow managed to blind and disorient Aria. Layers and layers of scrumptious furs covered the mattress, and pillows of all sizes rested at the head of the bed.

"It'll be suitable."

From the bedroom window, Aria could overlook the Gaulic forest. She watched as the iridescent fairy folk zoomed through the trees underneath.

"Thank you," Aria continued, "I think that I would like to get some rest now."

Raask offered her a piece of the bread that he had brought into the bedroom from the living area, to which Aria declined, eyes lingering on the crumbs falling with each bite.

"Alright, you'll be vetted first thing in the morning. If you need anything, just yell, someone will certainly hear you."

"Goodnight," she whispered before shutting the door behind the prince and the servants, who followed close behind.

Aria was alone again.

It wasn't long after she buried herself under the soft furs that the cobalt tea took over her tired body and she fell into a deep sleep. While she slept, she dreamt of the thick, salty waters of the Dahs and the sound of tails whipping in the darkness.

Sunlight awoke Aria in the early morning. Still groggy from the heavy dose of cobalt she had scarfed down the night before, she was admittedly slow to rise. Although Aria was no stranger to the powers of lithe, she had never before been completely surrounded by charged white lithe for long periods of time. While her body felt overcharged, buzzing with energy caused by the presence of strong magic, it tired her mind out.

After several minutes of coaxing herself into it, Aria got out of bed and out of the warm protection of the heavy blankets. She couldn't help but wobble slightly as she first stood on her two feet.

When Aria finally entered the living area of her chambers, she was shocked to see a steaming loaf of brown bread waiting for her. Someone must have been in the chambers with her recently. Unsure how she could have not awoken by someone entering her rooms, Aria did a quick check of her area to ensure that she was good and truly alone.

After checking each cupboard, under all of the furniture, within the chimney, the entirety of the bathroom and even knocking on the walls of the castle to ensure there were no hollow hiding spots—Aria was sure that she was in fact alone.

Now, comfortable in her solitude, she yanked a chair out from under the grand table and ripped a piece of bread from the brown loaf. And taking the plate of butter she found on the opposite counter, she dug her bread into the cold, salty butter, taking huge globs of it onto each slice of bread. After one or two bites of that, she rummaged around for the salt bin she saw earlier and began sprinkling additional salt onto each bite as well. Aria didn't know if it was because she was starving or if somehow the palace cooks had found a way to use their rich abundance of lithe to make the food more delectable. But it was by far the best bread and butter she had ever had.

Parched from the breakfast, Aria rinsed a mug out from the cupboard and filled it with the hot water sitting above the fire. She drank several mugfuls of water before deciding that she was ready to finally bathe. Peeling her filthy clothes off, she got a good look at the damage done to her body. Her heart dropped down to her liver at the sight of her own self.

Her arms and legs were covered in stitches ranging from the size of a snail to ones that raced up her limbs like a snake. Where she once had carried pounds of muscle, she was now nothing more than bones and gnarly wounds. *This is temporary*, Aria told herself over and over again before putting her clothes into a bucket in the bathroom. She then added warm water and soap and began scrubbing at her clothes while the tub filled with water. When it was finally ready, she slowly lowered herself under.

She watched as the blood from her black hair leaked out into the water in swirls of red ribbons. With great effort, she began to scrub at her bloodstained and throbbing limbs. The strong, suffocating scent of roses and chamomile, that seemed to have been infused within all of the products here at the palace, gave her a clawing headache but she didn't stop her scrubbing.

She did everything that she could to remove all traces of the Dahs from her frail and broken body, unable to bear any reminder of the seas left on herself.

When she was done, she drained the bath and repeated this ritual over and over again until she was able to bathe without her wounds turning the water red. It took three baths before Aria felt clean enough, although she detested the strong floral scents that seemed to reek from her every pore.

Aria stood and stepped out of the bath and slipped a lush, snow-colored robe over her body. It had been left on the counter for her along with a small tub of balm, for her injuries. Selby had even left instructions on how to coat her wounds—they'd thought of everything. The softness of the furry material soothed her wounds as she pressed the water out of her hair and back into the tub to drain. She watched it swirl around like a little tornado as she liberally applied and the soothing balm to her skin, silently thanking the Gods that it wasn't rose scented.

Wishing for another cup of water, Aria stepped out of the bathroom and into the living room. To her shock, a man was sitting at the birch table with a cup of steaming tawny lithe. Without tightening her robe, she took the seat across from him.

"You must be Aria," the man said, his voice thick like the honey added to a too-sour tea.

"And you are?" Aria asked, reaching for a chunk of the bread loaf that the man must have brought up with him. It smelled like cinnamon raisin. More sweetness to hide the bitter, but she wasn't one to complain about an excess of sweets.

"I am the one who will be vetting you this morning," the man answered in a condescendingly short manner.

He lifted the mug of tawny lithe back up to his mouth, and loudly slurped the drink. Aria didn't bother to hide her disgust at the noise. "Would you like some?" the man asked.

She shook her head no as she reached for more of the cinnamon raisin loaf. It was, as suspected, as delicious as it smelled.

The two sat watching each other for a few minutes, falling into a pattern of sorts. The man would loudly slurp his tawny, Aria would snarl her lips in disgust at the Gods-awful noise, in between eating giant slabs of bread and butter. She carefully watched and observed.

His eyes, a rich, dark brown that reminded Aria of the whiskey the elders would drink on the nights of remembrance. Not quite as dark as hers, but almost. His hair, like hers, was as black as the Dahs itself. He was tall, she could tell this even with them both sitting, the man's body towered over her. But where she was previously lean and toned, he was wide with muscle that must have taken years to bulk on.

Some part of her, a nagging itch, couldn't help but think that he was another version of herself. That maybe if she was born in Etra, and as a man, she would be the one to investigate any potential corruption or threats to the Morloks.

It was a deeply unsettling thought for Aria, to consider a realm in which she worked for the Morloks. Protecting them even.

Breaking the silence and her negative spiral of thoughts, Aria finally asked, "So? Are you going to vet me or not?"

The man watched her face, apparently searching for any hint or clue that she was out for blood, before finally proceeding with his questioning. His dark eyes scanned her face like it was a puzzle, mirroring her own gaze. "Why were you in the Dahs?"

"Our ship was attacked a few nights ago."

"How did you survive?"

"I hid in a barrel that was thrown overboard."

The man watched her with an intensity and alertness that matched her own. Did he see in her what she saw in him? Warriors recognize one another. In their body language, their movements. Even if he wasn't built like a tree, she would have recognized his anger in the way that he held his cup too tightly or the lingering assessing stares across the chamber as if he was silently determining which items could be made into weapons. Was he born for battle or sharpened into it?

As she was busy pondering what in this man's childhood made him like her, he was busy preparing for what he obviously thought was the killing blow. "There was no barrel with you when you were found."

Aria loudly sighed. This was tedious and unnecessary and quite frankly, embarrassing on his part. "I was attacked by a sea wraith a few hours before I reached shore." She held up her wrists which did in fact still bear her scars, only no open wounds.

The man raised his eyebrows in disbelief that this woman could survive the brutal attack of a sea wraith. It was a fair assumption, Aria had seen sea wraith victims before. They'd always been returned in pieces. She could only assume he'd seen the shreds of their prey at some point too.

"I stabbed it in the eye with a shard from the barrel," Aria explained.

His brow raised and a brief flash of respect passed across his face. "And that killed the sea wraith?"

Aria shook her head, and looked down to her hands and at her scarred legs. She was grateful to still bear her scars, but she was not stupid. To remain within the walls of the House of Morlok, she needed this man's approval. And right now, this was the only place she could possibly be. There was nothing left for her at home anyways.

Forward. She must move forward. Unfortunately, forward meant the House of Morlok for now. So, she looked down at the history of her life that was etched upon her body in scars, feigning great sadness. And with a swell of pride, and a puff of her chest she finally answered him. "No, but it bled enough to attract the larger sea wraiths. *They* killed it." She paused for a minute and rubbed her wounds, as if she was trying to smoothen out both the aches and the memories. "If you're going to ask me why they didn't kill me, too, I don't know. I wondered the same thing for the long hours until I was finally able to spot land. I didn't even recognize it as the capital until I had been taken into the palace to be treated."

That ought to shut him up.

"Why am I to believe you?" The man asked, finally getting to the point. His dark hair fell across his face as he cocked his head at a slight angle.

Aria ripped another hunk of bread off and took her time chewing it. What could she possibly say to convince this stranger that she was not a threat?

She chewed the thick bread around her mouth and swallowed. "Because I was alone with your prince several times last night." Her eyes narrowed, deciding to not leave any room for ambiguity. "And if I wanted to kill him, I had plenty of chances then."

The man nodded, but she didn't miss that he had stopped scratching at the stubble across his cheeks. "He is not your prince?"

Skullin's Scythe . . .

Her stare grew cold.

"My family are lithe miners," Aria allowed the man to fill in the blanks himself this time. If her family were lithe miners, she must have come from Surtr, "It is still very recent for us, and I sometimes forget that Prince Raask is now my prince."

The tall man nodded and resumed scratching at his chin. She could tell he was figuring out what to make of her being from the one portion of Skierka under rebellion. A newly-acquired colony, rich with the two things the Morloks valued above all else: lithe and slaves.

He finished his glass of tawny, taking his time. "You will be allowed to stay here. But you will be under constant watch from my guards. We will also continue to lock your door at night until sunrise when a guard will come to let you out. Do you accept these terms, or do you wish to return to the Dahs?"

"Make it an hour after sunrise, I won't be up for it anyways."

Aria watched as the man smiled briefly at her joke. The chair groaned as he took his weight off the chair and stood. The man gave her a dismissive nod—not kind but not rude either.

As he walked out of Aria's new chambers, he called over to a guard named Zaries, commanding him to take the first shift with her.

"You never said who you are." Aria asked a moment before her door slammed shut with a heavy thud. From far down the hall Aria heard the man's footsteps growing softer and softer, ignoring her request for his identification.

Chuckling at his abrupt exit and Helk, the strangeness of waking up in the Morlok Palace, Aria excused herself to her bedroom in search of clothes. After deciding upon a long, black silken dress with red lace trimmings and a black fur shawl over top, Aria went back into the living room to search for a pair of suitable shoes to explore the castle in. It was within the closet next to the entrance door that Aria found stacks and stacks of shoes available. It seemed that all of the shoes for females were created to hinder their mobility and comfort. Aria finally settled on a pair of slippers made of a buttery and warm fabric that managed to not upset her shredded feet.

It was then that Aria realized another loaf of cinnamon raisin bread was sitting on the table waiting for her. A tub of heavily salted butter sat next to it. She devoured the bread and watched as the guard had started a fire to warm up the icy room. As she watched the flames flicker, and begin to catch, she was reminded of the king who roamed these very halls. The Fire Monger King, King Morlok. The man who had enslaved her kind. And Aria wondered, if her ancestors had been the ones to have been taken into the palace of Morlok, what would they do?

CHAPTER 2
RAASK

Raask waited for Viggo outside the locked gates of the Cloud Corridors in which Aria was staying. He heard Viggo's signature loud stomps heading towards him long before Viggo actually reached the door.

Although it was quite clear to Raask that Viggo's stomps were the steps of a leader and a warrior, he still couldn't figure out how Viggo was able to remain so remarkably well-hidden during his stealth missions, with steps loud enough to wake the whole keep.

"Can we keep her?" Raask asked jokingly.

Viggo locked the door behind him using only his lithe-tattooed thumb. Members of the royal family, and only the highest leaders in the Skierkan military and guards were tattooed with white lithe on their thumbs. The white star tattoo, created with a combination of ground white lithe and heavy metals, was able to lock and unlock any door in the entire palace.

"She is from Surtr." Viggo said, looking up at Raask's eyes and registering the shock that briefly ran across his face. "You didn't know," Viggo continued.

Raask stiffened, "She told me she was from the countryside."

"Did you bother to ask which countryside?" Viggo asked.

"I assumed Skierka's countryside."

Viggo leaned onto the window behind him as he delicately watched the young Prince. "You know you are to ask for the specifics." Raask ran a hand through his hair and looked out the window down onto Etra in disbelief.

"What did you do with her body?" Raask asked, his voice cold and sad. He wasn't sure why, but the thought of her dying had scared him. Hurt him even. How strange.

Viggo laughed, "I didn't kill her, Raask."

"But she is from Surtr?" Raask bit his lip, Viggo had only just won the war in Surtr so recently. His body was still slightly tanned from battling on the islands.

"And Surtr is no longer our enemy. They are now a part of Skierka," Viggo sighed before continuing. "Her family are lithe miners. I'm guessing she was aboard a lithe cargo ship when her boat was attacked. I'll take a team to look into it this afternoon."

Raask, without Viggo's explicit words, understood this to mean that his brother would once again be leaving the palace for an extended period of time. Time traveled strangely on top of the Dahs, and even then, they couldn't be sure where to find the lithe cargo ship. And they certainly couldn't risk diving for the lithe. The Dahs was filled with more vile creatures than Helk itself. Any lost ships were claimed by the Dahs. And to violate the Dahs would be a death sentence that even Viggo, blessed with the magic of death, wouldn't wish on his greatest enemy.

"So you don't think that she's a rebel?" Raask asked, hoping for a window into his brother's thoughts. As they grew older, and Viggo began to rise in ranks in the military, while Raask prepared for a life as king, he began to receive fewer and fewer windows into the world of his brother. His first friend. His only family left, really.

"Did you?"

Raask knew Viggo was testing him. "No." Of course he knew. He was always being tested. And he didn't have a good reason to believe she wasn't a rebel, only that he had fallen asleep thinking about the girl who crawled out of the Dahs. The girl with a back full of the same whipping scars as his, was it her father who did it to her too?

"I didn't think so either. But to be safe we will be locking her door when she goes to bed at night and unlocking it at eight in the morning. She will also be escorted around the palace with a guard at all times."

Raask nodded. Although he thought it was overkill to keep Aria so heavily guarded, he knew better than to question Viggo's orders "I'll ask her why she didn't say she was from Surtr last night."

With the recent conquest of Surtr, it was essential that the palace did everything they could to ensure confidence from the Surtrians. "We don't want to add any fuel to the uprisings." He paused for a moment before finding the right words.

"Make her comfortable enough here so that when she returns to Surtr she will tell stories of our generosity and kindness."

With an eagerness to keep his brother's respect, Raask began to unlock the door to Aria's corridors. With a palace of treasures and Raask himself, he was certain it would be easy to keep a Surtrian girl pleased.

"Where are you going?" Viggo asked. "Did you forget about your training?"

Raask smirked, "Of course not." Raask had always hated his combat training and diplomatic classes, but as the second son to the King it was his responsibility to lead the kingdom. And as the first son of the king, it was Viggo's responsibility to lead the army. An army that was seemingly constantly at war trying to conquer another foreign land. He hardly ever got to train with Viggo himself anymore.

"Come brother, we'll start with a jog to the training grounds," called Viggo, as he was already several steps ahead. Raask didn't miss the smile he heard in his brother's voice.

CHAPTER 3
ARIA

Zaries, the guard assigned to Aria, was annoyingly silent. Aria had tried several times to engage in conversation with the pudgy guard, only to be met with empty stares. Eventually she had given up and took to making cup after cup of tea. So far, she had tried peppermint, a tea of lavender, and even a lemon tea. But her favorite was a surprisingly spicy black tea that filled the room with an irresistible licorice aroma. She offered one to Zaries, who of course declined with silence.

Aria took her cup of tea over to the bookshelf. There weren't many books available to her growing up. She remembered having to share her school textbooks with her sister as a child. And when she was older, she would spend the occasional afternoon reading the same four children's books to the other children, over and over again. Although reading was taught to even the poorest of Skierkan children, in her clan only the wealthiest of families were able to teach their children how to read. Even a bookshelf of this size would have meant the world to the families of her clan. And here was a fully stocked bookshelf, one of hundreds in rooms that were hardly used.

She ran her fingers across the spines, and breathed in the scent of the old books. They smelled of dust and decay as they sat rotting in the palace of Morlok. Aria chose a pink book with a half-naked satyr caressing a young witch on the cover. She had never seen a book like it. After picking it up, she caught Zaries rolling his eyes out of the corner of her view.

"What?" Aria teased, "You don't like the *His Sweet Hooves* series?"

"My sister reads that kind of garbage," Zaries mumbled.

Aria laughed, "I think I'd like your sister."

"Yeah, you probably would, Miss. She's married to a wraithkin though," Zaries's face twisted at the word "wraithkin". Aria had heard of the wraithkins, but had only dealt with them occasionally. They were an ancient tribe that believed in living in harmony among the wraiths.

"Do they have a wraith?" Aria asked, she was unsure if it was just stories or the truth about the secret ways they used to tame the wraiths. She had even heard crazy stories of wraithkins riding their bonded wraiths..

"Gods, no," He laughed.

Aria clicked her tongue and opened the pink book that Zaries called garbage. Curling up against the soft white fabric of the couch, Aria began to read. She was completely entranced in the melodramatic book when Zaries's incessant coughing distracted Aria, causing her to re-read the same paragraph three times before she decided to make Zaries a cup of tea.

She wandered over to the kitchen and poured him and herself another cup of the spicy licorice tea into two large musg with lids. "I am allowed to leave these chambers, am I not?" Aria asked Zaries as she watched over the Gaulic forest out the window. Zaries thanked her and loudly gulped the hot tea. Aria cringed at the noise.

"Yes, as long as you are with an escort." Zaries followed Aria's line of sight, "Although I will certainly not be escorting you through the Gaulic."

Aria snickered before taking a few more generous sips of her tea. "You don't enjoy the forest?"

Zaries let out an exaggerated scoff at Aria's question. "Do I enjoy the forest?" He repeated her question back to her in disbelief. "No, I do not enjoy the feeling of constantly being watched at the very least or being hunted at the very most!"

Aria turned to look at Zaries, her eyes sparkling with snark. "I don't know if I am relieved or upset that the Palace of Morlok has so quickly decided that I am harmless enough to be assigned with such a cowardly guard." Zaries's eyes lowered as he let out an exasperated snort.

"I will have you know that my father, his father and *his father* have all bravely served the Morlok name." Zaries huffed.

"Oh please, Z. I was just teasing you. Now please be a dear and take me on a tour of the palace." Aria said sweetly.

After huffing yet another time, Zaries opened the door to the hallway for Aria. "Are you sure you don't want to change out of those slippers, Miss Aria?" Zaries asked, heavily implying that it was improper wear for the palace. Aria looked down at her sore and bloated feet. In defeat, she silently waddled over to the shoes and switched her cloud-like slippers with a pair of black leather pointed boots. After reluctantly sliding her feet into the constricting shoes, she tightened the fur shawl around her shoulders and followed Zaries into the halls of the enemy's keep.

CHAPTER 4
RAASK

Raask's legs were sore. After running to the grounds with Viggo, he had spent the rest of the morning enduring a grueling training session. It was a combat day, which meant that he spent half the time on hand-to-hand combat, in different scenarios.

He practiced in the hot spring, up in the trees, and in the dirt. Then he trained different weaponry with the Vermilli. He even went a few rounds against several Vermilli, as Viggo watched and threw out critiques. At the end, Viggo left to gather his squad to check out the boat wreck Aria must have come in on, and had instructed Raask to run along the shore of the Dahs until he couldn't see Viggo's ship anymore, and then to run all the way back to the palace.

Before parting ways, Raask held onto him in a tight hug that he was certain made his brother uncomfortable. Raask, who had not once ever felt self-conscious about showing love for his brother, smirked, enjoying the torture. And Viggo, who silently held him in the nights of his youth after terrifying nightmares had awoken him screaming, let Raask hold onto him without complaint for a few moments more.

It never bothered Raask that Viggo was not the type to tell him with words how much he loved him. It never even bothered Raask that Viggo couldn't accept a hug without going stiff. Viggo was his brother. The one he was constantly trying to emulate. The brother who was forced to act as his father as theirs was busy causing mass destruction and building empires.

Viggo would not tell Raask he loved him, or that he would come back as soon as he possibly could. Instead, he would make sure his swords were sharpened before he left and that his left hook wasn't sagging as it always tended to.

"Ferr bjort deh li." The ancient Skierkan words caught Raask off guard. It took him a moment to remember the meaning. *Walk well on the ice.* In the cold winters of Skierka, the land transforms from vibrant and lush greenery to a barren desert of ice and snow. To tell a Skierkan to walk well on the ice was to remind them to remember their family at times of war. To remember that if they were to misstep in battle, their family would be the ones to hurt. It meant to be cautious. And coming from Viggo, it meant *I love you.*

One of their ancestors had banned the phrase long ago, as they believed a soldier should only worry about the greatness of their kingdom. To die in the glory of battle was a great honor for a Skierkan. To tell them to be careful would be an insult.

Odd, that Viggo chose the statement as his goodbye.

Raask's eyes narrowed onto his older brother, who was always so clever and always testing him, trying to figure out what it meant. Unable to figure it out, he whispered it back in the modern Skierkan tongue, "Walk well on the ice, brother." They patted each other once on their shoulders and Raask turned to complete his run by the Dahs as his brother turned to collect his team to investigate Aria's shipwreck.

He hated running along the Dahs. He did it every day, rain or shine. But today was worse, of course, knowing that he was saying goodbye to his brother mere weeks after he had just come home. He was too overcome with grief to even notice the general eerie feeling of being watched from the dark waters of the Dahs.

He ran. And ran. And ran. Long after his brother's ship left his eyesight, he continued to run, until his lungs were nothing more than a burnt ember and he was too tired to worry about the loneliness he felt deep within his chest each time his brother left. A tumor. An old ache. An old friend even. Loneliness was something he was no stranger to here at the Palace of Morlok.

Running himself ragged during his training was the only thing that helped, although he would never admit it to his brother or his trainers. Instead, he enjoyed playing the role of the mischievously charming prince who hated and resented his trainings.

After many hours of running, and his legs having almost completely given up moving, Raask finally reentered the grounds of the palace and made a beeline to the medic chambers. The medics knew to expect him. They had a cup of tawny lithe and several ointments at the ready. He grabbed the concoction of soothing and strengthening lithe lotions, and drank his tawny as he quickly headed out and up to his own chambers, past a group of young medics in training. He gave them a quick wave and heard them giggling as he rushed past, not in the mood for any politics at the moment.

The walk up the hundred or so steps to his chambers was particularly brutal after the day's training session, but the cup of tawny gave him just the right amount of energy to make it all the way up. Thank the Gods for tawny. It's sweet bitterness and the rush of energy it gave him. Pure luxury.

Raask pressed his white lithe-tattooed thumb to unlock the heavy bronze doorknob of his own tower. He kicked the door shut behind him and hurried to the bathroom, not wanting to waste any of the precious tawny energy that he still had. Once in the bathroom, he drew the curtains open for proper lighting and inspected himself in the mirror. His long golden hair was covered in mud. His clothes were saturated with blood, both from his own busted lip and the Vermilli he sparred with.

Carefully, he peeled his musty clothes off and threw them into the basket by the door, before heading to the shower to start the hot water. As the bathroom filled with steam, Raask strutted back to the mirror. His jaw tightened as he blankly stared into his own blue-gray eyes. Like the sun's rays on a cloudless day, his eyes held a promise of joy and laughter. He grunted in dissatisfaction.

His mother's eyes were a similar shade. But where Raask's gaze held softness, hers held power. She was a frostbitten morning and the deadly current of the Incarno river all rolled into one. While Raask knew her as a loving and doting mother, who would rub his head when he was sick and listen intently to his neverending thoughts when he was cheerful. He publicly knew her as the almighty Queen of Skierka—the domineering authoritarian by nature who would choose kindness only for her family. Raask had to choose to look strong, it didn't come as naturally for him as it did his mother, brother or even father for that matter. After schooling his features into his own harsh gaze, he locked his facial muscles in and took a shower.

Once Raask was showered, he applied a thick coating of the medic-made healing ointment he'd grabbed earlier and put on his red long sleeved shirt with a white fur over top. Even though it was the summer, the great swathes of white lithe-bleached walls that built the palace, combined with the location on top of the hill, ensured that the palace was always cold.

He left the top of his red shirt unbuttoned, allowing for the Morlok crest inked on his chest to remain visible. The black sketch of a raven against a full moon sat proudly on his chest. In half a year's time, if Raask were to successfully pass his royal trials, the tattoo would be outlined with lithe-infused ink and Raask would be allowed to demonstrate the raw powers heralding from the Morlok blood, fine-tuned with the amplifier of the lithe-infused crest. Tattooing with white-lithe was illegal to all except the Morloks and the highest members of their court. It amplified any magic already within an individual exponentially.

While the tradition stated to wait until the passing of the trials, it was no secret to the people of Skierka that the royal family trained, from a young age, the ability to wield magic with the aid of lithe. In fact, training before the trials was the only way to possibly pass them. But that remained a secret to all but the Morloks and the highest-ranking members of their court. If the public knew that their training was essential to passing the trials, they would see a crack in the Palace of Morlok. And history had shown time and time again that visible cracks led to downfalls. So, they were trained to hide any weaknesses since they were young children, repeatedly taught that to show a weakness would be to condemn their kingdom.

Thus, for the most part, Raask' and Viggo's lithe training always occurred after dark, far from the gaze of the God of the sun and justice, Baldrei.

Raask had always thought that waiting until dark was a load of crap, but it wasn't really up to him anyway. He also thought that it was a gigantic load of crap for Viggo to give him such an intense combat lesson the morning of a lithe training night, when he knew that he wouldn't be able to sleep off the muscle aches. Raask made a mental note to ask for another hot mug of tawny as he stumbled down to the kitchens to grab a midday meal.

As the Prince of Skierka, Raask enjoyed certain perks at the palace. And just as they always were, his ointments were ready for him at the exact moment he needed them after his combative training. Raask preferred to move through the castle noisily, either whistling or walking loudly to give the staff warning of his presence. But he suspected that even if he didn't come down for his midday meal whistling, the staff would already somehow know he was on his way.

As Raask entered the kitchen, the staff bowed their heads out of respect and murmurs of "My Prince" echoed across the room. Raask waved them off as he grabbed the plate of roasted duck, duck fat-fried potatoes with a sprinkling of fish eggs on top, glazed carrots, buttered peas, and a hot roll, that was sitting by the door. Taking his plate with him, Raask walked through the royal dining room and out to the gardens.

Before the entrance of the royal gardens, lay benches and tables. These were a relatively new addition to the castle, added within his lifetime, unlike much of the palace. They were put in after his mother herself requested an outside dining area. She would take Raask and Viggo out here to snack, and learn to read. On warm days, Raask often liked to take his own meals out here and sit at the very same table that he would with his mother all those years ago. So, it was particularly shocking to see that his table was currently occupied by Zaries and Aria.

The wounds on the girl's face were already healing nicely, but he could sense she still carried a certain heaviness in her spirit. She sat with her knees to her chest, almost hugging herself. Her long black hair cascaded in front of her face as she tilted her head up to look at him. Zaries's eyes followed her gaze as he stopped speaking, to greet the prince properly. Zaries stood and bowed to Raask. Aria sat still, carefully watching him.

"May I sit here?" Raask asked as he removed his satchel of silverware from his pocket.

"It's your palace, do as you will." Aria answered.

He held back his laugh, taking a seat across from Aria, and motioning for Zaries to take a seat as well. "And how are you liking the palace?" He asked, taking a large bite out of his roll.

"From what I've seen, it's a beautiful castle. Z has just shown me around the gardens before we started on our tea break." Aria said, looking back at the extensive gardens.

Zaries straightened before adding, "I was going to take Miss Aria around the palace itself after giving her legs some time to rest."

The three sat in silence as Aria and Zaries sipped their tea and Raask worked on his massive plate of food. Zaries was the first to finish and loudly slurped the last bit of his tea. Immediately after finishing, Zaries looked around impatiently.

"I can watch over our guest until my courses begin. You can resume the morning shift with Miss Aria tomorrow," Raask instructed.

Zaries scratched at his head. "But who will watch Miss Aria tonight?"

Amused, Raask answered, "I'm sure I can find another guard when it is time for me to excuse myself."

"Right." Zaries said as he stood up, grabbing his empty teacup to bring back to the kitchens.

Before Zaries left earshot, Aria called out, "Thank you for showing me around the gardens. I look forward to trying your wife's tea blend."

Zaries stopped in his tracks as he answered Aria, "Yes, of course! I'm sure you'll love it. It has that sweet spice that you said you like. I'll also remember to ask my sister for the next book in your uh . . . series." Zaries blushed, as he rushed back into the castle.

"Do I want to know what books you are asking Zaries for that make him blush like that?" Raask asked while still chewing the duck.

Aria's lips tightened before cracking a wicked smile, "*His Sweet Hooves.*"

Raask nearly choked on his bite. In half a second, he regained his composure. "Yes, well we do have a library here at the palace. I'm sure we even have the *His Sweet Hooves* series in stock."

Aria nodded, taking a small sip from her tea. "We already checked. It seems that the second book in the series has already been checked out. And based on the look on the librarian's face when we asked her to check who it was, it must have been some high-ranking member of your court."

Raask immediately stopped chewing. "Do you have any idea who it could be?" Aria's smirk might as well have been a pointed finger. Raask put his fork down and waved his white napkin as if it was a white flag.

Aria laughed so incredibly boisterously, yet it was sweet at the same time. "Alright you got me," Raask admitted. "How could you possibly know it was me?"

"I didn't until I saw how you reacted to hearing the name of the series."

"You're quite clever, aren't you?" Raask asked.

"I guess it depends on who you ask." Aria offered.

"I'm asking you."

Aria's eyes scanned back and forth across Raask's face, leaving him feeling vulnerable and amused all at once. "Is the second book as good as the first?" She evidently decided to ignore Raask's own question.

Returning to his meal, Raask nodded. "It's honestly even better. I don't want to give anything away, but let's just say that they finally find the secret chamber."

Raask wiggled his eyebrows suggestively, which made Aria burst out into a fit of laughter. "What does that even mean?" She asked.

"Oh, you'll see," Raask answered. He took the last few bites of what was left on his plate. "Are you ready to see the rest of the palace?" He asked as he stood up.

Aria nodded and followed him back through the castle.

Raask dropped off their dishes to the kitchen, while Aria leaned against the wall, looking utterly and completely drained.

"They'll make you anything that you want," said Raask, as he let the door to the kitchens slam behind him. He took a big bite out of a piece of cinnamon raisin bread he apparently snagged from the kitchen, before handing a slice to Aria.

"They usually keep loaves of bread in baskets by the door for anyone to grab if they're hungry. And if you're extra nice they'll even pack you a blob of butter with it."

He led Aria down the halls of the palace. As he passed, the members of the court would tilt their head in slight bows. Everytime, Raask would give them a quick smile or even a handshake as he kept walking. After shaking the hands of several high-ranking court officials and walking out of earshot, Aria asked, "Do you truly know all of these people?"

"Of course!" He scoffed. "I am the crown prince, you know."

Aria nodded as they rounded yet another corner of the palace. Raask watched as she did her best to peek into rooms quickly and on the sly. Noticing her interest in each room, he began to slow down and try to imagine his palace from the eyes of someone who had never seen it.

It was a foreboding place, large and clunky by design. But each piece of furniture, each statue, each piece of art was one of a kind, and overflowing with opulence. The red rugs adorned with the black embroidery of the Morlok Crest, also painted stories of past battles of Skierka as well as of the Gods. Ancient mythology blended into modern-day politics throughout the entire palace in a way that made it confusing for Raask, as a boy, to understand what was real and what wasn't. Which creatures stopped existing at the end of the book and which creatures could he see crawling out of the Gaulic forest? He was never quite sure.

They walked past galleries, various forms of libraries, the jeweler, the servants' rooms, and dozens of other grand halls and rooms that Raask was sure Aria had never seen before.

It was only when they passed the music room that Aria called out to Raask, asking him to hold on.

"Do you need a break?" Raask asked, after remembering where they were he continued, "There is a terrace on the other side of this wall if you would like to sit. I could send for tawny."

He quickly looked at her, assessing her wellness. She didn't seem overly tired or injured. If anything, she looked intrigued by something.

Aria stepped into the music room with her mouth agape. The tall ceilings were adorned with ornate murals of all kinds of musical creatures, and humans playing on instruments. There were faery folk, banshees, trolls and of course syrens singing with the humans. Peacefully. *Must be old*, Raask thought, as the creatures have not been allowed entry into the palace in centuries—unless they were slaves of course.

The room was large and spacious, meant to seat the royal orchestra.

Raask stood against the corner of the door watching Aria with fascination. She idly ran her hand across the various instruments, stopping only when she reached the harp.

"Do you play?" Raask asked, although somehow, he already knew the answer.

Aria looked back at Raask with a softness that betrayed her, "Yes."

"So why don't you? Go ahead."

Aria's face contorted in confusion. "It's not disrespectful in your culture to play another's instrument without permission?"

Raask laughed. "You're forgetting that these instruments are owned by the palace and their musicians are also an asset of the palace. They are all technically mine."

"Owning an instrument does not make it yours."

"That's exactly what ownership means."

Aria sat at the harp's stool, still facing Raask. "You truly don't think that an instrument belongs to whoever makes it sing?"

"No, but you clearly do. So go ahead and play it and it'll belong to you."

He could tell Aria felt conflicted by playing the instrument, but her wish to create music trumped her wish to remain respectful. And it was a beautiful harp, even Raask could see that.

It was long and made of a form of lithe-infused gold and embellished with twinkling crystals that spilled down the instrument in the most alluring arrangement, that managed to just catch the light from the windows above. Aria pulled the harp back onto her chest as if it was an old friend that she was embracing. And Raask watched, mesmerized as something within her changed.

The music sort of just fell out of her. A melody poured out of her body, somehow aged, like a fine wine, and for once a smile that was not wicked crept across her face. It was a beautiful song played by an even more beautiful woman. Something about the whole thing brought an ache to his chest. He could tell by the way she held her breath, the way that her fingers gently plucked the strings, and how her body fell into an almost instinctual dance as she played, that she never believed she'd be able to play her instrument again. He wondered what it had been like stuck on the Dahs, if she was scared, if she heard this music in her head as she floated atop the wicked seas.

He could almost see it in his mind's' eye as she played and images of Aria swimming through the black waters, staring at the silver moon, danced through his head like fireflies.

The second she finished, Raask erupted into applause. "That was incredible." He said as he walked closer to her, brushing a tuft of his hair that fell into his face. "Have you always played?"

"It feels like it," Aria answered, picking an imaginary piece of lint from her corset. "Do you play anything?"

Raask shook his head. "No, my mother tried to teach me the organ, but I never really cared for it. But Viggo used to play the cello. I'm not really sure if he still does."

Aria led the way out of the musical room, "Viggo is the other prince?"

"Yeah. You met him this morning." Raask said as he passed Aria, putting himself in the lead once again. Aria fell into step behind him, as he led her through the thick green doors at the end of the hall.

"Your brother is the General of Morlok's armies?" Aria asked as they walked outside of the palace towards the stables.

"Yes," answered Raask.

"Does the general of your entire army usually individually screen everyone who enters the palace?"

"Of course not." He turned to see Aria's quizzical face and laughed. "Only the ones who somehow managed to crawl out of the Dahs alive."

"How are you doing, by the way?" He asked as they neared the stables. The 'horses' whinnying could be heard from this distance, as well as the occasional sound of livestock.

"I'm okay, still a bit sore, but better," Aria continued, "where are we going?"

"I want you to meet my horse!" Raask exclaimed cheerfully as Aria slammed to a halt. He watched her, amused by her sudden halt. "That's not a good idea," she warned.

"Oh, come on, you'll love her. She's such a sweetheart." Raask grabbed Aria's hand. It was warm and callused in all of the places where a sword would thicken the skin. "I don't know . . . Animals don't usually like me so much."

Raask shrugged off her concerns, "Don't be silly. These are highly trained and incredibly intelligent creatures, Aria."

She bit her lip as she thought it over. "Alright." She conceded.

Raask smiled and opened the door to the stables. As soon as he moved out of the doorframe and let Aria in, the horses within the stable began to spook and violently thrash within their stalls. Several were able to jump loose into the stable and ran out the back of the barn into the pastures. The servants attending the animals all dispersed, some attempting to calm down the horses still within their stalls while most ran after the spooked horses now galloping into the cow pasture.

Utterly bewildered, Raask looked Aria over. Her eyes were wild and her hair mussed from the frenzy.

"I told you animals don't really like me." She said quietly. And just like that Raask roared in laughter. The jewels across his fingers flashed in the air as he laughed.

After a moment, Aria finally joined in.

The servants buzzed around them in a whirlwind attempt to restore order. But Aria and Raask stood in the middle of it all. Raask, a lion's roar of a laugh, and Aria's, a quiet and melodic one set in a minor key.

CHAPTER 5
VIGGO

The cold, rough wind viciously slapped against Viggo's ship. In the distance, a pod of younger sea wraiths repeatedly breached the water. They spun out into the air doing somersaults and cartwheels, before effortlessly dropping back into the thick oil-like water of the Dahs.

As younger creatures, sea wraiths enjoyed living in large pods. Like most children, the young of sea wraiths enjoyed play. It was only when they grew older that they would isolate. And the agility that they spent years fostering through acrobatics and games, would eventually lead to what would make them such extraordinarily deadly predators. Viggo's thoughts drifted to the children of the court, his own friends and Raask's, and the games of war they would play as children. Most of the children of courtiers would only have those memories of war, as a childhood game, by the time they were sending others into it. A game.

Was he any better? Unlikely. He may have even been worse than them. But at least he knew that war was no game. There was no coming home to mother for dinner in real wars.

Silia, one of Viggo's lieutenants, watched the sea wraiths closely through binoculars. The clicking of her switching lens on the binoculars brought Viggo back to his place on the Dahs, watching the wraiths play as children do.

The wraiths themselves were too busy playing to either notice or care about the ship, it certainly hadn't been unheard of for the pods of wraiths to decide to *play* with smaller ships. And what young wraiths considered play was in fact deadly for most other creatures. Viggo's fists tightened against the ship's rails.

Better to be cautious. Always better to be cautious when others' lives were on the line.

On Silia's flanks, Emir and Skender worked in tandem to steer the small ship through the rough waters of the Dahs, made even choppier by the playing pod of wraiths.

Viggo stood in the back of the catamaran, keeping watch on their surroundings and the odd group of soldiers he called family. They had made voyage across the Dahs too many times to count. Each was different and difficult in unique ways. Sometimes they lasted months, sometimes days. There was no way to know. Viggo only prayed that they would all remain safe, that they lived long and happy lives.

The wind pressed against his back as he prayed, and the coolness of a comforting dark shadow brought a small smile to his tight lips.

Between the four of them, they carried several blades, swords, axes, and enough forms of both weapons-grade lithe and oxygen-laced lithe, to survive stranded in the Dahs for upwards of several weeks. If that wasn't enough, he would have to find another way for them to survive.

Silia, the youngest of the squad, bore her signature bow across her back. Her long blonde hair had been neatly tucked away in tight braids that were only loosened slightly by the whipping wind. Emir and Skender both preferred the swords their father had made them out of the metals mined underneath the God of War's temple, and infused with the poisonous purple blood of a syren. It was a famed technique of their kind and very, very valuable. The King had often demanded Viggo take them for the Morlok's war chest. Viggo, who long ago learned not to anger the King, would nod and go on his way. He would not take such heirlooms from his men. And even if he wanted to, he was unsure if he could.

Emir and Skender, the twisted twins of the North, signaled to Viggo that they were getting low on their silver lithe. Viggo drew two large rocks of it from the sack at his feet. Walking first towards Emir, he handed it to him, watching as took the lithe from Viggo and quickly crushed it in his palm, then snorted the harsh powder. Skender did the same when he received it, although he was more careful to crush the lithe into as fine of a powder as possible.

"You waste it that way," Emir yelled over the waves to Skender. Skender groaned. It wasn't the first time the two had had this argument.

"The wind blows it away when it's too fine!" Emir yelled again after Skender ignored him the first time.

"The big chunks make my nose bleed!" Skender yelled back. "Besides, you're supposed to be controlling the wind with this shit. Maybe I'm blowing the dust right back up my nose after I hit it."

Silia scoffed.

"Got something to say there?" Skender challenged. "We all know you couldn't blow lithe back up your nose if you tried, Sken." Silia retorted.

Viggo choked back a laugh. It was a well-known fact that Skender's power ran wild like a wraith in a potions shop. Where Skender himself was an incredibly careful man, his magic erred on the side of bluntness. Emir, his twin, was the opposite. Emir's magic was soft-tempered and agile. Emir's abilities were precise, while Skender's abilities were more of brute strength and power. Interestingly enough, it was Skender who was tall and lean bodied and Emir who was thick and burly. Viggo had always wondered if somehow their magic had swapped in the womb.

Despite the difference in stature, their browned skin and unique features gave away their familial background and their heritage as

Rakkei. They each had the smaller pupils of the Rakkei people, from generations of working in forges, wielding the most infamous weapons across the Arkts. Along with other Rakkei, they shared arched noses, a strong brow, and thick lashes—perfect for keeping flakes of flame out of eyes or blood when in battle. The Rakkei were warriors and great forgers. It was often said that if not for the Morlok's conquest of the Rakkei people, Skierka would not have the military presence it did today.

"What exactly are we looking for?" Silia called to Viggo over the harsh winds.

"Proof of a shipwreck." His eyes continuously scanned the horizon, always on edge and on guard. "Always with the half-answers," Emir muttered underneath his breath. Viggo wished he wasn't on a boat with his crew in extremely dangerous territory so that he could give Emir a proper eye roll at that, but he didn't want to risk taking his eyes off of the seas.

"Do we know anything about this supposed shipwreck?" Skender asked, focusing on controlling the winds and navigating the sails.

"Supposedly it's a large cargo ship containing shipments of lithe." Viggo didn't have to look at his crew to know that they understood how troublesome this news was. Silia, Skender, and Emir had all fought in the capturing of the Surtr Islands alongside Viggo. They were also all aware of the rebel groups beginning to attack Skierkan forces across the islands, and even their waterways. While Viggo did his best to subdue the rebel attacks without any acts of violence— or more importantly telling the King of his avoidance of violence—this would be something too big to keep from him. The Morloks carried a strong predisposition to magic due to their ancestors, the white lithe amplified these powers tenfold, and were only permitted to be used by the Morloks themselves.

If a rebel group had anything to do with the wreckage of a lithe-carrying ship, let alone the one full of white lithe that was supposed to have arrived two days ago, the King would consider it an act of war. More than that. He would order the deaths of thousands. And Viggo would do everything in his power to ensure that wouldn't happen. So, he started with verifying the girl's story. He had to get his facts straight. This was not something that could be taken lightly.

If Aria had been truthful about the amount of time she had spent at sea, given the currents and wind patterns of the past few days, any evidence of the cargo ship would begin to pop up soon. And with the magic in his blood, he should be able to spot any disturbances in the water or above, far sooner than any other human.

Several hours had passed with no signs of the shipwreck. The twins began to share nervous looks. Locking gazes with them, Viggo nodded. Without need for verbal commands, they knew to shift the wind patterns to begin searching the west side of the perimeter for signs of the ship.

More hours passed with no signs of an attacked ship. Only sea wraiths, colossal squids, and the fin of what looked to be a shark, broke up the monotony of the sea.

Eventually, the sun began to set, turning the sky a blazing orange before disappearing behind the black waters of the Dahs on the horizon. He and the crew knew the dangers of the Dahs during the sun hours compared little to the hours after the sun had set.

"We will need to rest for the night." Viggo called.

And with a huff, Emir threw down his hands which Viggo imagined sure had long ago grown tired from directing the winds.

Viggo took out his satchel and pulled out the loaves of bread, tinned fish, and cheeses that the royal kitchen had packed for them before they left. Skender was the first to rush over to the dinner Viggo had set up, followed by Silia.

"Skullin's Scythe," Emir mumbled.

Viggo, Silia, and Skender all looked up to where Emir was standing. His thick body blocked most of the light from the low sun, but just past his left shoulder the dorsal fin of a massive shark sulked into view. The fin itself was three times as tall as the sails of their ship and far wider. Silia's loud chewing of the dry bread continued as they each focused in on the fin.

"Damn," Skender said, staring at the shark in pure awe. Silia merely nodded in agreement.

Viggo took a bite of the salty cheese before ripping off a piece of the bread. It was as tough as it sounded, but it would fill his stomach up, nonetheless. Through his chewing, Viggo muttered, "Just wait to see what's coming up behind it."

Skender looked back at Viggo with a brow raised before looking back at the fin and attempting to look beyond. Besides Viggo, Silia was the first to see it. She gasped and instinctively reached out for her bow and arrow.

Long spikes that shot up through the sky, began to creep behind the shark. The unmistakable long and pointy needle-like spikes of a sea wraith's tail. Viggo willed his magic to push the boat further from the scene as his crew continued to eat.

The burning oranges of the sky turned into muted blues and purples as the sun clicked into place just past the horizon. In one motion, Viggo, Silia, Skender, and Emir turned their heads to the opposite side of the Dahs. Like a clock, the silver moon had just entered into their view. Several minutes passed, Viggo continued to slowly move the ship further away from the scene, but purposefully not fast enough to miss all of the action. Boredom was often even more dangerous than hunger or injury, when on a mission.

The second the silver moon became entirely visible on this side of the realm, the wraith fully submerged its spikes. Wraiths were incredibly prideful and showman-istic at their core. The long-scaled creatures were deeply intelligent and deadly. The entire crew tensed and held their breath in hot anticipation for the bloodbath. And when the wraith finally did strike, it did not disappoint.

Launching the shark *and* itself into the air, the wraith took hold of the shark's gills in its impossibly huge teeth. Holding onto the shark, the wraith arced through the air, whipping its entire body in a crescent shape before entering back into the sea. The gigantic shark's body floated lifelessly as a red stain of blood crawled across the sea and over to their boat.

A feeding frenzy would begin any moment now.

Willing his magic to quicken, Viggo sent a strong wind into the sails of the ship, moving their boat as far away as possible from the pool of blood that was certain to pull predators from across the Dahs. Over Viggo's loud winds, the sound of a strong cannon of pressure rang. The crew turned around once more to see the origin of the noise.

Reaching the height of the Gods themselves, the shark's gills that the wraith tore out were shooting across the sky. The crew laughed as they watched the gills enter back into the water with a splash that reached the spot that they just left.

"Fucking, Rahn." Emir chuckled. The crew echoed Emir's curse. Silia repeated it sarcastically, not one to miss a jab at the superstitious nature of the twins. Silia had always hated the old legends and folkloric explanations for things.

It was a story that all the school children of Skierka knew, the answer as to why the sea creatures stirred so restlessly during the hours ruled by Loor, the Goddess of the Moons. Rahn, the God of the Seas, held a deep and unwavering love for her. Knowing how much the Goddess of the Moon loved gore and carnage, he commanded his creatures to create spectacles for her as she entered this side of the realm. The creatures happily obliged.

The faded blues of the skies quickly turned to black. At this hour it was impossible for even one with magically enhanced vision, to see where the Dahs bled into the night sky. "Get some rest," Viggo ordered.

Knowing full well that Viggo could manage steering the ship and fending off an attack without lifting a finger—the crew happily obliged. They trusted him, and it was not something that he took lightly.

Viggo smiled as he heard the telltale sounds of his crew getting ready for rest. The scratch of the heavy blankets against the wooden ship and the nightly prayers of the twins. Viggo rested his back against the rim of the ship, smiling into the lightless night. To be trusted with the lives of his people, to keep them safe and happy, was one of the greatest honors of his life.

And for just a moment, Viggo pretended that everything would be okay, and that he was not betraying Skierka and putting everyone he loved into danger.

CHAPTER 6

CHAPTER 6
ARIA

"You weren't kidding, huh?" Raask smirked.

It took nearly an hour for all of the servants to wrangle the horses and get everything back into order. And it went without saying that Aria couldn't be anywhere near the stables without causing further chaos. It didn't matter how many sugar cubes she tossed to the horses. They simply refused to involve themselves with her.

Aria felt the ends of her mouth creep up as Raask approached the rock she was sitting on—at a safe distance from the horses of course. Her careful eyes watched him, how he moved with the smoothness that only came with years of training. But his eyes. His smile. The freeness of him. He had never seen a day of battle, of that Aria was sure. Why train for a battle he would certainly never fight himself? Although as she watched the glimpse of his abs that peaked through the bottom of his shirt as he moved, she figured she couldn't complain.

Distracted by studying him, she hardly noticed until he was right in front of her, lifting her off the rock and swinging her carefully to the ground. He brought her back to the soil with a gentleness that surprised her.

"You're heavier than I expected," Raask faked a wince..

Aria's brows furrowed and she stepped back. "And you're weaker than I expected." She shot back.

It took Raask a moment, in which he wore an extremely puzzled look, before he pieced it together. "Oh no, my darling." He laughed, not a roar, but a rumble of thunder on a hot night. "Don't you mistake it, I'm surprised Freyite lets you walk around like this."

"What do you mean?" Aria asked, cocking her head to the side. She knew exactly what he was implying by invoking the name of the Goddess of Beauty. But she wanted to hear him say it out loud to her.

Raask stepped back. His eyes slowly roamed over every part of Aria's body like a hungry dog. While she wore a large cloak that hid most of her body, Raask didn't hide that he obviously liked whatever it was he thought that he was seeing through the heavy thing.

"I mean, look at you."

"What?" She blinked her long eyelashes and pouted her lips, holding back a cackle.

Raask stretched his hand out to Aria, who had zero interest in holding his hand and simply walked past.

"Well, you do know Freyite is the Goddess of Beauty, obviously?" Raask asked, a little too happy to be following her lead.

Aria nodded. "Mmmhmm."

"Well, when the Gods walked the realm, she apparently had a habit of decimating any female whose beauty could possibly compare to her own."

Leading them on the trail around the palace, Aria answered, "I guess I'm not comparable to her then."

"Aria, love, why would you say that?"

She looked back upon the prince with one eyebrow slightly raised. With sass, she pointed to her legs. "Still walking around," she answered.

Raask bit back a laugh, the hungry look still in his eyes.

"Well, she obviously doesn't know about you yet." He waved off the guards they passed who had bowed, before continuing. He stepped in front and turned to face her. "Don't worry, my sweet thing. If she were to find out about your beauty I would guard you with an army. No. I would guard you with two armies. And I would keep you safe and sound."

He sounded like a child.

But somehow she had found this whole thing quite fun so far.

Now it was Aria's turn to look the prince up and down. She poked a bony finger into his chest. "One—has anyone ever told you that you're too much? And two—I am not your sweet thing." Aria continued walking.

The guard nearby nearly choked, watching her tell off the prince and future king of Skierka. Raask simply smiled up at them and shot them a knowing nod before chasing after Aria yet again.

"To answer your first question, surprisingly, very rarely am I told I'm too much. But truthfully it's not the first time I've heard it. And on the second part, we will just have to agree to disagree."

Aria rolled her eyes and groaned. "When does Zaries get back?"

"Whenever I order him to." Raask called, as he walked in the lead this time. Aria's jaw tightened as she realized that he was whistling.

He was actually whistling. While walking with his hands in his pocket. He was certainly an unbothered and unworried member of the royal family.

Then again, Aria knew better than to assume she knew a man's heart after only a day. And she knew better than anyone that a wolf could successfully hide as a sheep if it willed. Although she was doubtful that this was an act of the prince's, it was far more likely that he was a man without responsibility, thus a man without seriousness.

As Aria reminded herself to remember the damage done across the realm at the hands of the prince's bloodline, while he pranced around his kingdom, she couldn't help but notice yet again that the prince had an extremely toned body. Quite distracting even.

There was no doubt that the royal family had invested a great deal of time and resources into training their young in combat; the proof was in Raask's body. Aria's eyes had just risen to the point where she could admire the prince's freckles when she realized that Raask had turned to face her. "When you're done checking out my ass, I figured we could go get you some more food and check in with Selby."

Aria caught up with Raask and muttered, "Don't flatter yourself."

"Whatever you say, sweet thing." *Again*, Raask whistled.

The two walked back into the castle and headed straight to the kitchen. The heavy smells of the decadent food, and the clank of pots and pans grew with each step. Aria couldn't hold back a near-drool as her stomach rumbled. While she was used to going long lengths of time without food, the stress on her body from being stuck at sea had left her body completely malnourished, on top of years of famine. It seemed her body was trying to make up for decades of hunger, now that it had access to the best kitchen in the realm, with food at all hours of the day.

Raask opened the heavy door to the kitchen and within seconds a hot cup of tawny was slapped into his hand with a mumbled "my Prince," by one of the kitchen servants. Raask shot back the cup of tawny and lifted his glass, asking for another.

"And for you?" The servant asked Aria as he quickly brought the prince another cup of tawny.

Aria walked around the kitchen in amazement. "Well . . . What is ready?" She asked.

A big man entered the kitchen from the pantry, carrying a bag of potatoes almost as large as Aria. "You must be the special guest of the prince that I've heard so much about," the man said as he walked closer to the two.

"Ah, there he is! I didn't see you earlier when I grabbed my lunch!" Raask slapped the man on the back as he gave a slight bow of the head, before extending his hand to shake Aria's. "I'm Padge, the head chef here at the Palace." Aria shook his hand and introduced herself, "I'm Aria, it's nice to meet you."

Padge took Aria around the kitchen and pointed out each component of the meals that his staff worked on tirelessly, "Well, Aria, we have several roasted geese, two dozen boiled and breaded eggs, beef stew, smoked trout, mashed potatoes, roasted carrots, and an assortment of fresh breads."

Aria's eyes widened as they approached the pastry station. "I can see that you're excited for this portion of the kitchen tour." Padge laughed. Aria had always loved sweets more than anything else. While they were a rarity in her household growing up, she always looked forward to birthdays of any kind, as that was the only time they would splurge for some kind of sweet.

The last table was filled to the brim with dozens of sweets. Pies, custards, and cakes bloomed across the table, so bountiful and sweet that Aria couldn't help but fantasize about trying each and every one of them.

She looked up at Raask, wondering if he too was in awe of the pastry selection. She found him, not in awe but already deeply engaged, several spoonfuls into some sort of strawberry and cream custard. A sweet melody of laughter erupted from Aria's lips, "And what is *that*?"

"Strawberry shortcake," Raask answered, or at least it sounded like that through the mouthfuls of food he continued to pile into his mouth. "Padge, make sure you save her some of this."

Ignoring the prince, Aria looked back to the head chef, befuddled. "I don't understand, today is not a day of feasts . . . Is it?" She knew that her time in the Dahs had scrambled with her mind, but she was certain that the next day of feasts wasn't until the summer solstice..

"No, no. But we don't only make food for the Morloks, or the members of the courts. We also feed the servants and medics and anyone who lives on the grounds." Padge answered as he grabbed a plate for Aria. "What would you like?"

Grinning from ear to ear, Aria requested a plate of the smoked trout on top of the toasted bread. Raask was served a plate with a little bit of everything. After thanking Padge, they brought their plates into the room opposite the kitchen. The dining area contained several long and grandiose tables, all decorated with fine silverware and red table clothes adorned with the Morlok Crest. After stuffing their faces with two helpings of dinner and a serving of dessert, the clock chimed nine.

"When do your lessons start again?" Aria asked, speaking for the first time since they sat with their dinner. While Aria knew she was so famished from the recent stresses on her body, she had no clue how the prince was able to eat so much.

"Soon," the prince pushed the last few bites of his strawberry treat around the plate.

Aria carefully watched Raask before asking, "You don't enjoy your schooling?"

Raask's lips condensed into a tight line as he shrugged. "I mean does anyone really like school?" His eyes remained focused on his plate while he took the last few bites.

Aria sank back into her seat, slumped from such a heavy and rich meal. She did enjoy learning. "I really enjoyed history."

Raask's eyes reached Aria before the rest of his head followed. A small smile reached his lips. "Yeah?" He asked, voice gravelly. His smile grew even wider as Aria nodded yes. "Of course you did."

"What's that supposed to mean?" Aria asked, sitting back up. Always ready for a fight.

"All hot like history." She rolled her eyes in response to Raask's obvious flirtations. Warm butterflies in her stomach rose up to her chest like bubbly wine, and Aria did everything that she could to ignore them. She hated herself for feeling so bubbly by the slightest compliment from an overgrown man child. But when she looked up into Raask's vivacious eyes. Oh Gods, he looked at her like she was some beautiful masterpiece, the butterflies in her stomach seemed to grow just at the thought.

Desperate to suffocate the little nuisances, Aria asked, "You really don't enjoy any part of your schooling?"

"I don't mind learning the different languages and dialects. And combat training with Viggo is tough, but it's the only time I really get to see my brother, so I don't mi . . ." Raask trailed off at the sight of the Irridesci entering the dining hall.

Dressed in long red robes that trailed several steps behind them, the Irridesci were easy to identify by anyone who had heard their tales. While Aria had never seen one in person before, she had immediately recognized them. Silently, they walked over to Aria and Raask.

Judging by their silhouettes, one was a male and the other a female. They were both tall, and unnaturally slim. A distinct scent of creamy brine and ocean rot—from their use of white lithe—followed the Irridesci. Intermixed with the familiar scent of the white lithe, Aria wasn't quite sure what other strange smell tainted their auras. Something dark, and old mixed into their sillage, and while Aria hoped she would never get close enough to tell, she knew that the scent came from deep within their own biochemistry. The scent was oddly nostalgic for Aria, and that caught her off guard. It was almost too similar to the scent of the old books in the back of her elders' closet, that she would sneak in to read in the middle of the night as a child, but there was that earthy note that just smelled unnatural and wrong, that continued to throw her off.

As the Irridesci approached the table, they raised their gray hands in greeting to Raask. When Raask reached out to shake their hands, all four hands from the two Irridesci encircled Raask's, "*Meh beneditio a vitae*" the Irridesci whispered together in voices that cut through the air like a freshly sharpened blade.

The hood of their robes sunk over their heads, keeping their faces hidden by shadows. Stories of mortals who made the mistake of looking under an Irridesci's hood to see the twisted face underneath were often told around campfires. Aria herself heard several times as a child that if she didn't act right, her parents would send an Irridesci to speak some sense into her. A part of Aria had always thought the Irridesci were nothing but legends to incite fear. But what was standing in front of Aria was no myth but the reality of the twisted nature of the Morloks. To create deals with these creatures who claimed to speak with the Gods by maiming themselves and their own kind. Aria had lived through enough pain to know that it didn't get you any closer to the Gods as the Irridesci claimed.

And yet they roamed around the Bleached Palace as an entity that did not seem to answer to the king. Aria wondered what it was that the king received from them, and vice versa. Did they truly commune with the Gods, was that how the Morloks were so much more powerful than any other magic wielder in the Arkts?

The creatures twisted breathing brought Aria back to the present. Their breaths sounded harsh and forced—as if they had just spent the last several hours screaming. The palace told Skierkans that the Irridesci used to be human. And every few years, some babies would be chosen by the Gods to become Irridesci. It was considered a blessing of the highest, to have a child chosen to join the Irridesci. But how a human could be turned into such an abomination was a mystery to her.

It took Aria far too long to realize that the Irridesci had reached their hands out to her. She quickly looked at Raask, uncertain as to what she was supposed to do.

"Give them your hand, Aria." Raask softly urged. His eyes were warm, but the tension around them told Aria that he must have understood her apprehension to freely give her hand to these wrongful creatures.

Aria's lips tightened as she lifted her hand to meet the Irridesci.

And just like with the prince, they whispered their so-called blessing, "*Meh beneditio a vitae.*"

Like the walls of the caves Aria had loved to wander in as a child, their hands were chilled and damp to the touch. However, when exploring in the caves, Aria had always felt the need to explore just a little bit more, each time she ventured into one. They had always felt like they would whisper to her a secret that she needed to uncover, or the location of some lost land that was waiting to be discovered. But with the Irridesci, it took everything out of Aria to stay seated and not run as far away as possible, as fast as possible.

Aria forced a smile after receiving the Irridesci's blessing. Their hoods tilted forward. In unison they spoke again, their voices a song full of all of the wrong notes. "Hello Aria." They turned their hoods to the prince. "It is time for your lessons, Prince."

Suddenly, Aria understood why Raask seemed to hate his schooling so much. If she had to be taught by these vile creatures, she would have refused to learn altogether.

The prince stood, and waved the guards from the doorway in. "Would you be able to escort Miss Aria to Selby, and then return her to her chambers?"

"Yes, my Prince." The guards answered.

Aria watched as the Irridesci led the way out of the dining room. She noticed the crest on the back of their robes was not the familiar raven of the Morlok crest, but a tree with deep roots made of lace, that weaved themselves all the way down the length of the robes' train.

Raask followed in their wake. Aria found it particularly unusual that the creatures who answered only to the Gods and supposedly those of Morlok blood, would lead the prince—and not the other way around. It was a universal rule of the realm that royals led the way.

"Good night, my sweet thing," Raask called just before he carelessly let the door to the dining room slam shut behind him.

How Raask was able to stay cheerful around the presence of Irridesci was just another mystery Aria was going to have to add to her growing list about him.

Aria wasn't certain exactly how much time had passed between

Raask leaving with those ghastly creatures, before she was finally comfortable enough to breathe. Although the moment the Irridesci left the area, the temperature of the room returned to the comfortable, yet still chilly feeling of the palace.

Knowing that the only chance she had to gain comfort and warmth would be to drop herself in a tub, Aria made herself get up and ask the guards to escort her to see Selby. It took everything out of her to ask the guards' permission to see the medic, feeling completely ridiculous at having to be chaperoned, she did her best to hide her resentment from her tone. The looks from the guards assured her that she did not do an excellent job at hiding her dissatisfaction at having to be escorted everywhere. As someone who coveted her time alone, and freedom to explore, her stay at the Palace of Morlok felt more and more like a cage.

Aria let out a frustrated breath, which caused the guards escorting her to share a concerned look that Aria chose to ignore.

Tightening her jaw, Aria remembered who owned the halls which she walked through. She remembered watching her people being taken by the Skierkans and forced into the dangerous pursuit of lithe, along with other lowly and dangerous tasks that the Skierkans would force her people into. Descending into the deepest pits to retrieve the white lithe. Lives wasted away mining for a substance only legal to be used by a handful of people in the realm. Because of the Skierkans, her people were doomed to an eternity of darkness.

Aria bit back a shudder at the memory of her older sister, who was beautiful beyond comprehension. Her own stunning physicality had made her a target. Just like all the other times Aria had allowed her mind to wander to the past, it always led to an ocean of painful memories crashing through her head. To think about her sisters and her family was to relive a lifetime of heartache.

But Aria had learned how to cope with it all from a young age. Nothing quieted her anger like the promise of revenge. She envisioned a great and powerful wave crashing against the memories, ripping them apart piece by piece. A river of Morlok blood. And her people, swimming among it, smiling. Free. Finally free.

She couldn't resist the wicked smile that crept across her face like a thief in the night.

"Miss Aria," The guard called, seemingly not for the first time. Aria turned her head to meet the guard's irritated look, her eyebrows lifted, mirroring the guards' irritation.

"We're here."

The crow's feet of the guard who had called Aria several times crinkled as he stared down upon her. His annoyance with the girl was clear. The younger one with long curly locks that often fell over her face, shot Aria an apologetic look.

"I can see that." Aria knocked on the oversized doors in front of her. After a few uneasy breaths, Selby opened the door to let Aria in. She quickly shut the door, only for it to be caught on one of the guard's heavy feet. "Can I help you?" Selby chimed.

"We were ordered to escort Aria here." The portly older guard huffed.

Selby nodded, "Yes, and it seems that you've already done that." The guards shared a look of confusion. "You may escort her to her own chambers once I am done with her." The door loudly clicked shut.

Aria couldn't help but to smirk at Selby.

"Please," She offered Aria the seat across from her desk. Sitting down, Aria took note of the various oddly-sized vials filled with substances ranging from lithe to strange and colorful liquids. The sound of toads croaking creeped out of several of the jars with holed lids. Trying her best to remain friendly, something that didn't come naturally to Aria, she bit back her disgust at the toads. Selby followed Aria's gaze. "They're awfully misleading creatures, aren't they?"

Aria twisted her head curiously.

"Other than those who look at them in disgust, before quickly looking away, people walk past toads daily and for the most part they don't think anything about them. After all, they're just lowly creatures." Selby watched Aria carefully before continuing, "Very few know that toads, particularly warhic toads, carry a great deal of power in their odd little bodies."

Aria lifted a container, and carefully inspected them. "These guys are powerful?" She asked.

"Very. When crushed and left in moonlight, their eyeballs can cure a range of lithe-inflicted wounds. But when left in sunlight and turned into a paste, their eyeballs can cause paralysis.

Aria studied Selby. "Why are you telling me this?" After a breath, Selby smiled and reclined in her seat.

"I didn't want you to think that I was simply keeping these nasty little creatures as pets." Aria laughed. "As for the other peculiarities on my desk, you must understand that my work here at the palace isn't just as a healer, but also as a researcher." Selby reclined back into her seat. "But that's enough about me and my work. How are you feeling?"

"I'm doing okay." Aria's voice fell flat.

"Are you eating?"

"Ferociously."

"Good, and your scarring seems to already be fading." Selby's eyes looked over Aria's skin, scanning her wounds. "Does anything hurt?"

"It's manageable with the medicine that you've given me. Thank you."

With a wave of her hand, Selby dismissed Aria's gratitude. She pulled out several tubs of the lotion that she had given Aria before. "This one will help with the pain, and this one will help with preventing infection and scarring. Apply them minimally twice a day, and no more than five times a day." Selby placed the tubs into a large leather satchel she had kept at her feet and handed it to Aria.

Aria thanked her once again, and stood to leave. "After you," Aria said to the guards, before letting them lead the way to her chambers.

With slight hesitation, they started the long journey from the medical quarters up to Aria's hall.

She counted the steps as the trio walked up the endless loop of stairs. A hum of power radiated from the white lithe-bleached stone encompassing the small stairwell, causing a wave of nausea for Aria.

Finally, Aria saw the glimmer of moonlight from the upper section of the stairwell. Her body ached for a brief break from the magical hum of the white lithe-bleached stone. She sprinted the last steps until the glowing light of the moon cocooned her. She didn't miss the amused look that the guards shared. The scrawny one let a small laugh escape as Aria leaned against the glass windows of the stairwell. "You will adjust." The young and gawky guard looked past Aria and onto the forest below.

"You feel it too?" Aria asked, watching the stocky guard tread past them.

"We all do!" The older one called, trying to get ahead of the younger guard and herself, while they enjoyed the view.

Laughing, the younger guard nodded her head in agreement. "Yes, we all feel it. But it's something that you won't notice after a while. Then, when you leave and come back, it'll hit you."

After briefly inspecting each room in Aria's chambers, for what, Aria wasn't quite sure, the guards stood by the door. "We will see you tomorrow evening. Goodnight, Miss Aria."

She stood awkwardly in front of the guards, not quite sure how to dismiss them, or if she even had the ability to dismiss them. After a beat of uncomfortable silence, she decided to simply bid them both goodnight and shut the door after them. Couldn't they see that she was ready for them to leave? Did they mean to humiliate her? Show her that she couldn't sleep until they deemed it time. She let the door shut loudly and listened as their footsteps faded. She didn't move, barely breathed, until she heard the click of the door at the end of the hall. The nausea from the bottom portion of the palace's lithed walls still sat deep in her belly, refusing to budge.

She strode into the kitchen, eager to have more of the spiced licorice tea that she had been thinking about all day. Tea was a luxury to her people. Some of her rare, gentler memories of childhood involved drinking tea with her family after long and eventful days.

She shook the thought free from her head as she grazed her hand along the handles of the slate gray cabinets. Their handles, and the entire chamber were warm to the touch. No doubt a pleasant effect of the lengthy fireplace in the sitting area across from the kitchen. The teas that Aria had used yesterday had all been restocked. Curious, Aria checked the other cabinet. All the mugs and plates that she used had been cleaned and returned to their rightful place.

She attempted to open the jar to the tea blend and struggled. It was too tight, and she had grown too weak. A quiet anger, that resided deep in her bones, swelled.

Aria looked at her long and slender fingers that were connected to gangly and frail arms and snarled. Her time floating around the top of the Dahs had left her weak. An overwhelming storm of grief, despair, shame, and anger overtook her as she stared at the jar she had been excited to open all day. For a brief moment, Aria allowed herself to succumb to the anger that had eaten away at her bones since birth. With precision, she tapped a knife against the edge of the jar, hard enough to cause a crack. Once cracked, she easily removed the top section of the jar, removing enough of the tea and placing it into a mug.

Steam hit her face as she poured hot water from above the fire, over her tea. The cozy smell wafted up to her nose, bringing with it a sense of calmness.

Grabbing the creamy fur blanket that had been folded neatly sometime after she left this morning, Aria curled like a cat onto the cloud-like sofa. She reached over to read the new book that the librarian assured was similar to the *His Sweet Hooves* series. And before cracking open the book, Aria made a promise to herself that she would work to regain her strength tomorrow. She may even ask the prince to join his training sessions. Smiling at the thought of the prince's sweaty training, it wasn't hard for Aria to picture him as the love interest in her new book.

Charming, rich, and powerful. Raask was an ideal love interest for a novel about a peasant girl who somehow ended up in the prince's palace. It was a perfect story really, a story that she was counting on. Love and hope: the two easiest things to manipulate.

CHAPTER 7
RAASK

Raask's eyes never took too long to adjust to the darkness of the Irridesci tower. On every full moon since Raask could remember, he was escorted out of the Palace and into the Irridesci tower that sat in the darkest corner of the estate. While the darkness was something he grew accustomed to over the years, the bone-chilling air and stench was something that never grew tolerable.

Raask leaned back into his seat, ignoring the stiff wooden columns of the ancient chair that dug into his back. With the intense combat training Viggo put him through this morning, and the rigid chair, Raask was certain that he would be in a lot of pain tomorrow. Probably tonight, too.

The only sounds that seemed to exist within the tower came from the ticking of the clock above and the harsh whispers that radiated through the heavy wooden floors. Both sounds seemed to be on an endless loop, designed to irritate Raask. Across from him stood the ancient Irridesci who acted as his tutor in all areas of magic wielding besides, of course, anything that could be used during a battle. Viggo remained the expert in that area of lithe. Although he would never let on to how he learned to harness lithe in such violent manners, no matter how many times Raask had bugged him for the answer.

The only reason Raask even knew that Balk was ancient was because he had asked him as a young child. Children could get away with asking such questions. Now the time for curiosities has passed, and as Raask had never seen Balk or any other Irridesci's face, and they all sounded like crones, he just had to take his word for it.

Balk himself loomed overhead. His piercing gaze could be felt through the hood that fell over his face, for as long as Raask had known him. He had once told the young Prince that to look upon the face of an Irridesci was to glimpse the face of the Gods. And that was why it was so dangerous to peer under their hoods. Raask wasn't sure if he truly believed that, but he had heard rumors of egregious procedures the Irridesci executed upon themselves to bring themselves closer to the Gods. Any facial mutilation would be considered tame compared to the stories he had heard whispered through the halls. Either way, Raask had always kept his eyes low when dealing with the Irridesci. Better safe than sorry, he figured.

"You are not focusing, my Prince." Each word left Balk's throat like they were thorned.

Raask released a heavy sigh, ever careful to not breathe in the putrid air that surrounded the Irridesci on the inhale.

"Your father and brother had located their power alignments when they were mere boys," Balk spat. It wasn't the first time he had heard the same disappointed line from the horrific tutor. He had even heard Balk's half-decayed voice relaying the same disapproving line in his nightmares. Pushing past the pain and disappointment from his ancestral blood, and the cult of the Irridesci, Raask poured his power into the throbbing tunnel of his soul. Just as he had been instructed to on every full moon for the past decade.

There was no doubt among those who tested the young Prince that his well of power was deep, potentially even deeper than Viggo's.

It remained a mystery that his magic had yet to show an alignment to a particular element or purpose, as it had the others within his family. While Morlok magic was infamous for its strength and ability to cross alignments with only pure white lithe, it was crucial for the kingdom that his magic chose a natural inclination. His father was a fire-eater at heart. Morloks were able to twist their innate magic into the other forms—but for his father—magic always began and ended with flame. Announcing Raask's alignment was not only the first of the three trials that were set to begin in a quarter of a sun cycle, but it was also an indicator of the type of ruler Raask would become.

As a fire-eater, the king ruled with a great temper and intensity. It was crucial for Raask to find his natural alignment not only ascend to the throne, but also for the people of Skierka to prepare for the coming decades of the kingdom.

Essentially, Raask was running out of time.

Blood dripped down his neck. Mimicking the seconds on the clock tower in some horrific coincidence.

The immense concentration, combined with the impressive amount of white lithe he had snorted had caused blood to careen out of his ears. He knew from past experience that he only had a few moments before it started to pool out of his nose too.

Praying to the Gods that he could get his shit together before that happened, he harbored more of his power behind his thoughts. He pushed everything he had into the well of power that resided in his blood, focusing it into his gut, his brain, his heart, and every other part of his body that he could locate. From far away he could feel the warm drops of blood escaping from his nose and falling into his lap. The warmth from the blood provided the smallest of comforts to his too-cold body.

At some point Raask had started to hold his breath, giving over every ounce of his being to his ancestral magic. There was no room for his brain to process bringing oxygen in, while he attempted to herd his power towards an alignment. Any alignment for Gods' sake.

There wasn't much more time. He needed to find it. He needed his alignment.

He knew he was only a few moments now from blacking out. He was desperate. *Manifest yourself*, he pleaded with his own powers. *Manifest yourself*, he begged whatever Gods were listening, for their help. *Manifest yourself*. He heard it whispered in his mother's hushed voice.

Repeating the same phrase that the Irridesci claimed to be holy, over and over to himself. Supposedly the same phrase that an ancient God had whispered into the ear of the first Morlok to ascend to royalty. Unlocking the well of power within their line. The legends say the whispered phrase gave his ancestor enough power to pass the trials with no training. They say the phrase gifted his kin with their enhanced connection to the white lithe.

Raask wondered what it meant that he whispered the same phrase thousands of times to no avail. He wondered if the Gods had decided he wasn't worthy of an alignment. Or maybe they decided he wasn't worthy to be king.

Spots of blood began to encompass his body. The infamous Morlok blood that reigned a power nearly as strong as the Gods, was now oozing out of his every pore. And it was a waste. It was all a waste. He was pushing himself too hard. But it wasn't enough. It never was.

Black spots began to cloud his vision. The whispers from underneath the floorboards rose, as the blackness spilled across his vision like ink on a page. The last thing Raask heard before the blackness overtook him was the agitated sigh from Balk, and the untiring ticks from that Gods-awful clock.

CHAPTER 8
VIGGO

P ale sunlight cascaded across the black water of the Dahs. At some point near dawn, the twins awoke to relieve Viggo of his shift and let him have a few hours of rest. While the twins were steering the ship, and Viggo was catching up on some much-needed sleep, Silia softly snored in the hull of the boat. The crew had been fighting together since they were young and knew just about everything there was to know about one another— including Silia's tendency to stab anyone who woke her up.

It wasn't until midmorning, almost afternoon, that Viggo finally awoke. His brown eyes erred more on the side of hazel in the harsh light of the sun above. After grabbing water from his canteen, a bit of dried beef and an apple, he walked over to catch up with the rest of his crew. Skender and Emir worked the sides of the ship, steering the boat with ease now that the creatures had gone to rest during the day. Silia, who was now awake and seemingly hadn't stabbed anyone, crouched by the tip of the mast. A gigantic pair of binoculars sat pressed firmly to her eyes as she continuously scanned the horizon. Viggo felt queasy just watching her gently bounce from side to side with the sail.

"Any news?" Viggo's booming voice disrupted the silence.

Emir jumped, unaware that Viggo had not only awoken but approached his side of the boat. Viggo was naturally a quiet mover, something that came in handy more often than not. Emir tried his best to mask his surprise with a stretch, but Skender's laugh ultimately gave him away.

"Nothing yet, boss." Skender answered, as Emir's cheeks reddened.

Viggo snapped a bite from his apple, and wiped the juice off of his face with the bottom of his sleeve. After taking another particularly crunchy bite of apple, he heard someone's stomach grumbling. Unsure of who it was, he went back to his bag and grabbed apples for all three. Silently, he handed the apples to the twins and tossed the third up to Silia.

"Thanks," Skender muttered as he quickly ate.

"Don't mention it."

The crew loudly smacked down their snack as they nervously kept watch on the waters around them. The tides on the Dahs were notorious for lulling ships to rest and relaxation only moments before hitting them with massive ship-breaking waves. To relax while in the Dahs was as good as accepting death.

Viggo scanned the waters behind the ship. With the wind whipping into his face, he had to continuously push his black hair out of his eyes. He was in the midst of pushing his hair behind his ears, when he felt a stinging hit on the side of his head. He looked down to find a hair red ribbon had been flung at him from above.

"You would fling a ribbon at your own general?" Viggo cockily called to Silia above.

"I'd fling an arrow at your head if it would get you to stop tweaking out about your hair." Silia answered flatly.

Viggo choked on his own laugh, his throat already dry from the exposure to the salty water and winds that surrounded them. "I'm not going to use this!" He flung it right back at Silia, who caught it without even taking her eyes out of the binoculars and just as quickly flung it right back at him.

"Where are we anyways?"

Emir and Skender shared a nervous look, before gluing their eyes back to the waters ahead.

"We'll be above the Rigelus trench in a half hour or so." Skender answered. Viggo's sharp jaw clenched.

Any air of playfulness disappeared just as quickly as it had appeared. He moved to the center of the ship, and took a serious scan of the waters surrounding the boat. The sun was at the highest point of the day, blasting heat and light down upon the realm with the fierceness of a blade. But even at the sun's strongest point, it barely lit more than a hand's depth into the thick, dark waters of the Dahs. Even so, for any sailor to attempt to go near the Rigelus trench, the sun would have to be at its highest point. If they were smart, anyways.

Viggo cursed. He was annoyed that his crew hadn't warned him of their plans to venture over the trench when he first awoke. Helk, he was annoyed that they didn't bother to tell him before he fell asleep. If he knew, he wouldn't have wasted precious hours sleeping when he could be analyzing the seas for any hints of danger—or clues of Aria's ship. If anything happened to any member of his crew, it would destroy him.

He sighed as he realized that he inadvertently stumbled upon the very reason his own crew didn't let him in on their plan to voyage over the deadliest part of the realm's most viscous sea. For the most part, it seems that everything has been fine so far.

Afterall, Viggo trusted his life with every single member of his squadron, and he knew that they felt the same way. He also knew that they were smart enough to not take traveling over this section of the Dahs lightly.

It also made perfect sense to check over the trench for traces of Aria's shipwreck. The damn thing had an unnatural pull to it that seemed to drag things deep into its depths. Unlike the Zojz trench to the north, where white lithe was abundant and the waters were thick and cancerous. The Rigelus trench felt alive with the malicious pull that dragged entire warships down and called upon the sea monsters to feast. It was likely Aria's ship had been pulled by a strong current and had ended up here. It wasn't unheard of for the Dahs to trick even the most experienced sailors and confuse them of their path and current whereabouts.

The waters over the trench were so devoid of light, and filled with such a high concentration of lithe fragments, that its black currents could be seen stretching and pulling the seas around it during the lightest hours of the day. Rumors had swirled since the dawn of time over what lay at the bottom of the trench. Many explorers died in search of whatever glory they believed to be at the bottom. Sometimes they would simply never be heard from again, and sometimes bodies would wash up on shore with missing chunks of skin or even limbs. Viggo had always believed that the Dahs left their bodies so visibly on the shore next to the Salt district as an example of what it does with those who test it, a kind of warning from the seas themselves.

He told this to Emir once when they were sent to investigate the ravaged bodies that had been found on the shores of Skierka. He happened to believe the same, only that it was the creatures of the deep who left the bloodied victims for us to see, and not the Dahs itself.

Viggo shook off the gory memory.

He constantly lived on the edge of trying his best to forget the grotesque parts of his job, and forcing himself to never forget—as punishment for either not preventing these atrocities, or not bringing justice to whoever committed them.

The day they were called to the shore to inspect those bodies, only two out of the dozen were able to be identified. The rest had been so severely mutilated that any hope for identification was long gone. Viggo and his crew buried the bodies themselves, on the edge of the Gaulic forest.

Now was no time to be questioning what gnarly creatures swam beneath the surface, or if he would ever be able to identify all of the victims who had haunted his dreams. It was time to prepare for the possibility of battle.

And Gods forbid if there was evidence of the lithe-filled cargo ship being taken by Surtrian rebels, Viggo didn't even want to consider the destruction the king would order onto the islands. Or the destruction that would occur when Viggo told his father that he refused to lead another mission with the purpose of conquering. Or maybe even coming clean about what he had truly been doing in the Surtr Islands all this time.

Maybe he would do as he had in the past, and remain the ever-loyal little general in front of his father and his court; but secretly do everything in his power to ensure the safety of the Sutrians by making it *seem* like he was killing them.

It was an incredibly difficult line to toe, but he had saved thousands of lives by doing so.

As far as the average Skierkan knew, Viggo was nothing but a Morlok general that often succumbed to his savage bloodlust. And while the common Skierkan wouldn't exactly be wrong about that, they could never know how much innocent bloodshed that he prevented.

The loss of those lives that he was unable to prevent — in order to keep his cover—weighed heavily on Viggo's soul. He felt them each, like stones that rested on his chest; pushing down on his lungs and sending cracks into his heart. The uncertainty of the future of his kingdom—that Aria's possible shipwreck brought—was another stone added to his already heavy chest.

Deep underneath his scarred and callused skin, and even deeper than his bloodied heart, he knew what he had to do to save both Skierka and the Surtrian Islands. He knew the only answer laid in his very hands. But Viggo was almost in his thirtieth year, and he was already so tired of causing bloodshed. He couldn't admit to himself just yet that the only route towards peace was one of gore and carnage.

Gore and carnage. It was all he knew. All he was trained to know. Yet it was the one thing he ached to end by any means.

Tired of having the same haunted conversation with himself day in and day out, Viggo made himself useful. He quickly worked to ensure that each of their weapons were loaded and deadly sharp. Going the extra step, he even took his favorite crossbow out and slung it across his back. For good measure, Viggo loaded a few arrows in it, making the bow uncomfortable against his skin, but made him breathe easier knowing it was there.

With the crossbow gently tapping on his back with each of his long steps, Viggo went around to his crew and gave them each a raw chunk of crystal lithe, to help them go without breathing if the ship were to go underwater, and blooded lithe in case any of the sea beasts decided to act up.

Silia remained at the top of the mast, seemingly unbothered by the constant sway of the sail. "You see anything?" Viggo howled over the wind.

"When I see something, I'll tell you!" Silia hollered down.

"Alright, alright." Viggo muttered to himself, walking towards the edge of the boat. He knew these waters as well as anyone, and wanted to see the colors of the water to determine just how close they were to the trench. Viggo could just make out the heavy swirly patterns of the thick trench water under the ship. The currents pulled the slightly lighter water at the top of the Dahs into itself like a nest of starved snakes.

They must be getting closer to the trench now, if not already at the edge.

The hot rays of the sun beat down onto Viggo's olive skin, causing a few rogue beads of sweat to run down his face and into the water beneath. Silently, he watched as the drops were pulled deep down into the sea beneath. Just as he was turning to bring the twins more silver lithe, Viggo saw something twinkle from deep below the surface. His entire body tensed as whatever it was that sparkled disappeared.

"Something moved underneath us." Viggo yelled. "Stay alert." His husky voice boomed.

Emir and Skender continued working in tandem, pulling the winds to keep them moving. They made sure that they didn't move the boat too quickly, knowing that the most ancient predators had a thing for a chase.

Viggo searched the waters underneath the boat and around them for a clue as to what creature was able to visibly sparkle from not only within the Dahs, but by the Rigelus trench. His black hair fell over his face yet again, causing Viggo to push his hair back in a brief moment of distraction and dropped the red ribbon into the Dahs.

Suddenly, another silver twinkle appeared from deep below the ship. Seemingly moving slowly and all too fast at the same time, the twinkle grew in size before completely disappearing once more.

As Viggo remained so focused on the silver light beneath, he almost missed the sharp claws that pulled the red ribbon like a string off a harp and out of sight with an unholy speed. Growing frustrated at not knowing whatever creature lurked below, Viggo called to his crew, "There's definitely something here—maybe some-things. Don't adjust our course or pace. Just keep going."

Silently, Viggo pulled the crossbow that was slung across his back into his hands. Without fully realizing what he was doing, he plucked a piece of red thread from one of the blankets and dropped it into the waters.

His fingers shook with anticipation, as he held his gaze on the thread for as long as he physically could. After the red disappeared out of sight, Viggo kept his gaze locked onto its last seen location. His sculpted shoulders began to ache as he angled the bow further down, following the trajectory he imagined it would fall. Several moments passed where Viggo kept his bow at the ready.

As the general of the Skierkan armies, Viggo could maintain a fixed stance for hours, but it wasn't exactly something that was comfortable. He also knew that it was dangerous to hyperfixate on one point of the Dahs, and lose track of the rest of their surroundings. Just when Viggo was ready to move on from the glimmers below, he heard an enchanting giggle cascade from the waters behind the boat.

In sync, the entire unit's heads snapped to the waters just behind the stern. Silia, the only one at a vantage point where she could see the creature, angled her own bow onto the giggler. Her brows furrowed upon taking in the sight, "A syren," Silia yelled to the males beneath her.

Viggo cautiously walked to the hull. He kept his crossbow at the ready, as Emir and Skender kept watch for other surprises that could pop up on the other sides of the ship. The sharp sound of their swords sliding out of their sheathes vibrated across the ship. Viggo took a deep breath as he prepared to see the syren. He saw one once as a boy, his brother and father captured it and brought it to the Zojz trench to live the rest of her life as a slave. A small part of him briefly wondered if this syren knew her.

The syren's long hair danced violently into the wind, whipping back and forth in a dangerous song. In a mere moment, he was lulled from his thoughts on the enslaved syren from his youth and to the black cherries that grew around his mother's childhood home. The same color as this syren's hair. Her eyes even matched the dark pits that Viggo remembered sucking on as a child—savoring each and every morsel of juice it had to offer.

He had only seen the syren for a brief moment, and he was already transported to a deeply nostalgic area of his psyche. He was back in Etra's countryside, eating a slice of his grandmother's fresh cherry pie that he had been smelling all day. Viggo's heart physically warmed as he kept walking towards the beautiful creature that seemed to effortlessly lay on top of the Dahs as if it were a fluffed mattress.

Her lips were a dark red, almost purple, that shone under the sunlight. Seeing Viggo draw closer, the syren leaned back and flipped her hair behind her shoulders—exposing her full, perky breasts. Her dark eyes narrowed onto Viggo's shoulders, still tightly holding onto the crossbow. Suddenly his thoughts were no longer at the rickety kitchen table devouring a cherry pie, but in between the silky, ruby red sheets of a friend that he used to know. The syren bit her lip and blinked, before mischievously looking up into the general's face as if she knew exactly which memories had popped into his distracted mind.

"For a man who stinks of death, you're not too bad to look at." The syren's sweet voice reached over the waves and into Viggo's ears with an ease unknown to humans.

"Can I help you?" Viggo answered back, keeping his voice relaxed. He tightened the leash that held onto his thoughts, keeping himself from darting away to comfortable memories and seductive feelings. Syrens were one of the few creatures who had the ability to influence the emotions of humans. They could also plant false feelings of trust in their victims. Something about the way their magic worked caused all souls to want to trust them and invite them closer. The fishermen of Skierka would often tell lore of syrens sensing their victims' desires, both those that their victims were unable to admit to themselves, and the ones that lay at the top of their mind. He wondered what the syren would answer if he were to ask her what he desired most. If she knew the answers to the questions that plagued his soul.

Her head angled, as if she could sense the general's train of thought. "What is it that you want to know, Prince?" The syren asked, peering up at the general through a thick row of lashes.

"I'm no prince."

She giggled once again. "If you say so." She dropped her body just beneath the surface, remaining visible to both Viggo and Silia. Her long-scaled tail pumped her closer to the boat as she swam on her back, ensuring that the general's view of her chest remained unobstructed. When she surfaced, she glided effortlessly up next to Viggo, latching onto the boat and flipping her long hair behind her. Water splashed onto Viggo, who didn't bother wiping it off of his face. He couldn't afford any distraction from the creature. She had yet to identify her reason for appearing in front of the crew today. Simply glimpsing a syren is a rarity, an omen for death to come, even. Viggo couldn't help but wonder if the only reason he was led to believe that syrens rarely interacted with humans was because they left no survivors to tell their tales.

The syren's eyes narrowed onto Viggo's crossbow that remained tightly focused on her. Her brows furrowed and she snarled revealing teeth that somehow elongated and sharpened in a matter of seconds. Her once beautiful, dark cherry eyes flashed white, and her voice rang like a broken bell. "Either shoot me or put your weapon down."

"If I were to put my bow down, what would stop you from slaughtering me and my squadron?" Viggo challenged.

In an instant, the syren's teeth blunted. Her eyes became a sweet chocolate, a change from the cherry red, and all her facial muscles relaxed, beside her lips, which she kept in a dangerous pout. Viggo noted the change in her coloring, and wandered exactly how much of their appearance they could change.

She lifted herself up closer to Viggo. Her pillow-like lips grazed the finger he kept wrapped around the trigger. Suddenly a warm summer breeze hit Viggo, carrying with it the sultry jasmine scent of the syren. Aware of her powers testing his, Viggo kept his entire body rigid. He felt her warm magic brush against his like the tickle of a feather.

"Sweet prince, why would I want to kill you?" Like a ripple originating from her waist, her plum-colored tail transformed into impossibly smooth and slender legs that seemed to go on for days.

The syren pulled herself up onto the ledge of the boat. Her wet hair dripped down onto the wooden boards, causing a small puddle underneath Viggo's shoes.

"It is your people that kill my kind for sport. Not the other way around," The syren reminded him.

The general inhaled, allowing his lungs to completely fill before exhaling. The two kept their eyes locked on one another while Viggo decided how to proceed. Well aware that Silia would never lower her bow, Viggo brought his down to his sides. "Is that why you are here? For revenge?"

"If it was revenge that I sought, you and your friends' deaths would bring me no atonement."

"And what would me and my friends' deaths bring you?"

"A mild inconvenience," she teased, keeping a careful eye on the general.

"You asked what I want to know, Syren." Viggo carefully eyed her. While he was usually able to tell right away when someone was lying or manipulating him, syrens were master manipulators with thousands of years of evolution honing their ability to sense desire and manipulate others. And that's not even to mention whatever kind of magic coursed through their chilled veins. "I want to know why you are here."

The syren smirked and released a small, but condescending scoff. "How much longer will you continue wasting my time? Ask what you really want to know."

Viggo's jaw tightened as he sensed the syren's powers retreating. Whatever it was that she was here for, she didn't need her powers for it. "Who attacked Aria's ship?" He was certain that somehow the syren already knew what they sought in the Dahs. And for what it was worth, he would bet all of the lithe in his back pocket that the syren wasn't here to simply kill them, or even to look for intel.

The syren's smile grew a few sizes too large for such a delicate face. "Closer. But that's not the question that you want to know." The syren let out a hot and impatient breath. "I am growing so very bored of this little charade."

A dark and threatening laugh pulsed out of the general's mouth. "I am growing tired of these childish games." He took a step towards the creature and placed a gentle hand on the bottom of her chin. He tilted her head up towards his face. "While that may not be the question that haunts my sleep or twists my gut, it is the question that I am willing to ask you today. Understood?"

Her eyes wandered across the general's face with the intensity of an owl perched over a mice-infested plain. "I understand more than you realize." She hissed.

And all at once, the syren's already too-large smile grew three sizes. Her teeth sharpened into serrated blades. Thick claws, sharp enough to rip bone sprouted out where once dainty nails grew. The tail that had once sat below the beautiful creature's waist, that had turned into legs briefly, transformed once again into something far more sinister. Each scale protruded out with sharp edges that dripped with the syren's syrupy venom. Viggo watched in awe as he took in each detail of the syren's anatomy. There was no doubt in his mind that every part of the syren was designed to create the ideal predator.

He held a hand up towards his crew, signaling them to hold off from firing onto the syren. He was yet to be convinced that the syren was after their blood. He knew when a female was putting on a show.

Without flinching, Viggo was able to keep his gaze locked onto the syren's. His eyes were kept level, and his jaw relaxed. "Am I supposed to be afraid?" He dared.

The syren released the same sweet laugh that she had used to give her position away. Only it was even odder now that it escaped the twisted and sharp mouth of her true form.

"Am I?" She challenged, flicking her gaze towards Silia, whose bow was angled straight at the creature's heart.

Viggo sighed, allowing himself to look all too bored with the interaction. "Lower your bow." He ordered. The general didn't have to look back to know that Silia followed the order, he also didn't have to look back to know that she was probably pissed about it.

"Why are you here?" Viggo demanded.

"I'm holding up my end of a deal."

His eyes narrowed. "What kind of a deal?"

With a ripple, the syren fell into her humanoid form. A sinister smile was all that was left of the wicked creature that she transformed into, now back into the body with lean legs instead of a muscular tail.

Taking another moment to study the general's face, the syren whispered, "The answer that you seek will be waiting for you at home." And then after raising her voice, loud enough for Viggo's crew to hear, she said, "Your shipwreck is close. Turn your course due east and you will be there by nightfall."

Without another word, the syren allowed herself to fall back into the dark waters below. Like a powerful wave, her body quickly transformed back into the body honed for hunting. Nothing was left of the beautiful creature but a spot of her purple blood on the sharp wood edge of the boat.

Her long, spiked tail was the last thing Viggo saw before she disappeared into the darkness.

CHAPTER 9
ARIA

"Why do you reek of blood?"

It had been several days since Aria had last seen the Prince taking off with the Irridesci. She had spent most of that first day reading whatever romance novels she could get her claws on. Sometimes she would explore the seemingly never-ending palace with Zaries, and occasionally they would run throughout the grounds—as Zaries was trying to lose some weight, and Aria was trying to pack on some muscle.

The first night that she hadn't seen the Prince at all, she had come back to her chambers to find a fantastic harp awaiting her. Crafted from the bone white lumber of the osseinic tree, with intricate carvings of ravens and skeletons that raced up the pillar and all the way to the crown of the harp, it was easily one of most beautiful things that she had ever seen.

Since then, she had spent hours each evening playing the harp. She had started with the same songs she had memorized as a child, each note coming back to her with ease. Every time she played, she felt the pit in her stomach shrink, only to swell again once she stopped. An air of peace and tranquility surrounded Aria as she played the harp, just as it had when she learned as a child, on a tiny and bruised imitation of a harp. Her father would always tell her that the harp was a holy instrument among their people, originally gifted to them from Freyite, the Goddess of Beauty, herself. While Aria held many doubts about the stories of the Gods, the holiness of the harp was not one.

Eventually, the evening guards, Orin and Skye, would bring her new sheet music each evening. Occasionally servants, students, and all those who resided in the palace would make their way to Aria's quarters to listen to her play.

Tired of escorting Aria's audience, the Vermilli began to leave the hall to her room unlocked while she played. The door to Aria's chambers still remained locked, and to enter people would knock so very softly. Orin would camp by the door and let people in. Everyone would enter as quietly as possible, to not disturb Aria's little 'sunset concerts' as they eventually became known around the palace.

Once word got around that Aria had a particular love of the spicy licorice teas, sugary breads, and strong wines, the people would also begin to bring her little gifts along with the song requests, most being lullabies they remembered their mothers singing.

The most she had seen of Raask was out of her window, coming back from his run along the shore of the Dahs. Like clockwork, he would come and go at the same time every day, and Aria would watch out from her window. So, when Raask had finally appeared at her door one morning for breakfast, reeking of blood, Aria was more than happy to continue being rude to him.

"It's nice to see you too, sweet thing." Raask smirked as he brushed past her and into her chambers. He took a seat at her table and helped himself to a boiled egg and piece of her brown bread.

She gave him a piercing look and crossed her arms, still standing by the door. "I asked you why you reek of blood." Zaries sniffed from the other side of the table and muttered, "I don't smell anything." That comment earned him a glaring look from Aria.

Raask eyed her carefully, not used to being spoken to like a common dog. "And I ignored you." He answered, before taking a large bite out of the bread and thanking Zaries for saying that he didn't smell.

Aria scoffed as she shut the door and walked back to her seat at the table.

"I noticed." She challenged, before blowing onto her hot tea, keeping an eye on the prince's reaction. And when his head tilted to the side, and he smiled at her with that cocky know-it-all grin, it took everything in Aria not to throw the hot water right into his smug face.

"If I didn't know better, I would say that it seemed like you missed me."

"Good thing you do know better." She rolled her eyes, taking a slice of bread and slathering it with an ungodly amount of butter. Raask watched with amusement in his eyes. "If you don't answer why you reek of blood, then I will have to ask you to leave."

"Truly, Aria, I don't think that Prince Raask smells." Zaries pleaded with her, not wanting to have to refuse her request to throw out his own prince.

Raask took one long look at her, drinking her in like a drunkard. And when his eyes traveled to her lips, she made sure to give them just the right amount of pout. She knew that he would answer any question that came from a mouth as pretty as hers. All males were the same in that sense. "I've been practicing my magic in the dark hours. Sometimes it makes my nose bleed."

Aria's shoulders loosened just the slightest. She took a sip from her tea while she thought for a few moments. "Is your magic supposed to hurt you? Make you bleed?" She asked between sips. Zaries' eyes grew wide. His chair scraped against the floor as he stood up too fast. "I think that I have some business to attend to in the gardens." Before he exited out the door, he turned to Aria and said, "I will be by the gardens if you wish to find me later." They locked eyes, and she nodded, biting back amusement by Zaries' timid nature around the prince.

Raask waited until the door clicked shut. "You ought to be careful which questions you ask a prince." He reclined back into his seat and poured himself a glass of tawny. "Some may consider your question an act of treason against the kingdom of Skierka."

"Do you?" Aria asked.

"That depends," The Prince answered with a smirk. Aria watched Raask as he drank his cup of tawny, nearly finishing the whole thing in only a few gulps. She cringed as the prince put the glass back down onto the birch table with no coaster in sight. The tiny drop of tawny that had dripped down the glass was on its way to permanently mark the beautiful table that Aria had become quite fond of.

Unable to watch Raask's carelessness ruin the fine wood, with the speed of a great tide, she yanked a coaster from their hidden compartment in the side of the table and shoved it under the Prince's cup. As she wiped away the drip from the side of the glass, she noticed Raask watching her.

"What does it depend on?" She challenged, and overcompensated with a fierce tone after feeling a little insecure after her display.

"Well, if you're truly just a Surtrian girl from a long line of lithe miners whose boat was destroyed, who *somehow* washed ashore on the beach in front of me, and is then a little curious about magic, then it's a fine question to ask, I suppose. Although an illegal question to ask and you should note that." He took the last remaining sip of his tawny, careful to lick the dribble that ran down the edge of the cup, before placing it back onto its coaster. Aria's eyes widened at the display, but remained silent. "But, if you're a spy who was sent here to learn our secrets, then that would obviously be an act of treason. Would it not?" Raask's face remained the same as before, but his voice grew cold. Like a fearful switch inside of him had suddenly been flipped, alerting him to the potential vulnerabilities and responding the only way he knew how. She'd observed many nobles of the Morlok court respond in similar manners during her weeks exploring the castle with Zaries. The Skierkans were so strange and prideful. She couldn't understand for the life of her what exactly they were so proud of. Every great thing that had come out of Skierka had come from their occupation of another culture.

Aria flashed him a too-sweet smile, potentially overcompensating once again. "To commit treason, doesn't one need to be a citizen?" She could feel she was pulling the wrong strings and reacting in all of the wrong ways. Deep inside of her bones laid a predatory hunger that would always react with violence in response to a challenge. It's what had kept her alive so far, but would do her no favors in her current position. She had stumbled upon entry to the Bleached Palace. She was on speaking terms with the prince. And she felt the eyes of her ancestors upon her.

"We conquered the Surtr Islands. The Surtrians are now Skierkans." Raask said evenly.

She bit her lip and furrowed her brows as she zeroed in on a spot just behind the Prince. After several long moments passed, Aria said in an uncharacteristically small voice, "You are correct; your people have conquered the islands."

The Prince's angry stare softened in response to the hurt in her voice. He silently reached a hand out across the table to Aria, and delicately lifted her hand into his.

"I don't know why I said that." Raask gently massaged the rough skin on Aria's hands, as she avoided his gaze.

"Well, I do." Aria said.

She turned away and quickly blotted at her eyes with a thick napkin, before turning to look back at the Prince. "If you are waiting for me to say something that will convince you that I am no spy, then you are wasting your breath." He surveyed her face, searching for a hint as to her thoughts. She could see his regret in the lump that swelled at his throat. She could nearly feel it in the heaviness of the air.

But when his eyes instinctively darted back to her lips, Aria watched his muscles ease and a tongue run across his lips. How quickly men moved from regret to hunger. And how quickly hunger could turn to violence.

She needed to ensure that Raask saw her as nothing more than a girl who needed help from a shining prince. The love story, where he was one of the leads.

"I am not one for eloquent words or speeches." She paused, allowing her words and the ache behind her voice to be registered by the prince. "All I know is that my family is gone. And I am alone in a strange place."

It was these words that broke the prince. Just as she knew they would. She could feel the aching loneliness that sat behind his gaze, as heavy and hidden as a secret identity.

In an instant, Raask was at her side, clutching her head to his chest as she held onto him. And she was crying.

She was crying so hard that it was a miracle she could breathe at all.

Her salty tears soaked the prince's shirt while he gently rubbed her back. When her thunderous tears began to slow to a drizzle, Aria drew back. Raask tucked his fingers underneath her chin, and tenderly tilted her head up. She fought the instinct to flinch at the touch of his calloused fingers, surprised that the Prince of Skierka's hands were not soft from years of pampering, but rough and thickened like hers. His other hand wiped away the last of her tears as he whispered her a promise.

"Viggo and his crew are inspecting the shipwreck to identify the responsible party. And when he does, I want you to know, that nothing in this realm will stop me from gutting them." He lowered the hand he was using to wipe her tears and ran his thumb down the center of her lips tugging slowly at her bottom lip. "That is my promise to you."

Breathlessly, Aria asked, "And what if I would like to be the one to take revenge? To gut someone? Would that scare you, Prince?"

Her chest ached, hollow and cold as she awaited his answer. Almost as if she really wanted to know if he would accept her for who she truly was? *Ruthless. Violent. Bloodthirsty.*

Why do you care? Her own voice, cruel and sharp, snapped within her mind with the fierceness of a cracking wave. And as the wave broke across her mind, a chill raced through her body. Her eyes scanned Raask's. She noted him for more than his muscular build. And she noticed the concern in his eyes. The warmth in his smile.

A part of her reacted in anger, to the ease of softness that he could feel. But, somehow, a part of her felt a lulling pull into him . . . A longing even. Perhaps she was just jealous of his easy life. Yes, that must be it . . .

Aria watched carefully as the Prince's face transformed from momentary shock, to a true and genuine smile. Her toes curled beneath her as she watched it. *Why do you care?* She heard her own voice ask again, quieter this time, as her own heart was beating too loud to hear it.

And when he gripped the back of her head, before pulling her into an aggressive kiss, her body reacted instinctually. She wrapped her arms around his neck and jumped up into his arms. Effortlessly, and with what Aria assumed was perhaps too much practice, Raask held her against the wall. From far away, Aria could hear her own inner voice telling her that this was all wrong.

She was not supposed to enjoy the kiss of a Morlok.

But she did.

His lips felt like endless sips of a bubbly spirit, and she couldn't help herself from wanting more. *More. More.*

She was not supposed to enjoy the kiss of a Morlok.

To kiss for survival, for trickery, for fun, was all fine.

But this was something else.

Aria pulled away from the kiss and made her way over to his ear. She tightened the hold her legs had on the Prince's waist, before she pointed out that he had never answered her question.

With a dark thunderous laugh, Raask finally answered. "If it's revenge you want, it's what I'll give you."

She examined his face, uncertain if he was telling the truth or saying whatever he thought would get her to allow him into her bed.

Still uncertain, she hopped out of his arms. Standing on her own two feet, she refused to distance herself from him.

"Prove it."

He bit his lip and gave her one final look up and down before heading to her door. Hurt, and then angry, Aria watched him leave her room. And when he didn't bother to shut the door behind him, her anger turned into a white-hot rage.

"Are you coming, love?" Raask called from the end of her hall.

Stifling a smile, Aria grabbed a long fur cloak and hurried after him.

CHAPTER 10
RAASK

Raask couldn't suppress the smile that crept across his face at the sound of Aria's hurried footsteps padding towards him. "You didn't think I was leaving, did you?"

As soon as she caught up, she hurled her fist into his bicep with a punch that bordered on playful and painful.

He led her down the winding stairs and halls of his family's palace as he asked Aria questions about the other books she'd been reading since he last saw her. It took until they were at the entrance to the palace before she finally started to relax, and tell him her real thoughts on the books and the ridiculous characters, and they were actually exiting the castle by the time she finally told him about her little sunset concerts. She told him of the songs people would bring for her to play, and the way it made her feel free. Raask nodded along and asked questions about her background with the harp, pretending that he had no clue about her nightly concerts.

After the disappointing night with Balk several days ago, that took place after a long decade of many disappointing and painful nights spent in the Irridesci tower, Raask felt too ashamed to be around people. So, in his spare time, when he was not training, he wandered around aimlessly. Sometimes he would scurry to the back corner of the library, scouring for answers on his elusive but powerful magic. But mostly he stuck to the aimless wandering around halls and hidden corridors he had discovered long ago. He was in no mood to travel down to the pubs.

It didn't help that Balk had decided to increase his monthly training to weekly, in what felt like a feeble attempt to find his alignment before the upcoming royal trials. Raask was becoming more and more desperate with each passing second. He spent every moment of his life in preparation for the throne, and it would all be in vain if he couldn't find the true conduit for his magic. A task—that he was often reminded—that didn't typically require any effort of most Morloks.

Whenever he would get close, he would hyper-focus on his heart and the heartbeats of those around him. He would hyper-fixate on their breaths and his own, until it drove him positively mad. It always went the same way until he would, of course, black out. A truly exhausting cycle with seemingly no end.

The only respite to his misery was the harp music that swam through the halls of Morlok Palace each evening. He knew, without having to investigate, that it was Aria's playing he heard. He would listen carefully as Aria made her way through the music the people of Etra would bring for her. Yesterday he had even paid off a young servant to bring Aria the sheet music to one of the songs his mother had sung to him as a child. As she played, Raask was transported back to a time when his mother was still alive and his only concern was having enough time to play with Viggo.

Once she finished playing the song of his childhood, Raask made a pact with himself that despite his own internal misery, he would speak with her the next morning.

Just as the sound of her harp pulled him into seeing her again, the sound of her voice breaking had him ready to give her anything and everything this world had to offer. And the fact that all she wanted was to take her own revenge on the bastard who killed her family made it official, Aria was the most remarkable creature he had ever met.

But if he was to keep his promise to her, as he intended, Aria was going to need to learn some basic combat skills. There was no way he would put a civilian into a dangerous situation, let alone the beautifully violent creature that walked beside him. Zaries had also let him know that Aria was trying to gain her strength back, so he knew that she would be happy to join him in training.

"We'll take an easy pace and do a quick loop. And we can take as many breaks as you need." Raask said, beginning to stretch.

"I won't need a break, but you let me know if you need one." Aria ran off, shrugging off her coat and getting a head start. Laughing, Raask quickly caught up.

He had no idea how fast or strong she was before the shipwreck, but whatever muscle mass Aria had built from her past was gone. Her breaths became heavy, and she started to drastically slow down before they had even made it to the shore.

"You sound like shit."

Aria's scoff was buried underneath her panting, but it was there alright. "Well, you look like shit."

It took them longer than it generally took for Raask to complete his entire loop alone, before they finally made it to the Dahs.

Aria remained a few paces behind Raask, trying to mask the sound of her heavy breathes. Giving up on Aria asking for a break, Raask asked her if she wanted to come with him to visit an old friend. The baker who would generally nurse his hangovers in the Salt District was not far at all from where they were, and he knew that the baker would be kind enough to not say anything about her obvious physical distress. Aria quickly agreed, which surprised Raask, as she had always been an incredibly disagreeable creature.

Raask decided this must mean she was even more exhausted than he thought, and wondered if it was a bad idea to take her on this loop for her first day. But it was too late now anyways.

The smell of warm, fresh bread wafted down the cobblestone

streets, slicing through the strong scents of smoked hallucinogens and spirits that permanently stained the Salt District. Ilana's apartment over the Mink's Den was not far, but Raask found himself hoping that she wouldn't see him and Aria together. He had yet to see her since he had ditched her steps from her apartment over the Mink's Den and sprinted towards as she crawled out of the Dahs on that cold, cold night.

While Ilana was kind and generous with him, he knew that he was one of few—if not the only person—who was able to see that side of her. Most saw her as a cold, manipulative, and greedy woman who had somehow charmed her way into the prince's heart. Raask had seen her conduct business enough, to know that those people weren't exactly wrong, but they weren't exactly right either. Ilana could be cold, and even vicious, but she did what she had to do, and she did it while protecting her girls.

Aria had washed ashore without family, her own possessions, and a way to make her own money, at the moment. She was all-in-all the perfect target for Ilana, who he knew was currently recruiting more girls.

Raask couldn't take the risk of Ilana seeing them and giving Aria her little recruitment spiel that somehow transfixed almost all who heard. Helk, listening to her give her spiel with the bright eyes and warmth that she reserved for these pitches, sometimes he considered running away to the Mink's Den himself.

Ilana had a gift of convincing others to do what she wanted, while they thought it was what *they* wanted. And Raask just couldn't allow it to happen to Aria. He wasn't sure what it was, but from the moment he heard her cries, he'd felt a need to protect her. Even more than that, he felt the need to serve her.

The sound of a sea wraith rumbling from somewhere close brought Raask back to his senses. Looking back to the sea, and briefly at Aria to ensure she was alright, Raask realized it was no sea wraith's growl but Aria's stomach.

Blushing, Aria said, "What? I'm starving all the time now, okay!"

"Do you have some kind of beast in there?"

He laughed as Aria scrunched her nose and hurried her pace. Her long, wild black hair bounced with her steps as she followed the decadent scent of fresh bread to the green entrance to the bakery.

The bell chimed as Aria opened the door, Raask followed close enough behind that he nearly brushes against her. The smell of fresh pastries and loaves of thick bread smacked them in the face as they walked towards the counter, listening to the sounds of kneading dough and pots clanking coming from the back. "One second!" The baker called.

"Take your time!" Raask yelled back. The sound of kneading stopped at Raask's voice.

Out from the kitchen came a tall and stocky red-haired man covered in flour. He smirked at Raask and gave Aria a welcoming nod. "I haven't seen you in a few weeks, your Highness."

Raask waved off the *your highness*. "Yeah I've been busy lately." He pulled out a stool from under the counter and patted it for Aria before taking his own seat.

The baker smiled at Aria before bringing out two huge glasses of fresh water. He winked as he passed it to Aria, who had—for the most part—appeared to have caught her breath by now. "Thank you," she said, surprisingly sweetly. So she was capable of being polite.

The baker smiled. "Anything for one of Raask's friends." The baker, who Raask had long assumed had part-Rakkei in him—with his dark skin and small pupils—gave a kind smile despite the long scars across his face.

"We aren't friends really," Aria said.

"No?" The baker asked.

Raask stifled a laugh before shaking his head. "I'm working on it, Arthur."

"I see." Arthur responded, taking a few moments to watch the two together. Without saying a word, he disappeared into the back.

Aria's big brown eyes looked at Raask in confusion. Smiling, he dragged her chair closer to his and whispered into her ear, "Don't worry, this is kind of his thing."

Before Aria had the chance to ask, Arthur had come back from the kitchen carrying two loaves of bread. He quickly sliced them and handed Raask a piece of cheesy bread, with butter thick enough to look like a slice of cheese. And for Aria, Arthur had chosen a swirled cinnamon raisin bread, with some kind of sweet brown butter spread over the top.

Raask watched in wonder as Aria's eyes grew six sizes at the sight of the cinnamon bread. Her often-pouty face switched into the rare radiant look she seemed to save for sweets. Her glow and joy felt like a blessing from Svati, Goddess of Kindness.

Aria took a big bite out of the bread and her eyes nearly sank into the back of her head in pure bliss. "This is the most delicious thing I've ever tasted." Aria said in between bites. Raask's laugh filled the small bakeshop, "I think you got it right." He said to Arthur.

Arthur beamed with pride. "I'm honored, Miss Aria."

She sucked the sweet butter off from her fingers and tilted her head to the side in a manner that Raask couldn't quite decide to be lethal or playful. "How did you know my name?"

"Not every day a pretty girl crawls out of the Dahs." Arthur shrugged.

He went ahead and sliced another piece off for Aria and slid her new plate over. Arthur's ever-careful gaze looked at Raask, lingering on the bags underneath his eyes and the tightness in his shoulders. Hoping to deflect Arthur's incoming line of questioning, he was the first to ask how he had been since last seeing him.

"Fine. Ilana was asking about you." Arthur took a sip from his own water before continuing. "I told her I haven't seen you in a few weeks."

Raask nodded, noticing that Aria's chewing quieted at the mention of Ilana.

"Yeah, there's been a lot going on with the trials coming up so fast." Raask had known Arthur since he was too young to understand that not every child had a team of guards told to kill first and ask questions later. Arthur was one of Raask's personal Vermilli escorts who wore robes in a shade of red so dark it was almost black. He had stayed on as Raask's personal guard for many years after he had earned his retirement from the Vermilli. That was when he went off to open his own bakery in the only area of Skierka that he could afford. Since then, Raask would visit as often as he could. It was no coincidence that Raask's running loop took him through the Salt District and right past the bakery.

Raask and Arthur spent a few more minutes catching up before they bid him farewell. Arthur had promised Aria a loaf of the cinnamon swirl if she ever stopped by again. She promised to be back tomorrow on their morning run with the seriousness of a call to war.

After gorging themselves on Arthur's breads, Raask had decided it would be best to walk the rest of the route up to the palace. They trudged past Raask's favorite pubs, views of the city, and the homes of his favorite palace guards. He happily told Aria all about the best spots in the city to find a good breakfast, tawny, or even a good time. Even though the walk took much longer than the run, it seemed to have gone by faster with their conversation. Surprisingly, Aria listened to all of it, and asked questions. She took jabs at him whenever the occasion arised, but she'd always laugh afterwards in that way that Raask couldn't get enough of.

He watched her carefully. Her light steps. The way she seemed to take note of her surroundings constantly. She did not blush—nor run— from the stares from his people. No. She puffed her chest up high and scowled.

He saw it in her, the way she held herself. She was cold, yes, but there was more to it than that. She moved and spoke like she was constantly challenging anyone and everyone. He was entranced by it. His entire life he *had* to be friendly and charming. She did not hide behind pleasantries, she laid her feelings out for all to see.

When they arrived back at the palace, Raask had been ready to call it a day on training, but Aria insisted on training basic combat moves as Raask had promised earlier. She called him a liar if he didn't do as he said this morning, and train her. She yelled it, actually yelled at *him*. The Crown Prince of Skierka.

So he took her to the training arena. He didn't want to be a liar and he'd do anything to forlong their time together. While she wasn't as strong as he would have liked her to be in order to take on whoever or whatever attacked her family, he was impressed with her determination. She was flexible enough to contort her body into odd angles that even advanced wrestlers had a difficult time succeeding in. And in short spurts, she was able to move incredibly fast, ducking and hitting before Raask was able to see where she was. It seemed that her angelic face and soft curves were the perfect disguise for the beautiful little savage that she hid inside.

The next several weeks bled slowly into each other. Their morning runs along the Dahs went quicker each time. Every day, Aria had to take fewer and fewer breaks during their runs and their training. Raask showed her the basics in weaponry, hand-to-hand combat, and even basic anatomy, so she would know where to best target any attackers.

While it was easy for Raask to see that she had some background in fighting—from the way she naturally stood in the correct stance for archery, or the way that her hands naturally and correctly palmed a dagger—it was even easier for him to not care to ask. She was sour and bitter and playful and sweet all rolled into one little creature that he couldn't quite get enough of. A mystery that he liked too much to solve too quickly.

As the time passed, her once frail limbs grew muscular. She was getting stronger each day and her soft curves grew—along with her muscles—giving her a silhouette that made the guards begin to look back at her as she passed. It was at one of these moments, when a nasty member of the court had all but dropped his jaw as Aria walked in front of him, that Raask had realized it. His fists tightened at his sides. It took every ounce of his self-control to not sign an execution sentence for the miserly member of the court from the southern shore. Instead he had seen to it that he had been sent away on an *important mission* very far away from the palace.

In a short matter of time, he had grown absolutely enchanted with Aria.

He obsessed over the way her lips moved slightly as she read the books that Zaries would bring her. And when she would occasionally bite her lip when thinking really hard about something—it was enough to drive him positively wild. When she made tea, she'd give it a good smell before drinking and smile so smugly that it appeared that she was proving someone wrong about how delicious it smelled.

She felt like a rough gem hidden in a bucket of overly polished stones, that managed to feel raw and true against a sea of sameness. His life had always been so polished and proper. So regal.

And his anger and resentment towards his own magic, his own blood and his own high standing in the court, had always been something he hid deeply from the courts. Helk, he even hid it deeply from himself when he could, for he knew that it was not proper of a prince to be so angry. It was not right to carry darkness in the heart. To be resentful over the blessing of a crown would be foolish, he knew that.

And in knowing that, he knew he was a fool.

With each year he grew more and more into a puppet, willed by his people, his father, the Irridesci. He was nothing but a smiling face and source of charm for the court. An agreeable figurehead who entertained the women of the court and visiting diplomats. Raask was nothing but a jester. He knew it. His father knew it. And the higher courtesans knew it.

But Aria . . . She felt like an angry storm that threatened to light the whole realm on fire, and Raask was nothing more than the moth that kept coming back, begging for her burn.

CHAPTER II
A CREATURE

Nobody knew that she came up to the shore to watch.

The tides closer to the land of Etra were uncomfortably warm. The sun baked onto her scales as she sat and waited and waited and waited. Each morning for years she had come to watch the Prince of Skierka run past.

Butterflies took over her entire belly each time he ran into her sight. His golden hair and tanned skin is what she always saw first when she watched him, followed by his impressive muscles, and then his sweet smile.

For years she would swim along the shore while he ran. Watching.

She watched as the prince would buy iced treats for sweet and naughty children, alike. She watched as the prince would bring coats for old drunks and dirty loiterers in the cooler months. She watched and loved him from afar.

It was dangerous for her to watch. Yes, so close to the shore was a dangerous place for a creature like her. Syrens were hunted for sport and trophies by the people of Skierka. But she knew in her heart that her prince would never hurt her or any of her kind. He was mistaken to believe her kind were all nasty and rotten, the evil kinds of syrens who would trick sailors into love. She would never do that to him . . . or anybody else, for *that matter. She knew he would change Skierka, he would fix the laws. He would free her people, if he only knew that syrens were more than what their stories told them. They could be soft and gentle. They were not born evil, as the Skierkans were taught.*

She could see the kindness radiating from him like sunlight.

It was dangerous for her to come watch him, but she did it anyway. She would watch, and she would love him. It hurt her that he didn't know that she existed. But it was something that she had come to accept in time.

But no . . . who was it that ran with him . . . how could she be there . . .

CHAPTER 12
VIGGO

The darkened edges of Viggo's dreamscape would be eerie to most, but for Viggo it was comforting. He felt at home in the darkness.

But the darkness faded, as it always did, and Viggo knew without any certainty that this was no dream.

The chilled suffocating air let Viggo know that Kel was close by. Kel, the God of Death, Darkness & Destruction, was a bad omen to almost all creatures of the realm besides himself.

For Viggo alone, meeting Kel was a joyous occasion. For what son would not want to see their loving father.

A visit from Kel was like any other fatherly visit, if others' true fathers and their mothers' affair had been kept a secret from the world—including his public father and younger brother. Oh, and if most fathers happened to be the God of Death, Darkness, Destruction, and the underworld commonly referred to as Helk.

Kel had summoned Viggo into his study, which meant two things. One, that Kel needed to discuss some important matter, most likely political. And two, that his mother—who had faked her death rather than admit to the king that she loved another and wished to run off with him to the underrealm which he ruled—did not know that Viggo was summoned.

Viggo sat back in the chair across from his father's empty seat. The chairs in Helk were all stiff, and made from various bones, except for single one. As a child, Viggo complained of the rigidness of the chairs in the underrealm. At his next visit, the chair across from his father's desk was replaced by a plush chair made of some stuffed furs. It was warm, soft, and incredibly comfortable. Really it was the only item in the underrealm that could be described as any of those things.

He was certainly no ordinary father, but neither was the one that Viggo had to publicly accept. And between Kel and the king, there was no competition. Although death radiated from Kel's every pore, he was a loving father to Viggo, guiding and protecting him in ways he was certain he would never even know about. Kel sacrificed everything for Viggo, his mother, and even Raask—who Kel had guided and helped without the young prince ever realizing. Kel did everything in his power to love his son, and his son's half-brother whom he considered family just as well.

The hairs on the back of Viggo's neck raised, and goosebumps covered his exposed flesh. Even though Kel was silent, Viggo was certain he had entered the room behind him. The smell of rot and dust began to seep from him as his powers began to pool in a subconscious response to the feeling of his father's great power coming closer.

"My boy!" Kel cried.

Viggo unleashed a true and genuine smile, a rare thing for him to do since his time in battle. Immediately his magic dissipated as his unease vanished. His magic had been far too temperamental as of late, and he lost control more than he cared to admit.

He stood up as Kel closed the space between them, and fervently accepted his embrace. After Kel patted his back a few too many times, he took his seat across from Viggo.

Made from the bones of an abberack, a similar creature to a moon wraith, but fleshless and with horns the size of trees and wings the length of ponds, originating from the pits of Helk, Kel's chair was properly imposing and horrific.

"How have you been? How's mother?" Viggo asked.

Viggo caught the grimace that flashed across his father's face only because he knew to look out for the crinkling at the corners of his eyes.

"She is good, truly . . ." Kel said.

Sensing a *but*, Viggo angled his head at his father. "What is it? Is she alright?"

"Yes, yes. She is okay. She is safe and in good health. But she does worry for you and your brother." Kel's lips tightened into a line. There was something he wasn't telling Viggo. After several moments passed, Kel let out a heavy breath. "What's going on?" Viggo asked.

"I hear the Gods whispering. Their voices echo to me, even when they communicate in silence, I can hear. Even the my brothers and the other Gods forget that the silence falls under my command."

Viggo nodded, carefully watching his father. It was rare for Kel to discuss the other Gods, so when he did, it was almost always to raise the alarm of something great or something tragic. Whatever it was . . . it was always *something*.

So when the Gods and their hidden agendas were brought up by the ruler of the underrealm, one of the most ancient of the Gods, Viggo knew it was vital to listen to the words left unspoken.

The light lines around Kel's eyes crinkled, and his nostrils flared just the slightest. "A prophecy has been foretold."

Viggo's entire body stiffened. It had been centuries since the last prophecy had been foretold by the wicked sistros. The three sisters who held the secrets of time itself were long thought to be dead. But something deep inside of Viggo's psyche, maybe his own genetic connection to death, told him that the sistros were not yet dead, they had simply given up on this realm.

"And what does it tell?" Viggo asked.

Kel spat, "My arrogant brothers seem to think it's proper to keep secrets from me." Kel's anger summoned the darkness into the room. The temperature dropped, causing Viggo's arms to raise in goosebumps and his breath to fog.

Viggo bit back the surge of his own powers that ached to be released. While Viggo, like his father, could call darkness and the cold from the depths of the underrealm, unlike his father, it affected him deeply. His body was not built for the eternal darkness and frigid temperatures that it could so easily conjure.

"Viggo," Kel's already quiet voice was softer, gentler. Kel allowed the warmth to enter back into the room. "I believe that the prophecy speaks of you, and possibly your brother."

His heart dropped. Viggo could handle anything that the Gods threw at him. He was the feared and blood hungry general of the notorious Skierkan army, leader of the deadliest squadron in the realm, and son of the ancient God of Death, Darkness, and Silence. The Skierkan Bruin. But what he could not bear, was a threat against his brother. It was for him that Viggo endured the king's cruelty. It was for Raask that Viggo went to such great troubles to hide the rebellion he was beginning against his father.

It was all for Raask. It would always be all for Raask.

And in a cruel joke of the sistros, his beloved brother was now in danger. A danger that he possibly couldn't protect him from. But he knew that he would die trying. "Do you know anything else?" Viggo asked, aware of his father's ever-watchful eyes.

"I have sent my scouts to dig up any details that they may find." Kel paused and fed the fire in his hearth. "While I remain in the dark on the content of the prophecy. It goes without saying that most are grim." Viggo noted the unsaid, *especially for mortals and halflings,* that his father had left out. "I urge you to be careful. You must consider every decision going forth. You must weigh the costs of each pathway and the futures that may be found at the end of every decision. You will need to decide what it is that you value the most, what it is that you would sacrifice yourself for."

Viggo knew that his father hadn't meant 'sacrifice his life for', but, his legacy. As a warrior, legacy was the ultimate test of his character. He swallowed once, and then swallowed again. "I understand." Viggo said, in a voice softer than he intended.

Magic stronger and more ancient than even his father's prevented the Gods from interfering with a prophecy uttered by the sistros, and Viggo understood that his father risked a great deal by offering the aid of a warning to his own flesh.

Once the ugly matter of Viggo's legacy and survival was out of the way, Viggo and Kel spent the better part of the next hour catching up. Kel informed his son about the latest onslaught of abberacks from this past breeding season. He had bred this specific batch with the hopes of finding ones that would excel in stealth. Occasionally he would pat the handle of the abberack's carcass that now sat as his own desk chair. The bones from his once favorite and prized abberack held the honor of making his seat. His father had ensured that his soul was pampered, occasionally it would wander out of its circle and back to Kel.

Viggo prattled on about the missions of his squadron, the missions assigned to him from the king, and his own personal missions to allow the world to see him as the monster the king saw him as, but with minimal bloodshed of the innocent. When Viggo had come to the part in his story of the syren that had invaded his ship, he noticed a slight furrow in his father's brow and the crinkle of worry at the edge of his eyes.

"Peculiar creatures . . . are they not?" Kel scratched his chin as he looked into the corner of the room at a painting of a bloodied syren eating her young. Viggo turned from his chair, and looked at the painting. He took in the egregious sight of the syren ripping the heads off of her own litter, the myth of the first syren unknowing that her own kind's purple blood served as the only poison capable of killing herself. He turned back around and continued filling Kel in on his own life, but beforehand he gave a slight nod, confirming to his father that the message was received.

◈

Viggo had spent the greater part of his morning throwing up over the side of the boat. Before he had left the palace, he'd swiped several tins of the herbal concoction Selby made for him whenever his missions took him into the Dahs, and he had run out of the minty medicine the night before, when they had finally arrived at the shipwreck.

The syren had not lied, but she certainly held back some of the truth.

Viggo and his squadron spent an entire day arguing whether or not to listen to the syren, and head due east. Eventually they had decided to simply stay put for the night and get some much-needed rest while they could.

The next morning Viggo, Silia, and Skender were all in agreement to head east and see if the shipwreck was where the syren said it was, and if it wasn't, they would be prepared for battle. Truthfully, they were always prepared for battle anyways.

But Emir wanted no part of that plan, and just wished to get ashore as fast as possible and as far away from the wicked air of the Dahs.

Viggo didn't blame him, and if it wasn't his duty to investigate Aria's shipwreck, he would be right there with Emir in trying anything to at least get out of the Dahs. The oily black waters produced the strangest smells and gnarliest of creatures. The tides would change, giving no natural rhyme or reason. Worst of all, it seemed the Dahs would play tricks upon the sailors that would attempt to brave it. Along with the strange tidal patterns, time itself seemed to lose all rules along the Dahs.

They were just about to call it a night with plans to turn around in the morning when Silia whistled from above. Viggo, Emir, and Skender immediately silenced and turned to where Silia's long fingers pointed. After several drawn-out seconds, the wave retreated, and a singular bloodied board was floating. The red bloody stain stood out against the black waters like a flame in the night.

More planks began to float into sight. Some were bloody and split roughly down the middle, and some, miraculously, were left unharmed.

Viggo held his breath as he searched for any hints of the barrels of lithe that were on the ship. But as he searched the seas, it was only wooden planks and scraps of cloth that floated along the top of the waters.

The warm, pinkish sky faded into a cold blue as the sun set.

"Keep going?" Skender called from the back of the ship, already heading to grab a heavy fur cloak from his satchel. Emir carefully watched Viggo, awaiting the answer he knew was coming, but didn't want to accept. Silently, Viggo nodded to Emir who grumbled a select number of curses underneath his breath, while obeying his wordless command to anchor here for the night.

While this team wasn't new to being in uncomfortable situations, they had all been growing more irritable by the day. Viggo wasn't quite sure if it was the lack of sustenance from all the throwing up, the warning from Kel, or something to do with the Dahs itself, but he knew he wasn't feeling great himself.

Viggo stalked towards the back of the boat and withdrew his own cloak. Made from the rich obsidian skin and fur of a Skierkan bear, the cloak was a gift from his younger brother. Raask had hunted the bear himself, to give to Viggo on the solstice he was named the official general of the Skierkan armies. With his large stature and strength in battle, Viggo had earned the title as the Skierkan Bruin long before his promotion.

The soft fur warmed his body nicely as he laid against the bedroll. He didn't have to check with his team to ensure that Silia was taking the first watch. She always did. Just as Emir would take the next, then Skender, and then himself. That was one of the great honors of working alongside the same crew for years. Knowing your place, and having your own routine was a special sort of luxury that Viggo knew to never take for granted.

Viggo looked towards the sky as he started to doze off. He ignored the sounds of Emir and Skender bickering, just as he did so many other nights just like this. And as he fell asleep, he wondered what they would find at the bottom of the Dahs in the morning.

CHAPTER 13
RAASK

Blood trickled down Raask's face and onto the pristine copper sink of his private washroom. The red and black sparring leathers he was wearing were caked in a combination of mud, rain, and a teensy bit of his own blood. He washed off his face, careful around the nose that now bled into the sink. Aria had accidentally hit him while he was teaching her the basics of swordplay.

As he walked to the bathing pool the servants had already filled with warm water, he noticed the odd silence of the Gaulic forest beneath his window. The Gaulic was an enchantedly beautiful, yet terribly cruel forest. The magical creatures and fauna within produced a buzz, a sort of tug even, that—with Raask's tower being so close to the forest—had grown to be a comfort.

Yet that constant buzz that he had grown used to in his years was silent.

Curious, Raask peered out his window. And even the countless hours training with diplomatic tutors on keeping a straight face couldn't stop the smile that took over his face.

Out by the forest floor, next to a thin stream that ran at the edge of the palace and by the entrance of the Gaulic, Aria sat. Still dressed in the sparring leathers he had commissioned for her a few weeks ago, she sat with her toes in the stream.

A breeze ran past the stream, gently pushing her long onyx hair to the other side of her face. Her lips were moving, although no one was near enough to her for her to be talking to them. Raask concluded that she must be talking to herself.

Suddenly, he couldn't help but feel jealous for the first time in his life. He wished he was the stream that kissed her feet. He wished he was the fish and lizards inside the stream, to hear the thoughts that she only spoke out loud when no one was close enough to hear. And maybe most of all, he wished he was the breeze that caused her to turn, that pulled her hair, and kept her secrets.

It wasn't until more blood began to trickle down his face that Raask realized he was biting his lip. Using the bottom of his leather sleeves, he carelessly wiped the blood off his chin. And when he looked back down onto Aria, he saw her eyes meet his own. He gave her a slight nod, too happy and at peace to bother wiping the dopey smile off of his face.

But Aria didn't wave back.

Her eyes widened and brows furrowed. She seemed to be screaming something, but Raask couldn't hear what. She seemed to be looking up at him in horror . . . was it his bloody lip that drew so much fear into her heart? He wiped again at his face.

Raask looked back out at Aria, who was now standing and screaming something to him. The two guards who now watched Aria in place of Zaries, who had taken the day off, were pointing their own swords up at him. They were also screaming.

And it didn't occur to Raask, that they were looking just past him in horror, and not actually at himself in his private tower. No . . . It didn't occur to Raask that he was in danger within the palace of Morlok, the palace of his ancestors, the stronghold of his people.

Not until a gigantic, winged shadow flew over Aria did Raask understand.

CHAPTER 14

ARIA

Aria's stomach dropped at the sight of the lunar wraith.

In a second, the creature's long talons swooped low enough to grip onto the edge of Raask's tower. Chunks of heavy stone rained down as the wraith perched just above Raask. The lunar wraith, now securely above the stronghold of the Morloks, let out a triumphant roar. Screams of terror errupted as people fled.

Aria's entire body stiffened, did they not know of a wraith's prey drive? Running from a wraith would do nothing but cause more carnage. More blood lust. More death. But the wraith did not turn from the window of the tower. It was then that Aria finally noticed the rider. The rider wore a tall hood that left their face in shadow, hiding everything but the glimmer from a silver scarf masking their face.

This was no wild wraith. This was an assassination.

Arrows flew from all directions, all with the one target in mind. Did the stupid Morloks not know that no normal arrow could breach the thick scales of a wraith? Everything they did was wrong. And the wraith was getting closer to the window she had just seen Raask in.

Aria's heart quickened as the beast angled its body so that its tail swooped down into the window. The masked rider swung off the saddle and raced down the creatures tail into Raask's tower. Two long swords were strapped to the rider's back.

If Aria stayed put, Raask would die. He could beat an assassin maybe, he had trained for many years, but a lunar wraith? No human had killed a lunar wraith since the first Morlok King. And Raask... He liked to drink. He liked to dance. He liked to make people happy.

He was no warrior.

A pit fell into her stomach, large and horrible. *He was not a warrior. But a good man.*

Aria sprinted to the castle. Her legs, already sore from the sparring earlier, moved as quickly as she possibly could. She threw herself, one foot in front of the other, until she reached the bottom of the prince's tower. Footsteps of guards running to save the prince echoed from behind her, but they were too far away. And far too slow.

Aria whipped her body around the base of Raask's tower and sprinted up the steps, taking two or three at a time. She was halfway up the tower when it began to shake with the power of the wraith's roar. The sounds of terror and stones falling continued her entire sprint. Aria increased her speed, doing everything in her power to get there in time.

Raask had to be fighting this masked rider. That must be the reason why she hadn't run into him yet. He had to be dueling with them. The stupid stupid man must be dueling with the rider. Left foot. Right foot. She barreled onwards and upwards.

Faster, she had to go faster.

Aria's lungs burned as she sprinted full force up the tower. She whipped around the final bend to the prince's chambers and didn't stop when the metallic stench of blood hit her like a stallion. The familiar clank of swords dueling warmed her heart. He was still fighting.

She flung the heavy door open and thanked whatever God was

responsible for Raask leaving it unlocked. As the door swung open, hitting the wall behind it, the wraith's head, now merely a few paces away, let out a realm-shattering roar. The first thing she noticed was the creature's fangs, as long as her fingers, and sharp enough to ensure that any bite from the creature would be clean, and deadly. That's when she finally noticed that the creature had torn a hole into the side of the tower. Its claws were still gripping the top of the tower, and with its long neck it had craned itself into the prince's chambers—to watch after its rider or in a bloodlust induced frezny—Aria wasn't sure.

Raask was fighting. He was strong and he was fighting. Only he looked at Aria and his eyes widened in horror. "Aria, Run!" He screamed. But the precious moment he gave to command her to safety, was all the masked rider needed. The rider hit his head with the hilt of the sword.

The prince collapsed.

Aria roared as she raced across the bloodied floor. Her body slammed into the rider as hard as she could. With hands tight around the masked assailant's throat, Aria pinned the rider down. Nails as sharp as she imagined the wraith's teeth scratched across Aria's face as she crushed the rider's windpipe.

Another roar, this time a battle cry, the wraith desperately tried to find an angle where he could reach the rider.

Out of the corner of Aria's eyes, she saw the prince rising and stalking towards them. He raised his sword high into the air, angled to behead the rider, who Aria held between her claws. Thick, warm, blood began to trickle down Aria's face from the scratches. Her eyes closed momentarily, and in that *moment* precisely four things happened.

One, the door flung open from the guards who were at last here to save the prince. Two, the wraith tore an even larger hole into the tower, attempting to reach his rider. Three, Raask started to swing down to behead the assassin. And four, in that singular moment where Aria was temporarily blinded by the blood dripping into her eyes, the rider was able to twist her, so she now sat at the point of target of Raask's swift blade.

Pure terror swept across the prince's face as Aria's head now sat in the position his blade was swinging towards.

In the split second that she was finally able to see the sword coming down onto her, she gripped onto the assassin and began to roll. In that same moment, the prince pushed his sword to an angle, inches away from where Aria had just laid.

His sword stuck into the floor of his room. And before he could wriggle it out, before the too-slow guards had time to do anything, Aria and the masked rider were now inadvertently rolling towards the gigantic hole in the side of the tower.

"Stop!" Raask screamed to the mass of twisting limbs that was Aria and the rider as they traded hits and scratches. As they tumbled towards the hole. "*Stop!*" Raask cried again, his voice tight in desperation.

Unaware of the hole getting closer and closer to her skirmish, Aria continued clawing at the assassin. The instant before her and the assassin's bodies fell through the hole in the side of the tower in the sky, she felt her blood curdle and heart stop as she finally heard the desperation in the prince's command.

The last thing Aria saw before she tumbled out of the tower was the prince's panicked face, and a bloodied fist hammering straight towards her own.

Down.

Down.

Down.

She was falling.

Not just falling, but being mauled. The rider, seemingly accustomed to occasional drops, continued to scratch at Aria. A fist to her left temple like a hammer. A scratch to her right cheek. None of it even registered to Aria as she sliced through the sky and down to the hard dirt she knew waited beneath. Her head ached from the savage beating of the masked rider. And her heart dropped to her stomach as gravity pulled her to her death.

It all hurt and none of it even mattered.

In those moments, when Aria was certain she was about to die, she couldn't help but wonder if they would buy her body underneath Skierkan soil. Would anybody think to take her home? Not that they knew where she called home anyways.

But it wasn't the unforgiving ground that Aria's body slammed into. Not the dirt she prayed she never found herself under. It was the rough and thick leathers of a wraith's hide that crunched Aria's nose. For a stunned second, Aria silently watched her blood gush onto the beast's back, and drizzle down the long fall to the ground beneath.

Arrows whizzed past her ear. Too slowly, she turned around to find the rider already standing on the creature's back. Whoever this masked rider was, they were used to falling onto their beast's back and must have known a trick to stick the landing. Effortlessly, the rider was able to stalk to Aria's side.

The rider didn't waver even as strong winds pulled the silver scarf back. But it wasn't the sharpened teeth that Aria noticed, it was the lips themselves.

A female. The masked rider seemed to be a woman, or at least a female of some sorts.

Aria cataloged this information into the back of her brain. If she was able to survive this attack, it may be useful in getting down to the bottom of what happened at the Palace of Morlok on this late summer day.

The rider now loomed overhead. She retrieved a jeweled dagger from a sheath that lay hidden on her thigh, and angled it at Aria's chest.

The masked rider dove, ready to plunge the blade into Aria's beating heart. With the strength of the muscles she'd packed on in the past few weeks, she was able to grab onto the rider's wrist and stop the blade from penetrating into her chest. The rider's eyes widened as she pushed with everything she had onto the blade. But it wasn't enough.

Aria shoved her bare foot into the rider's core. Muffled by the scarf that once again covered the rider's mouth, a select number of impressive curses managed to float their way into Aria's ears. Aria flipped her long and wild hair out of the wind's course, as she managed to jump to her feet and tower over the rider strung across the beast's back. A feral hiss escaped from Aria's mouth as her claws once again found their way around the rider's tanned neck.

With cruel satisfaction, Aria watched as that exposed lip turned from an enviable shade of pink to white and then all the way to blue.

The rider's chest stopped rising.

Aria panted as she gripped the jeweled blade. Aria glimpsed the ground that remained too far away for her liking. She wiped the blood from her face with her battered training leathers, and stalked to the neck of the beast. Like a horse, she pulled on the reins of the saddle, begging the creature to take her to ground. But it was a mistake, and a costly one.

Whether it be her scent or the feeling being all wrong, or maybe even some invisible tether between rider and beast—somehow the beast became all too aware that it was Aria who now tugged on its reins—and not its mistress.

The beast began to violently sway and flip as it flew with unnatural speed. But Aria managed to keep her tight grip around the creature's thick neck. Her fists turned white as the violent swaying and thrashing threatened to cause the contents of Aria's stomach to make a sudden resurgence.

Still panting, and now dizzy enough that the threat of passing out became more real with every second, Aria turned the blade in her hand around before she began to saw at the thick hide of the creature's neck.

Screams from below, whizzed past her ears, along with arrows. Somehow the creature must have twisted and turned so much that they managed to come full circle and now headed back towards the

Palace of Morlok. Aria was vaguely aware that in the beast's frantic flying, it occasionally dipped close enough to the ground for her to simply jump off. But if the beast wished for Aria's mercy, it shouldn't have threatened *him*.

The blade was sharp, but the hide of the beast was thick. Aria continued to saw.

And to saw.

And to saw.

Until finally thick, green blood began to drip from the beast. Its rancid smell hit Aria, and in bloodlust she began to saw faster. The green blood mixed with hers and the attacker's, thoroughly coating her face and hair. It obscured her vision. But Aria didn't have to see to finish this job.

The grinding of the knife was the only noise Aria heard before the creature finally succumbed to its wounds. And as a final act of loyalty towards the rider, the beast refused to cry out in pain. No. It only twisted to its side, hoping for one last chance to kill Aria. To squish her into the hard ground beneath.

With the ground getting closer and closer, Aria threw herself over to the belly of the beast with one final heave.

Her body was so slippery. The blood covering her made it nearly impossible to get a good grip onto the wraith's leathers. And half of her body was still stuck on the wrong side of the beast when the ground had finally come.

But Aria never hit the ground.

At least not consciously.

For right before impact, right before a certainly realm-shattering pain, blackness overcame Aria's vision. And she was spared the feeling of her body breaking as she slipped into unconsciousness.

Red, was her last thought. *All the red blood.*

CHAPTER 15
VIGGO

By the time Emir, Skender, and Silia woke up for the day, Viggo was just about finished making breakfast. With a large metallic canister, Viggo even managed to brew some fresh tawny. And using the bottom of the hot canister, he toasted some old bread then spread a thick layer of a strawberry jelly.

Silia, as per usual, had two massive mugs of tawny before her eyes even managed to lift open all the way. Silently, Skender traded his pieces of dried pork for Emir's toast.

As the sun hadn't fully risen, it was still quite cold. The four sat with their furs pulled tight around themselves, grasping the warm tawny mugs tight against their chests. In a few hours, once the sun made its way above the Dahs, they would all be unbearably hot and sweaty. But for now, they sat close together, shivering.

"We're going under, aren't we?" Skender asked quietly.

Viggo nodded, to which none of the others looked even remotely surprised. He reached into his leather bag and pulled out a raw chunk of crystal lithe. With the end of his sword, he broke off a few smaller chunks. It took a few tries before the lithe eventually cracked. A long spider-web like vein ran through the rock. Again, with greater power, Viggo struck.

"One of us will go all the way down. One of us will keep an eye on the horizon for any incoming ships. And the other two will go down at different intervals to be able to watch for any signals from the person above them." Viggo continued to break apart the lithe. The clear lithe, harvested from the salt caves along the coast of the Dahs, bore a heavy scent of sweet lemon.

"I will go down. To the bottom. As far as I'm aware, no other person has ever reached the floor of the Dahs. I will not have any of you take that risk." Viggo's tone was strong and definite. He spoke, not in the friendly voice of the male who had just made their breakfast, but as their general.

Silia took a bite from her toast. "I will keep watch above water." Silia's wraithking heritage gave her far better sight and agility than any human. And from what Viggo had heard, her brother inherited unnatural strength that made him quite successful in the circus circuit. Her sister was a whole other story.

Emir carefully watched Silia. Despite the chilled breeze that swept across the boat, Emir's expression warmed.

"How will you signal to us if someone is coming? Or how would I signal to Viggo and Emir if I see some creature coming?" Skender asked.

Silia smirked, "If you see a red arrow shooting past you, then you better signal to the others to get the Helk out of there."

Skender nodded and grabbed a piece of crystal lithe from Viggo. "How will we even see down there?" He asked.

Viggo had dreaded this very moment. While he took pride in his crew, and he knew without a doubt that they were all worthy of his trust . . . There were some things that Viggo was too ashamed to tell them. And the king's little experiments were one of them, for sure.

It wasn't enough for the king to enslave entire nations of people. Nothing was ever enough for that man. He now conducted secret experiments on slaves, testing the capabilities of lithe and attempting to create new forms of the magical mineral. The fire lithe, hidden in a deep compartment of his leather bag, was one of these experiments.

Viggo withdrew the six, tiny amber stones that seemed to glow, like the final remnants in burnt coal.

"What is that?" Silia asked.

"My spies within the castle informed me that the king has been experimenting with lithe. While they haven't been able to break into the lower levels . . ." Viggo shuddered, thinking of the screams that his spies had described coming from far below the palace. "One of them hid in total darkness, without food and with whatever water he could lick off the stone walls for six days in order to retrieve these stones and inform us of the experiments that he had been able to see."

Without hesitation, Emir and Skender muttered, "*Tsu kyomo attai*." An ancient prayer of the Rakkei, urging Tsu, the God of the Sky and Keeper of Paradise, to accept a great warrior into the Kingdom of Paradise.

"It appears that the king has decided that white lithe alone is not quite powerful enough," Viggo continued, "This stone of fire was once a hunk of silver lithe. When activated, it will create a bright fire that can stay lit without oxygen."

Silia eyes narrowed onto the stones. "Why would the king need this?" She asked.

Viggo shook his head. "I don't know." He handed a piece to Emir and Skender. "But I know that it's how we will communicate and see down there."

He slowly and carefully explained the plan. Skender would remain closest to the surface, and Emir would be halfway between himself and Viggo. If any of them were to see trouble, they would create pulses in their fire lithe. They would swim quickly and efficiently, as they searched for evidence of who hijacked Aria's lithe ship. It was a simple plan, but dangerous. For most, it would be a suicide mission.

Viggo walked Emir and Skender through how to light the fire lithe, and then showed them the trick the spy had overheard in how to make sure the lithe wouldn't burn the person who ignited it, and how to keep power over the magical flame.

The twins swapped their usual long swords for shorter daggers to avoid the extra weight dragging them down. And Viggo decided to rely on his magic, strengthened by the white lithe tattoo that swirled across his entire back and over his shoulders.

The crew didn't say much to each other as they got ready to take their positions.

It was a dangerous mission, but they were no stranger to risky assignments. And they all understood the importance of locating a cargo ship's worth of lithe.

Eventually they all finished their breakfasts and headed towards the rear of the boat. Viggo grimly looked at his crew. His face was tight, and his voice soft with a killer's edge. "We all understand our roles?" Viggo asked.

Emir and Skender nodded before they popped the crystal lithe into their mouths. Silia patted Emir on the back, before climbing up to the top of the sail, binoculars slung around her neck.

Viggo placed a large piece of the crystal lithe onto his tongue. The overwhelmingly sweet flavor of lemon ran down his throat and through his sinuses. The immediate relief took over as he enjoyed a deep breath enhanced by the lithe. He gently sucked on the stone, careful not to suck too hard, too soon. The breathing magic in the stone only worked as long as the user kept it in their mouths. Viggo may have been overly cautious by packing two extra stones for each of them, but he figured it was always better to err on the side of safety.

Without wanting to waste anymore daylight, Viggo gave one short and strong nod to his crew. To his friends. He wished them good luck in the language of Emir and Skender's warrior ancestors, the Rakkei. "*Vittai santito.*" As a tradition, and show of respect for their bloodline, Viggo always wished them a blessing of luck in the language of their own people. For if the King of Skierka had not conquered the Red Peaks, home to the Rakkei, Emir and Skender would be the princes, and one day Kings of the Red Peaks.

"*Vittai santito*," Emir and Skender answered, thumping their chest, giving Viggo the blessing and goodbye of a warrior. "Walk well on the ice, brother," Skender added, showing respect to the Skierkan traditions.

Viggo thumped his own chest back in response.

Without another word, the three of them dove into the Dahs. Viggo took one large breathe and braced his muscles for whatever impact these dark waters would have on him. The waters splashed around them in far too big of a wave for these predator-heavy waters, and as he dove into the Dahs, Viggo sent a silent prayer to Rahn, God of the Seas, for his mercy.

Viggo hit the waters like a stone, sinking into the vile sea. Everything about this water felt wrong. It was thick like a syrup, and seemed to beg to enter Viggo's nasal passage and crawl its way down his throat.

He could *feel* the water's energy and matter, and knew that he didn't belong. It wanted, more than anything, to drown him. To enter into his body and never leave. It wanted to weigh him down as its own creatures feasted on his writhing body.

The combination of heavy salt and extreme cold immediately sent a shock into Viggo's system, causing his heart to race. He was panicking. And he couldn't even see far enough into the water to know how his brothers in arms were handling.

Willing his divine strength to surge through every muscle, he pulled himself deeper into the Dahs. Each foot gained felt like a mile, but it was progress. The muscles he spent years packing onto his frame, through training and warfare, began to burn. And the fire lithe, lit in his palm, managed to do absolutely nothing to penetrate the absolute darkness of the Dahs. If he wasn't so screwed right now he would find it laughable. This would be the last time he would ever rely on one of the king's abominable experiments.

Viggo pushed and pushed, lowering himself further and deeper into the Dahs with each push of his legs and pull of his chest. The pressure, while only being a few feet deep into the waters, was already building much too fast. And somehow all too slow.

Everything was building.

Everything was aching.

But Viggo kept pushing. Kept pulling. Finally, the initial desperation and intense feelings of despair that immediately arose as Viggo dove into the Dahs were fading. And it was replaced by a much more familiar feeling, even a comfortable one: he was pissed.

He'd be damned if some wrinkly old hags thought they knew his and his brother's destiny better than himself. And he'd be damned if some nasty ancient waters were going to keep him from the answers that he needed.

The waters were becoming darker, but Viggo kept pushing. Deeper. Deeper. He had to keep going. He could no longer see his hands stretching in front of him. No, his hands appeared to end somewhere along his forearm, where the darkness had become too thick for his eyes to penetrate.

And if the water was all this heavy and thick, it couldn't be long until he found some proof of the shipwreck that he could grab onto and bring back up onto the ship to investigate. There was no way the board could have sunk into the depths if the water was this heavy. Not unless someone ransacked the lithe. Or some creature dragged it down.

He didn't allow himself to linger on that thought for too long.

He knew there were creatures in these waters. Wicked and vile creatures, that like the waters that they called home, would love nothing more than to shred his body apart and taste his blood.

Suddenly, Viggo noticed the pressure on his ears begin to lessen. He delved deep into himself, deep into his divine dark powers and sent waves of energy ahead of him. The smells were changing. He was certain of it. The initial reek of rot was turning . . . sweet? Maybe it was just in his head. A cruel trick from the waters that bore syrens, who were known for similar tricks. Or perhaps it was a syren tricking him now.

The clouded waters were beginning to disperse. Viggo could once again see his fingers as he continued to dive. He was sure of it.

But he could sense something ahead. Either by his own magical powers, amplified by his lithe tattoos, or from his own warrior-like instinct from over a decade at battle, Viggo knew something was ahead.

His dark powers came back to him. Like a sonar, he could send silent clicks into the world to get a greater picture of what lay ahead, to the sides, and behind. His suspicions were correct.

Ahead there seemed to be some massive wall that stretched as far as his senses could tell to either side. No . . . This could not be the bottom of the Dahs. Even in normal waters, it would take hours for a magic-wielder to swim to the bottom. Had it been hours? It certainly hadn't felt like it . . . But it was no secret that time traveled differently when crossing the Dahs, it wouldn't be so unheard of if, somehow, traveling through the Dahs itself warped time as well.

The wall was getting closer and closer as Viggo continued to dive. The rotted scent of the Dahs had almost completely faded at this point. And now the sweet scent of freshness and life surrounded him.

Arms aching, and legs throbbing, Viggo gave one last push. He was almost to the wall. Viggo continued the dive into himself, preparing his dark powers that screeched in pleasure in Viggo's blood as he braced for impact.

An impact that never came.

For the wall that Viggo had sensed was a break in the waters.

As Viggo swam, angled down towards the bottom of the Dahs, it wasn't complete blackness that he saw. No, everything was bright. The thick waters that he had trudged through sat on top of a well of cerulean waters. Vibrant fish of all shapes and sizes swam in gigantic schools, acting as one creature. This was not the Helk-like realm that his people had always thought it to be. This was a paradise.

Sensing someone's eyes, Viggo looked up to see Emir and Skender already past the layer of cruel waters, waiting patiently for him.

They all knew that their time was limited, at best, because of the diminishing crystal lithe stone sitting on top of each of their tongues, and at worst, because of the deadly creatures that no doubt lived in this paradise. As the top unit in the Skierkan military, they had each established internal clocks that never wavered. And even with this internal clock ticking down, they couldn't resist the urge to take in the beauty below them.

Viggo didn't have to ask the brothers to know that they were sending prayers of thanks to both Rahn, the God of the Seas, and Freyite, the Goddess of Beauty, for a moment of peace and beauty—that had been far too rare for the warriors.

Silently, Viggo prayed too. But it was to Voskulle that Viggo prayed—the ancient God of Warfare. He prayed for Voskulle to continue to rest. To not stir.

To allow Viggo more time to find all of the hidden pockets of beauty that this realm had to offer. *A fool's prayer,* A little voice deep inside of him rang. But he prayed anyway.

CHAPTER 16
ARIA

A ria had to pee.

It was this deep and intense pressure in her bladder that had awoken her. And it was the only feeling that she initially noticed upon waking up, once again, in the medic quarters of the palace.

The sunlight was too bright, even though there were no windows in the cave-like room, it was all too bright after Gods knew how long she had been unconscious. Her hands flew up to her face as she rubbed her eyes and let out a groan. But it was only her right arm that blocked the light from her eyes. She reached to bring her left arm up.

There was no answer.

There was no familiar weight hanging off of her left shoulder. There was nothing pressing against her left thigh.

Aria couldn't breathe. She was sucking in loads of air, but no oxygen was reaching her brain. The familiar blackness began to cloud her vision once again. Panicking and terrified, she screamed. A warm liquid seeped between her legs. She kept screaming.

Aria vomited before the blackness once again overtook her.

It was dark by the time Aria woke, either hours or days had passed. It didn't really matter which. The lack of vomit and piss meant someone must have been in here to clean her up. It meant that while she slept, weak and vulnerable, someone had come in here to wipe the vile fluids off of her. They changed her sheets, and her gown . . .

Aria sniffed at her hair that covered her face, her hair must have been cleaned as well for it now smelled like those Gods-awful rose soaps that had been in her rooms. Whether it was kindness or some-one's duty to clean her and take care of her, Aria couldn't help but feel violated. There was nothing left inside of her but the bubbling rage that had coated her every atom since she was just a young girl who saw too much.

For as long as Aria could remember, she couldn't stand to show any signs of weakness. She would deny being sick, even when her running, red nose would give her away. She would never admit to the sadness or loneliness that usually plagued her bones and soul, as she worked and bled while most children played.

To know that some unknown person, most likely multiple people, had seen her in such a vulnerable and disgusting state filled her with such intense shame and repulsion that she wanted to drown the entire palace and watch as the hope left their eyes. She'd seen enough of her own people drowning in their own sorrows. Let the Skierkans develop a taste for it.

She would have rather awoken to dried vomit and piss stuck to her body, than the knowledge that the workers of the Morlok Palace had scrubbed her naked body. Her nostrils flared, and jaw tightened. Aria would find whoever did this to her, and speak with them about the matter. The cruelest parts of her began to sing, opening up in response to the humiliation of being vulnerable.

She was lying down, flat. Her heavily perfumed hair still rested on her face, partially over her eyes. Annoyed, nauseous, and ready to speak to whoever had done this, Aria reached up to move her long hair out of her face. It was then that Aria finally remembered what had caused her to puke her guts up.

The arm that she beckoned to move the hair out of her face had not answered the call. For where her left arm had once hung off of her shoulder, was now a stub.

Aria did not scream. Not this time.

She held her breath. For a moment. For two moments. She held her breath, unable to process the stub that hung too lightly from her shoulder, and to convert oxygen at the same time. It was too much to ask of her body.

Or whatever was left of it.

Concentrating on her breaths now, Aria forced herself to breathe. She closed her eyes, unable to look any longer at the thing that hung where her arm should be. *Inhale. Exhale. Inhale. Exhale. Repeat. Repeat. Repeat. Repeat.*

The anger that lived inside of her began to swell. The hatred that rested in her soul, that intertwined with her very essence, rose like bile in her throat. The Morloks had taken her arm. They had taken a piece of her.

They had taken her family, her culture, the precious and holy lithe that belonged to her people. They had taken her people's food supply. They had ransacked the gems and finery of her own palace. And now: it was her arm.

Her ancestors had been warriors, turned to miners and slaves by the Morloks. Now she would be neither. No, she would not be wielding a pickaxe or a trident again. She would not feel the swing of a blade, the hallowed actions of her ancestors.

Her warrior heart would starve.

She felt the gaze of her ancestors, long gone, looking down at her. She felt their shame, and embarrassment.

Her blood was poison. Her blood was holy. Her heritage, her ancestors were warriors, who fought against the Skierkans. They prayed and blessed their Gods with the blood of their enemies. And now, after generations of slavery under the Morlok rule . . . After years and years of defeat at the hands of the Skierkans . . . The Morloks had taken her arm . . . her strength . . .

Aria bowed her head in shame. She bit back tears.

No, the Morloks would not receive her precious tears. They would not take that from her too.

She didn't know how long it was until sleep came for her. But she welcomed it when it did. She had to sleep, to escape this world. It was the only thing she could do right now if she wasn't doing what she truly wanted and massacring them all.

And when she slept, she dreamt of the crisp waters of her homeland. She dreamt of whipping around the reefs using both arms to swim against the playful currents of her home.

She dreamed of laying with the great waters on her back, and looking up towards the sunny skies. Both hands resting underneath her head. Floating. Peacefully floating.

When Aria awoke, she couldn't decide if the dream of what once had been, was a comfort sent to her by her ancestors, or a reminder of what would never be, of what she had lost. Were they taunting her or comforting her?

She knew the answer.

To her people, prayer was found in battle, never in the ostentatious churches of the Skierkans. Her people did not believe in comfort.

Anger.

Rage.

Revenge.

War.

Their intention to send a message of the peace she would never have again, was clear.

Do not forget the enemy.

Do not forget the world that their children could have.

None of it was for her.

Not even for her baby sister, although she wished more than anything that it could happen for her.

It was for their people who had yet to be born. So maybe they could know the peace that she would never have.

CHAPTER 17
RAASK

Raask Morlok felt his own heart shatter, over and over again. A different kind of decimation, and a different kind of ache than what Aria had survived.

He had been close enough to her when she crashed into the ground that he heard her bones break. He heard the initial crack, and the dozens of softer ones as the wraith had landed on half of her body. She looked so small underneath the monstrous creature that she slaughtered near moments ago.

She looked so small, as she fell through the sky.

It was a week later, and he still hadn't given much thought to the fact that he had used his own powers to ensure that Aria had not been conscious to feel the moment she hit the ground.

It was the first time his magic had worked without the use of white lithe, or any form of lithe for that matter. Eventually, he would have to think about what that meant for him, about what kind of power he had that allied itself with the own internal mechanics of the body. To control someone's consciousness . . . But for now, he had been spending all of his time watching over Aria.

She was so beautiful when she slept.

He had taken each of his meetings within earshot of her rooms. The Vermilli increased their numbers around the palace. And the ones that had been ordered to protect his private tower on that day, who had been off Gods knew where, had each been executed. Raask saw to it that their bodies remained hanging in the front entrance of the palace.

Maybe if they had been quicker, Aria would not be in pain.

Their rotting corpses baked in the late summer sun. The entrance of the palace was high enough that the entire capital city of Etra could see them swaying in the wind. Occasionally, bits of their rotting meat would slide down their decomposing bodies and smack onto the ground beneath with a wet splash.

Raask often wondered, as he sat in the corner of Aria's room, if he had been too lenient by merely hanging the failed Vermilli. It wasn't until after the hanging that it occurred to him that he could have done more. He could have made them pay more. He sat in that stiff chair, imagining the torturous things he should have done to his own men who had failed him, for most of the week.

And when Raask could sense that she would awaken soon, he would stalk out of the room and into the hall. He would still watch her through the thick glass though. He would not be fully leaving her side anytime soon. He couldn't bear the thought of it. It wasn't like he could run to his private tower anymore, anyways.

But he didn't want her to be totally alone when she awoke, missing a part of herself. Aria . . . so proud and so violent.

He had used his strange powers again when she woke up that first time and started to panic. Like a cool sheet, dried by the strongest of winds, Raask used those strange powers to put her to sleep. To end the terror behind her eyes, or more likely to delay it.

Raask wasn't sure if it was for her or for himself that he continued to knock her out. He couldn't handle knowing that she had been saving him when she lost her arm. It was his fault that she screamed like a banshee into the night. It was his fault that her eyes, her lovely and powerful eyes, bulged out of her skull each time she awoke to find her arm gone.

He would never forget the haunted look or the screams.

It was on the tenth morning after the incident that Raask overheard a few of the medics mentioning that Selby would be coming back later that afternoon from whatever trip his father had taken her on. He didn't understand what his father had needed of the lead medic, or where he had taken her. But he truthfully didn't really care either.

With Selby coming back to the palace, Raask figured he would consult with her over Aria's options, before finally waking her for good. He had been keeping her blissfully unconscious for long enough. It was time for her to wake up, to begin to learn how to live her new life.

Raask saw to it that the best blacksmiths of Skierka were creating a somewhat-working arm for Aria. He spared no expense to ensure that she would be as comfortable and capable as possible. The team of blacksmiths worked on the mechanical arm, day and night. And they often visited Aria to double-check the proportions against the other arm. But with all of the modifications Raask had requested, it would take weeks to craft.

It was after one of the blacksmiths had come up to ask the prince about coloring for the prosthetic arm, that Raask decided to wash Aria's hair once again. He had requested everything to be rose-scented. It was the smell that he knew she must love, as she always smelled like it.

Selby had entered the room as Raask rinsed out the hydrating oils from Aria's hair.

"She is very lucky to have someone fuss over her with such love," Selby said softly, smiling gently.

Only to Raask, warmth in her voice felt revolting. This was no time for kindness. And gentleness had no place in the Bleached Palace, especially not after his own failure had caused Aria such pain. Everything was broken and yet everyone just kept going on, business as usual. Nobody had even blinked when he sentenced those Vermilli to death.

He didn't feel guilty over it, but he did feel as if somebody should have tried to stop him.

Raask didn't bother to look up as Selby entered. He picked up another pitcher of warmed water and poured it over Aria's hair and into the bucket beneath.

"It is my fault that she cannot wash her own hair."

Selby's steps made their way over to where Raask sat. He could hear a slight limp in her gait that hadn't been there before she left.

She tugged a nearby stool, and sat next to him. "You will not deny that it is my fault?" A test and a plea, rolled into one question.

"Would it make a difference if I did?" Selby responded, watching him as his fingers gently scrubbed Aria's scalp. The perfumed oils filled the space with a heavy sweetness as he worked his way around her scalp, rubbing soothing circles onto her head.

"I suppose it wouldn't," he answered.

The two sat in silence. Raask poured another pitcher through Aria's hair, removing the final remnants of the products from her scalp and hair. He even considered applying more or plaiting it. Anything to do for her. He needed to take care of her, in some way, after failing to protect her.

"Her hair will be much stronger now, with these healing oils," Selby said. Exhaustion showed on her face; deep bags sat underneath her eyes. It seemed that she must have just arrived back from whatever trip she had taken with the king and had come directly here. Raask knew better than to comment on a woman's state, as a prince he was trained to be proper.

"Congratulations," Selby said quietly.

A flash of rage crossed Raask's face. How could she congratulate him at such a tragic event? What could she possibly be thinking—to be so impolite at the time like this?

Selby noted the prince's anger and continued, "She does not sleep naturally. Does she, Prince?"

Raask had no clue how Selby had guessed that his strange powers kept Aria's consciousness at bay. His head angled towards Selby, in question and demand of an answer.

"I am the lead medic at the Palace of Morlok. Don't think that I can't recognize the signs of magical intervention of a patient."

Raask gave a slight nod in response. His long arms reached over to the table holding an impossibly soft linen towel. Strong, calloused hands worked their way through Aria's hair. Scrunching the bottoms up to the top, mimicking the way one of the med students showed him a few days ago, Raask dried her wavy hair.

"Have other Morloks had a similar gift?" Raask asked.

Selby raised a brow. "Viggo, perhaps." She looked down at Aria's hair, avoiding eye contact.

Raask was all too familiar with his brother's dark gifts. Through his intensive training and even from sibling spats, he had been on the brunt end of his dark powers all too many times throughout his life. But Viggo's powers felt different to Raask's.

"I don't think I've ever seen Viggo put someone to sleep." Raask muttered.

Selby's gaze wandered into the distance. Her freckled nose scrunched slightly, as she clearly had to do some kind of deep thinking. About what, Raask wasn't sure. So he simply continued working the towel through Aria's hair. Scunching and unscrunching.

"Viggo holds the power of darkness, death, and destruction," Selby said.

Raask didn't allow his own internal confusion to show on his face. Viggo could certainly be deadly. There was a reason he was nicknamed the Skierkan Bruin, afterall. Growing up, Raask had often heard his older brother's name whispered as a scary story around fires.

Viggo's tales in warfare certainly seemed fantastical to Raask. But to him, to the young prince he once was, Viggo would always be his older brother. A kind and caring man, and a God at some points. It didn't make sense to Raask that Viggo, a soft-spoken man who had doted on him his entire life, could carry the powers of death in his blood.

The idea of it all began to click into place for Raask. He thought back on his experiences with Viggo's magic. He reminisced over the stories of killing entire battle fields with the snap of his fingers. And the soothing darkness that Viggo would conjure to comfort Raask as a young boy who had just lost his mother . . .

"You think that I am also blessed by Kel? Like Viggo?"

"No," Selby shook her head. "When Viggo puts someone to sleep, it is permanent."

Selby looked the young prince over. She let herself take in the sight of him. Raask had little doubt over what she was thinking of the man who had every wish, and every command answered to, anticipated even, who was now fussing over a young creature who had been a stranger not too long ago.

"Can you not feel your powers? Its own inclinations? *Your* own inclinations?" She asked.

Raask bit back the groan of annoyance. He had spent his entire life not being able to feel or describe his own powers. But now that he had used them for something, now that it was something tangible . . . No . . . It didn't feel like Viggo's dark magic. Viggo's magic felt definitive. Powerful. Soothing. Raask's magic... It felt alive. Playful even.

"It feels like a wind, or a storm. Although I haven't had any strength controlling the air." If he did, he would have stopped Aria's fall completely, not just knock her into unconsciousness.

"Maybe it would do you well to read up on your family's history," Selby said. The stool creaked as she got up and headed towards the door. With ease, she opened the glass door out of Aria's room. Just before it clicked shut, Selby called, "I will go shower, and then I think it is time to finally awaken Miss Aria."

CHAPTER 18
VIGGO

Vibrant sea creatures spun all around the Dahs. They ranged in size from little, tiny fluorescent orange blobs to white-and-black striped gentle creatures that were nearly the size of a horse.

Even under the water, the thicker and darker water from the Rigelus trench could be seen in swirls that all led to the west. Viggo didn't need to dive into the trench to know that it was likely filled with water that more closely resembled the top layer of the Dahs, than this cerulean paradise. Was the Zojz trench, where white lithe was mined along the northern coast of Skierka, a paradise underneath? Or were the waters as black as these currents from the Rigelus? Had it all been lies?

While this lighter water was easier to see through, and swim through, the crew still would not be able to see the bottom from this location. They would need to dive deeper.

Skender, with his tall and lean frame, would be the one to stay towards the divide between the dark top and the calming cerulean water below. He would stay in this location to keep watch for any signs of trouble, either from Silia's warning arrow from above, or a sea wraith looking for a snack from the flanks. If he would need to warn the others, he would signal with the fire lithe still burning in his palm. Which luckily, seemed to work fine from the clearer waters down here than the black waters uptop.

It was a simple plan, but a dangerous one.

Viggo and Emir kept diving.

Their strong arms parted easily through the welcoming waters. Small bubbles, courtesy of the crystal lithe, continuously escaped from their noses. If something was hunting them, these bubbles would be a dead giveaway. Viggo increased his speed. Like a good soldier, Emir followed.

When Emir could just barely make out his brother's flame from above, he motioned for Viggo's attention. By pointing up towards Skender, Viggo knew this was as far as Emir would be able to go to still see if Skender were to send a distress signal. With a curt nod, Viggo continued his trek to the ocean floor alone.

Luckily, due to his genetics, Viggo was able to see much farther than the average human. Although there was no way to know if he would even be able to see Emir from however deep the floor was, or if the shipwreck was in fact down here. He continued diving. Going down, down, down.

The immense pressure of the water on top of him started to build. His ears and sinus cavities ached with each push further into the depths of the Dahs. The water became colder and colder the further he went. And although he lied to himself, and saying it was simply a trick of the mind, the water was certainly darkening. Not just darkening . . . but thickening as well.

He passed a school of red fish, each the size of his arm. It wasn't until they came close enough to investigate him that he realized they each had rows upon rows of disgustingly sharp teeth. Viggo hoped that like wasps, they wouldn't bother him unless he bothered them. It seemed he was either right or that more likely, they weren't inter-ested in taking a big bite out of him. Down, down, down.

The sweet lemon from the crystal lithe sitting on his tongue continued to take over his senses. The overwhelming strength and sweetness of the flavor made it so Viggo had not even realized that he was bleeding. The pressure from being this far deep must have been too much for his nasal cavities—that now dripped blood into his mouth and out of his nose.

He continued diving. The water was indeed both darkening and thickening. But he was able to continue swimming. Luckily, this was nothing like those wicked waters that sat on top of the Dahs. Well, not yet anyways

He angled himself back down and dove further and further. His body was aching, and he was certain he was still bleeding. But he kept going.

Something nudged against his leg.

Viggo twisted his body to look behind and see what had touched his leg. He prepared for the worst. He prepared for serrated teeth, a barbed tail, or penetrating eyes. But it was none of those things at all. No, it was a sleek silver creature with a rounded belly and eyes as big as the cattle raised outside of the palace. Viggo smiled at the creature, and didn't resist the urge to pat it on its bubbled head.

Viggo turned to continue diving, when the creature bumped into him once again. More urgently, and harsher this time. *This thing must really love being pets,* Viggo thought. He happily obliged and scratched under its chin.

"Thank you, they do feel nice, but you must leave now." The creature spoke, in Viggo's mother tongue.

Viggo's eyes widened, and he instinctively swam further back, putting space between him and the creature.

"You do not need to fear me. But the others are coming," the chubby creature continued. It was then that Viggo realized the creature was not truly speaking. But it was communicating directly into his mind.

"The others?" Viggo responded, hoping the creature could somehow hear his response. At the same time he prayed that this creature did not have the ability to read his mind, or honestly that any of these creatures could.

"I was able to drink up your blood that leaked. Even a whiff of it could send them into a frenzy. But they can still smell your fear. They hunger for it." It nudged Viggo again. "Please, you must go. Now."

Viggo spared a moment to watch the creature. Its wide eyes watched him back. "I am looking for a shipwreck. I need to find it. The fate of two kingdoms lay within it." The chubby creature seemed to nod knowingly.

"You are searching for the lithe?" The creature spoke into Viggo's mind. Even for Viggo, whose father was the God of Death, and whose mother faked her own death, this was an odd experience.

The creature's sweet eyes drifted slightly to Viggo's left, and down to the bottom of the sea and the den of shadows beneath. "It is gone. The ship was destroyed by your kingdom's enemies. Whatever was left of the lithe was taken by the Dahs itself." The big eyes once again met his, before it continued, "Please, Viggo, you must go."

The vibrant sea life that had encompassed the area had now disappeared completely. The thriving energy that lived within the cerulean waters died down. And just past the doe-eyed creature that could speak telepathically, a gigantic shadow grew larger.

"Why should I trust you?" Viggo asked.

He could have sworn the creature scoffed with annoyance. "You must not think that I would truly lead the son of Kel astray?" With more questions than answers, Viggo decided that he would listen to the creature. He shot one last glance towards the part of the water where the creature looked, where Aria's shipwreck must lay, and swam up towards his crew.

The light in Viggo's palm flickered as he signaled to his crew to vacate the water. When he looked up to see if they listened, he saw that they were already signaling for him.

"My court has already warned your friends," The creature said, smiling. Odd.

"Thank you," Viggo said.

The current seemed to naturally pull him towards the Rigelus trench. The dark, spiraled waters tugged Viggo's skin, latching onto his body, pulling him towards the same dreaded shadows that the sweet creature warned Viggo about.

Apparently frustrated with Viggo's slow pace, the creature nudged his legs once again, before swimming upwards in a way that caused Viggo to startle and grasp onto him.

"Hold tightly," the creature advised, giving just the quickest of warnings before shooting up with surprising speed.

It took the creature less than a minute to swim what took Viggo seemingly hours.

The cool water rushed past his ears at dizzying speeds. The combined effort of the immense speed and pressure caused the flesh on his face to go gaunt. He had to do everything in his power just to make sure he didn't choke on the hunk of crystal lithe sitting on his tongue.

Miraculously, they created no bubbles as they shot through the waters. And as promised, both Skender and Emir had left their posts, apparently already aboard the boat. If they weren't, well he didn't have to worry about that unless it actually did come down to that.

Once Viggo and the creature reached the layer of dark protective waters that sat on top of the Dahs, the creature halted.

"I cannot help you through the rest. One must go alone," Viggo's brows furrowed before the creature continued, "it is simply the way of the Dahs."

It nudged his leg one last time before swimming towards the big shadows—or the others as it had called them earlier. Viggo called out a *thank you* in his mind, to the creature that most likely saved his friends and his own life . . . who also somehow knew that his true father was Kels . . . Burying that thought for another time, Viggo extended his arms towards the darkness and pushed on towards his friends.

Not another moment could pass before ensuring that they were okay.

The dizzying and aching sensation of the darkness affected Viggo a little less this time, maybe knowing that it would end soon, or that his crew may be in trouble, made it easier to forget about the pain and focus on the goal of getting through it. Whatever it was, Viggo was eternally grateful when his head finally popped out of the Dahs and into the air.

It only took a few seconds before a pair of familiar hands grabbed Viggo and pulled him out of the water and onto the boat. "We have to get out of here," Viggo ordered. His heart still raced from the adrenaline of the toxic water layer, and from being thrown around by Emir.

Emir and Skender had evidently already crushed enough silver lithe to use the winds to bring them back to Etra. He heard the sound of them roughly snorting the lavender-smelling stone, and noted Silia's bit lip and odd silence. She always had some snarky comment to say . . . But he didn't push. He knew his crew well enough to know when to let them come to him.

Utterly exhausted, Viggo leaned against the bundles of equipment. Without much thought, he reached into the food reserves. Every one of his muscles ached. Helk, it felt like those black waters even did a number on his soul. He just needed a bite of something bright and sweet, to get his energy back.

Aching hands reached to lift up the bag of apples he had left by his bedroll. He braced himself for the all too familiar burn that would rush down his entire body by bending over to lift the satchel after hours of burning energy swimming. A long exhale passed through his mouth, twisting in the crisp air of dusk.

His fingers clenched around the sun-damaged strap, and lifted. The bag soared right on up. It was practically weightless. Viggo did not have to look inside to know that it contained at most two or three apples. He could feel Silia's eyes on him. Slowly, he tilted his head up to meet her anxious gaze.

Wind bit at his skin, along with a thousand thoughts and worries.

"How long?" Viggo asked quietly. He didn't have to look at the Twisted Twins of the North to know that their bodies tensed, as they willed the wind to push them further and further away from the creatures, and closer to home.

No, Viggo knew his crew well. He could feel it in the air when any one of them tensed. From several feet away, with the wind rushing past his face, he knew that their jaws were tight, and their eyes were locked on the horizon. And Viggo's eyes, they stayed locked on Silia's. She was the only one who had stayed above the water.

He felt his powers begin to pool, coursing through his body like a thick poison. Too much was happening. Too much had happened. And way too much had fallen onto his shoulders. He was drowning in the fears of failure and what it meant to his people . . . to his brother. He did his best to put a leash on his dark powers, but he could feel them surging, as if one day he would lose control over himself and rain death over all that he wished to save.

Silia's chapped lips tightened, anticipating Viggo's question and his dread.

"A long time."

CHAPTER 19
ARIA

It had been precisely six days, fourteen hours, and twenty-two minutes since Aria had awoken from her coma. If she added a week or so to that number, she would know the exact amount of time since she had lost her arm. But she never did the math to figure it out exactly.

She wasn't even sure how long it had been until they'd decided to cut off a piece of her. Was it right away? Or did they at least try to save her arm? Did they at least try to mend back together the broken pieces of her before resorting to simply chopping off the problem? Aria had grown up always hearing stories of the Skierkan's brutalism. She had little doubt that if the wraith had crushed her arm at her homeland, her own healers could have fixed it.

But she wasn't in her homeland anymore.

And she didn't know. She would probably never know if they made any effort to save her limb. It was probably better that she didn't know.

A sword whined through the air, and the already growing bruise on Aria's side began to ache once again. "You'll need to either twist away from blows on the left, or block it with your sword," Raask instructed.

The only thing that stopped her from mauling him was the fact that he wasn't pulling any of his blows. If anything, he was going much harder on her than he had done before the accident. She hated to admit it, truly hated it, but she needed him to. She had no idea how to fight with only one arm. No idea how to function with a piece of her missing.

He held her for so long in those days after she first woke up. She had screamed at him. Tried to maul him even. But he stayed and took it all, holding her all throughout the night and well into the morning. He promised her everything would be okay. And for some reason, when coming from him, she believed it.

He didn't let her wallow in her sadness or fester in her anger for long. After three days, he told her it was time to start training. Surprisingly, she didn't mind the thought of training with him once again.

But her balance was constantly off. She stumbled around, taking hit after hit from Raask's blunted training swords. Of course, she would still get a few strikes in as well, but she was slower now. She needed the help in order to stay strong. So they trained each day.

"Come on, sweet thing. You going to let me leave you black and blue?" Raask taunted.

Pissed, Aria shot forward. She raised her own sword over her head, ready to bring it down onto Raask's shoulders. She fell right into his trap. He left his leg sticking out and brought her to the ground. Aria's skull bounced against the rough dirt as she bit back a dozen or so curses. She felt the blunted tip of the prince's sword resting on her chest in what would have been a killshot in a battle.

"Again," Aria spat as she accepted Raask's hand to help her stand.

They continued sparring throughout the rest of the morning, stopping only when they were properly covered in bruises and dirt. But the training didn't stop there. They jogged across the shore of the

Dahs. To correct her balance, Raask had her running barefoot on the sands. The rough stones, shells, and bones that rested along the shore sent shocks of pain into Aria's foot each time she stepped.

But she didn't mind. Truthfully, the pain was something that she embraced. A familiar sting, an ache, a distraction; it was what kept her going.

So she pushed harder and harder, thankful that Raask was able to keep up.

He was a silent presence on today's run. And she couldn't help but note that he looked longingly towards Arthur's bakery, a place that she hadn't visited since she lost her arm. If it was up her, she wouldn't see anyone, but a little voice deep inside of her felt bad that she was the reason the prince hadn't seen the baker.

"Why don't you grab us some bread to take back?" Aria asked.

"Won't you come in?" Raask said.

Aria bit her lip as they ran towards the shop. The intoxicating scent of fresh bread hit her like a wraith.

Ouch.

She was not ready to see anyone like this. Raask, who could sense her moods somehow, smiled reassuringly at her. He was kind. She hated that about him. It made this whole thing so much harder. "It's okay."

Aria sat on the edge of the shore and the cobblestone streets, as the prince caught up with his baker friend. She listened for the sound of the bell, indicating that he had finally gone in, and had stopped staring at her to make sure that she was okay.

Once the bell had rung, Aria slunk down into herself. She held her knees to her chest as she listened to the waves.

A long sigh passed through her lips. Down the beach from her, a few dark-coated Vermilli seemed to have been exchanging duties. She recognized the one from that night. The older one with a cloak as dark as the wines her people drank. The guard nodded his head at Aria, before taking post behind her. She wondered if the guard had fought in the Skierkan army, as many of the Vermilli had.

She wondered if he had slaughtered her kind at the orders of the Morloks. And she wondered if he had, what she would do about it . . . It was probably best that she didn't know, and better if she never asked the weathered guard his background.

There was too much hatred in her heart. Too much anger already.

Let him be the kind guard who carried her. And not the man who slaughtered her people. Oh how confusing it felt to find kindness in the eyes of the enemy. To realize that they had families, too. To realize that, like her, all they truly wanted was to protect their own. Hunger was hunger. And blood was blood.

To him, her people were bloodthirsty savages that needed to be contained.

To her . . . she would let him be the one who carried her out of that cold night and into the warmth. Not for him. But for her own dark and angry heart.

A doorbell rang behind her. Aria brushed her long, wild hair off of her shoulder. It was utterly untamable and unbraidable now that she could only use her right hand.

A stolen glance confirmed that it was indeed Arthur's door that had opened, only it let in a mother and her two young daughters, rather than let out a prince. Aria watched through the glass doors as they bowed to Raask. In a flicker that most would miss, Aria watched as Raask transformed into the prince. He waved off their bows, and pinched the cheeks of the ecstatic children. He was charming, yet authoritative. The People's Prince. It was a part of Raask that Aria realized she had hardly seen in private. A skill that she wished she had.

She watched as the prince bought the family various breads and treats. His smile and demeanor were friendly, yet his clear blue eyes rang royal. Aria scoffed as she thought of the Prince of Skierka who had been following her around like a lost puppy.

Undoubtedly, he must have felt guilty. She could see it in the way his eyes would crinkle whenever she would try to reach for something with her missing arm, a phenomenon that unfortunately happened far too often.

Aria had not seen the guards that he had hung in the front entrance of the palace, but she had overheard a few of the young medic students speaking of the incident while she had laid, pretending to sleep. She pieced together that the old, grumpy guard who had been on shift during many of her harp escapades, Orin, was one of them.

She should have been furious at Raask. He slaughtered his own people who had risked their lives protecting him. But it wasn't fury that coursed through her veins when she heard of Raask's executions. After all, a few less Skierkans was not such a terrible thing to her.

Even though Raask was in fact Raask Morlok, High Prince of Skierka, Son of the Fire Monger King, and heir to the kingdom that ripped Aria's apart, somehow her rage did not extend to Raask. Or maybe it did. Okay, often it did.

But when she had heard about the massacred bodies that dangled over the palace until they rotted, the thought did not make her furious. She wished, more than anything, that it had been done by her hands. Their failure led to her breaking. Blood for blood. It was one of the highest laws of her people.

Raask was right to let them rot.

Oh, but to know that her sweet prince with shaggy golden hair and a smile that could turn a stone soft, held that kind of rage and violence within . . . A wicked smirk crested across her face. A smile that was all too close to a display of sharp teeth.

"Are you smiling thinking about me or Arthur's raisin bread?"

"Arthur's raisin bread, of course," Aria teased. Seconds later, she felt Raask's muscled body slamming into the sand next to her as he sat down. He handed her a sandwich of the sweet cinnamon bread with a thick layer of sweetened butter in the middle. Aria bounced in excitement and squealed at the sight of her favorite post-run treat. She took a massive bite from the sandwich and let out a groan.

From the corner of her eye, she could see Raask staring at her, as he often did.

When Aria was younger, she would read a fairytale to her younger sister. It was a retelling of the legendary love story of Voskule, the God of War, and Svati, the Goddess of Kindness. Aria's younger sister would beg for the book each night, and would stare at the page illustrating the first time Voskule had locked eyes on Svati and had immediately fallen in love. It was that story, and that drawing, that Aria thought of whenever she caught Raask staring at her. She silently continued eating, tearing apart massive bites, and pretending she didn't see the prince watching her.

Pretending that she didn't enjoy being watched by the prince.

That night, Aria twisted around in her furred blankets, tossing and turning, doing anything and everything to try to ignore the constant itch of a limb that was no longer there. It didn't help that the Godsdamned room was now colder than a sistro's tit. Even during the hottest summer days, the castle remained cold. Now that autumn was right around the corner, her bed chambers were constantly freezing.

Between the goosebumps, frigid air, and itchy stump, Aria had given up on a proper night's rest. She threw off the sheepskin blankets and wrapped herself in a wolf's fur robe. After saving the prince from the rebel attack, the Morloks had decided she was trustworthy enough to not have her room locked up at night. But after hours of training each day, exhaustion had come for her each night, and she still had yet to explore the palace in the dark hours.

Her feet slid into the cozy slippers, that were just as silent as they were warm, and she opened the heavy door to her chambers. She walked past the books Zaries brought over from his family, and the harp that she hadn't touched since the attack.

Silently, Aria stalked into the hall. When she reached the guarded doors to enter the rest of the castle, Aria smiled sheepishly at the guards and offered to grab them a bite from the kitchen, an excuse for her late-night wanderings that she was certain would be reported to whomever they answered to.

Luckily, they declined any food from the kitchen.

Aria cascaded down the steps. Her feet padded silently down, further and further, to the bottom of the palace. Although the excuse to head to the kitchens was only a story meant to be reported, the smell of the bakers preparing sweets slithered into Aria's throat. She took a detour and headed straight towards the smell of sweets.

She was in the kitchens before anyone even noticed her.

"Are any of the pastries ready?" Aria asked.

Padge jumped. Recognizing her voice, he smiled as he turned towards her and patted a stool for her to sit. But his eyes darted to the left sleeve of her robe that hung limply at her side. He quickly looked away, but she still noted it. Just as she noted it every other time a nosey Skierkan gawked at her like she was some circus freak.

Aria faked a yawn. "Maybe a sweet wasn't the best idea, I think I should be heading back to bed." She was already irritated and couldn't stand the looks of pity from the servants in the kitchen.

Padge shook his head. Gingerly, he placed two wheels of amia onto a plate. It was one of her favorites, a soft, chewy cookie made of almond paste and dipped in chocolate. A weak smile escaped his lips as he passed it to Aria.

"A sweet is never a bad idea, Miss Aria," he winked.

She smiled back, noticing Padge's flinch. As she whipped out of the kitchens, she realized that perhaps she had used too many teeth in her smile at the cook.

❖

Moonlight gleamed across the cool, silver blades of the daggers Aria took from the armory. Their plain wooden handles told her enough about the daggers to know that they wouldn't be missed among the hundreds of other weapons stored in the palace's armory.

They now sat on the wide birch table in the center of Aria's chambers, soaking up the precious moonlight. A practice done by her people when claiming a blade as their own. Loor's Kiss: the tradition was called. A connection to her ancestors, who undoubtedly looked upon her with great shame already.

The fire roaring behind Aria managed to warm her chambers. Combined with the strong mead she grabbed behind Padge's back, she was finally warming up.

The crisp air tore into the palace like claws. And in the quiet of night, the buzz of the lithe-bleached stone was harder to ignore. Indeed, she had grown more accustomed to them, but at night, when all was quiet, the buzzing was her only salvation from her own thoughts.

Aria mindlessly chewed the almond cookie Padge gifted to her. It certainly wasn't a common treat in her homeland, but she recognized them from the scraps of the Skierkan nobles. She hated to admit it, but sweets were the one thing that the Skierkans got right.

Her people were not ones to make treats. Food was always a means of survival to her kind, even when it was abundant. These cookies were shaped to look like their namesake, Amia's Wheel. The pottery wheel that had supposedly created the universe.

All cultures within the Arkts accepted that the realms and everything began in the wheel, but different species, and cultures within the various species, argued for centuries over who was the one to wield the wheel. In modern times, and along the western half of the realm, it was now believed to have been wielded by Amia. The Goddess of the Arts was gifted the powerful relic from the King of Gods, the Skies, and the Keeper of Paradise, Tsu. Stories say that it was what won her over and convinced her to marry him.

She thought it was odd to pay tribute to Amia, the wheel, and the creation of the universe with a cookie. But she figured it was an incredibly human thing to do as well, and the more she thought of it . . . She wouldn't mind having a sweet made and eaten in tribute to her.

Long ago, she once heard a sailor discussing the spicy and sweet delicacies created in Luru, the nation southeast of Skierka, on the mainland just below D'Ami Cos. She wouldn't mind at all, having a sweet that packed a punch named after her.

Aria popped the second cookie into her mouth, and decided that her sudden interest in naming a cookie after herself indicated that it was time to get to sleep. She had just been about to hide the daggers when movement outside the window caught her predatory gaze.

His golden hair and wild blue eyes gave him away immediately. She would recognize those eyes even through the dark waters of the Dahs.

A distinct curt nod at the guards—who bowed as he walked—told Aria enough about Raask's mood. She had come to know him well in the past months. And she wondered if the Vermilli understood how different his nods were, how when he breezed past with a tight chin tilt it meant that he was upset. And when he grinned like a fool as he dismissed the bowing guards, he was acting as the ever-charming prince character, playing a game he had no choice in since birth. It was the small, tight-lipped smile that grew to be Aria's favorite. The one that she often thought about before sleep. The one that was too small to be an act or a show, a true genuine smile in a sea of shadowed intentions and cover-ups.

He never smiled when he came back from that Gods-awful tower. The home of the Irridesci.

She couldn't bring herself to come close to it herself, or even the slews of pale mushrooms that grew in its wake. The general fog of wrongness that emanated from it was too thick. Too otherworldly. It felt offensive to her very soul and blood. In the same way Raask seemed to carry an overwhelming sense of sameness and home to her cells, the tower seemed to repel her.

It reeked of leather, metal, and the white lithe that they used for their religious ceremonies. Even from her runs, where she made sure to stay very far away, she could still smell the vile scent of whatever their kind was, of whatever they did to become closer to the Gods and 'ascension' as they called it. The practice that supposedly charged the white lithe that gave the Morloks their power.

The disgusting spores from the funghi that grew wherever they clustered provided Aria enough awareness to know just how far away to remain from the vile creatures. A shudder ran down her spine as she imagined their wicked fingers of pure bone, and the slither of their long cloaks following after Raask.

Aria didn't move until his golden hair disappeared into the safety of the palace. Then she waited several more moments, watching the forest. She searched for the slow movement of the Irridesci. And when the only movement came from a pair of mischievous sprites looking for a dark corner of the forest to continue their affairs, and the occasional slithering of a serpent, Aria determined Raask was safe enough. She burrowed deep under the blankets of her decadent furs and laid down in bed.

It was there, and only there, that Aria allowed herself to sing the songs of her people. The music she once played on the harp. The harp she could not play anymore.

The music that her very bones, or whatever was left of them, had missed deeply.

While she dozed off, she sang the stories of her ancestors, the tales of bloodshed and carnage that were sung to her when she was nothing more than a sweet, little thing. The tales of gore and revenge that she was raised on, and understood to be love stories in their own ways.

CHAPTER 20
RAASK

Raask slammed open the palace door, leaving a bloodied mark on the lithe-bleached stone. The heavy door banged into the wall behind it with such ferocity that it left a dent in the palace itself.

Now with his powers' natural alignment unlocked, a floodgate had opened within him, an endless reservoir of raw power. Balk told him tonight that whenever his father either died or renounced his throne to him, Raask would inherit the power of the kingdom as well as *'the gift of the Morlok crown,'* Balk had called it. He didn't know how powerful his father was without the gift of the Morlok crown, but if it was anything like what Raask had, he couldn't imagine adding to it.

The power lived inside of him now. It breathed, and thundered, and ached to be used. It clenched to his ribs like a baby to its mother. He didn't know just yet what it fed on, but he could feel it feeding within him, or most likely on him. And the worst of all, was that what the Irridesci instructed him to do, lessened the pain of the power.

Their twisted ideas of prayers and tributes to the Gods left his body feeling stronger, his power leashed and heavy, but his soul crippled. Each act of cruelty and bloodshed in the Irridesci's tower felt like a weight being lifted from his shoulders. Every time Raask twisted a bone, slashed a wrist, or filled a throat with the blood of their own lungs, he felt chain after chain fall from his reservoir of power. He was becoming limitless, and the key to it all was suffering.

He felt better than he ever had, and nothing hurt him worse.

So entranced within his own internal battles, Raask almost didn't notice Ilana. She stood in the shadows of an empty window on the second floor of the palace. It was the familiar scent of jasmine that made Raask aware of the Coquette Queen's presence. Silently, Raask took a spot next to his old friend.

"I heard the palace was attacked," Ilana whispered. Her feathery black hair fell over her face as she looked out at the forest. With the autumnal equinox approaching, a few of the leaves had already begun to turn to gold and silver. Some part of Raask remembered that the autumnal views had always been Ilana's favorite.

"I saw the bodies that you hung. I didn't believe my girls when they told me it was you who ordered it." Raask wondered what it was that made her finally believe it, but he did not ask.

"The traitors have been dealt with," Raask answered.

Ilana's wide doleful eyes looked up at him at last. For a glimmer, Raask saw the hurt in her eyes, before she disappeared it away, to sit with the other hurts she'd buried deep within herself from over the years. "There is a price to everything, Prince. Including the blood of traitors," Ilana warned.

"The stronghold of your kingdom was attacked. My life was threatened. Do you not think that the taking of lives was justified?" Raask asked, his voice quieter than he willed.

Ilana's lips tightened into a line before she asked, "Is she worth it?"

Raask didn't have to ask who she meant, or how she had heard what she had become to him.

He knew Ilana had powerful nobles within her clientele. An

appointment with one was most likely how she had gained entrance into the palace this evening. She never revealed her clientele, nor the lovers she took on the side, he had never even asked. And until now, she had never asked of any of the women he had taken notice of either.

Her eyes sharpened on him, and just as quickly, they turned to a look of amusement. Ilana must have noticed his pitiful face, and known what an arrogant bastard he was.

"Raask, I do not love you in that way. That is not why I ask." Ilana shook her head before continuing, "I am not asking if she is worthy of your love. I am asking you if she is worthy of your cruelty."

Raask's face twisted. "I would never be cruel to her."

Ilana's smile warmed up once again. "No, but you have proved that you will be cruel for her." Raask nodded, and allowed himself to think of her. He grew up reading fairy tales of sweet princesses.

Yet Aria was the furthest thing from those stories. When she looked at him, Raask knew that she was looking at him, and not the ever-charming Prince of Skierka. She was wild, and lively. She was unpredictable and sweet if one only knew where to look.

"Yes," Raask answered. She was worth a prince who cared to do more than simply get by.

He did not share that thought with Ilana. But he realized that he thought Aria was worthy of a greater ruler than even his father. He never considered what kind of ruler he would want to be, that he thought would be the best for his people. His father had bred a lust for blood and glory into him. A need for more. More land. More slaves. More power. More. More. More.

But was that right? If he thought Aria was worthy of a greater ruler, a great kingdom . . . He had to figure out what that looked like. He had much to think about. A lifetime of playing cards and drinking that he should have spent learning.

He was no great student. But he had to try.

Instead of saying all of this to Ilana, who loved only the prince she knew, he offered her a carriage ride home from one of his riders. When she declined, he wished her a good night and left. Before he was out of earshot, he heard her small voice calling out to him, "You reek of blood."

Raask turned towards her. And with the carefully crafted smile of the prince she loved, he winked.

The next morning, the nobles and higher-ups of the court shared looks of shock to see Raask not just on-time, but early to the meetings. Their eyes widened as they filed into the rooms, one after another. Raask hadn't slept at all that night. Not one wink of it. No, he didn't want to waste another moment.

He knew that as a child of the recently conquered Surtrian Islands, Aria didn't hold any love for Skierka. How could she? When the kingdom that had blessed him had cursed her?

Raask was determined. He had never given much thought to the lands conquered by Skierka. They had always been chess pieces on a war board, part of a game that his family was winning, and in turn, he won, too.

Maybe he would have felt ashamed, for not thinking of the children who grew up in these ransacked countries. The children of war. But he was too busy for shame. For *once* he felt a need to serve. Maybe as prince he should have felt this call to service much sooner, but he was busy playing the ever-charming and unbothered prince.

Now it was time for his next role. He would find a way to create Skierka anew, in his own vision. He would change the vicious rule and land-hungry reign of his father, and create a kingdom that Aria would not only love, but proudly serve alongside him . . . He would do it. And he would do it for her.

But kingdoms were not made, nor remade in a day.

So Raask attended the meetings the advisors and nobles had begged him to attend for his entire life. He took dutiful notes. He asked questions, but only for clarification. He could not change a system that he did not fully understand. And at night, after the dinners he spent coaxing a smile or a blessed laugh from Aria, and training with the Irridesci, Raask drew up plans for his reign. Whenever his father was ready to abdicate the throne, Raask would be ready.

CHAPTER 21
RAASK

Raask wasn't ever entirely sure how to care for Aria when she was like this. It always started the same. She would not show up for training, and Raask would know that she was stuck in bed with that hollowed look on her face. Today, she allowed him to sit on the bed next to her, and stroke her hair, while she stared into oblivion. At least there was that.

When he wasn't able to sit with her any longer without risking being late for his meetings, Raask kissed her forehead. And although she wasn't responsive, he told her that he would be back to bring her lunch in the afternoon. The only answer was the rushing sound of rain banging against the lithe-glass windows.

After grabbing a steaming cup of tawny, Raask headed into his day of war planning, diplomacy, and court appearances. But several long minutes and a full cup of tawny later, Raask realized nobody else was coming in to the war rooms. He maybe should have taken the hint when he had to ask someone to light the torches and the fireplace that were usually already lit. He hunted down the first servant he could find to ask where the sistro's tit the other nobles and courtiers were, and when they didn't know, he kept asking around.

Raask's hands turned into fists at his side as he grew more and more certain that they were secretly meeting without him. While he hadn't been vocal about his opposition to the tactics used in bending the Surtrians to their will, and the ideas of conquering the snowy island of Morrill in the northeast next, he hadn't exactly been hiding it either.

Unsure of how to find them in the giant palace when either the servants were lying to him, or they truly didn't know, was daunting, but he figured he would head to the stables to see if their carriages had arrived. And maybe pay off one of their drivers to see what they heard about the day's meeting locations. It was as good of a place as any to continue his search.

The thick, red woolen cloak was little protection from the heavy rain that fell on the path from the palace to the stables. Even the prince's fine, sea wraith leather boots were not enough to keep the heavy downpour from wetting his feet. Raask fought off the urge to shiver, something about it was so un-princely and un-commanding. And right now, he was pissed, and he needed to show it.

So lost in his own thoughts, Raask nearly rammed right into his own driver. Cristo, per usual, smelled like he had drunk an entire pub's worth of ale.

"Your highness!" Cristo croaked in surprise. Raask straightened his cloak out, making sure that the Morlok crest was unwrinkled.

"Have the other courtier's carriages arrived?" Raask asked, looking around for the ridiculous show ponies that the courtiers preferred.

Cristo shook his head. "No, didn't you hear? All court appointments have been canceled today and all of the darkest coats from the Vermilli have been summoned to the Dahs."

Raask's brows furrowed. "Why?"

Cristo laughed incredulously. "Why? Look at all of this rain!" He motioned his arms to point to the rain as if Raask had completely missed the whole thing.

"The Dahs is flooding?"

"Not yet. Gustav told me it was only about a foot higher than it usually is at this time. But I guess all the rain has the sea wraiths making all sorts of weird cries. And earlier, one of the crocodillos stalked up onto the beach and dragged one of Ilana's girls down into the waters." Cristo's eyes widened at the thought, making it very easy for Raask to see how dilated his pupils were from the fuschia lithe he had obviously been inhaling.

"Gustav said that the witnesses didn't even see the crocodillo until it opened its fat mouth, and they saw the pop of pink of in its maw. Heard that its jaw was the size of the lady's leg, and she was known for her long legs too." Cristo shook his head and spat onto the stable floor. "But I guess the thing was so pissing ancient that it was as black as the sand itself, and its eyes too!" Cristo rubbed at his bad shoulder that he always seemed to complain about when it rained.

"Bloody Helk," Raask muttered in shock. Even he couldn't hold back the chill that ran down his spine at the colorful image that Cristo spun.

Raask had little experience with the ancient beasts, but the ones that he had seen were never by the capital's shores. Occasionally, Raask would see them on a hunting excursion on the eastern coast of Skierka, but it was always the pale ,white babies that were more drawn to the shallows. He'd even thought at the time that the little albino creatures were quite cute—with their crocodillo smile and large, milky eyes. One followed him and the other courtier's sons around for a whole day like a puppy. It didn't leave them alone until it ate an entire water sprite in one bite.

It was the last thing Raask wanted to do, but he knew that if Viggo were here he would already have been out on the water hunting for the crocodillo. With a heavy sigh, Raask walked towards his own favored horse.

"You're not going down there, are ya?" Cristo asked.

"Somebody must," Raask answered.

Cristo snorted. "And you are the one to go?" He stumbled after the prince. "I'm sure the Vermillli have already sent a troop onto the water after the beast!"

"So I will take another." He pushed his boot into the stirrup of the black stallion and swung his leg over with the grace of a royal who had ridden horses since before he could walk.

Cristo stammered in absolute drunken shock. "Do you even have a weapon to kill the beast?"

Raask lifted his cloak to reveal the long, dual swords hung across his back.

Cristo's eyes widened. "Baldrei's balls!" He spluttered. "What are you doing with those things strung on your back? You didn't even know about the crocodillo when you came out here!" Cristos demanded.

Raask shifted in his seat before finally looking into Cristo's eyes with a coldness that would freeze even the King of Morrill. And when hurt ran across his old drunken friend's face, Raask urged his prized stallion out of the stables with a bump of a heel on the horse's rear.

Raask had grabbed the dual swords earlier, as he passed the armory, as a precaution in case he couldn't find the meeting of the courtiers. He wouldn't waste a whole day looking around for them, so he figured he'd head to the training ground and practice sparring with two swords. He was fine with the dual sword technique, but he wanted to become better. Of course, Raask didn't tell any of this to Cristo because he thought it made him look possibly more prepared and brutal if people thought he just walked around armed nowadays.

Raask and his favored horse, Bjor, made their way out of the stables and turned back as they passed Cristo. "Are you coming or not?" Raask called to Cristo. He was starting to feel bad for acting like a jerk to one of his eldest friends, and could truthfully use the help anyways.

Grinning like a child, Cristo hopped onto Tratta, one of the palace's horses, and took a running start towards where Etra met the Dahs. The thunderous gallops from Bjor and Tratta warned the Vermilli and those hanging around trying to catch a glimpse of action, to make room for their arrival. Bjor and Tratta, like most horses, refused to even go onto the onyx sand. So they left their rides next to the other guard's horses and sauntered over to Gustav who seemed to be giving some kind of orders to the other less-decorated Vermilli. The twitch of Gustav's mustache upon seeing the prince this close to the dangerous waters was the only emotion Gustav would ever give away while on duty, but it was enough for Raask to know that he would have to pitch a fight to get onto the waters.

Raask swaggered closer to Gustav and the huddled Vermilli, who bowed upon seeing him. "I'll need a boat and a team of three to four Vermilli to go after the beast." Raask demanded.

As Gustav was often stationed by the sinful Salt District, where Raask and Cristo and the other courtier's sons would drink until they couldn't remember their own Gods-damned names, he knew that Gustav was surprised to see him not just sober, but volunteering to do dirty work too.

"Absolutely not," Gustav answered. And then after remembering who he was speaking to, quickly but still sternly added, "Your Highness."

"I don't think it's up to you to give me orders, Gus." Raask answered, with a charming crocodillo smile.

"I will not have the Crown Prince of Skierka risking his life to go after an oversized lizard with teeth the size of thumbs!" Gustav puffed with an already reddening face.

Raask lifted his brows in response, refusing to dignify the war hero's orders.

"I won't do it, your Highness. I won't. And you can bring me in front of the king and tell him that I refused, and Helk you can even execute me if you'd like. But I will not let my children and grandchildren be known as the descendants of the man who let the Crown

Prince of Skierka rush to his death after a creature we make armor out of!"

The other Vermilli avoided the prince's eyes.

"You would let Viggo go," Raask answered, using the same authoritative, rumbling voice he had heard from his father more times than he could count. A tone that promised punishment. A whisper even, for the truly powerful didn't need to shout. For a moment, the only sound was the onslaught of raindrops, before Gustav finally spoke.

"Viggo is the General. He is the Skierkan Bruin. He's massacred entire battle fields with the snap of his fingers and a snort of lithe. And Tsu forbid if something did happen to him, at least he is not next in line for the throne. One of his commanders would take his place and life would go on. There is no one to take your place, Prince."

Raask was two seconds away from tearing into Gustav's head when a younger guard with a bright red cloak cleared his throat.

"Please, Your Highness. Truly, it's not worth putting you in danger." After seeing that nobody was stopping him, the young guard continued, "We would be honored to hunt the beast, for the people of Skierka. And for the same people of Skierka, we also keep you safe." The young guard gave himself a nod, before looking back to the ground.

Raask carefully looked over each Vermilli before him, from the young men with bright cloaks to the old-timers like Gustav, and even the young woman with a red cloak as dark as the ruby necklace his mother had worn.

Finally, Raask drew in a long breath. "Very well then, Cristo and I will be on our way."

He swung around and headed back towards the horses with Cristo only a few steps behind. "Raask, come on. We're already down here. It's pouring out. Let's stop at the pub." Cristo begged. "Raask! Come on! I'm soaked to the pissin' core over here. I don't want to troop all the way back to the palace. I want to get dry, and warm up with a few glasses of that sugar liquor shit they brought back from Surtr."

He made it all the way back to their horses, before he stopped to consider Cristo's offer. There was a time, not too long ago, when getting Dahs drunk at the pubs with his friends was the only thing he was interested in. It was the only thing that he wanted, the only break from the heavy weight of being a Morlok.

And maybe it was because the horses seemed to agree with Cristo's wish to stay dry, hunkering underneath the tents outside one of their favorite gambling houses. Maybe it was because it had been a while since he hung out with Cristo. Maybe it was because he was also soaked to the pissin' core. Whatever it was, he flung open the familiar creaky door of the Gray Goblin and threw Cristo a slight smile before disappearing to their old favorite table.

The Gray Goblin was just as it always was. Gamblers and drunks gathered together over the bar, the card tables, and every other dark corner of the place. At the piano, a group of absolutely blasted gnomes sang a song of a garden gnome shacking up with the lady of the house. Raask nodded at the gnome that sang the loudest, recognizing him from the meticulous shrub sculptures that he often pruned in the palace's gardens. The gnome's small eyes narrowed even further at the nod, before his brows shot up and his jaw dropped.

"Why, it's Prince Raask!" The gnome called.

All at once, all other noise from the pub halted. Dozens of eyes immediately met the prince's, studying him. Just as the silence fell at a moment's notice, so did the uproar. The gnomes now stood on the piano, cheering for the charming prince with heavy and loose pockets. The drunks lifted their mugs up in greeting; and the females gave a playful smirk. His father may technically still be the King of Skierka, holding on to the people's loyalty with fear and violence. But Raask, he was already the King of the Drunks, the Gamblers, the Whores, and all the rest of the sinners.

As Raask stood there, dripping from the heavy rain, he realized that seeing and getting to know his people may be just as important as the courtier's meetings when it came to ruling a land. And in fact, maybe all of his time drinking until he was sloppy, was not spent in vain at all.

He lowered his hood and smiled. "This round's on me!" He roared. The crowd answered his roar with one of their own.

Yes, he decided, *he would make a fine King for his kingdom one day.*

It only took three, maybe four ales, and a roll of emerald lithe before it all seemed dreamy again and Raask finally stopped cringing at the sticky floor and the general stench of ale mixed with sweat.

It certainly didn't hurt that the prince was cleaning up anyone and everyone who challenged him to a game of Four-Footed Monk. The prince had always been good at cards, mostly because he needed to learn the language of faces before he even understood what all of the creatures and characters were on the cards themselves. He was good enough at Four-Footed Monk that he understood how to lose without making it too obvious. Nobody liked when the prince cleaned up the whole bar in cards, before running off to his castle. So he even lost a few rounds too, and in a way, getting away with the loss also felt like a win to him.

Raask was so caught up in the thrill of the game, that if it weren't for Cristo's well-hidden nudge, he wouldn't have noticed the witch in the corner. She wasn't what he was expecting from Cristo's nudge, normally he reserved those for particularly curvy women. On second thought, the witch did have some nice curves . . . Yup, Raask was now remembering why he stopped smoking so much emerald lithe.

A few more rounds went by. Raask made sure to lose a large sum of his earnings to Cristo—who often refused the gifts he would try to give him. The entire time, the witch watched. Her long, stringy, gray hair hung over the edge of the bar like the thorny vines that climbed the palace. Her yellowed teeth reminded Raask of the wasps that buzzed around the top rooms of the Irridesci tower.

"I'll play you, Prince."

Raask was almost certain that the witch's mouth hadn't moved, but they all heard the croaked request, and there was no doubt that it had come from her.

He gave one of the smiles he saw his mother constantly make when with bad company. "Let's have it then!" He answered. "What will you play for?" The prince asked, making room for the witch at the table.

The witch stayed seated at her corner of the bar, her pigeon-colored eyes tracking his every movement. "The better question, Prince, is what will you be playing for?"

Raask didn't let his annoyance show. "Why don't you tell me?" He asked, assuming that the witch had something specific in mind.

A smile that seemed to curve into itself immediately weaseled its way across the witch's face. The strange smile did at least seem to explain the odd wrinkles that went sideways across her cheeks.

"If you win, I'll break your curse." The raspy words hung in the air of the Gray Goblin like the first echoed steps onto a battlefield.

"I hate to be the bearer of bad news, my friend, but I am not cursed."

The witch let out a phlegmy laugh. "If you say so, Prince."

Raask's eyes narrowed on the witch. He didn't wish to gain a witch as an enemy, but he was nearing the end of his rope. "What will it be, witch? Will you be playing?" He tapped the cards with impatience.

Cristo tensed, his muscled legs shaking up and down underneath the table. He'd been afraid of witches since he was a kid. Raask and the others used to tease him about it when they were children, and chase him throughout the palace on broomsticks. It didn't seem so funny anymore after seeing this gnarly creature up close.

"Can't you see?" The cards on the table began to move on their own, but slowly and shakily, as if a great deal of magic was being used for this parlor trick. "I've already started," the witch taunted.

If the witch thought this feeble magic was impressive, he ought to keep her alive long enough to see his first trial upon midnight tomorrow. Then she would know what it was to challenge the Prince of Skierka. Then she would know how the other side of fear felt.

With slow shakes, one card began to creep its way in front of him. And then another, from the opposite end of the table. Finally, a third card slid on top of the others.

"Witch, we are playing Four-Footed Monk, not a charlatan trick of the Three Sistros."

Sharp clicks of her tongue echoed through the quiet pub. "I am sacrificing myself, Prince." Her own twisted mouth grimaced at her own words. "You do not need to trust me. But trust the sistros. They speak through the cards."

Raask was all too aware of the attention the witch's little display was drawing. It was one thing to be challenged and lose in a game of cards. It was another to lose a witch's challenge in front of an audience.

"I will flip your cards." The witch nodded smugly. Raask continued, "But only if you buy me a drink first."

The gnomes spit out their drinks in laughter. The one who worked in the gardens of the palace let out a soft, "this guy."

The witch's lips upturned in a near smile. She reached into her hole-ridden cloak and took out a copper coin that clunk against the bar.

It was a deal.

The first card was the Orphan. A sad child stood on the cover, crying by the sea.

The Knight of Vengeance was the second card. In Four-Footed Monk, it was a good offensive card to play. Raask wasn't sure what it meant regarding the reading of his future, and truthfully he didn't really believe any of it. Witches and witch-pretenders were known to play gullible tourists and convince them to play the Three Sistros and then sell them the 'potion' that would cure their destiny.

The final card was the Skullin and his infamous abberack, Cryos.

Skullin was the harbinger of death. He was the creature who took souls to the underrealm on the back of Cryos. Some tales told of him as a gentle creature, and some told of him as wrathful. Again, Raask wasn't entirely sure what any of this meant or if it meant anything at all. And truthfully, he just wanted it to be over. The rolls of emerald lithe and pints upon pints of ale were starting to make the room spin.

Ale spilled from the drink that the witch had bought him, pulling him away from his thoughts of the cards. "Is now when you sell me a talisman that will keep me safe from the Knight? Or a potion to ward off the Skullin?"

The witch's eyes looked hollowed. Somehow more so than before. Her gray skin wrinkled in a frown. At the hiss of another card moving magically from the pile and into the Prince's hand, the witch's eyes widened.

"What is it?" The witch whispered, seemingly in surprise. Or at least she was a pleasant actress. Maybe instead of witching she should have worked at the Royal Theater.

Reluctantly, Raask flipped over the additional card to reveal Freyite with a swollen belly, Goddess of Love and Beauty, and often forgotten, the Goddess of Birth.

The witch gasped, "No." She shook her head in horror, "It can't be." She stumbled off her stool, screaming and crying.

"Enough!" The Gray Goblin himself came down from his office above the bar, swinging from the chandelier to the top of the bar with ease. "You must leave now!" He screamed.

It didn't matter. The witch fell to the floor screaming. The wraiths, already agitated today due to the rain, answered the witch's call and joined in on her screaming from the Dahs. The witch covered her eyes with her hands and began scratching at her face. Blood dripped from sharp nails. Chunks of her face were left behind as an agitated troll finally dragged her out of the bar and flung her out back. The screaming cries could still be heard, but only faintly.

The Gray Goblin sniffed the air. "Play," he commanded one of the bartenders who rushed to the piano to start playing and sing a lively sea tune. The Gray Goblin then gave a nod to the prince, the most respect he would ever show a human, before turning back around and leaping up to his office high above the bar.

"Can we go now?" Cristos croaked.

CHAPTER 22
ARIA

At some point in the day, Selby had brought Aria a plate of dark rye and pickled herring, with a bowl of sugared cherries on the side. And of course, a cup of cobalt lithe to put her to sleep. The herring was salty, and the bread felt nice on her stomach. But the deep sleep from the cobalt was what really did the trick.

It was dusk by the time Aria woke up. The strong scents of ale and emerald lithe rolls emanated from Raask, who snored on a chair that he must have dragged in from the other room while Aria slept. It was not a peculiar thing for her to find the prince in her bedroom. After losing her arm, he stayed with her throughout the night, trying to ease her mind and coax her to sleep. He started out on the same chair he slept on now. Eventually, after waking up from a few too many nightmares, she began to ask him to stay in bed with her and hold her while she slept.

Nothing more had ever happened between them. Too much was on her mind. And at the end of the day, he was still a Morlok. She tried not to think of it, on those nights he woke her up from nightmares, the only warm thing in her cold life.

She was so lost in her thoughts, the confusion of being comforted by those that brought tragedies to thousands, that she did not notice when the prince's eyes had opened. Light blue with flecks of violet. Aria blushed, slightly embarrassed to be caught staring. He stared back. Eyes warm and kind. He was the man who brought her a harp when this palace was foreign and empty of things of comfort for her. The one who brought a seemingly endless supply of cinnamon bread to her table. The one she wished to see when waking up from nightmares. Yes, that was Raask.

"Why didn't you come into the bed?" She asked.

Raask yawned and ignored her question. "You look beautiful."

She did not know what he saw in her. Of course she was beautiful. Her entire family was beautiful. To her it never meant anything other than as a potential weapon, to lure and to entrap. But she didn't mind hearing it coming from him. He seemed to see in her things she never saw in herself. She was violent. Cruel. Mean, even. But he looked at her as if she was the entire night sky.

Aria's eyes briefly shot to the window. Her reflection did the same. Oh Gods, she looked at him with a similar look. She had never seen herself looking at him, and she wished that she still hadn't. How could she care for Rassk while his family had damned the entirety of the Arkts. He yawned once again, bringing back the smell of strong ales.

"Are you drunk, Prince?"

He chuckled and for some reason his eyes darted to the floor. "No, no. Please, I can handle myself." Raask smiled a little to himself before resting his head on a fist, as if the weight of the world lay on his own two shoulders.

It was then that Aria finally saw it. Something was wrong. Raask never sat this far from her. He did not joke or play. He was quiet. She was always wishing he would shut up, now that he had, she found it disturbed her.

"What happened?" She asked.

He didn't reek of carnage like he usually did after leaving the Irridesci tower. So it couldn't be that.

"Nothing." He rubbed the spot between his eyes with two fingers.

Aria carefully observed him.

And when his eyes came back to focus, Raask observed her observing him and chuckled. He then did the unthinkable and booped her nose, "my little bloodhound."

Even Aria's cold heart couldn't resist a small smile at that.

"Tomorrow is my first trial. To deem if I am worthy of ascending to the crown."

Her eyes narrowed. "You're lying." That wasn't it. She could just feel that there was something more, something that he was scared of.

Raask smiled sloppily, letting his drunken stupor show. "I'm afraid not, sweet thing. Tomorrow is the autumnal equinox."

Aria rolled her eyes and gave Raask a playful shove. "Yes, Prince, I'm aware of the date." She was not. She had forgotten it was already autumn, but no matter the fact, she knew that wasn't what was upsetting him. "What's really bothering you?"

Raask rubbed his eyes and looked out the window, before looking back to her. "A witch came into the Gray Goblin."

Aria recognized the name of the gambling den from Raask's stories and their running routes. Raask looked outside once again. She'd seen the fear sat heavily in his eyes, and with it aggression boomed from deep within her. She did not like that he was afraid, nor that he was upset. She didn't understand why, but it was all very troubling to her.

"She hurt you?" Aria asked, her voice hoarse.

Raask shook his head and smiled warmly. Something about this entire conversation was making her sad and fearful, even though she was certain no witch was going to get to her. He reached out for her hand. His calloused palms, now more than familiar to her, felt warm against her cold skin.

Then she caught the twinkle in his eyes. The pale blue with flecks of violet. A lightness rested in his gaze that wasn't there before.

Slowly, he lifted her hand up to his mouth and kissed it. Her heart quickened, and cheeks reddened, as she let herself become slightly undone. His kiss felt like those first gulps of air after being under for too long.

Her long fingers wrapped around his hand as she led him into her bed. She buried him under the shaggy fur blankets with her, and held his hand tightly into hers.

"What did the witch do?" She whispered, letting her curiosity get the better of her. She wanted to hold him tightly.

"Typical witch shit," Raask said. "It's just that, it reminded me that no matter what, as a born prince, I'll always be a target for these crazies. And anyone with me, becomes a part of that target too." He yawned, no doubt utterly exhausted, and ready to sleep off whatever concoction of stimulants he had been ingesting all day.

Aria reached onto her nightstand and gave him the last sips of her cobalt. He was snoring only a few moments later. He would need his rest for the trial tomorrow. And more importantly, she had to be sure that he wouldn't awaken.

She didn't waste a moment of time. She slept all day anyway, so she had plenty of energy. Quietly, Aria slid into her training leathers. She still hadn't gotten used to the modified bows, and the swords were still too heavy for her one arm, so she opted for the little daggers that Raask had commissioned for her. Her leather boots were perfect for slinking around the castle unheard.

She made it out of the castle with ease.

It was unlikely for anyone to recognize her, but just in case, she kept her face hidden in the shadows of her long hood and distorted her voice slightly, mimicking the timbre of the kitchen servants who spoke with a certain rasp and twang to it that most others didn't— besides a few random guards here and there. She also stuffed an old satchel into the left sleeve of the cloak to ensure that no one noticed she was missing the limb, a certain giveaway to her identity.

Aria easily found the witch's cottage and only had to ask two humans and one overworked goblin assistant, before locating it.

The cottage sat on the edge of town, nestled between the Incarno river and the Gaulic forest. There seemed to be no fires lit within, and the front door was slightly askew. Aria slinked in without a sound. It took only a few seconds for her eyes to fully accept the darkness that she had grown up with. Her heart stammered and leapt at the sight of the utter blackness. It felt like coming home.

Her eyes adjusted to the darkness immediately, giving Aria only a second before she noticed the figure on the rocking chair.

The figure, most likely the witch based off of the unnatural stench emanating from her, sat facing the empty fireplace. An old rickety thing that was probably once well-kept by whatever family lived here before the witch ate them.

Aria had to resist the urge to cough and gag from the mixture of metallic blood, witch-scent, and dust that heavily occupied the air. Her nostrils flared as she unsheathed one of her daggers from her thigh. Her silent footsteps felt heavy as she assessed the witch from behind. The witch's raspy breaths echoed across the mostly empty room. The only confirmation that the witch was alive in this dump.

A phlegmy cough escaped from the witch's lips. Awake. She was definitely awake now. Aria's entire body stiffened as the witch began to loudly sniff the air around her.

"You reek of the Dahs, girl."

The witch's piercing laugh was more shocking than her acknowledgment of Aria. Adrenaline flooded her blood as she sprinted towards the witch.

Heavily mutilated hands with missing fingers and nails raised in surrender. "I'm not going to give you any trouble, girl. I know why you're here." The witch rasped.

Aria nearly threw up at the sight of the witch's face, or whatever was left of it.

Deep red scratches ran down her skin, matching with the long nails that were still on the mangled hand she kept raised. Chunks of the witch's gray, sullen skin were hanging by mere threads. And while one eye was completely missing, the other was hanging loosely off the side of her face. A long gray nail remained stuck in the pupil.

"When you reap your reward," the witch mused, "do not forget to mention me to the scribes who will write of your ascension." The witch coughed up a hunk of green phlegm onto the floor below. "Do not forget that it was me, Ylva Krog, Heir to the All-Seeing Throne, that sacrificed herself to be the catalyst." The witch took a deep breath in. "Now get it over with, girl."

Aria had absolutely no clue what the batty old witch was talking about. But the gist that she was getting was that the old thing wasn't going to put up a fight. It was honestly a disappointing turn of events. She'd been itching for a fight. And truthfully, it was a little offensive. However the witch figured that she was some sort of catalyst, it didn't make sense to Aria. The catalyst of her life, her drive, came years and years ago. She had no intention of letting a cranky old witch take the credit.

With a roll of her eyes at the dramatics of witches, Aria slit the witch's throat. The papery skin parted easily. Aria made quick work of removing the head and plopped it carelessly into the leather satchel that had been crammed into her left sleeve. She felt a sense of relief, now that she had squashed what was causing Raask so much distress. She had solved the problem, and owed him a little less for all of his kindnesses.

She whistled gleefully the entire walk back to the palace.

CHAPTER 23
VIGGO

The children of Skierka learned at a young age that time traveled differently across the Dahs. Perhaps, being more than familiar with the odd phenomenon from his dozens of trips across the black waters, Viggo should have expected that time would also travel differently when diving into the Dahs itself.

Silia was tough, she'd lived through and caused enough slaughter to have to be. But she was noticeably shaken from the experience of living up here while the others dove into the depths of the black waters. She refused to move the boat and search for help, in case any of them were to come up. It was on the third night, she later told the crew, that she realized that time might be moving differently underneath. So she stayed and began to ration out her food.

Not much was left now.

Skender's belly loudly rumbled, loud enough that they could hear it past the racing winds. No one dared to eat the creatures from the Dahs—except *other* creatures from the Dahs. And they didn't plan on finding out what happened if they tried it. So they had each snorted large piles of silver lithe and booked it towards home.

Sweat ran down Viggo's brow as he held his concentration. With the swirls of white lithe-infused tattoos that ran across his back and arms, he was able to control much more magic than the others. It also didn't hurt that he was technically a Godling.

A night had come and passed, this time they decided two would stay awake at a time and continue hauling the ship closer to the capital city, Etra. For once, Silia was one of the first to fall asleep, tired from all of the waiting and worrying.

By Viggo's calculations, he was almost certain that his brother's first trial was either happening in the next few days or had already happened. Calculating the time difference from on the Dahs and on regular land was tricky and depended on exact coordinates, which Viggo of course didn't have. But nonetheless, he prayed to whatever Gods would listen that he could make it back to see Raask's first trial.

When he left Raask hadn't even found an alignment to his powers. Realizing this, Viggo sent another prayer to the Gods that Raask had found his natural alignment by now . . . He would have had to by now . . . Viggo could never figure out why it was so hard for his brother to find what came so easily to the Morloks before him. He often stayed awake late into the night, worrying that maybe like Viggo, Raask was not truly a Morlok. And where Viggo's true father had magic of his own to impart into Viggo's blood, maybe Raask's true father didn't carry such a thing. But then by morning, Viggo would take one look at his brother and see the king's face looking back at him, and then that was that.

For Viggo, the call to the darkness and destruction came easily and swiftly. If anything, it was much more difficult for him to control yielding the darkness. He accidentally broke many sets of silverware and darkened many paintings as a child. Whenever he would fall asleep, he would wake up to a room coated in darkness. Even worse were the rare occasions he would lose himself in the madness of his powers. He would always come to and see the damage he had done and nearly die from the shame of it all. The time in the military helped with that thought.

By now, he was certain that if Raask hadn't found his alignment, then he was clever enough to trick the palace into believing that he had. Raask had always been clever in the ways of the courts. He understood how to use charm and words to control others. Maybe he didn't even need the magic to become a good king, afterall he'd have Viggo by his side, anyways.

He reached into his pocket and drew a fistful of crushed silver lithe. The immediate buzz and sensation of power ramming into him was enough to wake him up. It was getting dark again. The silver moon was just now rising over the black seas.

Skender coughed pointedly, snatching Viggo's attention to the opposite horizon where the long spikes of a sea wraith poked out of the water. Seven spikes in all, with the middle fourth one being the tallest and widest. The sea wraith seemed to be in no hurry, and was luckily swimming away from the ship.

"Glad we didn't run into any of those when we went under," Viggo grumbled.

Skender twisted his head slightly, in confusion. His tall and lean body, noticeably even leaner from this trip, stood harshly against the horizon. Skender angled himself away from Viggo, watching the wraith's spikes swim slowly into the edge of view.

"So you didn't see it, then?" Skender asked quietly.

Neither Emir nor Skender shared much of what they saw under the Dahs. Viggo figured they had all experienced relatively the same thing, and only shared that Aria's ship had been attacked by the rebels. Another thing to add to his list of prayers, finding a way to calm the Surtrian rebels without the king's knowledge.

"No," Viggo answered.

Skender didn't elaborate. And Viggo didn't push.

They had all gone to war together. They committed treason dozens of times. And had slaughtered entire battlefields. On top of it all, they had lived together everywhere from tiny rat-infested shacks to grandiose foreign palaces. The four of them were a unit. And they understood, more than anyone, that it was better to sometimes leave things unsaid, and in the past. Where they belonged. Where they couldn't hurt anymore.

The moon was now just above Skender and Viggo's heads, meaning that it was about time to wake up Emir and Silia for their watches. No one spoke of, or asked why Silia suddenly preferred the second morning shift, but it was accepted and moved on from.

Skender yawned and stretched. Their bones were both rigid from the constant muscle use tied with the lack of sleep and nutrition. Viggo hated to admit it, but Emir, Skender, and Silia were at a greater advantage at working without food. As children of conquered lands, Emir and Skender were used to the tiny rations of food and the necessity of hunting and foraging for their nutrition. Silia's family had lost their fortune generations ago, but were generally too busy smoking roots and ingesting hallucinogenic fuschia lithe compounds to hunt or earn enough coin for food anyways. Viggo was the only one among them who had grown accustomed to regular eating schedules filled with high quality meats, vegetables, starches and even fruits from all over the Arkts.

The lack of sustenance was certainly getting to him. His stomach clenched in on itself, and Viggo felt like the entire realm of the Arkts was spinning around him. He rushed over to the edge of the boat in preparation of heaving whatever was left in his guts out, when a pale hand glowed against the all-consuming darkness of the Dahs.

Panting, with his head off the side of the boat and his eyes locked in on the hand that seemed to magically wave at him, Viggo managed to whistle an alert. He didn't need to turn around to know that Emir and Silia had awoken to the whistle and most likely reached for whatever weapon they tucked in next to themselves while they slept.

"What in the Skullen's Scythe is that?" Skender asked, silently appearing next to Viggo with his famed sword already drawn. Heavy footsteps joined Skender behind him. A warm and comforting pat on his back, as Viggo began to puke his guts up off the side of the boat, proved it to be Emir. The gigantic muscular creature was the only one of them with a comforting bone in his body.

"It looks like a hand," Emir answered. Silia's scoff from the crow's nest could be heard over the roaring waves *and* Viggo's hurling.

"Looks like she's clinging onto that barrel for her dear life," Silia reported.

Viggo vaguely gestured to his water skin. "Weapons?" He asked.

"Negative," Silia answered.

Emir handed Viggo the water skin. With his eyes locked onto the mysterious hand, Viggo rinsed out his mouth. Emir gave him another pat on his back before drawing his own famed sword, twin to his brother's. Again, Viggo's eyes drifted back to the mysterious pale hand, raised high to Tsu's Kingdom of the Skies, waving to them —presumably a call for help. The hand, delicate but strong, held out as a beacon of hope. A piece of Viggo's heart slid into his stomach at the sight of the frail hand.

"Could she be from the same wreck that Aria was in?" Emir asked.

"Could be another syren," Skender quickly added.

Viggo looked at Skender briefly, took in his tight lips and tense shoulders. Were none of the others feeling what he felt? Could they not feel that this hand belonged to someone who would mean everything. There was such a strong lure to it, a deep need to save the girl in the Dahs.

"Silia toss Skender the binoculars." Skender took a closer look at the hand, now waving frantically in desperation, and cleared his throat. He had to remain rational.

"Do you recognize the creature?" Viggo asked quietly, still unsure of who or what Skender and Emir saw during their time under the Dahs.

Skender shook his head. His brows remained furrowed, obviously not trusting whatever creature desperately waved for their help.

Emir grumbled annoyedly. "We can't just leave her in the Dahs, Sken."

They both looked to Viggo.

Skender looked like he was about two seconds from losing it all entirely. "Forget about a syren, she could be anything. We don't know. But it doesn't seem likely that there's a human who has survived this long out here, from Aria's ship. She could be a creature in disguise," Skender pleaded.

Viggo's throat bobbed, he knew that Skender was right. This could be any creature.

"We will save her." His eyes stayed on the girl as he spoke. "Silia and Emir, take a hit of the silver and get us there as quickly as possible."

Skender's fist tightened on his famed sword. But if the girl was a Skierkan or Surtrian, it was their duty to protect her, or at least that was how he justified following his desires. It was their duty to protect. Skender had to understand that—he had to know it. And couldn't they feel it too? That damned pull to the girl had to mean something, as the last time he felt it, it was drawing him to meet Kel.

"Don't forget that we are also wicked creatures." Viggo reminded his squadron.

If his gut feeling was wrong, they were certainly not defenseless in their own right. Viggo summoned a comforting smile to put Skender at ease, before walking towards the discarded weaponry that littered the planks of the ships. Within seconds he found his crossbow and pocketed white lithe.

Swiftly, Emir and Silia crushed the minty silver lithe and snorted just enough to get them towards the stranded woman and quickly away if need be. The winds changed as Emir and Silia began to twist the channels of air, and the ship made its way closer to the pale hand. The burning smell of the fire lithe made its way over to Viggo. Seconds later, the warm orange of the fire lithe was burning bright in Skender's hands. He held the fire high up in the air and walked towards the front of the ship, acting as a beacon of light against the darkening skies and the darker waters.

The burnt orange flame wasn't much, but it was enough.

With the help of the lithe-led winds, the ship drew close enough to see more of the girl.

At last, Viggo could see her. Her hair was the bright red of a sweet cherry, and her frail arms did in fact seem to be holding on to a broken barrel for dear life.

Viggo magically amplified his voice by pressing his lithe-infused thumb tattoo to his vocal chords. "We are an official ship of the Skierkan military. We will be throwing out a rope for you. If you attack, we will not hesitate to kill. Do you understand and accept?"

Wide green eyes shone against the silvery light of the moon and the burnt orange of the fire lithe.

"I understand and accept." The girl choked on her own voice. Viggo's own heart throbbed at the sound of it.

He threw the end of a long, red rope, and held on as she pulled herself and her barrel to the boat. When she came close enough, he gripped her by the waist and pulled her up onto the boat. Her cold and soaked body shivered against his chest as he carried her to a stool, and gently placed her on top of it. She was so cold against him.

Skender held onto the fire lithe with white knuckles as he brought it closer to the girl, Viggo watched, worried Skender was planning on burning her, only to feel shame when he realized Skender was merely warming the girl up.

Silia and Emir kept their weapons drawn and facing her.

The girl, or actually woman, quickly wrapped herself up in Viggo's blankets. Her shivering could be heard over the roaring waters below.

"Thank you," She whispered, to nobody in particular.

"Who are you?" Skender asked, not bothering to blunt the untrusting edge in his voice.

Her big green eyes carefully looked them all over, although she looked obviously fearful, she didn't seem too surprised by the bow and sword drawn inches away from her face.

"I am Mayta." She looked back towards Viggo, somehow recognizing him as the one in charge. "I was on a cargo ship, carrying lithe to Etra for the king. We were attacked."

Skender and Viggo shared a look with one another.

"How have you survived this long?" Viggo finally asked.

Mayta looked back towards the Dahs. "I'm not really sure. All I remember is an explosion, and waking up in that barrel."

"When did you wake?" Skender asked.

"I—I'm not sure," Mayta stammered.

"How many nights have fallen since you woke up?" Skender asked again.

"This was the first night that I've seen." Mayta answered.

Silia caught Viggo's eye and went closer to him. She leaned towards his ear, keeping her eyes on Mayta. "If she was in a barrel of white lithe, it wouldn't be unheard of. The magic might have kept her alive." Skender, who obviously overheard, gave Silia a look as sharp as his own blades. Silia continued, "It may have even been enough raw magic to knock her out, if it overwhelmed her."

Emir's brows furrowed as he considered the plausibility of it all, he did not like going against his brother's wishes nor did he like going against Viggo's.

Viggo's eyes rested on Emir's as he wondered what he was really thinking about the girl from the Dahs.

"I am not going to hurt you." Mayta's raw voice croaked in the darkness.

Viggo didn't need to hear anymore. He knew the second he held her shivering body against his own chest. He knew deep in his heart that this creature was made for him. And he was made for her. Viggo was half-God, and as everyone knew, love for Gods is not comparable as the love humans stored for one another. The love of a God was blunt and all-consuming. Gods had killed entire kingdoms and realms for the ones they loved, the ones that they had only merely glimpsed, before feeling the wrath and glory of a Godsly love.

Viggo's eyes remained focused on her. He couldn't breathe.

Who was she?

The question bounced around his skull as his eyes rested on Emir's, the quiet giant, and so he saw it when Emir sniffed, so subtly and so silently.

Yes, what was that? That smell? It had to be coming from the girl. How did she smell faintly of flowers?

CHAPTER 24
RAASK

Raask, on the most important day of his life, woke up to a bloodied head on the nightstand.

His heart fluttered at the grotesque sight. Although he woke up alone in her chambers, he knew that it was a gift from her and his heart swelled as he took in the decrepit state of the witch's head. A part of him had hurt greatly when he killed those guards, but he knew it was the right thing to do. While on duty, they drank and snorted, taking for granted the reputation of the impenetrable white palace. They had to be taken care of. A message had to be sent.

And Aria, so clever, of course received it and sent one back herself. But did it mean what he secretly ached for it to mean? Did she think of him too? He knew that she found comfort in him, in how he held her closely at night when she would thrash awake from a nightmare, and how he would challenge her even after she'd lost her arm. He felt something for her, he did, he wanted to be with her always. To protect her. To be the one that she confided in. It was an odd feeling, and one that he attempted to make sense of during many nights. But each morning, he'd find himself tripping over himself just to get closer to her again.

Raask ran out of Aria's bed and headed towards the kitchens. He grabbed an assorted plate of boiled eggs, meats, and crisped potatoes along with another plate of cinnamon rolls, doughnuts, and toast with a hazelnut chocolate spread. He rushed outside towards her favorite breakfast bench by the strange-smelling black flowers. Of course, she was there. He could already smell the licorice spiced tea wafting from her spot.

He knew that she could hear him approaching. And her little bloodhound nose could probably smell the sugared pastries from a mile away. But she sat still, sipping her tea, and watching the hummingbirds drink nectar from the little black flowers which grew wildly, and thorned.

With a slam, Raask dropped the breakfast plates in front of Aria and sat across from her, as he did every morning.

"I got your gift," Raask said, trying his best to keep his voice even.

"Oh?" Aria was obviously fighting off a little smile as she looked down upon him. Her long wavy hair blew behind her with a gentle breeze that carried with it the sweet scent of the gardens.

"How did you do it?" Raask asked. To sneak out of the castle was no easy feat, and to find the witch . . . It was incredibly impressive and, not to mention, quick.

He had understood in some part of him that she had a violent nature to her. He could see it in her face and in her knuckles, and the way she sparred. Violence certainly flooded her dreams. It meant something to him, and to her, that she did not hide her kill from him. Did she too know what it felt like to find glory in bloodshed? He hoped that she did, so that he wouldn't be alone. He had changed so much since the dramatic shift in his trainings with the Irridesci. The blood he had shed in the trainings with them, it satiated the hungry magic that coiled around his organs and spine like a snake. It had brought him peace, even if only for a few moments.

"It was nothing," She shrugged. "With the sharp daggers you commissioned for me, her head came off easily."

Incredible. Those daggers were quite small, it would take an awful lot of strength, especially for her—since she only had the one arm to work with.

"You truly are remarkable," He breathed.

Aria rolled her eyes and began to pick apart a cinnamon roll. The roll stretched apart in her fingers, as the gooey insides stuck to her palms. Raask watched as she plopped a chunk of it directly onto her tongue.

"Will you stop staring and eat?"

Aria dropped a piece of ham, a too-big piece if Raask was being honest, into his mouth, surely as a way to get him to stop staring.

As it was finally the autumnal equinox, Raask and Aria hadn't bothered with training that day. Instead they had decided to spend the day outdoors, walking the grounds and seeing Etra. It was when it began to rain that they ran into Aria's quarters with a basket from the kitchens.

The fireplace crackled behind them. The juices of a ripe, purple spriteberry dripped down Aria's face. She hadn't recognized it in the kitchens and Raask immediately knew how much she would love it for its sweet, almost cinnamon-like flavor.

"I wish they made this stuff into soap instead of that Gods-awful rose smell they put into everything," Aria said after eating multiple handfuls of them.

Raask angled his head upon hearing her words. It took a moment for them to truly soak in. "You don't like the smell of roses?" He asked quietly.

She snorted, as if roses were truly vile. "No." She grabbed another spriteberry from the pile, and dipped it in the jar of honey that lay next to it. When the berry was good and coated in the sweet nectar, she plopped into her mouth and sucked her fingers. "I mean, on the plants they smell fine." She clarified. "But in the soaps here they're way too strong. Like sickeningly sweet."

He didn't realize Aria could find something to be sickeningly sweet, not after personally watching her eat family portions of many desserts. But roses were where she apparently drew the line. He was embarrassed and humiliated as he had thought she loved the smell of them. He had been making sure everything she had was rose scented.

Raask pushed the bowl of spriteberries closer to her.

Aria continued, not before stuffing her mouth full of more berries and honey, "You at least get a nice, earthy mint smell in your soaps."

"Would you prefer the earthy mint scent or a spriteberry scent in your soaps?" Raask asked.

Aria swallowed another hunk of honey and spriteberries, which of course would be a cloyingly sweet combination for most. "I think spriteberry. Or maybe cinnamon raisin."

Raask couldn't help the laugh that escaped from him. "You're meant to wash with it, not eat it, sweet thing."

Aria rolled her eyes. "I know that, but it wouldn't be too bad to smell like sweet cinnamon all the time. But on the other stub, I think it might make me too hungry. So we should make it spriteberry."

Raask watched as Aria sat, happily eating and drinking. He saw as her eyes wandered to the edges of the room as they often did when she became lost in thought. He hated to interrupt her when she was like this, but there was something he needed to tell her. "Aria." Her name was a roll of gentle thunder coming from his mouth.

She looked up from her thoughts and saw immediately that this was something serious.

"I don't want you to come tonight." He told her, as he silently prayed it wouldn't cause her alarm. He reached for her hand. He held it firmly in his own hands and rubbed careful circles. His calloused thumbs scraped against her rough palm.

He realized that he had drifted away into each callous of her skin.

Raask smiled lazily, hoping to Tsu that it covered his thoughts.

"And why not?" She asked, her body already stiffer than it was mere moments ago.

Raask sighed before popping a piece of dried pork into his mouth. It was the chewiest selection on their platter, and he knew it would give him time to think of his answer. After too long, he swallowed. Her gaze never wavered. He forgot that he was the impatient one, not her. "I'll be revealing my power's alignment." He paused. "They want a show. So that's what I'm going to give them. It won't be pretty, and it won't be kind."

"You don't want me to see you be unkind?" Aria scoffed. "You must know by now that kindness is not something that I value."

Raask played with a spriteberry on the platter, twisting it around the plate. "I know what my people want from me. I know what you want from me. And if I was more in control, I would want you there. But I can't . . . I won't be able to follow through with my plan if you are there, I can't be worried about hurting you, when I am playing the part that I must tonight."

Aria nodded, he could see her grasping onto every word he said, along with the words that he didn't. "Will you not at least tell me of your plan?" She finally asked.

So, he told her his plan.

And to his delight, she smiled at his wicked thoughts.

CHAPTER 25
KING MORLOK

King Morlok lazily reclined on his throne. Carved out of a singular slice of pure white lithe, the throne emanated raw power. The back of the throne was raised in dozens of sharpened edges, permanently stained red. It was Morlok tradition to hang the heads of the leaders of conquered lands on the spikes of the throne until they rotted off. During his fiery rule, King Morlok himself had added several heads to the back of the throne. They had all decomposed long ago.

Behind the king, the Morlok crest hung high over the revelry. The black raven against the blood-red banner stood watching. One of the first decrees of the current king had been that each household must fly the Morlok crest, or be treated as an enemy of Skierka. The next day, the crest flew proudly above each household and business of Skierka. And the ones that didn't were burned with their owners inside.

Beside the throne lay two gigantic torches with red flames that stood high above the throne. The flames were a signifier of the king's own power alignment. He was the Fire Monger, and he never intended for his people to forget it. As for his second son, tonight would be the night to figure out what would lay next to him when he took the throne. If he was anything like his brother, perhaps a preserved carcass would be suitable for the power of destruction and carnage. But from what it sounded like from the Irridesci, Raask's powers were something a bit more colorful.

That was a good thing, as there was no hope in the power of death and destruction. And while the people of Skierka and beyond had to know that the Morloks were deadly, it was more important that they believed they had something that they were fighting for, when they fought to conquer other lands. King Morlok knew better than anyone that the fear of death would not bring loyalty. Fire. Passion. Violence. A literal flame. Now that was something that could incite fear and nationalism.

The king watched. His people had already taken their seats in rows. He had skipped the music and the dancing, but the sweat that gleamed down his people's faces was enough to show that it was a festive time indeed. The drums began. They were loud thumps that began slow. In unison, hundreds of drums boomed as the drummers struck the crocodillo-skinned instruments at the same time. The beat became faster. The drummers began to chant the ancient primal song that was sung at each of the first trials of all of the kings of Skierka. And when the beat was going so fast that each new note was almost indistinguishable from the last, Prince Raask entered the room.

As tradition, he wore his battle leathers. The shiny black leather made him a beacon. The king's own flames reflected against the long leathers—even from across the giant room. A black leather, made from the rarest of obsidian moon wraiths, draped across his back. And his chest was bare, showing off the Morlok crest tattooed onto him as soon as he became of age.

Yes indeed, his once scrawny and party-obsessed son had grown into a fine man. And tonight would show if he would be suitable to be a king. It took more than attending a few diplomatic appointments and growing muscles to be a suitable king, but he wasn't sure if his son knew that. He wasn't sure yet if his youngest son was ready to be a killer. A conqueror. A ruler. When did a boy become a man and when did a man become a God? Did Raask even understand that to rule over Skierka, was to play God?

Raask's heavy pointed boots pounded the floor as he walked towards him. It was a long walk, and his son was smart enough to maintain eye contact with him the entire time.

Not a soul spoke or moved the entire time the prince crossed the room. This was not the prince that they had all known and loved and drank with. No, this was the first time they had seen him as a threat. A leader. Hah! Who knew he could do it?

A cruel smile escaped its way across the king's lips. A smile that his boys had learned long ago to run away from. But not today. Pride oozed from the king's chest and across his face when his youngest son echoed his cruel smile with one of his own. Maybe the boy was indeed ready.

His son's echoed steps stopped as he stood at the bottom of the stairs that led up to the lithe throne. And for the first time in his son's life, he would not bow to his father. No, the first trial was the first time the future king began to be accepted as king. In a way, this was the first test of the night.

The king's late wife's eyes stared up at him. It sometimes alarmed him to see her face in his. After several long moments, the king gave a tiny nod to his son and to his people. The people of Skierka sat. Prince Raask's shoulders loosened, only slightly.

"Prince Raask, are you ready for your first trial? Are you ready to show the people of Skierka your worth? Are you ready to be judged for your worthiness as future King of Skierka?" The king spoke the ancient words that long ago had been spoken to him.

"I'm ready, my King." Raask's voice didn't waver.

The king lifted his palm up and quickly flipped it over, closing his hand in a tight fist. The roaring fires next to the throne immediately shot to the sky before vanishing. And only the fires at the end of each row lit the dim space.

"You may begin, Prince Raask." The king used his son's formal title as a reminder that today he was not his father. Today he was a king, judging the future of his kingdom.

Raask slowly lifted his head. His eyes looked like they could have borne a hole through his head. The king silently wondered if the Irridesci had been lying, had his son not found his alignment, still? Wrath flared across the king's face. The world could not see weakness in the Morlok line.

The little shit now had the audacity to laugh. The Crown Prince of the Morlok dynasty was laughing at the sight of his king's rage.

The king decided he'd had enough. And that maybe he was not above burning the hundreds of Skierkans who had ventured out to bear witness to the future king's alignment ceremony. Maybe he was not even above burning his youngest son alive.

He raised his fist, ready to make the kill. Thirsty for it, even. When he finally noticed the quietness of the room. It was quieter than any human ever could be, especially hundreds of humans in a tight space.

The king finally noticed his son for what he was, for what he could do. And in response, he let out a savage laugh. Without even lifting a finger, his son had stopped the heart of every single person in the room other than himself and the king. A wicked smile crept onto the prince's face. While the king continued to laugh, the prince started the Skierkans' hearts once again. At this, the king's laugh grew into a roar.

He wondered how long the prince could hold their hearts as prisoners, keeping them dead before they were too far gone. What a neat, little trick his son had perfected. Not at all like his eldest's rotten magic that tended to cause as much destruction and stink as possible.

The king continued to laugh cruelly as Prince Raask left the ginormous hall. Confused spectators looked back and forth from the king to the prince, unaware of what had just occurred. Unaware that their crown prince had just revealed himself to be a Blood Screamer.

The first Blood Screamer since the first Morlok King even. A blessing from Voskule, God of War, it must be.

The King's cold, cold laugh echoed across the lithe-bleached walls of the palace, and continued throughout the prince's restless slumber.

CHAPTER 26
VIGGO

"It was like the ancient ones had given me a push towards her. And I knew that she was mine and that I was hers, and I was willing to do anything for her." At the time, Viggo was a young boy who had just learned that the king—the man who had beaten him down again and again, and trained him to be nothing but a brutal killer—was not his father.

It was the same day that he learned his mother had never truly died. She only lived among the dead with his biological father, the God of Death. It was a lot for him to take in. And his mother did not smell the same anymore. Viggo was confused, and even a little bit betrayed. The only thing that helped in the beginning was seeing how much Kel had loved his mother, and how much happier she looked living among the dead than in the white palace.

He also enjoyed hearing how they had kept close tabs on him, and helped him without his knowing. Kel also helped him learn to harness his powers better, to prevent those terrible outbursts of decay and fury.

It was this conversation that Viggo kept thinking about as he sat with Mayta; his father's words on how deeply he loved his mother upon first seeing her.

It was nauseating.

Mayta hadn't talked much since they pulled her out of the black waters. But she watched them all carefully. Her wide, green eyes gave her fear away. And although it was freezing, and everyone else would shiver, flesh ripe with goosebumps, she never once indicated that she was cold. Maybe she didn't trust them enough to reveal any sort of weakness, including the cold that was tearing the rest of them apart.

Viggo pulled a small wheel of waxed cheese out of his satchel, and brought it to Mayta along with the last piece of stale bread that he had. He sat down on the creaky boards of the ship, making sure to leave a respectful gap between them. Silently, he handed her the last bits of food that he had.

"Thank you," she said quietly, voice hoarse.

"Are you thirsty?" Viggo asked, as he passed her his own water-skin. She took it, and gulped it down. Viggo ignored Skender's glare that shot up the second he heard her drinking water at such fast amounts.

"Thank you," Mayta said again.

"Are we almost out of food?" She finally asked. Eyes stuck on the gold horizon. It wouldn't be long until the sunset and they would be stuck in another nightfall.

Viggo solemnly nodded. "We are, but we should be home soon."

Mayta looked to the meager piece of cheese and bread that Viggo had brought her. She broke it apart into four, equal portions and handed them to Silia, Emir, Skender, and finally, Viggo. He waved off the last portion that she tried to hand to him. Her small, pale hand shook as she tried to grab his hand to make him take the food.

"Please, I'm not hungry. And I'm certain you have been out here longer."

He smiled, ignoring the emptiness in his belly, "I'm fine."

A sweet, small smile danced across her face. The first one he'd seen from her. "You need your strength to get us to land. I am fine. Really."

Viggo took the food into his hand, and twisted the cheese and bread into even smaller pieces. He still ended up giving her a larger portion, but the small bites were enough to stop the rumbling of his stomach. "Thank you," Viggo said.

Silia took the empty spot next to Mayta. She kept her back to the edge of the boat. None of them, besides Viggo, trusted Mayta just yet. Silia clamped her jaw down on the stale bread. With a twist and a pull, she ripped the rock-hard bread and took a massive bite. Silia was the one who had been conscious for the longest amount of time on the Dahs. Although she was always able to keep her muscles intact through creative exercises, the weeks were beginning to show on her face—and in her manners. She was a twitchy sort of creature, as if she always had more energy and strength than she knew what to do with. But ever since Viggo and the twins dove into the depths, her demeanor had calmed. Her eyes were now sullen, and her face red with burns from the harsh sunlight.

"Your family on the ship?" Silia asked, luckily only slightly more crassly than she normally would have.

Mayta chewed on her bottom lip. Her eyes lowered to the hem of Viggo's old cloak that she now wore. She played with the stray stitching. "They're gone."

Emir stood on the bow of the ship, snorting a conservative amount of the silver lithe. Emir let out a pointed cough. It snapped Mayta's attention away from the stray thread. "Well, we at least have a friend for you back in Etra. I'm sure you'll be excited to see a familiar face."

Mayta stared at Emir for a long while. Although she had a generally calming air to her, something had shifted in that moment.

Emir let out a cautious laugh. "What?" He asked, feigning amusement. Skender's face snapped up at the sound of it.

Silia studied Mayta's expression as she chewed the large lump of hard bread. Her lips smacked over and over again before Mayta's face slowly softened.

"They hurt you on that ship?" Silia asked.

Mayta sighed and stared out at the seas. "No, nothing like that." She finally looked up at Silia, who was still chewing so pissin' loudly it was driving Viggo insane, before explaining. "It's just that . . . I didn't think there were any other survivors from our ship."

"Were there any other lithe ships that had gone missing?" Skender asked Viggo.

"Not before we left," He answered. He didn't have to see Skender to know that he was giving Mayta a pointed look.

Emir chimed in, "Well, didn't you lose consciousness? Maybe you had already passed out by the time Aria had stowed away in one of those barrels." Viggo watched Mayta as she twisted her head to look at Emir and then back to Viggo. He almost lost it when he saw her lower lip tremble. Just as he was about to tell them off for harassing her, after she had already been through so much . . . too much. She spoke.

"Who is Aria?"

CHAPTER 27
ARIA

A slick sheen of sweat gleamed across Aria's face. She had expected Raask to want to sleep in the day after his first trial, a day that Skierkans certainly had a lot of speculation and rumor about him. That wasn't the case though. Before sunlight spilled through the cold glass of her chambers, the bed began to stir with Raask's unease. Aria could feel each turn and anxious fidget.

"Raask?" She asked, pretending she didn't already know that the prince had obviously been awake for hours.

He faked a yawn, "Mmmmhmmmm?" He could have been auditioning for the role of the sleepiest prince at the Royal Theater.

A few hours later, Aria and Raask had sparred about a dozen different times with a dozen different weapons. Raask had commissioned specialty bows, axes, swords, pick-axes, and just about anything and everything deadly so that she could use them with one arm. She was still getting used to shooting with the new bow, but the rest had already become second nature. And when it was Raask's turn to spar with his instructors, Aria was happy to practice with a target, or run drills on her own.

She had spent most of her life training, doing physical work of some kind. It was comfortable for her. She felt her freest and happiest when practicing with weaponry and pushing her body to its absolute limits. But when she looked back at Raask and the others, training with traditional weapons, the way her ancestors fought, the way she was taught by her very own family, her chest tightened and her breath halted.

Aria took a break from jogging back and forth around the training arena, and headed towards her waterskin. She tensed her fists, and if she closed her eyes, she could swear her left arm was still there. Of course, it wasn't. Of course, there was nothing but a stump where her left hand had been once. What would her parents say, if they knew she crippled herself to save the prince of the nation that had conquered hers? What would her people say, if they knew that she would do it all over again?

She unscrewed the cap to her waterskin, holding the bottle tight between her legs. The cold water hit her tongue and washed away all of the questions. She gulped the water until it hurt, and let it rinse away all of her internal criticisms. Her eyes narrowed on the specialty weapons that Raask had made for her. It was kind of him. But they made her feel weak, lighter than most other weapons, to account for her single arm.

These wobbly legs and missing arm, she decided, didn't make her weak. Thick muscles now corded her body once again. Maybe it was time to show the Skierkans who trained among them.

"You, you, and you." Aria pointed a long finger at the three biggest Skierkans in the arena. She jerked her head to a mat and didn't check to see if they followed. At this point, she had a reputation for being the prince's 'plaything'. She had even caught the redheaded brute snickering at her a few weeks ago. They would know what a mistake that was now, not because their prince was warming her bed at night, but because she was a force of her own.

Her specialty sword, ironically named Arachni for the many-armed spider-descended warrior folk that had gone extinct centuries ago, whined as she drew large circles with it at her side. When she finally got to the mat that was across the arena from Raask's, she turned around to see that the three oafs hadn't brought weapons with them.

"Miss Aria?" The burly, blonde woman seemed confused.

"Why did you not bring your weapons?" Aria asked.

"You would like us to spar for you?" The short, thick man with a long beard asked. "I'm sure there are many other ways we could entertain you." They all snickered. Although they were too cowardly to say that loud enough for the prince to hear. Their mistake in thinking he was the bigger threat.

She smiled with too many teeth. "I'll allow you the time to reconsider. And choose your weapon wisely." They shared another look of confusion and stayed planted in the same spot. The idiots still didn't understand. "You will all be sparring me."

The redhead balked. "You are a cripple. We are four of the best trained soldiers in all of Skierka."

The burly blonde felt the need to add, "We would be dishonorable if we were to spar with a citizen."

Her nostrils flared and her head tilted down towards them in a maneuver she mastered long ago. It gave the appearance that she was looking down on them even though she was much shorter than most. "You will all be sparring me." She repeated.

"I would do as she says," Raask's cool voice, a thundering heartbeat, echoed across the arena. "She can get quite testy if she doesn't get what she wants." He smirked at the four soldiers who had disobeyed her order to spar. She heard his familiar heavy gait heading their way. Steady and loud. She turned to him and fought the smile that seeing him brought to her lips. "I would definitely choose whichever weapon you feel best at. I wouldn't want the show to be over too quickly." He threw a wink at Aria.

The short, bearded one shrugged and grabbed the wooden hatchet. The blonde woman grabbed a training sword. And the redhead seemingly felt confident enough without a weapon. It was his mistake to make. Another costly one. He'd find that out soon enough.

But Aria didn't want there to be any confusion. So, she dropped her own weapon. Arachni clanged against the floor. The entire training arena had halted their own sparring and started watching Aria. Many were too cautious of upsetting the prince to make it too obvious that they were watching skeptically, but many didn't share that feeling, and practically pulled up a seat to watch the prince's new cocky plaything get her ass handed to her.

"You may begin," The prince announced.

The one with the hatchet swung at her. He was big and swung with the force of his entire body. Aria ducked and rolled. Before he even knew what hit him, she jumped on his back and gripped his throat with her right bicep. He released a shocked exhale. He knew she had him.

The nasty brute retaliated by flinging himself onto his back and onto her. Her body smashed into the floor and the wind knocked out of her lungs. Her grip on his throat tightened as his massive weight sandwiched her onto the floor. His ear was turning red as he struggled against her grip. She tried not to think about what color her own face was turning as the fat man squished her onto the hard floor. The woman with the sword decided she had enough of watching the spectacle and finally took a swing. Aria twisted. But she was too slow, too stunned by the man crushing her bones. The sword caught in Aria's braid.

The blonde smirked, all too aware of where her sword laid in her hair. She pulled the sword back up, dragging Aria's scalp up with it.

Hair pulling? Is this what they taught the Skierkan army? With no left hand to get her braid out from the sword, she was forced to twist her body out from underneath the bearded brute and let go of her chokehold.

The sudden release of the tension on her scalp was a quick moment of pure bliss as she took advantage of the brute's coughing, and focused on the woman now. Redhead stayed on the edge of the mat, apparently he didn't like to share, and was patient enough to wait. Unlike blondie.

She placed all of her weight onto her back leg, leaning back and leaving herself exposed. The blonde took the bait. She whipped the sword, aiming for the side of Aria's head. But her head wasn't there anymore. Aria spun around and kicked the blonde woman's head right in the sweet spot that put her unconscious.

Beard was still coughing up a lung on the floor. His whole face had gone violently red. Aria released a cold laugh as she grabbed blondie's sword and drew it to his throat. If it had been a real battle and a genuine sword, it would have been a kill shot, and Aria's hair would have been cut shorter.

"Two down, one to go." Raask's voice sent a thrilling chill down her spine. Other trainers dragged Blondie and Beard's bodies off of the mat, leaving more space for her and Red's battle.

Aria gave a teasing smirk to him. "Well, what are you waiting for?"

Red laughed, spit shot out of his gnarly mouth with it.

Aria looked towards Red's empty hands, and threw Blondie's sword outside of the ring.

"You sure you want to do that?" Red taunted.

"I don't need any weapons to humiliate you, big boy." Aria could practically imagine Raask's amused face at that. "In fact, I can do it one-handed." Aria mocked.

Red cracked his knuckles, and then his burly neck. Left then right. "So let's see it then." He charged towards her. He was surprisingly fast for someone so big.

He aimed for her waist, going for a takedown. She allowed him to grab her and bring her up in the air. At the last moment, she flung herself onto his back. But he was smarter than beard. He didn't give her his throat, he kept his chin tucked down. She couldn't choke him like that. They both knew it. She hopped off of his back and kicked him in the liver before he had the chance to turn back around. Red grunted in pain and swung around with his arms like hammers.

She saw stars the second his fists collided with the side of her head. Another fist collided with the opposite side of her, towards her mouth. Warm, thick blood coated the inside of her mouth. Her feet drew herself back and she spat out a chunk of blood and released a truly joyous laugh. "I decapitated the last creature to make me bleed." She laughed again, even harder. "If only we battled off the palace grounds, and I could discover exactly how brainless you are."

With that, she charged towards him. In an unGodsly speed, she was in front of him again. Her hand grasped onto the back of his skull, and she threw it down. She brought her knee up and rammed it into his head. While Red was still stunned, and blood poured off of his face, Aria threw herself into his core and knocked him into the ground.

Once on the mat, Aria straddled his waist and delivered punch after punch. She lifted her fists up high above her head and continuously smashed his skull. A bloody dent formed onto Red's head. Aria didn't stop. She didn't hear anything else but the beat of her own heart and the beat of her fists. She swallowed the blood that had pooled in her own mouth and let it drive her deeper into her blood-lust. Strong hands gripped Aria from underneath her arms, pulling her off of Red. The strong scent of mint and training leathers flooded her senses. Raask.

He pulled her off of the mat and twisted her around, breaking her eye contact with Red. His face was nearly unrecognizable. It looked like he had survived a wave of stones. But what did it matter? He was a Skierkan, fought in their military in fact. Maybe her ancestors were watching and maybe for once they were pleased.

She laughed and laughed as Raask dragged her off.

CHAPTER 28
RAASK

The warm scent of salty caramel and sandalwood flooded Raask's nose as he carried Aria away from the Vermilli. Sweet, wicked, loving, and cruel Aria. She tore through some of the best Skierkan soldiers in his brother's army, literally one handed. It was the most incredible thing he'd ever seen.

He whisked her up and carried her up to the palace. He wanted to kiss her, but he'd settle for just being near her. It was hard to ignore her violent tendencies, and even harder to ignore the feeling of understanding. She loved to set the world afire. And a part of him did, too. They were an odd pair, but he felt he could relax around her in the way he could with no one else.

After a heavy meal of roasted goose, spriteberry jam, and boiled greens, Aria had eventually calmed down. She fell asleep not too long afterwards.

Raask no longer dreaded the long minutes it took for him to fall asleep. Even on the nights he had to train and travel to the Irridesci tower, where he would shred creatures apart molecule by molecule, none of it mattered anymore, not as long as he had Aria to come home to. After losing his mother, and with his brother's busy sched-ule, he had spent so much of his life alone. And if he wasn't alone, he was playing a character.

When the morning came, Raask couldn't help but bask in the freeness of his heart. He felt as if he finally had a purpose and a person to share it all with. Yesterday, Raask's workers had told him that the metal arm he had commissioned for Aria would be ready by the afternoon. He could barely hold onto his excitement.

He planned to take her for a run where he could work out all of his excitement, and hopefully not spill the secret before grabbing breakfast at Arthur's bakery. Knowing her well enough, Raask knew she would want to train with it right away, so he wanted to wait until the afternoon, for the ship of soldiers to come back from the Surtr Islands. The one-armed Skierkan battle hero, Maltho, would be on the ship and he would certainly have tips for Aria on how to adjust to a metal arm. Or at the least, he may make Aria feel less lonely in her predicament. Loneliness was an awful sort of feeling. He wanted to keep it as far away from Aria as possible. Gods knew she had already been through enough. He'd seen the horrified look on her face as she awoke from her nightmares. The scars on her body. The way she cautiously eyed anyone who yelled.

She had been through enough already.

His feet smacked against the soil as he ran, and hers were as silent as always. Luckily the wind and cool autumnal breeze proved to be excellent running conditions. His country was beautiful this time of year, at least he had always thought so. The sky was grayer than he hoped, but not enough to block out the brilliant golds and silvers of the trees that had held onto their leaves. Raask began to lag just a hair behind Aria as he took in the beauty of his land. Of her.

Her sloppy braids always came undone on their runs, but she never seemed to notice.

"Come on! Keep up!" Aria teased over the roar of the Dahs.

"Last one to Arthur's is stuck with the egg loaf!" Raask yelled as he sprinted towards the familiar green doors. Aria's sweet laugh caught up to him as quick as she did, and in no time she was in front again.

He was lost in the bliss of it all and hardly noticed that Aria had stopped dead in her tracks. He smashed right into her, but she merely stumbled and caught herself.

"Baldrei's balls, Aria! What was tha—?" Raask's words were cut off once he noticed why Aria had stopped. On the end of the cove, all the way at the other end of the Salt District, was his brother's stealth ship. The Morlok flag flew above, in recognizable bright red and black colors, with a raven that matched the one tattooed to his own chest.

Raask couldn't hold back his grin. Viggo had met Aria, but only briefly, and before he had found family within her. He couldn't wait for them to really meet. He just knew that they would get along and love each other. Viggo and Aria were both vicious, but kind in their own secretive ways, and Viggo would love to hear of how Aria had sawed off the lunar wraith's head when it had attacked the palace.

"AYOOOO!" Raask cried at the top of his lungs at the sight of his brother walking towards him. But his brother did not complete the call, the same one that they had both done so many times before. How long had it been for Viggo? His brother was gone for months sometimes, but he claimed that on the Dahs it only felt like a few days. Maybe the opposite happened . . . Maybe to Viggo it had felt like years, and he had forgotten the tradition.

Raask rushed to the black sands of the Etran shore. He saw the familiar little clan that followed his brother around everywhere. There was Silia and her impeccably neat braids. There was Emir and Skender, with their massive swords and stalking forms. But next to Viggo was a girl. The first thing he noticed was her hair, the bright red of a fresh cherry.

The girl seemed to have a serious case of the sealegs. She wobbled and wiggled as she walked. Her wide seafoam eyes looked all around in what looked like fear.

It was then that Raask noticed his brother's arm stabilizing the girl. Raask threw his head back and let out a loud and warm laugh at the sight. It seemed he wasn't the only Morlok to find love in the past few months. What a day!

"Aria! It's my brother, don't you see?" He turned to look at her.

Her sun-kissed skin had somehow reverted to the sickly pale color she was when he first found her on these very sands.

"Are you alright?" He rushed over to her and placed the back of his hand on her forehead. She wasn't warm, so no fever or sickness. She nodded, but wrapped her arm around her belly. Maybe she was hungry . . . They would stop and grab a loaf at Arthur's with Viggo and his clan. Arthur would love to see Viggo too, especially since he was one of the few who actually enjoyed those egg loaves.

Raask looked back to his brother.

This time he noticed it.

Viggo, his older brother, the general of the entire Skierkan military, the Skierkan Bruin himself, who had always held such a tight leash on his powers, was leaking death. A black and gray mess of an aura encompassed him. Where he walked, death followed. Pure death, decay, and destruction radiated out of his brother from every pore. The already quiet street of the Salt District in the day, had completely emptied. The sounds of doors locking and curtains closing echoed across the district. Only his brother, his clan, the woman they traveled with, Aria and he, stood on the beach.

Raask didn't know what was going on, but he had a feeling that was what his brother wanted. It was so rare for his brother to display his power's deadly alignment to the public, and not at some nationalistic showcase. Something must be wrong. Or maybe, his brother had lost control again . . . If he did, Gods save them all . . .

Raask reached a hand out for Aria and he pushed her behind him. If his brother accidentally expelled too much of his power, let it hit him and not Aria.

Her cold and clammy hand gripped his in return. This was not the Viggo he wanted her to see. "Don't be frightened, he won't hurt you." Raask whispered. Although, he wasn't sure if it was the truth.

It was then that Viggo lifted a steady hand and pointed it at Aria. A whip of darkness crashed against her. Raask caught her in his arms before she could fall to the rough sands. In pain and confusion, Raask looked up at his brother's dark eyes and saw the violence that was promised in them. Viggo cocked his wrist up and down, another spiral of dark magic came shooting out of him and towards Aria. This time, Raask was ready.

A whip of blood magic came from Raask, and wrapped around Viggo's dark magic, halting it in place. Viggo looked to Raask, eyes widened. His brother sniffed the air, sniffed the metallic, repulsive, purely gory scent that came from his magic and nodded.

"A blood screamer?" Viggo asked, from across the beach.

"Explain yourself!" Raask called, bringing himself and Aria steady, and onto their own feet.

Viggo looked between them and spat. "Why don't you ask your lady to do just that?"

Raask asked again, "Explain!" This time his voice was quieter, and a kernel of pain echoed within it.

Raask looked at Aria, who clutched tightly to him. He looked back at his brother and his clan who stood close enough to interfere if need be, but far enough for the image of privacy. "And who is *your* lady?" Raask asked.

"She is the sole survivor of the lithe cargo ship. And she does not know of any Aria."

Raask's eyes darted to the redheaded woman. But it was not him that she was staring at, it was Aria. The redheaded woman nodded, confirming Viggo's story.

"She is lying." Raask snarled. He scooped his palm into the air and brought it back down into a fist with a powerful and swift movement. The redheaded girl began screaming. She clutched at her head and fell to the sand.

"Raask! Stop it! She is not the enemy!" Viggo cried.

Raask ignored him. He stared the woman down. "Admit you lied," he called, voice deep and steady even though he felt nauseous due to all of the power and the confusion. As a Blood Screamer, he could manipulate blood and organs and any other living matter with ease. And right now, he was increasing the temperature of the redhead's blood. Soon, her brain would boil in it and the threat against Aria would be finished.

The redhead thrashed against the sand. Her screams echoed against the cobbled empty streets. Viggo took a few steps towards Raask, his dark aura pulsing. "Raask, let her go, I do not want to hurt you."

He did not let go. He couldn't, for if he did, she would never admit to lying and Aria would be put at risk.

She had already been through so much. Too much. And she, who had saved him from that wraith, needed his saving now. "Admit that you are lying!" Raask screamed with enough force that his throat felt raw, as if his words were thorned with hope. *How could this be happening? Who was this redhead? Why did his brother believe her over him?*

He tightened his fist, and the redhead screamed as he began to bleed her. Soon blood would be flooding out of her.

"Raask . . ." Aria called from what felt like miles away. Her voice barely registered as he became all too consumed with his blood-hungry magic, and the need to protect.

"Raask!" Aria screamed it this time, and he immediately ceased his blood magic.

The redhead sank into the sand, sobbing and shaking uncontrollably. Viggo went to her and held her against his chest. Raask turned to Aria, who was watching the redhead with tears in her eyes.

"Raask," Aria whispered.

She looked at him and her eyes held the intensity of her wildness, her primal nature apparent in every piece of her. And in her eyes he saw it: the look of a trapped animal.

"She is not lying, Raask."

He took in how she held herself together at the abdomen, with a tight, clawed hand wrapped around herself. He saw how her wavy hair shook as she held back her tears. He wouldn't have believed it if it came from anyone else.

He didn't know if he believed it coming from her either.

If she was a monster, who had lied and manipulated, it wouldn't be pain in Aria's eyes, it would be satisfaction—or anger at being caught. It couldn't be true. She had killed for him. She had loved him in her own way. He knew it. He grew up in a court of liars and peacocks and showmen, and he knew a liar when he saw one. Her love had been true. He just knew it.

"No," Raask whispered. "You're lying."

"I *was* lying."

He watched Aria swallow, and take one long look at the redhead Viggo cradled, before looking back into his eyes. "I am from the Dahs, Raask. It's my home." She looked back towards the frigid black waves. "You did not rescue me that night."

He ran a hand through his golden hair, suddenly completely unaware of what he normally did with his hands. Unaware of how he stood. Unaware of how to be himself in a world where Aria was not the girl he thought she was. And he was suddenly all too aware of his awkward body and broken heart. All alone again. "Nobody is from the Dahs."

"No *human* is from the Dahs," Aria answered, even quieter.

In a sudden realization, every encounter with Aria rushed into Raask's thoughts. The salty scent of her. The way she moved impossibly fast, and her incredible strength. The familiarity of weaponry, like she had been trained before. The way her emotions pushed and pulled like waves in a storm. That's exactly what she was, the rocky waves of a storm. Or maybe more accurately, it was where she was from.

Desperation and panic struck Raask. He suddenly seemed to lose the ability to breathe. For the life of him, he couldn't draw breath. His vision turned blurry, but he didn't need much sight to know that his aura was now an aching, bleeding, pulsing red. He was feeling all too much and all too fast and like a protective shield, his powers cocooned him.

"Your harp?" Raask asked, his voice gravelly—for his mouth had dried up.

Aria smushed her lovely lips together until they were nothing but a strained line, and shook her head. No, then, she hadn't had to use any powers to get Raask to love her. He wished she had said yes, and he could blame this all on magic. Then it wouldn't be his fault at all that he had fallen in love with one of the realm's most deadly creatures.

"A syren?" Some twisted part of him needed to hear it from her.

"Not a syren, Raask. *The* syren."

"What is that supposed to mean?" Raask's bloodied aura pulsed more viciously with each moment. His bloody magic flared in sharp darts that landed like fireworks all around. This was too much, all of it was too much.

"I am the rightful heir to the throne of the Abisian syrens."

A princess... A queen to be.

Raask was more than familiar with the Dahsian syren that lived within the Dahs, and had tormented sailors for centuries. He had even hunted a few down as a boy, as was customary for the young boys of noble families. But the Abisian was not something he recognized. What did it matter anyways?

"Raask?" Viggo's voice drifted over from the dark sands where he still held the redhead.

Raask looked towards his brother, and gave a gentle nod to confirm approval of a disgusting thing.

Dark tendrils that smelled of rot and death itself shot out of Viggo and wrapped themselves around Aria's wrists. Raask stood still as he watched his brother's dark gifts restrain the only creature he had ever revealed his true self to. He stood still and watched as his brother got up from his spot and placed a bag over her head, then wrapped her body in his cloak. His brother, who was bringing his love to the dungeons no doubt, took the time to hide her identity and protect Raask from shame. Raask didn't recognize the kindness his brother attempted by hiding her identity, until later that night as he laid in a too large bed.

Alone again.

CHAPTER 29
ARIA

The dungeon reminded Aria of home. Her body quickly acclimated to the twisted angles and the weights of her shackles. The stone floor was not unlike the cave floor she'd slept on after her little sister was born. And the guards brought her porridge and other bland meals; none of which included Arthur's sweet breads, or even a cinnamon roll. But at least she was eating.

She'd always known she wouldn't have long to enjoy the sweets and comforts within the palace. This had always been the plan. She knew Raask would have to catch her. She knew her future, and had even concocted it herself. So, Aria was completely dumbfounded as to why she couldn't stop crying.

Crying was for weak children who had nothing better to do with their time but wallow. And while she obviously didn't have anything better to do with her time, as she was locked up for the rest of her life in a dungeon, she still thought of crying as weak and pathetic. For some reason, reminding herself of how weak and pathetic she was for crying didn't make her stop crying, she only cried harder.

She didn't sleep at all the first night. No, she kept her ear pressed against the western side of her cell, hoping to somehow hear if the prince cried for her as she did for him. It was utterly pathetic, but it did at least pass the time.

Aria counted the stones in her cell six or seven times. Each time she reached a new total. She sang songs from her childhood, songs from the palace, and the songs of the beasts of the Dahs. But mostly she slept, curled up in a ball by a puddle on the floor in the corner of her cell. Besides the guards who brought her meals three times a day, who refused to even acknowledge her, Aria had no interaction with the outside world.

Based on the meal schedule, it had been about four days and was sometime in the evening, when she received her first visitor. The clank of the key against the bars of her cell woke her up. She remained still, and kept her breaths even and her eyes closed. She listened as whomever was trying to get into her dungeon obviously struggled with the key.

Aria peeked open an eye.

"What are you doing here?" She asked, her voice low and deadly. She hoped whoever it was couldn't see how hard she had been crying.

Mayta's big, teary, green eyes met Aria's for only a brief moment before Mayta erupted in silent sobs. Her vibrant cherry-red hair shook with each sob. Over and over she silently mouthed the words, 'I'm sorry, I'm sorry, I'm sorry.'

Aria sat up and brushed the dirt off of her side. Without thinking, she used her right arm to itch her nonexistent left arm. Mayta noticed the movement, as she'd noticed everything since she first opened those big eyes and began to shake with her silent sobs.

"Mayta!" Aria hissed. "I'm fine. Get ahold of yourself." She did not want her sister to see her like this. Mayta needed her to be strong. So she would be.

Mayta's hands continued to shake as she struggled with the key to the dungeon.

Aria rolled her eyes. "Will you put that thing away?" She begged, already getting a headache from the incessant clanking. Not to mention that someone was bound to hear it sooner or later.

"I'm going to get you out of here, okay? I learned the guard's schedule and I poisoned the one that is normally on shift now." Aria looked up at Mayta with annoyance written all over her face. While Aria had mastered the art of brutal slaughter, Mayta had developed a knack for poisons. She had an unnatural ability to grow and maintain plants, and had managed to keep a small garden of poisonous plants tucked away on a tiny, forgotten island. If Mayta had already killed one of Aria's guards, it would greatly complicate her plans.

"No, I didn't kill him!" Mayta cried, far too loud after seeing Aria's face. "He'll only be stuck in the toilet for the night, and maybe some of tomorrow." Finally, Mayta unlocked the door. It swung open with a loud creak and a boing as it hit the bars on the opposite side.

"Mayta!" Aria hissed through her teeth. "I told you to put that thing away!"

Completely ignoring her, Mayta rushed into the cell and over to Aria. She gently inspected the shackles that bound her wrist and ankles. "I'm going to save you!" Mayta desperately pat Aria's body down, as if reassuring herself that Aria was fine and alive. "I hope you trusted me enough to know that I wasn't going to let you rot down here!"

Aria's jaw tightened. It was always impossible to get a word in with her. "I don't need saving, you idiot!" Mayta dropped the chains on the stones out of surprise and shock; Aria so rarely used a harsh voice with her little sister, and she was already feeling bad for it.

"What do you mean?" Mayta asked.

Aria watched as Mayta began to put the pieces together. "What is going on, Aria? Why did you come here and . . . and . . . seduce the prince?" Aria heard the heartbreak in Mayta's words. "You are my sister, and you know I've loved him for years." And at that sentence, Aria's own heart broke once again. Loving him was never in the plan. "I was so scared when I saw you with him... I just, I just knew you were going to kill him and I couldn't stand the thought of it!"

Aria stiffened. "And that is why you are going to marry him." The words hurt coming out of Aria's mouth. Her chest tightened and ached. She was feeling hollow again.

Aria had watched her little sister pine for the human prince since she was a young girl. Her little, sweet sister, who was so profoundly fascinated with the humans who hunted her own kind, that she would hide in the shallows and watch.

A silly, little girl. A lovely, little girl.

Mayta watched and loved many of them. But she had only fallen in love with one. The Crown Prince of Skierka, whom Mayta had sworn had hair of sunlight. She had evidently seen him as a young boy visiting the pastry shop often, and the whorehouse more as he grew older. She watched him save a young harlot. She watched his kindness to the villagers and his silliness on late, drunken nights, and she decided—somewhere very deep in her heart—that he was supposed to be hers. So Aria made it happen, in the only way that would benefit both Mayta and their kind.

It took her years to concoct the plan, and even longer to grow the courage to run towards her death.

While Mayta watched with hungry, loving eyes, Aria watched with power-hungry ones. Aria understood that to marry a prince was to one day be queen. And to be queen was to rule.

That was the one thing Aria had wanted more than anything, for the humans who had hunted and enslaved her own kind to be ruled by one of her own. She wanted the humans to know fear in the way that they had instilled it in the syrens. She wanted them to understand how it felt to be hunted in their own homelands. Aria's palms began to bleed as she held her fist too tight into itself.

"Marry him?" Mayta demanded. "And why would he propose to me when he loves you?"

It wasn't supposed to happen like this. The prince was not supposed to feel like home, not to her anyways. She was meant to be the monster of the story. And that was supposed to be fine.

"He may think he loves me for now. But you will eventually be the one who saved him from marrying an awful creature like me. You will be his savior, his light. And he will learn to love you as every male does, sooner or later." They both knew that every male Mayta had come into contact with had developed at least some form of a crush on her. Mayta couldn't help but exude a natural light and loveliness that drew all to her. She was a sun, and the rest of them had orbited around her. Just like *him*.

Whereas Aria was nothing like that. She was a beast of the dark waters, a wicked and cruel thing. The monster of the story.

That was supposed to be okay. She was never meant to want more.

She didn't have any warmth or love radiating from her. She was dark and angry and cruel, even. And where Mayta would dream of sweet, lovely, silly things, Aria dreamed of power and revenge. She was the darkness that was necessary to protect her younger sister. It was a role that she accepted long ago.

"But Aria . . . I am also a syren. He will have to know sooner or later."

Aria shook her head at her sister's words. She wouldn't like the scheming part of this plan, but she must follow along and do her part. Afterall, gaining the trust of the Skierkans would come effortlessly for her, Mayta was a syren and a strong one. She oozed feelings of trust. It would be nearly impossible for any human—or less powerful creature—to not immediately trust her and beg for her closeness.

"He must never know who you truly are. He will only know you as the sweet and loving soul that you are. He will love that you hate violence and that you care for each and every living creature. And for those reasons, you will ban the hunting of our kind. You will remove the term Dahsian syrens and allow us to keep our natural name." Aria had always hated how they not only enslaved their kind, but renamed them too. Apparently 'Abisian' was too hard for the Skierkan tongue to say, too confusing. "He will be none the wiser that you are one of us."

"I just . . . I don't understand why you had to come here first."
Mayta's voice, even while scared, managed to sound like the gentle
chimes in a spring breeze.

Aria blew out a long breath. "It was all I could come up with. I
didn't know how else to make sure that he didn't see you as a threat
to his people, but as a savior. I also wanted to make sure I wasn't
marrying you off to some wicked prince."

"He is no wicked prince, Aria. I already knew that."

Aria bit her tongue from telling Mayta how truly wicked the
prince was, but she knew Mayta wouldn't understand. And more
importantly, she knew Raask was not wicked in the way that he
would harm Mayta. No, he would keep her safe.

"So why must you stay locked up in this dungeon? I can bring
you back to the Dahs. You can swim back to our people and lead
them again." Mayta pleaded.

Aria clicked her tongue. "They are not stupid, sister. If I were to
escape, they would know that the other girl they pulled from the
Dahs had something to do with it." She paused, playing with the
chain around her right wrist. "No, now we must wait. Bide our time
until you and the prince marry and then we will wait until you are
appointed queen. And at some point the people of the court will
forget that I exist, that I have been left to rot in these dungeons, and
only then will we release me back into the seas." If she was still alive
by that point. She didn't have the heart to tell Mayta that she heavily
doubted she would live that long.

Mayta sniffled, wiping her eyes and nose with the sleeve of her
tunic. "Why didn't you tell me any of this before you left?"

Aria's small smile wavered. "You know why," she mouthed. They
were the only family that they had, and goodbyes had never been
easy for either of them.

Mayta returned Aria's small smile and choked back a combination of tears and a laugh. "And how the Helk did you get used to
walking with these damned things?" She motioned to her new legs.

To that, Aria gave a full laugh as a response. "They're just positively awful, aren't they? But at least we have developed fine asses from having strong tails. The humans all have those skinny, bony butts!"

Mayta clasped her hands around her mouth, holding back her laughter.

And with the sound of her sister's cheerful laughter, Aria was once again reminded of a home she would never return to.

CHAPTER 30
MAYTA

Mayta had been obsessed with humans for as long as she could remember.

She would watch the boats of men and swim just underneath, eavesdropping on their strange habits and conversations. She would come to the shores of Skierka, and when she was older, she would come to the shores of the capital city, Etra, and just watch and listen from the safety of the black waters.

Even after years of studying their kind, Mayta was still at a loss for some of the strange things she observed in the palace. Quite frankly, she had no clue how Aria had been able to slip past their suspicion for as long as she had. Luckily, they assumed she was from the Surtr Islands.

That was another thing she found strange.

Mayta had only been to the Surtr Islands a few times in her life. While there, she observed that the humans of the islands were a much darker color than the pale Skierkans. And as Mayta and Aria hailed from the Abisians, where the black waters halted the sun's rays, they were both quite pale.

And while Mayta and Aria both had the wild, wavy hair of the

Abisian syrens, Mayta was fairly certain that most of the Surtrians wore their hair in long, elegant braids. She thought it would be obvious to the humans that she was not a Surtrian. But so far nobody had indicated any sort of suspicion, well besides the tall one in Viggo's unit. Perhaps her syrenic aura was working a little too strongly, but as long as it was working she saw no reason to pull it back.

Mayta had watched a sea wraith give the tall one in Viggo's unit a good fright a few days before she revealed herself to them. While she commanded the wraith away telepathically, it still had time to torment the poor human. She missed her wraith already. The bond between syren and sea wraith was holy among their kind. And after learning of her sister's plans, it may be a long, long time before she saw her girl again.

Mayta swallowed that thought and the sadness that came with it, until they were both buried deeply within her. This was simply the way things were, and the cards that she had been dealt. That was that.

With a huff and a sigh, Mayta took another bite of her porridge. Like most things she ate in Skierka, it was too sweet for her. But with a heavy mug of bitter, black tawny, she managed to eat most of the porridge. She had never had this energizing, bitter drink before, but had often watched the Skierkans walking around with giant cups of it in the mornings. Now at the palace and in the gardens, where much of the staff and even the nobles chose to eat their breakfast, Mayta enjoyed noticing how various people took their tawny. She liked it bitter and strong, much like the food of the Dahs. But most seemed to take it with the milk of a cow and some sort of sweetening.

Mayta couldn't get enough of the stuff. She had maybe five or six mugs of it a day! And the delectable buzz she got from the tawny was the only thing that drowned out the incessant buzzing of the lithe-infused palace walls. Of course, syrens were not accustomed to such a thing. The syrens left after their enslavement by the Skierkans, were tasked with mining the rare and powerful white lithe troves hidden deep below the sea, primarily in the Zojz trench, where the purest white lithe could be found. She'd heard from a few other syren that now their Surtrian sisters were tasked with mining the lithe that came from their waters, and even the Surtrian humans were forced to mine the small troves of white lithe found within their caves.

Under the sea, Mayta would often wonder how the humans were able to use so much lithe at once, in their ointments and drinks and even walls. Now from within the palace, she couldn't help but wonder how she had gotten by so long, without all of the help from it.

She enjoyed her tawny lithe, which gave her energy during the day, and her cobalt lithe at night to help her sleep, and fuschia lithe which gave her such fun and silly hallucinations to pass the time with the young women of the palace. She spent most of her time so far wandering around, a kind but stiff guard named Zaries often following her, and she played with the different forms of lithe and wandered the gardens some more.

Eventually, Mayta requested to help the garden gnomes with the upkeep. Most mornings, she spent her time carefully pruning the bushes and tending to the flowers. It was calming and beautiful, and gave her a great excuse to observe human nature from afar, while she was still getting used to all the strange mannerisms and expectations that came with being a human girl.

Of course, Mayta also took her time tending the flowers on the side of the gardens closest to the prince's tower. She avoided looking up at the top windows that had obviously been rebuilt—as they were made from a far shinier material than the rest. When she asked Zaries about it once, he told her the story of the masked rider and the wraith, and how a girl had lost her arm defending the prince. Zaries seemed to have liked Aria before Mayta exposed her.

It made her heart arche. Not many people ever liked Aria. She was a little thorny on the outside, but when she loved and cared for someone, she would do anything in the world for them. And now because of her, Aria was locked in a dungeon . . .

But the more Mayta thought about it, the more she realized that it wasn't truly her fault. No, it was all part of Aria's plan. Her smart, smart sister knew that Mayta would assume that Aria had only infiltrated the Morlok's to kill, and of course Aria knew that the thought of the golden prince dying would be heart-breaking for her and she'd come to stop Aria from killing the prince that she loved. It was all a part of her plan that she now played into . . . Or at least she tried to. Mayta wasn't happy about this plan. She didn't exactly appreciate her sister's manipulations, or her lies in keeping the truth of her whereabouts from her. But it was too late now. And she trusted Aria.

What a long game her sister had planned? And the prize? Mayta would marry the prince she had always dreamed of, the syrens would be free, and Aria would be imprisoned. Mayta did not like it, but she was not one to make plans, only to follow her sister's lead.

But Prince Raask was not making it easy.

Mayta hardly saw him. And when she did, he reeked of liquor and stumbled around. The warm, blue eyes she had loved and watched for many years were now hollow. And he did not look at her with the same kindness she saw him give to the hundreds of villagers she must have watched him interact with over the years.

He must have felt very strongly for her sister to act so foolishly now. But like the rebuilt glossy section of the prince's tower or the stub on the end of Aria's arm, the prince's love for her sister was another thing that Mayta didn't like to look at for too long.

Finished with her breakfast, Mayta took her mug and empty bowl back into the kitchens. Padge already had a mug of tawny left out for her, sitting next to the ovens where it could stay warm. They even had a handy mug with a lid and a sucking tube for beverages on the go, it was probably Mayta's favorite human contraption so far.

Mayta gave the old chef a kiss on the cheek for his kindness and was off to the gardens to help the gnomes remove the beetles from the lunar gardens. The gnomes loved the autumn for this exact activity, they happened to find the beetles' crunch to be very satisfying, and all the more tasty. Mayta tried one, hoping they would remind her of the yummy snail snacks from home, but the beetles were simply all wrong in texture—and they tasted too much like the soil of the Arkts for her liking.

Mayta took a moment to adjust the bodice of her long, pale blue dress, before heading out for the morning. She didn't have many options for clothes and often found herself re-wearing the same light blue dress, with sleeves that flared at the ends, and a skirt that graced the tops of her feet. Every day, the bottom of the skirt and the sleeves would get muddy from the gardening, but somehow the servants knew some amazing way to remove the stains like nothing ever happened.

Most Skierkans seemed to have an affinity for wearing their national colors: black and red. And when not wearing black or red, they often wore creams or browns. It was dreadful and sad.

She found herself fixing the bodice about ten times a day. She wasn't sure how the women of the palace were able to tighten the ribbons so tight on themselves, and push their breasts up so high. But it was just another thing Mayta would have to get used to for now. Maybe as queen she could have some influence over the fashions at the white palace.

She finished adjusting her bodice and moved onto adjusting the braids she wore her hair in, as an attempt to remind others she was supposed to be Surtrian.

"Miss Mayta?" A dark voice asked from behind her.

With her hands stuck in her hair, trying to pin back the too-short layers, she whipped around. It was Viggo of course. "Yes?"

The general had cleaned up since returning to the palace. He had a clean shave that showed off the sharp edge of his jaw, and trimmed his hair so his once-shaggy black hair now was cropped to just above his ears. She watched as his dark eyes brightened and his full lips gently turned upward at the edges, at the sight of her obviously struggling with her hair.

"Do you need some help?" He asked, biting back a laugh. She wished he wouldn't hold it back. She only heard his laugh a handful of times on the ship. It was warm and comforting, an odd thing coming from such a physically intimidating man. She loved when things didn't match up.

Mayta pinned back what she could from her shorter layers and shrugged. "No, it's alright. The short pieces always fall down a few minutes into gardening no matter what I do anyways." Her hands stung slightly. The work in the gardens had pricked her hands all over. She ignored the pain but couldn't hold back the slight hiss—as the cool metal of the pins rubbed against a particularly sore spot from a nasty thorn in the lunar garden.

Viggo's eyes immediately narrowed at her hiss of pain. He looked at her hand and gave a slight nod at the answer to his silent question. When he must have decided it wasn't worth commenting on, he looked past her towards the gardens out the windows. "They look lovely this time of year."

Mayta brightened. "They really do. I'd heard that the trees in Skierka turn vibrant metal shades in the autumn, but I thought they would be muted. I never realized how shiny and bright they became." She could only see the very tips of the metal-turning leaves from the Dahs, and in person, they were far more beautiful than she ever hoped.

"They'll be falling soon." Viggo scratched mindlessly at his chin.

"Before the winter?" He nodded in answer.

Mayta was surprised that the general of the most feared army in the Arkts had enough time to discuss the seasonal habits of his lands with a virtual stranger, but truthfully he was easy on the eyes, so she didn't mind.

"Yes, it gets cold here in the winter. The leaves all fall and wilt, and get covered in snow." Viggo answered dryly, as if Mayta had never heard of such a thing as weather.

"That sounds wonderful," she responded, unsure of what else to say.

Viggo shrugged, clearly unimpressed by snow.

"You prefer the warmer months?" Mayta asked.

"The cold is what I prefer . . . it is less stressful for me . . . in the warmer months when everything is so alive, I have to hold my powers in check tightly. In the cooler months, I have more freedom to relax without worrying about killing off the flowers."

Mayta laughed. It was an odd sight to picture, a general of death, who was strong enough to leak his powers when not keeping a tight restraint on himself, loving flowers enough to avoid killing them.

"Come help?" She asked, giving him a gentle tug on the arm to lead him to the gardens. She watched a "yes" form on his lips, and the beginning of a step towards the doors, but the harsh sound of a wooden door slamming into the wall behind it halted both of those actions.

Prince Raask stumbled into the great hall. The strong stench of spirits hit Mayta like a flood. His golden locks were greasy, and if she wasn't mistaken, there was some blood in them too. Old blood by the smell of it. Viggo rushed to his brother, holding him up against his side and steering him back towards the halls en route to the prince's chambers.

Raask threw himself off of Viggo, obviously not wanting to go back. "Viggo!" Raask called affectionately. "Thank you for steadying me, but I will be needing a piece of the palace's finest chocolate cake."

"I think you need to get some rest and sleep this off. I'll bring you up a nice big cup of tawny and a piece of bread and you'll feel much better, okay?" Viggo whispered into his brother's ear. If it wasn't for Mayta's syrenic hearing, she wouldn't have heard his words nor the begging in his voice.

Her heart hurt at the sight of it. The loving and compassion and pain in Viggo's heavy dark eyes. The broken air around the prince himself, who was once a human of light and play and love. A man of the sun. It was too much for her. Mayta turned around and headed toward the gardens. Her movement alerted the prince to her presence.

"You." Raask spat.

Slowly, Mayta turned around to face the human she had loved for so many years, who now apparently loved her sister enough to ruin himself over.

She blinked at the prince. He was an inch or two taller than the general. And his piercing blue eyes, that once reminded Mayta of the breezy, careless summer skies, now looked haunted. She understood why he blamed her for outting Aria, but as far as the humans were concerned, she was another human who was looking out for the royal family. She should be regarded as a hero among their kind, and not be treated like this. The few interactions she had with Prince Raask were all cold and hostile. He made it clear he disliked her by constantly storming out of the rooms that she entered. Mayta didn't embarrass easily, but even she had her limits.

"Yes, it's me. The one you blame for your broken heart. The one who hasn't received but one thanks for saving you from a liar." Mayta put her hands on her hips and stared down the prince and the general. The latter looked quite impressed by her response.

Prince Raask straightened, standing up to his full height. A twisted smirk spread across his lips, eerily similar to the ones she had seen Aria give many times before. "Sounds like the little, island girl found her voice." He drawled.

"Don't be cruel," the general warned his brother. "She's right, she did save you. She saved all of us actually."

Raask's lips twisted in disgust at the general's statement. "Yes, yes, I guess we should all praise the little girl you saved from the Dahs, for identifying the other one that we saved from the Dahs, as a liar." He laughed, coldly and cruelly. "You really want me to believe that Aria meant me harm? You really want me to believe that you are some savior to us?" He took a step closer to Mayta. She made sure not to oblige her body's gut reaction to put distance between them. Instead, she took a step closer to him as well.

Mayta's brow furrowed. She hadn't been prepared for the accusation. Luckily the general decided he had had enough and put a hand on Raask's chest, pulling him back and away from Mayta.

The rage in Raask must have sobered him up. His gaze was steady, and he stood strong against Viggo's hand. Mayta couldn't help the hurt that throbbed in her chest at the sight of Raask's pure hatred. After all, this was the same prince that she'd watched for years giving kindness after kindness to his people.

During those long days of basking in the shallow waters, Mayta had dreamed of speaking with her prince. She'd dreamed of explaining to him that she was also a princess, and that she understood the power and the burden of it all. She did not dream of her prince hating her. And she certainly did not dream that he would be in love with her sister.

The brothers must have seen the hurt racing across her face, as Raask backed away slightly, and Viggo pushed more force into the hand holding his brother back.

"We could be friends, you know?" She asked. Her slightly too-sharp teeth bit into her lip, nervous for his reaction.

Viggo's grip tightened on Raask's arm. She could feel the general's silent pleas to his younger brother, asking him to send her kindness. But Mayta should have known that there was no kindness in the prince's heart for her. Viggo pulled Raask back towards the door. His knuckles were white and his jaw clenched so tightly, Mayta could hear his teeth grinding.

But despite Viggo's best efforts, Prince Raask called out, "My first order as king will be to torture your secrets out of you, and then publicly execute you. You have my word of that."

The echo of his threat rang throughout the hall, stopped only by the slam of the door, as Viggo quite literally dragged his brother out. Mayta managed a small smile to the people who witnessed the prince's outbursts. Most looked at her with pity, not believing the prince's story, thankfully. But some did look with suspicion. Mayta ignored the muffled curses of Prince Raask being dragged across the palace and into his tower. And she headed into the gardens, a little later today than usual. As she plucked the beetles off of the flowers, Mayta thought and thought about her precarious situation. People had always fallen in love with her without any effort on her part. But the prince would be a challenge that she supposed would be worth it. So, like her big sister, Mayta began to scheme a way into the prince's heart.

CHAPTER 31
VIGGO

Viggo had seen the look in Mayta's eyes. He saw it every time she was around his little brother.

His younger brother was handsome, charming, and would one day be king. Viggo was a general, known for his savagery, and would be lucky to make it to forty years old. Helk, he felt lucky he had somehow made it to thirty. He had always been happy for his brother, it wasn't his fault that he was the second born and, thus, the one set to inherit the throne. In fact, Viggo had spent much of his life giving whatever he could to his brother. He loved him deeply. But that didn't stop the seed of envy that now sat heavily in his chest.

He wanted Mayta to look at him like that. He wanted Mayta to look at him with adoration and want. But maybe it was better this way, anyways.

Viggo ignored Raask's drunken curses that had continued all the way out of the great hall and towards Raask's chambers. It was nothing he wasn't used to after being with his army for most of his life. Although, he had never seen his brother be anything but charming and stupid while drunk. This whole drunken bastard spiel he had taken on since Aria's imprisonment was new. And quite frankly, it was time for him to snap out of it.

Raask continued yammering about how he couldn't trust anybody, and nobody knew the real him, or something like that. It was hard to discern exactly what he was saying. It seemed the general gist of it was all "woe is me" bullshit.

"Enough," Viggo said.

Raask's eyes widened, surprised by Viggo's order. Technically, Raask would outrank Viggo one day, but today Viggo was the general and Raask was a young prince throwing a tantrum. "Get ahold of yourself," Viggo continued.

"You'll never know what it was like growing up here," Raask muttered.

Viggo could have smacked the drunk out of him. But he didn't. He rubbed his temples and took a deep breath. "Raask, maybe you are forgetting. But I am your brother. I know exactly what it's like to be raised in this den of wraiths."

Raask leaned against the wall. They were now only one simple turn from entering the stairs to Raask's tower, and safely far away from any listening ears. "You were sent off though. You weren't forced to stay here, alone."

"I was sent off to war, brother." Viggo's dark eyes bore into his younger brother's. "Would you have preferred to have spent your second decade of life in barracks learning to slaughter? I was forged into a weapon and used as one. I've maimed, killed, gutted, and done much worse—all before my sixteenth year. And I did it happily, knowing that it was keeping you safe." Viggo opted-out from admitting that he had also learned how to manipulate a battlefield to look like a victory, while keeping the victims of the Morloks safe and hidden. Now was not the time to reveal his treason.

Raask scoffed. "And you think that you were the only one fighting?" Suddenly, he launched himself off of the wall and directly in front of Viggo. Raask's entire body was rigid and electric. His aura turned metallic, and faintly red. A sadness crept across Viggo's vision, remembering what it felt like to be so little in control.

But while Viggo had Kel to train him, it took until now for him to realize that Raask had only received guidance from those wretched Irridesci. It took Viggo years of intensive training to learn to reel in his powers, and the temper that came from withholding Godsly power in a half-human vessel. Even to this day, he would sometimes lose his temper and need to recuse himself until he could let off some of his magic.

And it was true that Viggo had been gone for most of Raask's life . . . He never truly realized that until now, watching the sadness and anger that twisted his brother's soul, from the lack of guidance and love ever since their mother had died, and he himself had left for war.

"Swords are not the only instruments of war, *brother*." Raask spat. "You think that just because you were the only one to be sent to an actual battlefield, that I have not been fighting as well?" The red aura surrounding Raask darkened and thickened with each word. And the unmistakable scent of blood cocooned the entire hall. This was not good. It was one thing to be a prince throwing a tantrum, but it was another altogether to be a wielder of blood magic with so little control.

"Please, you need to sleep this off. I can go get you your cake. Okay?" Viggo pleaded. He broke eye contact and turned his back to his brother. Maybe the sugar and starch of the cake in his stomach could absorb some of the substances he'd been hauling into himself, and then they could have a real talk about his behavior.

But the second Viggo took a step away from his brother, the entire hall turned red. The deep, dark, and wet red of blood magic. "You will listen to me!" Raask screamed. "You will not run off again." Raask's fist hit the wall of the corridor with the sound of a thump followed by the cracking of the walls.

Viggo coughed and coughed, the thick wet musk of the blood magic began to overwhelm him. His stomach rolled in his gut, and he could hardly get any oxygen into his body. Each breath felt wet and heavy. He was drowning in his brother's blood magic. Viggo's own dark powers attempted to rise in self-protection. It took everything in him to subdue himself. He had no idea whose magic would win, death magic versus blood magic. Nonetheless, he had no intention of finding out. Raask would need to learn control the same as he did. "Pull it back in. Quickly. Raask, you need to pull your magic back in." He coughed and coughed, falling to the floor and clawing at his own throat now. The blood magic was thick like a mucus. It clung to his chest and lungs and slowly climbed down his throat. It was filled with anger and hatred and so much sadness and at its core, deep, down inside of the magic, in a place where only Viggo would know to look, it was Raask's soul itself. "Please," Viggo said, choking out the word between coughs.

The red pulsed back into Raask, who was on his knees next to Viggo in an instant. Viggo rubbed at his brother's back and tears dropped down his face. "I'm so sorry." Raask whispered. Over and over again, he just kept saying it. "I'm sorry, I'm sorry, I'm sorry."

Viggo fought for his breath. He coughed up several chunks of gooey blood clots that had made their way down his throat. "It's okay." He answered each one of Raask's apologies, telling him that it was okay. Over and over again. The brothers held each other in their arms. And for the first time in Viggo's life, he realized that maybe he was not the only one wielded into a weapon. Maybe he wasn't the only Morlok brother who had been fighting all these years. And Raask . . . Raask was in danger.

✧

Raask's snoring was the only sound in his chambers. Although how Raask was able to sleep in such a space was a mystery to Viggo. After Raask's explosion, they both headed up to his brother's chambers. It took everything in Viggo's powers to not react to his brother's current living situation. The once white lithe-bleached walls, were now covered in the red splatter of his brother's uncontrolled blood magic. The overwhelming waft of bucket after bucket of rotten blood took over the entire space, mixed in with hints of emerald lithe and what smelled like an entire brewery's worth of ale.

After he brought his little brother a bowl of lamb stew with golden raisins, and a fat piece of chocolate cake, they talked for ages. Viggo rehashed some of his war stories and even spoke about his time in the battle camps. Raask told Viggo about what it was like in the palace after their mother died. About the Irridesci's teachings, how they fueled his power with violence that he now craved and feared that he now *needed*. The Irridesci were awful, but at least they provided some guidance, and some knowledge to the magic in the Morlok blood. Somehow, from their wicked prayers to the Gods or their routine soul searches, they understood the magic within Raask. Finally, Raask told him about his time with Aria, about how she was the first real connection he'd had since their mother.

There was so much he hadn't known about his brother. And so much he didn't know about him. Viggo had not been there for brother. And when he did come back, he'd stripped him of the one who had been there, who had loved him.

Some brother he was.

"You blame Mayta and I for Aria," Viggo said and asked, at the same time.

At that point, Raask's eyes were struggling to stay open. They had split the cake and talked for hours. The crisp, purple light of dusk poured into the room. Viggo knew it would be dark soon, and his brother had drunk an entire bar's worth of liquor.

Raask stiffened. The black fur blankets were thick and wrapped around most of his body. "I know you are not at fault. But I can't help but be so angry at you and her." He twisted off of his side and onto his back. "I see how you look at Mayta." Raask admitted.

Suddenly, Viggo understood. Viggo had come back and not only taken away his brother's love, but had someone that he loved all on his own. "She doesn't feel the same for me."

Raask chuckled, "I know." Although Raask's comment stung, Viggo couldn't help but laugh. "She will though. She just needs to get to know you." Raask yawned, and Viggo was transported back to many years ago when they were both young. Their mother was still alive. And they fell asleep almost every night in the same bed. It had been ages since they spent time together like this.

"Emir told me that you hadn't spent much time together, and that Mayta was mostly silent on the trip."

Viggo sighed. He wasn't sure how to explain it even to himself, and he sure as Helk wasn't sure how to explain it to someone else. "I just . . . I looked at her and I knew that she was mine and that I was hers. And ever since then, I just can't . . . I can't think about anything else. She's in all of my thoughts and all of my dreams, and yet, to her, I am nothing."

Raask yawned again, barely staying awake. Long after Viggo thought Raask had fallen asleep, he heard his little brother mutter, "At least you are not her enemy."

CHAPTER 32
ARIA

Aria had already lost track of how much time had passed since she had been locked in the dungeons. She had started a tally in the corner of her cell, but at some point, realized just how utterly and completely depressing it was to see a reminder of each useless day's passing, as her only decoration within her cage. So only ten or so marks were etched into the corner of the wall.

She spent her time mostly doing the exercises the human trainers had taught her before her imprisonment. Meals were fun—she did her best to draw them out. She ate each pea individually and made sure to chew it at least ten times before swallowing. But more than ten was even better.

As a kid, her mother had once told her that chewing more made the jaw more pronounced. Her mother's teeth were sharper than hers, but she still managed to eat slower than both her and Mayta. The thought of her mother made her lose her appetite. She was a wicked and vile creature. But she still loved her, and missed her.

Tears began to form in the corners of her eyes. Actual tears, just from the thought of her mother. Oh, and she got her cycle the day before, so that combined with the lack of nutrition, the lack of sunlight and wind and company altogether, had Aria crying all too frequently lately. She hated it. Weak. Pathetic.

Her tears hit the stone beneath her. Eventually they would form a puddle, and she would get cold. And then she would spend the rest of the day huddled in a ball, praying to Freyite that her cycle would end quickly, or in the very least for her cramps would go.

The dim lighting in the room was beginning to turn a deep purple. Aria assumed this meant it was evening. Dinner would be soon. So when the door to her dungeon creaked open, she hadn't suspected anything.

When she heard the clumsy and heavy footsteps into her dungeon, she didn't bother to look-up. The guards who brought in her dinner were never keen to chat anyways. It was when she heard two other pairs of footsteps that she finally looked up from her wet corner.

Red, the bearded guy, and the big blonde all stood in her cell— the three guards she'd fought that day while training with the prince. A malicious smile was spread across each of their lips.

This couldn't be good.

She didn't bother to scramble back. A long chain kept her in place, and even if there was no chain attached to her, she was locked in a dungeon. So she stayed curled up in her ball in the corner.

"Miss us?" Big blonde teased.

"Not particularly," Aria answered. "Shall we get this over with then?"

"Get this over with?" Beard asked. "I don't think we'll be getting anything just over with. I want to take my sweet, sweet time with you." He hawked a loogie that landed directly on Aria's side.

Red started to laugh now.

Big blonde actually snarled at that. "I will go first, and when I'm done you two can do whatever you want." She pulled a little blade out from her sheath. "Hold her down." Big blonde ordered. Red and Beard obliged.

Their clammy hands gripped Aria's body and held her down onto her back. The smell of their tobacco and sweat made Aria recoil, but other than that she didn't bother to fight. She'd known when she made her plan that the chances of someone coming down to the dungeon to extract revenge on her were high. And she went through with it, knowing. Knowing that violence from men was a more-than-likely price to pay for the avenging of her kingdom.

But for Mayta to become queen and marry the man she had loved for years, all while saving their people from slavery, this would be worth it. For her sister. For her people. She would deal with a million human men and women like these sick bastards, and she would do it happily time and time again. Okay, maybe not happily. But this was the price to pay.

Big blonde kneeled down, placing her knee just between the apex of Aria's legs. With her knife, she cut down from the collar of Aria's smock down to her belly button, and then ripped the rest off with her bare hands. Aria kept her stare directly onto big blonde. She would not shy away from this. She would make sure that they saw her defiance and pain. She needed to watch this. To remember this. Humans. Skierkans. They all loved to feel powerful by inflicting pain on those they deemed below them.

Chills ran down Aria's body as her chest and stomach were exposed to the crisp air of the dungeon. She bore her teeth in a silent snarl at Big Blonde. But Blonde, along with Red and Beard, were too busy gaping at her body to notice her sharpened teeth. Blonde lowered the knife down onto Aria's abdomen and began to cut. Based on the strokes, she was cutting a word into her. But Aria didn't plan on giving her the satisfaction of watching the knife, instead she watched the ugly beast who wielded it. Her eyes stayed locked in on Big Blonde's face. She memorized the light mustache above her lips. The slight bruise on her neck. The high collar in an attempt to hide the bruise. She noticed it all, and kept looking at the beast, instead of allowing herself to feel the fear and pain the beast so wanted from her.

"Will she even feel this?" Beard asked Red, "Do they even feel pain?"

It was at these words that Aria finally lost her will to stare down her attackers. Because it did hurt, and she wasn't sure she could hide how much it hurt, any longer. The strength to hold on for it all. The lingering parts of her soul that were capable of good and love. Everything. And after Gods knew how long, when they had all finished their business of cutting, picking, and hurting, when they finally left her dungeon with smug smiles that reeked of her, Aria finally looked down to see what they had cut into her. And after crying for what felt like weeks on end, even Aria wasn't prepared for the laugh that erupted out of her at the sight of her torn up belly, because those stupid humans did not realize that the game was far from over.

CHAPTER 33
RAASK

His books were all put away and neatly organized. His training leathers and assortment of cloaks were all hung up in his closet. Viggo had left a pitcher of water next to a glass with lemons, on Raask's nightstand. He choked down several, crisp glasses of the lemon water, before getting out of bed and rushing to his wash closet. It was only when he came back from relieving himself, brushing his teeth, and doing all of the other aspects of his morning routine that he'd been forgoing, that he came back and saw the note that Viggo left.

Come down for training if you're not puking your guts up. Afterwards,
we'll be cleaning your room and working on some magic drills.
Tread Carefully on the Ice,
Viggo

ALTHOUGH RAASK HAD BEEN NEGLECTING HIS TRAINING SINCE THE WHOLE Aria debacle, and he was severely hungover from weeks of drinking himself stupid, he was weirdly excited to spend the day with his older brother. So he didn't mind when Viggo demanded extra laps or criticized his form. He didn't mind when he made him clean off the blood magic stains with buckets, even though typically the servants would do it, and he didn't mind the massive migraines that came with the magic drills he taught him. No, he didn't mind at all.

It was actually the best day he'd had in a long while. Unlike the Irridesci's tactics of only teaching how to wield the blood magic, Viggo also taught Raask how to control it, and how to use it for some of the 'simple magics'—as he called it. Raask could now lock and unlock doors with a simple thought. Okay, not just a simple thought, it took him a good bit of concentration. But Viggo assured him that eventually it would be as simple as using an actual physical key.

The next day was similar. And the day after that. And the day after that. Until it truly was as simple as just thinking about the magic, and having it happen.

Some days, Viggo's little group would join them for training. Some days, Raask had to miss training with his brother to attend important meetings concerning the war, or taxes, or other courtly responsibilities. And some days Raask would go out with Cristo to the Grey Goblin after training was done. Occasionally, Raask would see Mayta around. She almost always had someone walking with her. It seemed she made friends easily. Whenever she would see Raask, she would follow him around like a little puppy dog. The old Raask would have probably messed around with her by now and moved on. But now, whenever she would follow him around, he would make sure to talk about Viggo and bring her to him. He wasn't sure if she was catching on to the bit, so he mostly tried his best to avoid her all together.

That was a difficult task in its own right. It seemed like she always knew where he would be, and conveniently found herself waiting in those same places. Mayta was nice though. She was bright and cheerful. He could see why Viggo felt so strongly for her. But to him, anyone who wasn't Aria didn't really matter.

Days passed. Weeks passed. Raask found himself heartbroken and moping less and less. While the ache of her absence was diminishing, he didn't stop thinking about her. No, his mind never strayed too far from the syren who was chained far below him in his very own palace. He would see her wild hair in the breeze against the pine, and her eyes in the depths of the Dahs. She was in the wind and the tides and the glow of the moon and the warmth of the sun. Aria was everywhere. He did his best to try to distract himself from thinking of her and the love that he still felt for her, regardless of her betrayal.

It helped that all of his time had been spent training for various responsibilities or in meetings. It also helped that the second trial, to prove his worthiness of the crown, had finally come.

Unlike the first trial, which was all pomp, and didn't really require any particular skills other than a simple show and tell, the second trial was a far deadlier operation. Historically, the second trial was the one that weeded out most of the blood heirs for the kingdom. If Raask were to fail any of these trials, it would open up an array of Skierkans challenging Raask for the crown and months—if not years—of duel after duel to prove his worthiness for the crown.

He had to get this right.

This was not a trial that was shown to the public. Only the Morloks themselves, and a few advisors to the royal family were aware of what the second trial entailed. Even Raask wasn't exactly sure what the objective was, only that he was to travel through the Gaulic forest under the light of the Harvest Moon, and meet with the Keeper of the Wood. Balk didn't say any more or any less than that, and the wording never changed, even in the slightest. He wouldn't say where the Keeper of the Wood was located, or even *who* the Keeper of the Wood was. Raask had lived in this palace his whole life, and had ventured in the Gaulic forest dozens of times, but had never run into a keeper of any sorts. He'd seen hundreds of strange and dangerous creatures, even a few cute, little ones, but certainly no 'Keeper'.

Viggo came out with Raask to the edge of the wood. The two brothers sat on the lush grass and silently watched as the golden daylight transformed into darkening shades of blue, until the only light came from the Harvest Moon. Raask had always loved the Harvest Moon. It was generally a night for celebration, where Skierkans would revel in the fields under the ochre light.

Skierkans would pray to D'Ak, the God of the Harvest, through spilling spirits onto the soil of the Arkts. The dance and revelry of the night of the Harvest Moon was considered a sacred prayer. Even young Skierkans would spend the night dancing in the fields, spilling watered down ales. The king himself would even show face. He would be the first one to spill his drink to D'Ak and say a few words about the bountiful harvest that was sure to come both from the soil —and through the conquering of other lands. Then his father would take a few women and men back to his private tent for their own revelry. As a child, Raask always hated that part. When he got older, Raask learned to distract himself from his father's escapades by running off with his own women or men. And the first Harvest Moon since his mother's passing, he couldn't look his father in the eye for a month, without feeling heat swarming his cheeks and immense shame twisted with rage.

This was a dangerous trial, but a part of him was glad to miss the night of the Harvest Moon festival. Sitting on the grass with his big brother, sipping from the same bottle of ancient barley liquor, was infinitely better than the chaotic partying happening down at the fields. He did love to dance and kiss to the primal drums, but in Raask's world post-Aria, it wasn't something he was interested in anymore.

So the two brothers poured some of the ancient, spiced liquor onto the soil and watched as it flooded down towards the Gaulic forest. The old liquor coated and bubbled past the red mushrooms, and curved around the warty toads. It seemed to have a mind of its own, pulled into the soil and roots of the forest by D'Ak himself. Viggo took a large pull from the bottle before passing it to Raask, who gulped it down in several large swallows.

"You better slow it on that. You don't know what will be waiting for you out there," Viggo said. He didn't need to remind Raask that no matter what happened in the forest, Viggo would be prevented from interfering or helping in any way.

Raask wiped his mouth with the back of his hand, not minding that the spirit dripped down onto his bare chest. The liquor quickly absorbed into his lithe tattoo that curved along with the muscles of his chest. The raven of the Morlok crest seemed to take sips from the spirit on his chest, sucking up the drops of barley liquor that landed onto its beak. Maybe Raask had had too much to drink already.

"We've been playing in the Gaulic since we were young, I'll be alright." Raask's grip on the bottle tightened. Viggo looked towards his brother, his shoulders tensed, and his eyes slowly drifted to the darkest sections of the woods, before switching back to Raask. He gave a weak smile and slow nod. They both knew that they had been playing in the Gaulic since they were young, and they both remembered hiding in the holes between trees from creatures that would later haunt both of their nightmares well into adulthood. The only reason they had survived each time had been Viggo's powers of death. This time Raask would enter the wood alone. Raask was not ashamed to admit he was scared, but he also knew that he was not without power of his own.

Sure, he brought a sword, a couple of daggers, a vial of poison, and a wraith's claw—that would surely kill most creatures that inhabited the wood. But none of these weapons could come close to the power that surged through his veins. The power of blood. The power of the natural order. Raask could stop a heart, could will blood to leave any part of a person's body. He had studied anatomy and the sections of the brain, and had the power to move blood to different areas of the brain, and away from the parts that controlled vision or hearing, to make them blind or deaf or both. He was a weapon that had been worked tirelessly by the instruction of the Skierkan Bruin and the cruel magistrate of the Irridesci. He was ready for whatever the Gaulic had in store for him. Raask could not afford to be afraid, for fear would disrupt the division of his powers. Fear was repellent to the Morloks' magic. It diverted their energy and powers away from the magic and into the doubts. With a deep breath, and a final swig of the barley liquor, Raask stood.

Viggo quickly followed and pulled Raask into a tight hug. The brothers clapped each other on the back.

"Vittai santito," Viggo thumped his chest twice, indicating that it was not just a goodbye but a goodbye to a warrior. It was the first time he had given his brother the warrior's goodbye of the Rakkei.

Raask knew what it meant, from years studying books on the Skierkan military and of course, The Linguistic Tendencies of Skierkan Commoners and the Lands They Conquered, 4th Edition. From studying, he knew that the exact translation was closer to a blessing and a prayer. He knew that the thumping on the chest was in itself a prayer to Voskule, the God of Warfare, that the Rakkei had worshiped above all other Gods. And from watching Viggo's unit, and Emir and Skender who hailed from the Red Peaks of the Rakkei, and descended from the ancient kings of the Rakkei themselves, Raask knew that it was not a gesture to be taken lightly. Raask knew then that his brother now saw him for who he was now, a man who would one day rule over the greatest nation of the Artks, not just the little, sniveling brother that needed Viggo's protection. Raask had grown. And Viggo finally seen it.

With a last look, Raask turned away from his brother and ventured into the shadows of the Gaulic forest with a final goodbye, "Walk well on the ice!" The sound of his brother's laugh was the last Raask heard before entering the Gaulic.

The buzzing of the insects and the chirping of the frogs dimmed with each step deeper into the wood. Warm light from the Harvest Moon trickled through the dense layer of pine and golden leaves. The orange beams of moonlight glazed across the metallic leaves of autumn and reflected across the wood. The rays bounced from one leaf to another, providing just barely enough light for Raask to see, without needing to light the torch he'd packed in his leather bag.

Raask sent a silent thanks to D'Ak for the light of the Harvest Moon. Gods knew what sort of creatures would be attracted to a torch in the ancient wood. Or maybe they would be scared of the harsh light after spending years accustomed to the darkness. Raask wasn't exactly sure, but ended up deciding against using the torch, and saving it only in case he absolutely needed it.

Metallic leaves halfway decomposed crunched under his steps. There was no use in attempting to mask his noise as the forest floor was littered with the crunchy, shiny leaves. He also knew that he was supposed to be looking for the Keeper of the Wood, and thought that maybe his heavy footsteps would alert the so-called Keeper. Again, Raask wasn't exactly sure if he was supposed to remain hidden, or call attention to himself. Maybe this was part of the test.

Hours passed, or maybe they were only minutes that had felt like hours, and Raask had seen plenty of sprites darting about getting up to mischief. He saw one or two torno bears who largely ignored him as they devoured whatever rotten carcass they found. Raask didn't get close enough to investigate. He had even heard the telltale screech of a lunar wraith flying above, and the answer from the wraith's brethren. If any of those creatures had been the Keeper of the Wood, Raask was screwed. But there was nothing he could do about it if the Keeper decided to keep their identity hidden and ignore Raask.

So Raask trudged along. One step in front of another.

Crunch.

Crunch.

Crunch.

Crunch.

Ooooph.

Suddenly the world had turned upside down and Raask was sporting a gnarly gash on the back of his head. Warm blood already began to trickle down the side of his neck. And before Raask could wonder who—or what—had knocked him out, he lost all consciousness.

✧

"Will you stop whining?"

"I didn't see you carrying a whole-ass prince across the woods!"

"Well, I offered to take him halfway through! It's not my fault you're too stubborn to accept my help."

Raask was barely conscious and held onto each word like they were his last hope. His head laid against cool stone, and his wrists and ankles itched from the scratchy rope that bound them. He kept his eyes closed and breathing steady, not wanting to alert them to his consciousness. He didn't recognize the voices, but was almost certain that they were young; one was male and the other was female. They did not speak with the quick drawl of the Skierkans from the capital city of Etra. No, their words were slow. Their sentences took time to speak, unlike the rushed and harsh yelling of Etrans.

It sounded similar to the dialect spoken in the countryside of the mainland of Skierka. But there was another accent in there that Raask couldn't quite place. Each sentence was a melody, and the conversation was a song.

A deep throb in Raask's skull reminded him of the head wound he'd suffered.

He had to focus.

Raask was to prove his strength. His cunning. His intelligence. Cruelty, too. Maybe this was a part of the trial. It would not do to simply incinerate their bodies from the inside out, Raask had to learn more. To know an enemy's wishes was often more crucial than knowing meaningless identities. Like a child, eavesdropping on his parents' conversations, Raask feigned unconsciousness, and focused enough to hear them leave. At least he thought they did, he heard a door opening and closing, but no footsteps moving. He kept his eyes closed in case it was some kind of trick.

Darkness came and went by the time they had come back. And by now, Raask's stomach growled incessantly.

"Get up, Prince." The female demanded.

Raask whipped his eyes open, annoyed and too hungry to continue the charade. The male and female were indeed young, or at least they appeared young. Their hair was a deep red that reminded Raask of Viggo's favorite jester's wig. Their eyes were somewhat too large as if in a perpetual state of shock, and their ears ended in a pointed tip. So not human.

Raask refused to rise before knowing who dared to give orders to the prince. "Who are you?"

His voice cracked from the lack of water, but he kept his demeanor cruel. In his mind's eye, he imagined his father. He saw him sitting on the tall throne in the meeting room, with the shadow of the fire cracking across his face in a violent untraceable pattern along his stiff jaw. He saw him giving the command to slaughter an entire race of people, until they had agreed to join Skierka, until they would submit. He saw the gentle lowering of the chin as he faced his children, a mockery of a parent who wished to listen and understand their children, before the crack of the whip on Raask's back from whichever servant had pissed him off the most that day, unwilling to stoop low enough to lift the whip himself.

Like many times before, Raask had turned his face into a mirror of his father's. For Skierka to survive, it could only be done with a cruel hand and a proud face. This much Raask knew.

At this point going forward, he would need to consider the state of his country before any decision. When meeting a potential ally or enemy, he would need to remember to wear the face of his father. He would need to shed the pieces of himself that loved and trusted and ached to be seen, in order to properly rule.

Like his Aria, he would need to learn to place his people over his own wishes for comfort. Like his Aria. Gods, it still ached to think of her. But what hurt Raask the most in her betrayal, was how he wished he could rule like that. Aria was a proper ruler, willing to give her life and death for her people. Even if she had failed, she had at least tried.

It was time he learned the lesson she gifted him.

The twin faeries looked at one another, obviously perplexed. "Weren't you looking for us?" The female asked.

"I am in search of the Keeper of the Wood."

The male blinked. "You mean the KeeperSSSsss of the Wood." He practically shouted the plural.

Raask shook his head. "I am certain that the scroll mentioned a singular Keeper of the Wood. As the Crown Prince of Skierka, I order you to untie me and bring me to the Keeper."

The two fae burst into hysterics, laughing so hard that tears welled up in both of their eyes. "What is so Gods-damned funny?" Raask spat.

The twin faeries took turns imitating him demanding to be released. Each time they mimicked his speech, it sounded as if they had somehow recorded his voice and played it back. Each time they laughed harder and harder.

"Enough!" Raask cried.

They wiped the tears out of each other's eyes. "Oh, Prince Raask, haven't you realized that WE are the Keepers of the Wood!" The male fae snapped his finger and the knots keeping him tied up disappeared.

Raask rubbed his wrist as he sat-up properly. "Bullshit."

This resulted in another round of hysterics and mimicry of Raask's voice.

He groaned in frustration. "How could you be the Keepers of the Wood? You look younger than myself, and you are written about in our ancient scroll."

"Hey, Dumdum," the male faery taunted, "We are 326 years old! But it doesn't matter anyways, that ancient stinky parchment was written about our great-great grandpapa, Dorik."

"And so you inherited your title?"

"Obviously." The female rolled her eyes.

"Well then, I am to receive a quest from you." Raask did his best to not let the muscles in his face relax.

"Obviously." The male echoed.

It was then that Raask realized it was not difficult to keep his father's look of annoyance and anger plastered across his face. He began to tap his foot, desperate to expel some of his anger in some way. The female faerie's eyes tracked Raask's tapping foot and sniffed rather loudly. Raask was certain he didn't smell the best, but it was hardly his fault. These heathens hadn't allowed him to bathe or visit a bathroom since he had been knocked out!

The female cocked her head at her twin who sniffed loudly on his own. The two shared a glance.

"Yes, I'm sure I stink. Now that we have everything cleared up, I would like a meal and a bath." His knuckles turned white at his side as he clenched his fist too tight.

The male looked at his twin and shook his head. "Why would your birdies not tell us?" He asked, completely ignoring the prince of the nation with the most advanced and brutal military, who also happened to rule over the forest in which they resided.

"Maybe they did not know." Her jaw loosened and she looked out the door. Raask sensed that whatever her birdies didn't tell her felt like some form of betrayal to the female Keeper of the Wood.

A cruel and cocky laugh echoed across the grimy cell. "Whomever your spies are, I guarantee they knew whatever you're not sure of and refused to tell you. The little fish that hide amongst us sharks love to keep little scraps for themselves."

The female looked at Raask and winced. Her too-large eyes wandered back to her brother, too slow and full of distraction. "This is not good, Dorid." She walked out of the cell with her brother close behind.

"Hey! Hey! You can't leave me in here! I am the Crown Prince of Skierka! I am *your* prince!" The door swung open again, creaking against the hinge. An apple and bread were chucked onto the floor, a moment later, a bucket was thrown in as well.

At least a day, maybe more had passed before anyone had come back to check on the Prince. Three more meager pieces of bread with either an apple or cheese, were chucked into Raask's cell. He passed time by working out. He did hundreds of push-ups, hours of planks, and Gods knew how many squats and lunges. His body ached from the hard stone floor and the grueling exercises, with not nearly enough food to counterbalance the movement. He kept going. Kept pushing. He did anything and everything he could to drown out his thoughts, as he wondered if the cell that housed Aria far below the palace, was anything similar to the one he was in now.

An itch in the pit of his stomach grew into a throbbing pain. His powers ached to be used. The blood magic craved the release of blood. But it was too risky to unleash it blindly on the captors. If they truly were the Keepers of the Wood, he was certain that killing them would not be fulfilling the quest that was necessary to pass the trials of the king.

The tension in his blood kept building. He panted for oxygen, palms slipping across the cold, stone floor, riddled with puddles of his chilled sweat. He didn't know how long he had been kept in this prison, but it must have been longer than a week. He had never gone a week without feeding his blood magic—not since it had originally aligned. It hurt. It ached. It kept building. His body was on fire and the pressure of the outside world began to demolish him.

He had to feed it.

Raask began to bludgeon his skull into the stone. Maybe a hole in his skull would help release some of the building pressure. Maybe the release of blood would put the blood magic at ease. Maybe it just felt good to feel something, even if that something was pain.

Sticky warmth encompassed his entire body like a swaddle. And by Gods it stopped hurting. It stopped aching. The release of his own blood felt like a euphoria, and the drumming of his unceasing heart decrescendoed into a steady pulse. The buzzing within his skull sounded like the angelic creatures that protected Tsu's Gates of Eternity. He was covered in blood, the fluid of life, the energy that flowed through all living things, and he was so Gods-damned happy about it. Yes, this was it. This was what he needed. He just needed to feel that hurt. He just needed to spill some blood, even if it was his own. It was fine, he had plenty. For if Aria had ripped apart her own body and soul and crawled into the kingdom of her enemies for her own people, Raask could bleed too. He would bleed, too. He would bleed himself dry so she wouldn't bleed alone.

A laugh that Raask didn't recognize as his own filled the chamber. And wrapped in the blanket of his own insides, Raask finally drifted into a dreamless slumber.

"What in the . . ."

"What did he do to himself in here?"

"Disgusting!"

Cold water splashed across Raask's face like a thousand little knives. Instinctively, Raask jumped up and began to attack. The faerie twins grabbed his arms easily and held him against the wall. "Settle down! We have just decided on your quest, and we can't bloody tell it to you if you're too busy smacking us up."

His wild eyes calmed, like a lighthouse in the sea of blood that covered the rest of his face. "My—my apologies," he straightened. "What is my quest?"

The Keepers of the Wood shared an uneasy glance before reciting in unison, "Crown Prince of Skierka, Raask Morlok, Heir of Bjor the Blood Screamer, as the Keepers of the Wood and Rulers of the Gaulic, we request that you fulfill our quest in order to receive our blessing and continue your path towards the gift of the Morlok crown. Do you accept?"

Raask's eyes narrowed on the two. "Well, what is the quest?"

Dorid and Dorida looked at each other and rolled their eyes in sync. "You must accept the quest before we grant it. Are they not teaching the basics in magical mannerisms up in the Morlok Palace anymore? Sheesh!" Dorida squeaked.

"Fine, I accept." It wasn't like he had much of a choice anyways.

"Very well then," Dorida answered.

Again, in unison, they continued, "As a Blood Screamer—in order to be a suitable king to the people of Skierka, and the many territories overseen by the Skierkan Government and the Morlok family, then you must first mend your broken heart." They both gave a little nod, as if proud of finishing their part.

Raask was anything but amused. "I do not have a *broken* heart. Now give me a real quest! There's no way my father had to put up with something ridiculous like this."

Dorida sighed in annoyance. "Of course you have a broken heart, no sense in hiding it! We can hear it rattle every time you move. It's been driving us crazy."

"And as a Blood Screamer, having a sound heart is of the utmost importance! Your father's quest was different, yes of course, but he is a Fire Monger. What's in a Fire Monger's heart is not nearly as important as a Blood Screamer's, of course. Fire Mongers must fulfill quests of humility. Blood Screamers must prove their hearts, to ascend to the throne with our blessing. Of course, without our blessing, you will not receive the magic of our lands and will be stunted in your crown's powers," Dorid said.

"So you better do what we say!" Dorida added.

Raask wiped the blood that had begun to drip from the side of his head. He would laugh at the absurdity of this all, if he wasn't so completely screwed by it. Couldn't they see that he had been trying to mend himself? To put himself back together again? Couldn't they sniff it on him with their strange, supernatural senses?

"And how would I go about mending my broken heart? When will you determine it is properly mended, and how will I know I have your blessing?" Raask wanted to throttle the two fae. What a ridiculous quest from two ridiculous creatures.

"You must either make your lover your queen or king, swear your undying love to them, and vow to protect them from here until eternity," said Dorid.

"Or you must kill them," added Dorida. "Either way, you'll know you have our blessing along with the entirety of your power when—"

The temperature of the cell rose a few degrees as Raask barely held together his temper. This was ridiculous and cruel and a waste of his time. If they didn't want to give him a true quest, then he would be fine to be known as the slayer of the Keeper of the Wood. In mere seconds, blood began to spill out of the faerie twins' noses and ears and eyes. Blood trickled down from underneath their fingernails, and they began to scream in pain.

"Stop! Stop! There is no need to kill us!"

Raask halted the blood magic, his entire body jerking with the force it took to stop the powerful magic in its tracks. "Yes?" He asked coyly.

"We cannot rescind our quest. But you do not technically need to fulfill it."

"What do you mean? Be specific." Raask ordered.

Dorida wiped her bloody nose with her already soaked sleeve. "He means that your father did not fulfill his quest either."

"He also threatened us with violence," Dorid muttered under his breath.

"But we agreed to keep it a secret that he never fulfilled his quest, as long as we could keep our reign over the Gaulic forest and the creatures within."

"And this is the same deal you struck with my father?" Raask asked. He mindlessly tapped his chin as he thought about their proposition. The twins nodded.

"Why wouldn't I just kill you?"

Dorid scoffed. "Then who would control the creatures of the wood?"

"I would," Raask insisted. Dorid slammed a palm against his

forehead. "Prince Raask, please, be serious. These creatures would chew you up and spit you out in a heartbeat. They do not respect you or the Morloks. They will only answer to us."

Raask stored this information away, in case it ever became relevant again. "Fine, so we will just carry on as if I fulfilled your quest?" His stomach grumbled embarrassingly loud. He was done playing this game with the fae. All he wanted was to go back home and enjoy a fat dinner and a warm shower.

"Fine. But you must know—" Dorida was cut off by Dorid elbowing her in the rib.

"What? What is it?" Raask asked, losing what little patience he still had.

Dorida looked at Dorid sheepishly, as if she knew it would have been better to not speak up. "By enchanting your quest aloud, we have already set it in motion. So while we can lie to our subjects of the Gaulic forest and you can lie to the Skierkans and the rest of Arkts, the magic has already been set."

"Meaning?"

Dorid groaned. "It means, Dumdum, that like your father, you will rule without the entire magic of Skierka empowering you."

Raask nearly fell backwards. This could not be true. All Kings of Skierk inherit the magic of the land, as well as the magic of the lands conquered. It was part of the curse of the crown and was what made the Morloks so powerful.

"You're lying."

"Of course we are not lying, Prince Raask! Now, you will inherit the other magics. But like your father, you will not inherit the magic of our Gaulic forest. But to be truthful, none of you Morloks have inherited the magic of our wood since the first Morlok King!"

Dorida sighed. "It's probably better off this way anyways, Prince Raask. Our magic is ancient and much too strong for the modern Skierkan man."

With another snap from Dorid's fingers, a bottle of wine and a basket of bread, cheeses and jams clambered onto the floor, somehow staying intact. "Now we will feast together before we bring you back to your Palace."

Raask knew from children's stories how important it was to never refuse a meal with a fae. So even though it was the last thing he wanted to do, he sat down on the bloody floor and tore pieces of bread for each of them. It was warm, and much softer than the bread that they had been throwing in for him. And the cheese was soft and nutty, of some strange variety he wasn't quite sure of.

"Wraith's milk!" Dorida squeaked, sensing his impending question.

"Wraith's do not have milk." Raask retorted.

"BingBonger! How do you think they feed the babes?" Dorid asked.

Raask had never thought of the nasty creatures containing any bit of maternal instinct. "And how do you get the milk from them?" He asked, horrified by the mental image of some poor creature attempting to milk the wraiths.

"You ask!" The twins answered in unison, happily munching away on jammy pieces of bread and handing the bottle of wine back and forth. Raask was growing tired of their singsongy voices and the metallic tang to the air of the bloodied cell.

"May we eat in another room?" He grumbled.

"No, humans are not allowed to see our kingdom, young Prince. Not even the magical king—so don't bother asking again," Dorida said.

"So how am I to leave?" Raask asked, and immediately regretted it.

As he felt the effects of whichever sleeping tonic they'd laced in the food, Raask couldn't help but wonder how an entire kingdom had sat smack dab in the middle of his nation that his father had yet to conquer. His eyelids magically grew heavier and his neck weaker. He didn't have much time before he would knock out once again. As Raask ran through all of the new information he learned today, he wondered if he would remember any of it when the magic wore off.

CHAPTER 34
VIGGO

Viggo hadn't moved from where he and Raask had split a bottle of barley liquor the night before. His back ached from the lack of movement, but every time he got up to train or eat, a shot of guilt rushed through his body.

He spent the day listening for any sounds from the forest that could be his brother in distress. His head began to throb from the concentration and agony over every single snap of a branch. But when he truly concentrated, the only thing he heard was the usual wildlife of the unbearably annoying croaking frogs and the sprites getting frisky all day every day.

The sun had reached the center point of the sky, and even though they were well into autumn in Skierka, Viggo began to break a sweat. He was a damned puddle by the time Mayta had joined him.

He could smell her before he saw her.

An aura of a sweet bouquet followed her wherever she went. Viggo couldn't resist thinking how she would be an awful spy, just by smelling the mix of flowers and sweet citrus, an enemy could know precisely where she was. She'd give away the location of an entire army if he were to ever bring her along on his campaigns. His lips curved upwards at the mere thought.

"Hello, Mayta," Viggo's smile was audible through the two, simple words.

"How did you know it was me?" She asked before sitting in the grass next to him. She handed him a sweaty glass of iced tea and held her own glass of lemonade.

"Don't you know by now that I have eyes on the back of my head?" He thanked her for the iced tea and drank it in a single gulp.

She erupted into a fit of laughter as she watched him chug his tea, and after she offered him her own drink, which he chugged even faster. Her laughter filled his ears, and his aches and worries left to make room for her.

Viggo wiped the tea that hadn't quite made it into his mouth with the back of his hand and apologized for his messiness.

"That's quite alright. I can be a little messy too, sometimes."

Viggo watched as she mindlessly played with the hem of her skirt. And even though he knew that she came not for him, but for his brother, he didn't mind, he was just glad that she came

"You? No. I can't imagine you being messy," Viggo retorted.

She playfully pushed him, with a gentle palm and fingers that he could have sworn lingered on his chest.

Her fingers returned back to the hem of her skirt, and her eyes back to the footprints left by Raask the night before.

"You haven't seen my room have you? Oh, the other girls here at the palace love to tease me about it! But I just really can't help it. I've never had so many options for clothes to wear, and every time I have to get dressed, clothes just end up everywhere. It's pathetic, truly."

Viggo smiled, picturing her throwing her clothes everywhere— how her room looked filled with skirts and blouses thrown about.

"I like this." He felt the fabric of her pale pink skirt and ignored the goosebumps that speckled her arms from his touch.

"Thank you." She smiled, the adorable kind that was somehow from the corner of her mouth. He stopped breathing. He stopped everything besides watching her. The way she gently swayed back and forth, like she was singing a song to herself. The way she smelled of everything beautiful and everything worth fighting for. She was brave, and wild ,and wonderful, and he couldn't breathe without aching for her; without needing to feel her touch, and he was tired of living without it, and tired of questioning why he was so infatuated with someone he barely knew—who obviously didn't feel the same towards him.

It hurt. It hurt in a way Viggo would never admit to, even to himself. He was a general after all. The Skierkan Bruin. A commemorated killer. An agent of death and destruction. He was not made to love, he knew it in his gut. He was made for violence. For brutality.

Oh, Gods, she was life itself, and he was the dark devastation of death and cruelty, and he had no place in loving a creature like her.

He knew if he were a better man, he would get up and grab something from the kitchens to eat, and leave her there. For now, he would have to be okay with just pretending.

So quickly, as to not lose whatever slight grip on reality he had found himself holding onto, he stood up and muttered a goodbye to Mayta. He rushed away from her and back towards the castle, stomping on flowers and toadstools all along the way. Never daring to look back at the woman he left on the edge of Morlok Palace.

No, he made it nearly all the way back to Raask's personal tower before he heard her gasp.

With an ease and speed that only came from years at battle, Viggo drew his weapon, and whipped around. A tall shadow was stumbling through the forest with a beard that hadn't been there the night prior, and several inches added to his hair—his brother was back from his quest. Viggo didn't remember running back to the edge of the forest, or sheathing his sword. But suddenly he was looking into his brother's eyes, their mother's eyes really, and he knew without words that time had traveled differently for Raask over the past day. He himself knew the haunting and jarring feeling from his many tours across the Dahs.

All at once, he collided into his brother. Their wide arms wrapped around one another in an embrace and for the first time in a long time, Viggo found his eyes had turned wet. Raask smelled of sweat and pines and other strange notes that he couldn't quite place. His clothes that had been perfectly tailored to his body when he left, now hung looser on him. Everything was different and yet, in their arms, somehow it was all the same really.

"You're alright?" Viggo asked, taking a step back to get a good look at him.

"Yes."

"It's been long—where you were it was long?" He could barely speak. He was never the one who was left home worrying for others, and it was not a feeling he envied.

"Yes," Raask looked back at Viggo for the first time really. Viggo watched silently as the realization that he was in the same clothes as the night Raask had left, set onto Raask's face.

"How long has it been for you?" Raask asked.

"A night and half a day." Viggo knew better than to push, a skill he learned as a general and not as a brother, but worked for both of his roles in Skierka. "Come, let's get you something to eat."

Viggo didn't miss the glow in Raask's eyes at the mention of food. The pair strode the rest of the way out of the Gaulic forest, ignoring the slithering of the gossipy snakes. And when the shadows of the forest had finally ended, and sunlight gleamed down onto them, Viggo realized he had completely forgotten that Mayta had also been there waiting for Raask's return. The blinding, hot rays of the sun finally changed their angle, and there she was. Standing so still. Biting her lip. Staring at Raask as if he was the sun himself.

"You're back so soon!" She bounced slightly, as if she was resisting the urge to come over and hug him.

Raask grunted and nodded in her direction as an answer.

Viggo tried to give her an apologetic smile, but she was too busy trotting after Raask to even notice. It seemed she wasn't noticing much at the moment.

Raask was beaten down.

Mayta either didn't notice, or most likely didn't see what Viggo saw.

He saw how his brother's steps were heavier and more focused. His hands clenched and unclenched into tight fists at his sides. And he stared at the sky and looked into the breeze as if a part of him thought he would never see such things again. Whatever had happened at the second trial, had changed something in Raask. But for how long, Viggo wasn't sure. He silently prayed it was temporary, both selfishly and selflessly. There would always be a part of him that would wish to protect his brother from pain and harm, even though he believed it was a necessary thing to become not only a man, but a king.

Mayta wouldn't stop following him like a puppy. She stayed half a step behind him, not realizing that she was trodding too close to a man on the edge.

"I'm so happy that you're back! The palace wasn't quite the same without you. Of course, we all knew that you would pass the second trial, but it's nice to know that it's all bing, bang, boom, done, and out of the way. And now you'll have to do the last one. What is that again? I've asked a few people, but nobody wanted to answer, so it must be awful, I bet. But I'm sure you'll pass that with ease just like this one! And I feel that—"

It took Viggo a moment to comprehend what exactly had just happened.

One second, Mayta had been rambling on behind them as they walked steadily towards the kitchens. The next, Mayta was staring at Raask with wide, teary eyes. Slowly, the tears began to pour down her face.

The smell of rot and decay building up inside of himself, begging to be released, was the only tether he had back to himself. He didn't hear what his brother had said, but a part of him ached to scream at him. Maybe even do more. The rot began to build within him. A blow for a blow began to seem reasonable to him.

Webs of darkness began to creep across his vision. And from somewhere so very far away, too far away, Viggo was aware of his humanity slipping.

Raask could be cruel. He'd probably said something awful to Mayta, but that did not mean he wanted to hurt him. Viggo reminded himself over and over again, that he loved his brother and that he did not want to hurt his brother. This part of him was not human, and it was not clean.

Viggo's death magic rolled like a tide in his ears and through his sinuses. Over and over again, he reminded himself of his deep love for his brother. Raask's face waking him up from nightmares. His little hands holding so tightly to his own. The death magic began to ebb. But too much time had passed. Raask was gone, and Mayta was still staring at the place he had just been.

"He should not have said that," Viggo said, both to himself and Mayta.

His words seemed to have snapped something in her. She quickly wiped her tears and straightened. With quick movements she dusted some imaginary dirt from her skirt. "Did anyone else hear?" She asked, voice steady.

"No. Not that I know of, unless someone was looking out from the castle. But nobody would be stupid enough to remark about it." That much Viggo was certain. As Raask had just passed the second trial, it was dawning across Skierka that the former party-loving king of debauchery, would soon be their High King. Nobody would want to be on his bad side, especially if his temper took after his father's. At this moment, everything Raask did would be highly scrutinized among the Skierkans, both the loyalists and the breakers.

"Good," was all she said.

He expected her to run off, hiding her wounds. It's what he would have done. But she didn't.

Rolling her shoulders back, and slowly relaxing the tensed muscles of her brow and jaw, she transformed before his eyes. If it weren't for her reddened eyes, it would have been like nothing had

happened. It was a magic in her own right, to be verbally struck
down, and summon the power to keep on. Her chin lowered, a
polite nod.

How did it feel to be polite in the face of violence? Did it feel
powerful in its own way—to react as a dignified person? Or was it
humiliating to not give a blow for a blow? A slur for a slur? Did she
ache for retribution? Was every hit and taunt that she ever received
left on a mental list for revenge? Did she want to hurt the ones who
hurt her?

Was she like him or was she better?

The tail of her bluebell skirt dragged against the dark soil just at
the edge of his peripherals. She was going, almost gone. He reached
out for her, grasping for her hand like it was his last chance at salvation. And when he felt her warm fingers clasping around his callused
hands, he knew the answer to the questions he had been too scared
to speak.

"I'm sorry," He said. Or maybe he had only mouthed the words.

"It's alright."

He watched her disappear into the gardens. And stayed there
long after the scent of flowers had left. Death magic curled around
his fingers, a silent and cold presence that hungered to be used. The
grass around Viggo had turned pale.

Everything was certainly not alright.

It was well into the night by the time Viggo was able to fall
asleep. Marked by the shame and rage of years of pretending to agree
with the Morloks' violent nature, pretending to even be a Morlok.

It had enraged him. He was better than them.

He refused to massacre thousands of refugees. He saved them.
Working his black-market connections, and finding nations to take
them in as refugees under the guise of a notorious smuggler. He was
fine to play this double role, to keep up this charade of being the son

of the Morlok king. He did it all for his brother, and he would gladly do it again.

But what did it mean to not let his brother know who he truly was? His brother believed him a savage, which he could be, but he liked to consider himself righteous as well. A protector. And Raask, he was raised to value violence above all. A conqueror. And Viggo had not been around to show him any other way. To be above the greed and the endless need for more. More land. More slave. More violence. His brother did not know he was better than that.

His blankets and long limbs were beginning to tangle. He thought back to the patch of dead grass outside of the palace. The wide eyes of those he had killed in order to create and maintain his image of the Skierkan Bruin. Viggo had death and violence in his very veins. A part of him worried that maybe, he was not so much better than King Morlok.

He felt trapped and twisted and cramped and so very angry. It was getting harder and harder to mask his hatred of the king, and the Skierkan nobles who sat in their padded chairs in the finest of silks, moving pawns across boards and sentencing thousands to their deaths, between sips of extravagant liquors.

It was no longer enough to quietly dismantle their power. He wanted to throw it in their faces. He wanted them to learn the identity of the notorious smuggler who stole and freed the Skierkan slaves.

But he couldn't do it. Not just yet. Too much was planned. Too much was already set into motion and required him to stay where he was for the moment. Raask had not yet even passed the final trial. He was still growing into the man he would be when he took the Morlok crown. And he needed him. Raask needed some form of kindness and love to stop him from turning into his father. Viggo needed to be the man that *he* had needed himself, so many years ago.

So he would stay. And take beating after beating. He would humiliate himself, all for Raask. His little brother. It would be worth it. If love and family were not worth humiliation and pain, then nothing was.

The tension of the blankets began to ease. Slowly, but surely.

The sound of a young Raask's pitter-pattering steps, that echoed across the entire castle, raced through his mind. The smell of his mother's hair, hugging him and his brother tightly. Wishing she would hold on for just a moment longer, but being too proud and too old to ask.

Gentle darkness began to invade Viggo's memories. The darkness and death that ran through his veins ran to it like a child to its mother. His body remained planted in his too-large bed in the Morlok castle, but he allowed his mind to succumb to the fall, unknowing of the destination, but knowing that wherever he was going he was ready.

That night he dreamt of climbing mountains. The eastern winds slapped against the Red Peaks mercilessly as Viggo climbed with one goal and one goal only: to confront the sun.

CHAPTER 35
MAYTA

Mayta was not at all surprised she had been humiliated by a human male. From the waters she had watched men do far, far worse. Abissian folklore would often speak of the cruelties of men. Their violent nature did not come to a surprise to her.

She was, however, deeply surprised that Raask was the one to hurt her so. She had watched him for years. Day after day, he would smile and provide comfort to his people. Didn't he believe she was one of his people?

Maybe Aria had been right after all. Maybe men were not to be trusted. Maybe he was just having a rough day, and she should have known better than to pester him.

Mayta wanted nothing more than to run to her big sister and ask her advice. For a hug. For some comfort and reminder of the home that they had both left. But Aria had warned her to only seek her out in the direst of emergencies, in order to avoid any suspicions.

Aria had given up everything for her. She sacrificed herself so that Mayta could be seen as a savior to the prince. Oh, but it hadn't worked out as she planned, had it?

Mayta couldn't let her sister's sacrifices go to waste. She was to marry into the Morlok family and one day become Queen of Skierka. And as queen, she would protect the syrens, and teach the Skierkan children to do the same. She would outlaw syren hunting and set them free from their enslavement. And she was to do it by marrying the man she had dreamed of marrying since she was a child. Her sister had devised a beautiful plan to make her happy and save their people, all while she rotted in a dungeon. But Mayta was failing.

Her room was large and outfitted with several thick furs on every piece of furniture. Although she came from the cold waters, cold air somehow felt colder to her. Various pairs of boots and pointed shoes and slippers, were thrown across the room along with cloaks and dresses and skirts. She missed her old clothes. Everything here was black and red to stroke the Morlok's ego. At least her hair was a deep red. Or at least it had been. In the Dahs, her hair resembled a deep, plum wine, but after spending many days gardening under the sun, it had lightened a great deal.

She studied her face in the mirror. Oh, how much could change in such a short time. Apparently a lot.

Mayta finally stood, wobbling a bit under her sore legs. Gods, she hated having legs. They were so long and awkward. Her tail had been beautiful. It was thick and strong and glistened under the moonlight. Her legs were pale, and her feet constantly hurt. She hated having feet. Even more so, she hated that all of the prettiest shoes of the court women hurt the most.

What a wicked cruelty to make a shoe so beautiful, yet hurt so much.

She slid her feet into a pointed boot, with a heel that made her considerably taller. It didn't take her long to note that wearing a higher heel among the Skierkans was a sign of higher nobility. And if she were to be queen, she ought to wear a decent-sized heel. She grimaced as she took her first step in the lovely shoes.

In fact, she grimaced with each step. Each click of the heel against the white lithe-bleached stone came with a soft snarl. It wasn't until she had left her long hallway and began to see guards and nobles, that she raised her mask and plastered the sweet and humble smile that she had practiced nightly.

She had yet to see any of her friends. They all usually slept well into the day each morning. It took either a roll of emerald lithe, or some mixture of liquor and juice, to get them out of bed. Mayta loved the feeling of the emerald lithe and the bubbles in their spirits, but certainly not in the morning. These were the humans who were in charge of writing laws and correcting injustices in their nation, and they spent most of their time out of their minds. Humans were very, very strange creatures.

She figured it was because of humans' love for the bottle and flame, that breakfasts were usually so quiet at the castle. Silently, she stuffed her face with spicy sausage and eggs. It was her favorite thing that they made here and she'd even begun requesting it for her other meals.

The quietness of the breakfast made it easy to eavesdrop. Apparently, Prince Raask had requested to move up his final trial to tonight. Another reason this particular morning was very quiet. Mayta wasn't sure what the final trial was, but she knew that it took a great deal of preparation on the servants' and guards' parts.

While she was gardening in the bright morning sun, she had overheard a few of the men of the court speaking about the trial. It was to take place at sunset, and only the highest members of the court were invited. All others were to be turned away. Mayta had no clue if that included her, but she doubted it.

It was during her teatime, when she sat on a bench by the Dahs, that she overheard some of the women of the court mentioning that it would take place in a building behind the palace. These particular women were deeply upset by this, as they believed it would be the same place that they often snuck into to smoke crushed thierry vines with their paramours. They decided, just to be safe, they would go in earlier to clean out their stash of the strong hallucinogen.

Maya wasn't quite sure why she had decided to follow them, only that the decision had already been made by her legs.

The women stumbled up the hill towards Morlok castle, taking a semi-hidden path just past the Gaulic forest, next to the stables. As the houses and trees faded away with each step, Mayta began to worry about staying hidden. But with the harsh wind slapping at their faces, she gently prayed that the women wouldn't turn around and question why the new girl had followed them so far up the secretive path.

The cold air rushed into her lungs, stinging her dry throat. It had been too long since she had been truly active, and after weeks of indulging in the courtly sins of emerald and fuschia lithe, and seemingly never-ending glasses of sparkling mead and liquored tonics, the simple path felt like a torturous hike. It was a wonder that the women couldn't hear her labored breaths, or maybe even a blessing from Tsu himself, that the wind decided to build into a roar at the most strenuous part of the path.

Cold air and wind was all she could hear, and all that she could think of. The wind roared and slapped against the wood in the Gaulic. It blew the tops of mushrooms off, bringing about clouds of their noxious spores. The poor soil and fire sprites were hanging onto the branches with their dear lives. Of course, the air and water sprites were riding the wind waves, twirling and flipping and daring each other. Mayta took a moment to give more space between her and the women rushing to hide their paraphernalia. She hid behind a fat tree that happened to also be sheltering a family of the soil sprites, that were saying particularly unkind things about her wind-blown hair.

She could see now where the third trial would be. Tucked away, far from the Morlok castle and the stables and the Irridesci tower, sat a stone building. Broad columns engraved with some sort of design held the structure together. As the women approached, they entered between the third and fourth column, grabbing something out of a hole in the design of the column and disappeared out of view. Whatever this building was, it seemed to have been dug into the ground itself.

Glad that she had just eaten a plateful of spiced butter and bread at the tea house, Mayta sank against the cold ground and waited for the women to leave, so she could investigate the space further. If she got lucky, maybe she could find a hiding space within the stone structure, so she could see the third trial for herself. She was certain that the third trial would have something to do with true love. All of the greatest tales of kings and knights included a true love's kiss. She had to be there just in case. And even if it didn't, she couldn't miss the biggest event in Skierka.

Anyone who was anyone would talk about this for the next several decades, and Mayta did *not* want to miss out on it. She loved the strange curiosities that humans tended to get themselves mixed into.

A sudden rush of wind, and the beat of mighty wings broke her concentration on the stone structure. She twisted her neck around the trunk of the tree, not daring to venture further into the wood to investigate. But the Gaulic was far too shadowed and full of violent movement from the windstorm to see anything clearly.

"You've sure got a thing for being caught alone out in storms."

Mayta followed the voice to the branches above her. On the tree directly diagonal to her, a blonde with a long braid and a giant bow slung across her back, crouched and took a crispy bite out of an apple that surely had to be soaked.

"Silia?"

Silia hopped down from the branch with a wet thud. "The one and only." She circled around Mayta, looking her up and down the way Aria used to when Mayta had been out later than she expected.

"What are you doing out here?" Mayta asked.

Silia snorted. "I could ask you the same thing. In fact, I will. What are you doing out here?"

Oh, Freyite . . . She couldn't tell Silia that she had been trying to sneak into the third trial. Although she didn't show any outward aggression towards her—like the tall guy did—she was obviously suspicious of her already. Mayta was also certain that Silia could detect wraithshit from an ocean away.

"I heard . . . I heard some women talking in the tea house in town. They mentioned coming here to hide some fuschia lithe, I wanted to see if I could get some." Mayta had bet on Silia discounting her for a vapid lithe-addicted woman of the courts.

Silia snorted yet again, and took another juicy bite out of the green apple. A color that she wasn't aware apples had come in, she'd never seen one in the kitchens or in the wood along the Dahs. "We both know you could score higher quality shit from any of the handful of sons of nobles that follow you around on the daily."

Apparently Mayta had bet wrong, but in an awful way it felt truly flattering. "I'd say *more* than a handful of men have been following me around since you and your friends brought me here." She didn't miss the smile that flashed across Silia's lips before her eyes zoomed onto the stone columns in the distance.

"Ah." Silia nodded, seemingly making a decision as to why Mayta was out in the woods in a storm. "You know, you could have just asked me?"

"I'm pretty sure I did ask you why you were out here, before you even asked me."

Silia rolled her eyes and continued chewing on her apple. "Careful with the sass, Red. Or else I won't sneak you into the trial— and I might even tell the Twisted Twins to keep an eye out for a certain mischievous redhead."

Mayta stood up straight and narrowed her eyes onto Silia. "What do you want?"

Silia whipped her long braid, letting it fall against her back. She hummed loudly, pretending to think about what she would ask of Mayta.

"Oh little Red, little Red . . . I can't quite decide just yet. How about this? How about I sneak you into the third trial, no questions asked. And in the future: you owe me a favor." Her eyes narrowed before adding, "No questions asked."

Mayta sniffed, considering if she really did *need* to be snuck into the third trial. "Alright, you have a deal," Mayta answered after deciding that she did need to be there. If she missed out on this not only would she be behind on gossip, it would also look as if she wasn't important enough to be at such an exclusive event. There was also the matter of her belief that *just maybe*, true love's kiss might be used during the trial.

"Superb. I'll come get you from your room a little after sunset."

"Fine."

Silia laughed and spun around back towards the castle. Not wishing to walk the whole way back with her, Mayta hung back a while.

When Silia was just out of sight, her sweet voice carried across the wind, "You know, Red? You're a lot more fun than I thought." Her laugh crackled against the storm like wildfire.

When her laugh faded against the wind, and Silia's silhouette became too small to see any longer, Mayta rushed back to the palace, stopping at the kitchens for a hot cup of tawny and a thick piece of fresh bread slathered with chili-spiced butter. She ate the bread in the corner of the kitchen, doing her best to stay out of the way of the servants who were rushing to complete the last-minute feast to celebrate Raask's third trial. Padge was slicing vegetables, kneading dough, and supervising all the other cooks, seemingly at the same time.

She had seen similar levels of concentration only from her sister when she was training or hunting. From experience, she knew that Padge probably knew everything that was happening in the kitchen without even needing to look.

Mayta couldn't resist watching the kitchen staff, how they zoomed in and out of each other—yet somehow never collided, it was mesmerizing. The heat from the stoves and the bodies moving with precision and focus warmed her up enough that she forgot that she was sopping wet.

"Miss Mayta?" A gruff voice drew her eyes away from the feast preparations. As she looked towards the doorway, the large, balding guard that her sister had told her of was removing his outer coat. "You're soaked! You must be colder than a sistro's tit!" Zaries carefully placed his coat across Mayta's shivering shoulders.

"What was that?" Mayta asked, laughing.

A violent shade of red crossed Zaries's cheeks. "Skullin's Scythe . . . I'm so sorry Miss Mayta. My mouth has a mind of its own sometimes. I should know better . . . I ought to know better by now." Even if Aria hadn't told her about Zaries, she would have known that they had been friends.

"It's quite alright." Mayta said. Suddenly sad at the mental picture of Aria bonding with this large, crass guard, she wondered if he went down to visit her at all, or if he felt betrayed by finding out Aria's true identity.

Did he suspect her at all? Maybe they had figured that like lightning, it was unlikely for two villainous women to strike twice in the same place. Above all, humans tended to believe that the bad days were done. They had this almost universal belief that things would get better; that the world was a happy place. They believed that people meant to do well. That all humans just wanted to make the Arkts a better place and cause no harm.

It was so very different from how her kind viewed the world, and what initially drew her towards humanity, what made her come back to the edge of the Dahs and watch them parading around their grim lives with fangless smiles, laughing and dancing along the way.

Syrens rarely smiled without their fangs. And when they hugged, they kept their claws out, drawing blood from whomever they hugged. To hug a syren without drawing blood is a sign of great disrespect. A dishonor on both parties. Mayta wondered if Aria had ever hugged this man, and if she did, if she'd remembered to keep her claws retracted.

She thanked him for the coat and made a mental note to get it cleaned, dried, and steamed before returning. As she went up to her rooms, she thought of bringing him some flowers from the gardens as a thanks. And after she showered and applied her lotions and tinctures to her clean skin, she hunkered down into bed under thick layers of velvety furs and quilts and fell asleep thinking about which kind of flowers to bring for the guard who was kind to her sister.

It was already dark by the time Mayta woke up.

The second she opened her eyes, she bolted upright and ran to the door to see if Silia was outside waiting. The note slipped into her chambers told her enough that she didn't bother to open the heavy door.

Meet me in the southeast corner of the Spikes. Stick to the trees and hoot three times.

— S

SHE SPRINTED TO THE WINDOW AND SAW THE LAST STRAGGLERS ENTERING the stone structure. From a distance, the columns looked like sharpened spikes jutting out of the ground. The tops even seemed to have a bloody hue to them.

The trial wouldn't start too long after they had each found their places. Skullin's Scythe, this was bad. This was really bad. She'd wanted to just take a quick nap, wake up and take her time getting ready. There was absolutely no time for any of that now. Thankfully she had at least laid out her outfit before falling asleep.

Quickly, she tugged the dove-colored gown over her body. The fabric was created by master weavers who could take apart pearls and raw aquamarine and infuse them into fabrics. It was worth a fortune and sparkled against the moonlight. The corseted top gently cupped her breasts, before the rest of the dress fell loosely against her bare legs. It was the perfect dress for Raask to notice her against the crowd, and choose her for his true love kiss. Just in case that was going to happen that is . . . And if it did, the rest would be history. Mayta would save the syrens and eventually free her people.

If she could only get there in time.

Remembering that she *did* have to sneak into the Spikes, she swung a cloak around herself, concealing the pearlescent dress. It was the biggest cloak that she had, Morlok black with a trim of raven feathers that ran along the train. She had to keep it squeezed shut with her hands in the front to prevent the waves of fabric from showing. For her shoes, she chose her black gardening boots that were already stuffed with padded cushions for her eternally sore feet. Seeing as the dress covered her shoes and she would have to sprint through the Gaulic forest, she figured these would be the best bet. Admittedly, she also wasn't quite used to having to choose shoes with each outfit.

Mayta hadn't even left the palace before she knew that she made the right choice in choosing the comfier boots. Cursing herself for not training more with her sister or whomever handled such things at the Morlok castle, Mayta sprinted as fast as she could. She didn't allow herself to consider what kind of creatures were lurking in the forest at that very moment, or why that damned Irridesci tower always smelled so Gods-awful.

Her legs carried her to the edge of the forest, and although it was already suitably dark outside, she ran behind the tree line just in case. Branches broke and creatures howled from the depths of the Gaulic, Mayta kept sprinting. And praying. The praying helped distract her from mentally running over the list of monstrous creatures that could have made the noises she was hearing.

It may have been her imagination, but she could have sworn a hylbra ran in the same direction as her, but just hidden enough in the trees that she couldn't quite make it out. It must have been her imagination, though. Hylbras weren't native to this area of Skierka, she thought they were native to the Red Peaks up north—but she wasn't sure.

As she continued to run, she began to see the beast clearer and clearer. It seemed to be running by her side—only, on the opposite end of a line of trees. It was tall. Taller than most horses. And its maw was massive. In her picture books the hylbra always reminded her of the dogs humans would keep, only ten times the size and with teeth sharper than wraith claws.

Mayta's feet kept going. She didn't have time to look directly at the beast. She didn't have time to think of what to do if there was a beast running along her side in the Gaulic forest. All she knew was that she had to get to the Spikes.

When she finally reached the meeting point, she flung her body against a tree and fell over panting. Through strands of red hair, she gathered the courage to look into the woods and at her running mate.

The beast's eyes met hers.

The pupils were tiny for such massive eyes. And the irises were gold with tiny silver flecks spotted across, as if someone blew pure silver into their eyes and all that was left was a few drops.

The hylbra stamped its leg and twisted its head. He was beckoning her to come closer, to go deeper into the woods.

"Do you speak?" Mayta asked in a mix between a yell and a whisper. The hylbra whined in response. Mayta straightened, still leaning against the tree. "Well, I can't go with you right now. I need to do something very, very important! But if you are here later I can go with you." The hylbra whined again and tugged its head in the direction of the center of the Gaulic.

Mayta studied the hylbra. She noticed how it lowered its head when addressing her. How its eyes followed her without being glued onto her. How it whined and yelped and begged her. Mayta knew predators. She knew predators well. And this beast was not here to hunt her.

"Please, beast. I need to go in there. And I will call a friend now who will help me sneak in. But she is very dangerous, and I don't want her to hurt you. Please at least hide for now, and tomorrow I will meet you here again if you still need me." She took another look into the beast's striking eyes and added, "I promise."

With a huff and a growl, the hylbra turned around and sprinted off into the Gaulic. After giving him a few seconds of distance, she hooted three times and waited for Silia to arrive. As she waited, Mayta pondered what the beast wanted from her, of all people.

A ruffle of leaves was the only sound that alerted Mayta to Silia's presence. Just as last time, Silia came from above, with only her blonde hair giving her location away. "Thought you changed your mind, Red."

Silia was in all black training leathers. Her bow was slung across her back and a variety of knives stuck out from her uniform for easy access.

"Are you on duty?" Mayta asked.

"Yup." Silia answered as she led the way to a particularly tall tree that came closer to the Spikes than the rest.

"No one will notice you leaving your post?"

"You think I'm a guard?" Silia asked, apparently amused by the question.

"Well, how else would you be on duty dressed like that?" Mayta asked. She followed closely behind Silia all the way until they got to the tree. As Silia climbed the thick trunk faster than a sprite, Mayta realized just how screwed she really was.

"You want me to do that?"

Even through the dense darkness of the Gaulic, Mayta could see the gigantic eye roll from Silia. After one solid deep breath in and a short exhale, Mayta thanked her past self for deciding on the comfier shoe option and began to attempt to scale the tree. It took her longer than Silia, but to her credit, beneath her cloak she was wearing a couture gown that she was doing her best to keep from harm. Eventually she made it up to the branch where Silia was waiting.

Silia lowered her long arm to help pull Mayta's hand up. "See kid? You're tougher than you think."

Mayta replied with a particularly offensive gesture that Silia quietly laughed off.

From this angle, Mayta could finally get a decent view of what the others had been calling the Spikes. The stones she thought looked more similar to columns from afar, now seemed to look closer to shards of stone. The intricate details carved within seemed to tell famous folklore from ancient Skierka. If she had more time, and more light, she would love to one day come down here and trace the carvings into a journal—to later study and compare with the stories she'd heard as a child.

Below the shards of stone, carved into the ground itself, were rows upon rows of seats before a stage of some sort. In an odd way, it reminded Mayta of the empty conservatory within the side of the trench back home in the Dahs, that once housed beautiful concerts and performances. Only this wasn't below a thousand or so feet of water and was filled with mostly humans instead of other water folk.

Most of the crowd were members of the high courts of Skierka. They all wore embroidered black silken robes with the Morlok crest sewn into the back in white and red thread. Based off of the nauseous buzzing sensation oozing out of the pit, Mayta was pretty sure that a lot of lythe-generated magic was being used down there.

Mayta scanned the seats and the stage—that was filled with large boxes with elegant sheets draped over top—looking for Raask, but unable to find him.

"Which one are you looking for?" Silia asked.

"Raask," Mayta answered as if it hadn't been obvious.

Silia's brow furrowed and mouth tightened. "He isn't out yet. But he'll be out once the ceremony starts."

"You know what the third trial is, don't you?" Mayta asked, scanning Silia's face for some kind of clue. This wasn't at all what she had pictured for the last trial for a soon-to-be king. Where was the pomp and frills? Instead of popping bottles of the finest spirits and singing the Skierkan anthem like she had expected, the people were sitting ominously. This was the opposite of a happy scene. It felt more similar to a funeral than a celebration of Skierkan pride.

Silia's signature playfully arrogant smirk was missing. While Mayta was scanning the scene for Raask, Silia must have grabbed her bow off of her back. Her right hand gripped the bow, knuckles turning white, while her left hand reached into her quiver and removed a nearly invisible arrow. If it wasn't for the strong buzzing sensation and the blurred air around the outline of the arrow, Mayta wouldn't have realized it was even there. Mayta watched, eyes agape as Silia took out a small jar of twilight lithe from her pocket, and dipped each clear arrow head into the jar.

"You will not tell anyone of what you see me doing. Do you understand?" Silia's eyes bore into Mayta's soul.

"Are you going to kill Raask?" She asked, breathlessly.

"No. I will not be killing or harming anyone. Quite the opposite actually."

Mayta didn't understand what she meant by that, but she also knew that Silia was a part of Viggo's unit. She knew that Viggo trusted Silia, and somehow in her mind she knew that if Viggo trusted this crafty, cynical blonde, then she could too.

"I won't tell anyone. But that counts as the favor that I owe you."

The edges of Silia's lips turned upwards in the world's smallest smile before she regained her focus onto the stage far below.

"What's going to happen, Sil?" Mayta asked, keeping her eyes glued to the stage. The only answer Mayta received was a hush from Silia and a chilled blast from the northern winds.

Just before Mayta was about to ask Silia once again what was going to happen and when it would start, a low humming began to emit from the pits below. Seven Irridesci emerged from some kind of stairs concealed beneath the stage. They each hummed the same low note that sounded like the incarnation of despair itself. Their long robes slid across the stone stage, following in each of their steps. Each Irridesci took a spot next to one of the large rectangular items that were covered by the embroidered sheets. When they each took their place next to their respective boxes, they stopped their humming at once, and looked up to the top of the Spikes where the King of Skierka had been watching from.

The king took his first step into the pits and ignited a dozen or so torches along the outer wall of the Spikes, along with a crown of fire hovering over his head. His steps were slow but strong, and they echoed far across the Spikes and all the way up to Mayta and Silia with ease.

The king wore a lavish red robe that trailed behind him, but unlike the robes of the Irridesci, this one didn't seem to glide effortlessly behind, instead it moved as an extension of the king's staggered footsteps. Flames licked the edge of his robe, all the way up and around the collar.

A few paces behind the king was Viggo. He wore the formal Skierkan military outfit, a black pair of trousers with a matching black jacket that rested against his bare chest, showing off his various lithe-infused tattoos. The Morlok crest had been stitched into the back of his jacket with a frayed bone-white thread. The only thing that distinguished him against the rest of the military as a member of the Morlok family, was the color of his crest and the crown. His crown was made of scorched bones with long silver jewels hanging off it. Mayta bit her lip watching Viggo cascade down the steps. Each step echoed across the pit with the eerie sense of his dark powers. Even from this great distance she could feel his magic tugging at her chest.

When Viggo and the king finally made their way to the bottom of the pits, they took their seats. The king, of course, sat in the largest throne, decorated with rubies and lithe in abundance. As he sat down, he lit the entirety of the throne in a dark red flame. Above the throne, a flame in the shape of the Morlok crest flickered violently. The fire raven even appeared to move, occasionally flapping its wings or cocking its head to the side. It was a miraculous display of powers. The Morloks, with their strange genetic predisposition to power and the gift to their bloodlines from the Gods so long ago, could handle more magic than any other creature. It was terrifying to watch from so close.

Viggo sat after the king had finished lighting his throne, their thrones sat across from the main stage and in front of the crowd, facing both Silia and Mayta. His throne was the smallest of the three, as he would never be king. His throne was fashioned out of a shiny black stone. It was sleek and unembellished besides the array of swords that fanned across the back, in an upside down half-moon shape. The throne of the general.

Viggo brushed his black hair out of his face as he sank into the seat. And there it was again! Mayta was *certain* she could feel that tug once again. Almost as if the darkness of the forest was pushing her closer to him.

Mayta looked down for a second, feeling heat rushing to her cheeks as she noticed him. His muscular build. The way he sat in the smallest of the three thrones, commanding attention and respect with ease. He looked and felt like power . . . Power . . .

That was when she noticed that the shadows from the trees were moving. While the trees themselves stayed firmly in place, their shadows were wrapping around Silia and Mayta in a protective cocoon. At once, her body recognized this kind of magic and the familiar thrum of power beneath it. She looked back down to Viggo, and swore he looked up at her and winked. But he couldn't have done that, someone else would have noticed it, right?

Distracted by the warmth of the shadows and the hug of Viggo's dark power, Mayta tried her best to pay attention to the king who had started to speak, magically amplifying his voice.

"The day has come. The day that I have been anticipating since I myself championed the Trials of the King. On a night, not too different from this, I felt the pressures of a budding nation on my shoulders. I remember feeling the crisp air of the Northern winds on my head. I remember thinking that it would be the last time I would feel a chill on my scalp because after that night, I would be crowned the King in Waiting." Not a soul stirred as the king paused his speech, looking towards the covered boxes on the stage.

"Tonight, I am honored to present the same opportunity to my youngest son, who I hope will look back in many years and do the same for a new generation of Morloks. Ladies and men, I proudly present the Crown Prince of Skierka, Raask Morlok."

With the mention of Raask, the entire crowd roared. From the opposite side of where the king and the general had descended the stairs, Raask appeared. He wore leather combat pants, with no sword or bow at his sides. Like Viggo, he forwent a shirt, showing off the now-moving tattoo of the Morlok crest carved into his chest, peeking between the edges of a long, dark cloak. He cascaded down the steps like storm water off a cliff, his steps echoing deep into Skierka itself. His long, golden hair was pushed back and held back with some kind of sleek ooze. It was no longer messy, and it no longer reminded her of sunlight.

It was only when he had reached the bottom of the pits that Mayta realized that the Irridesci had left the stage, taking the seats reserved for them directly behind the king. All that was left on top of the stage were the now uncovered boxes. Mayta gasped in pure horror as it slowly dawned on her what everyone else in the Spikes had already known.

Silia worked quickly. She shot the clear arrows dipped into twilight lithe into each box with lethal accuracy. If Mayta hadn't understood the mercy that Silia was giving, she would have taken a moment to sit in awe and terror at the talent Silia had with a bow.

The boxes. The cages. The prisons.

They all contained individuals. But not humans of course, the Morloks would never massacre a Skierkan human. Not publically at least.

A goblin. A ghoul. A sprite. Gods . . . a syren. A wraithkin. These were only the creatures that she could recognize. A handful of other creatures in which Mayta couldn't name had been trapped in the cages. These boxes . . . They held each of the humanoid creatures found within Skierka and its conquered lands.

Mayta had to slam a hand against her mouth to stop herself from crying out.

This was wrong. This was all wrong. She simply couldn't understand why they were doing it. How was this a trial to deem the worthiness of a king? To kill as a coward? To slaughter the creatures in which the Morloks ruled over while they couldn't fight back?

Mayta had been wrong. The humans were far worse than she had ever realized.

Tears coursed their way down Mayta's face as she watched Raask walk over to an open box containing dozens of varied weapons. Long swords, throwing knives, battle axes, war hammers, even a variety of poisons sat open and available for the prince's perusing.

She watched, clamping her hand over her mouth, stifling a scream. Raask made a mockery of the whole thing and the Skierkans were loving it. He slowly picked up and inspected each weapon. He would find a supposed flaw and throw it to the side. When he had gone through the entire box, much to the crowd's delight, he turned back to the creatures. And like the great showman he was, he waited for the crowd to quiet down. His smile straightened and his eyes scanned the entire crowd from left to right before walking to the first cage. The goblin.

With a single glance, the blood began to pour out of his pores. Before the creature had even died, Raask continued to the cage of the sprite whose entire body began to balloon until it popped, successfully spraying blood across half of the stage. As Raask moved to the next cage of a humanoid creature that Mayta couldn't quite identify, she forced herself to look at the syren they had captured—they held her in a large, glass box, filled with water of the Dahs to keep her in syren form.

The girl met Mayta's eyes. It was Alletta. The daughter of one of their cooks who had gone missing over a year ago. Had she been among the Skierkans the entire time? Aria had investigated the disappearance, but even she hadn't come up with any answers for her family. It was believed she was killed by another creature of the Dahs.

"You numbed them?" Mayta asked Silia, her voice hardly loud enough to hear.

"Yes."

"Thank you." Raask stood in front of Alletta now. Mayta held her breath in anticipation. Alletta always had something quippy to say, *she had to say something to Raask*. She must have prepared something good, knowing that this moment was coming.

But it was not any harsh truths that raced across Alletta's tongue. Instead, heavy, venomous syren blood poured out of her mouth like a faucet. The waters within the glass box shifted from dark, Dahsian waters to a pool of thick, violet blood. Raask moved onto the next box. But Mayta's focus stopped there. Like a coward, Mayta hid in the trees while one of her people drowned in her own blood.

The rest of the murders went similarly.

Afterwards, the king placed a crown on Raask's head. Red jewels cascaded off the crown like drops of blood.

Mayta didn't pay much attention to any of it. Instead, she began to think. She began to plan. An unfamiliar rush of cold anger surged through her body, and from some part of her DNA that was ancient, she understood what needed to be done next.

CHAPTER 36
ARIA

Aria had completely lost track of the days and the nights.

The buzz of the lithe-infused castle walls that she had eventually become accustomed to while above ground, were driving her mad now that she was stuck underneath it all. The palace's overload of lithe felt like the yearly lightning storms at the end of the winter, that stayed for weeks on end over the Dahs. The constant buzz and darkness drove the sea creatures further into savagery.

Those dark waters were her domain, her home. She drew power from the water itself. So when it rained, even on the dry land, Aria could feel a slight surge in her own powers. The strength she could draw from the waters used to feel like a shot of adrenaline. Now, while underground and so very far away from a home she would never see again, the slight pulsation of her own magics during storms felt like how she imagined a painless hug would. Warm. Safe. Familiar. Maybe she could pretend . . . Would it be so bad? Would anyone know?

She laid down in the corner of the cell where the hard stones could cocoon her side and her head. She could almost hear the patter of the storm, the gentle roll of thunder, Mayta's tail swishing as she came to spend the storm with her. Would she ever see Mayta's tail again?

Oh Gods. Would she ever see her own tail again?

She could feel it in her memories. The cool water of the Dahs at her back as she surfaced for rainstorms. How she would bring her tail up to the surface, so every inch of her could feel the droplets of water. It was the only time her anger ever quieted down, during the lightning storms. Eventually Mayta would find her, her light, tail swooshes echoing against the waters beneath her. And for a brief moment, everything would be okay. For the briefest of moments, the Skierkans would be too scared to travel over their domain, and they would be safe. Safe enough to sing the songs of their people.

From far away in a dry dungeon, Aria began to hum to herself. The low melodic hum of the lullabies of their kind. Songs of vengeance. Songs of brutality. Songs of family. The very songs she would sing to little Mayta, when she would startle from a nightmare. And when the lullabies ended, she began to hum the songs of the syrens' history. Songs of the syrens' fury and wrath. Songs of their battles. Songs of their devotion to the ones they loved. They poured out of Aria like wine. She lost herself to the world inside of her head.

During the spring storms, she didn't know what it meant to be caged or to have the future of her kingdom resting on her shoulders. All she knew was the dance of the Dahs and the skies, and the songs that coursed through the veins of her people. And it was only in this private world that Aria allowed herself to cry. Like drops of rain, she felt the tears sliding down the side of her face.

She cried for herself and her imprisonment, for what was a syren with no access to water?

She cried for her sister who only ever wanted to find love and live a simple life with a family of her own.

She cried for her people who had been slaughtered and abused.

She cried for herself.

For the feelings she had developed for the man who had hunted her own kind. For the shame of loving him. And for the little part of herself, in the deepest part of her heart, that wanted to forget about the responsibilities of her kingdom and run off with *him*. The little, soft piece of flesh in her chest that had refused to ice over with the rest of her, it continued to beat.

Shame mixed with generations of fury had not been able to stomp out the sliver of warmth in her heart. Weeks of imprisonment had left it as fresh as it ever was before. Aria was beginning to worry that she was not entirely a cold-hearted creature, but maybe, a creature capable of love.

Nothing scared her more than this.

To be a creature that could love.

It was foolish. It was human. It was desperate. And it was opening herself up to hurting more—and Aria already hurt so very much. Her claws and fangs made her a weapon. Her childhood sharpened her talents, refining her into not a weapon, but *the* weapon that the syrens needed. And it was all falling apart because of a prince who saw the beast beneath her skin and cherished it. And he did. He adored her. She could see it in the commissioned weaponry. The way he always found his way to her side. The cinnamon breads he would bring her. And the gentleness in those dark nights when she'd awake from her nightmares.

Slowly, the black, storming clouds faded into the edge of her vision, revealing the harsh, stoned dungeon. The soothing waves of home stilled into the painful floor. And the salty rain drops revealed themselves to be what they always were.

She opened her eyes, ready to look head on into the emptiness. Ready to welcome, with open arms, the anger that felt so much better than the sadness. But it was not loneliness standing in the door of her cell, but *him*.

He was there and he was drenched in rainwater. His hair of sunlight dripped onto the cell below, brushed back in a way that suggested he still ran his hand through his hair when he was anxious.

But he wasn't meeting her eyes.

No. His gaze was far below her eyes.

Aria looked down, following the aching look in his eyes to see that in her fit of sadness and loneliness, she had left her womb of scars exposed. She tilted her head back up, to look at him once again. For several moments, the only sound was the drum of their own hearts accompanied by the *tinking* noise of Raask's water dripping onto the stone.

And then it all erupted.

The aching despair and heartbreak that had been written all over his face was replaced by a look of pure rage. "Who did this to you?" The words seethed from his teeth like a war song.

Aria bit back the obvious answer.

Raask stepped across the cell, diminishing the distance between them in seconds. And with hands gentler than she could ever imagine coming from the Prince of Skierka, he carefully observed her scarring. Aria didn't shrink back. She refused to be ashamed of it. Any of it.

Tired of biting her own tongue, she spat out the answer she knew he didn't want. "Wasn't it you who sentenced me to the dungeons, Prince?" Aria asked coldly.

She watched his throat, knowing his tell before it even happened. Raask swallowed, keeping his eyes on her. Aria knew the look well from him.

"Who did this?" He punctuated each word like a hammer.

She sat up. Slow enough to hide the fact that every time she moved, a wave of dizziness overcame her. Raask's eyes quickly scanned the rest of her, holding her up steadily with a soft grip. She hadn't fooled him.

"You're not eating."

A statement, not a question.

"What exactly do you think you're doing?" Aria asked, leaning her head back against the cool stone. "You can't throw me in a dungeon and show up baffled when I'm not thriving."

She watched for Raask to swallow again, sufficiently smug when he finally did.

"You know that it wasn't a choice, Aria. Now, if you won't tell me who did this, I'll have to find out for myself."

Her lips tightened into a straight line, eyeing him defiantly. Why was he here? Why did he care who cut her up? Didn't he know they were supposed to be enemies?

A familiar rage blazed across his face before he looked down and met her eyes. Heartbreak was all that was left of him.

"I didn't know you were being hurt, Aria. I told them to take good care of you. Bring you good food. Attend to all of your needs. They were supposed to bring down your harp." His voice broke at the word harp. Like everything was finally catching up to him.

As if to not frighten her, he slowly brought his head down to hers. His forehead pressed against hers so very gently and carefully, yet their eyes bore into each other with the intensity of a spring storm.

They had been two creatures of hatred. He may have drank and partied, but on the inside he was just as lonely and angry as she was. They were nothing but two creatures made of and by cruelty.

Two creatures that loved each other in a way that nobody, including themselves, could ever understand.

"I'm sorry." Raask breathed the words into her. "I do not know the correct answer to any of this." He hopelessly laughed, "I just keep trying to flip to the last page, to see if there's an answer key or a way out of it all." His hands held her sides firmly, as if checking to make sure that she was all still there.

"Aria, I —" His words cut off. He regained his composure and continued. "I succeeded in the third trial tonight. I will be king. I can make things different. I can make it a better world for you. For your kind."

She felt his aching honesty, his desperation, she felt his longing as it was, a cruel mirror to her own. Each word, a promise more than a prayer.

Shame rose in her like hot bile. Suddenly, she could feel her ancestors' eyes on her, their disappointment and disgust a tangible, sticky film that she was trapped within. She could not want this. She could not want him. Not after everything his family had done. After everything he had done.

He was a Morlok.

The Morloks had destroyed everything sacred to the syrens, slaughtered the nature and enslaved the creatures.

"Why would I want you?" She snarled. He was a Morlok. And at the end of the day, that's all that there was to it. Nothing he could do would ever change his blood.

He was a Morlok. And that was that.

Suddenly, his arms had dropped from her side, leaving her exposed and cold. The strength and determination written all over his fierce gaze had dampened into a sadness that she had no business feeling sorry for. A piece of her wanted to cry out and beg for him to go back to telling her how he would change the world for her. She wanted his arms around her again, keeping her safe and seen. She wanted him to stay. But she could not say it. She wasn't even supposed to be feeling it.

Raask dropped his gaze, running a hand through his wet hair. Aria watched as the drops of rain hit the cold floor. She watched as he stood and as he left her. She stayed watching the cell door long after he gently closed it behind him.

After that, every time she heard any noise, she would look up to the door waiting to see the prince with hair of sunlight. But it was never him. And even if he did come back, it wouldn't change the fact that her plan was for Raask to marry Mayta.

Mayta, her sister, who had loved Raask since she was young, who was the first to see him as the man with sunlight hair, she was to be his wife.

And Aria, well she was never really supposed to survive any of this anyway.

CHAPTER 37
RAASK

As he did every year on the anniversary of her death, Raask walked through the gardens and picked any flower he thought his mother might have liked.

His bouquet never looked nearly as nice as the ones the gardeners made when asked, but it was something he preferred to do for himself. As a child, he remembered watching her always pick flowers that matched the colors of the House of Morlok. It wasn't until after her death that he realized her own family's house colors were different from the Morloks'. His mother had come from the ancient house of Hawthorn: orange, brown, and copper. While Raask could recite the history of the Morlok lineage with accuracy from a young age, it wasn't until after she died that he learned anything about the Hawthorns. In the days since seeing Aria in the dungeons, he'd buried himself in studying his mother's family alongside training his blood magic with the Irridesci.

The air was crisp, and most of the leaves had already fallen off the trees by this time of the year. Flecks of golden and silver leaves decorated the floor of the Gaulic, occasionally reflecting the light of the sun and blinding him if he walked into their line of light.

His mother's family was once a prominent house of loggers, back when most houses were made of wood—and not the stone that was more commonly used for the past hundred years. He chuckled to himself, picturing his poised mother using an ax and cutting down a tree. The most labor he had ever known her to do was occasionally cut her own food when the servers were busy.

"What's so funny?" The painfully sweet voice of Mayta brought Raask out of his daydream and back into reality.

"Nothing." He continued walking, hoping that she would go back to whatever it was she was doing in the gardens.

Like the other toothaches he had had in the past, Mayta was proving to be quite difficult to get rid of. Raask did his best to storm off, ensuring his boots crashed loudly against the ground and he was fast enough to feel a slight breeze against his face.

Of course, she merely caught up to him and joined him, easily keeping up with his pace. After speaking with Viggo, Raask tried to be nicer to the girl. But he had been hurting for so long, it was hard for him to be around someone so sweet.

"Prince Raask! Please, I don't want to spill." She squeaked.

"Spill what?" Raask grunted. Annoyed, but not forgetting his original mission, he stopped and plucked the little blue flowers he remembered mother often having by her bed.

"Well, if you slowed down you would see for yourself, Prince Raask."

Raask nearly snorted, hearing the slightest hint of agitation from the Queen of Pep herself. It was humorous enough to cause him to stop and take a look at her. Her long red hair was braided as a crown on her head with little daisies poking out at all sorts of odd angles. Her dress was long and white, the bottom was clearly hemmed to accommodate her shorter height, but was still caked in dirt. And in her hands were two large traveling mugs of tawny.

"I didn't realize that you drank so much tawny. You ought to be careful, it stunts growth," Raask said.

"I think we're a little late to the height thing." She extended her hand and offered one of the mugs to him.

After a moment of hesitation, he took it. "Thank you."

"No problem! I saw you heading out to the gardens and I was getting another mug for myself anyways and it's just so Gods-damned cold outside. You really ought to drink something warm when walking around. Or at least that's what I think anyway."

Mayta took a large and loud gulp of her tawny, before looking at the mini bouquet Raask was holding stiffly in his palm. "You're picking flowers?" She asked.

"Yes." He reached behind Mayta, plucking a few white-and-red speckled flowers on a bush just behind her. He ignored the goose-bumps that arose on her skin when his hand brushed against her.

"What for?"

"I pick them before I visit my mother."

He could see in her face as she went through the stages of remembering that the Queen of Skierka had died ages ago. Her portrait, hung high above the main hall, was probably the most she had known of his mother, if she even noticed it.

"It's hard without a mother. I'm sorry for your loss." Mayta played with the sleeves on her arms. Raask took a moment to inspect her. He didn't know if others felt the same way, but whenever he met anyone else who had lost their mother he felt a sort of bonding feeling between them.

"Yes well . . . I ought to go now. Thanks again for the tawny." Raask ran a hand through his long, golden hair, brushing it out of his eyes and tucking it behind his ear so the harsh wind wouldn't keep pushing it into his face.

"Wait!" Mayta cried, loud enough for several garden gnomes to look up from their raking.

"What?" Raask looked around to make sure there was no masked rider or hidden syren princess among them.

Mayta grabbed the bouquet out of Raask's hand with surprising strength and began to rearrange the whole thing. By the time she was done, the bouquet looked like something his mother might have actually liked, even if he hadn't been the one to arrange the flowers.

When she was done, she handed it back to him and shrugged. "I just thought that she deserved the best, you know?"

She was a little too cloyingly sweet. Painfully happy. But maybe she wasn't so bad. And she was one of his people, someone he had a duty to protect and rule over. Raask smiled and bid her a thanks before walking off. He did not miss playing his role of the charming prince, but it was his duty. And just as always, everything would always come down to his duty and his people.

Raask shouldn't have been surprised to see that his brother had yet to bring anything to their mother's grave for yet another year. He didn't know why it bothered him so much that it seemed Viggo never truly mourned their mother, but it did hurt.

So when Raask met Viggo in one of the palace's many war rooms, he didn't hug him or greet him with a great cheer. The fire in the fireplace was roaring at obscene levels and Raask couldn't help but feel like the ceilings were slowly closing in on him. It only took about one or two minutes before Raask suggested they take the meeting out by the Spikes. He even came up with some lie about the importance of privacy away from prying ears of the castle, Viggo was kind enough to act like he didn't notice Raask's panic.

They were both tall with long legs so the walk that would normally take at least twenty minutes, took them less than ten. Most of it was spent with their heads down, bearing the cold and disavowing idle chit chat on the anniversary of their mother's death.

"Did you visit her today?" Raask finally got the nerve to ask as they approached the Spikes. He didn't miss the look of dread that crossed his brother's face, and was glad to see some kind of emotion on it. Even if it was dreadful.

"No. I . . ." He stumbled on his own words. Raask noticed for the first time how long his brother's hair was getting. He usually kept it short and trimmed, "better for battle" he always said. It was now nearly the same length as Raask's. From his meetings, he knew that the conquering of the Surtr Islands were finished, but it took seeing Viggo's hair growing out to realize that for the first time in ages, Raask was the prince of a kingdom that was not at war.

"I just don't see the point. She's not there anyways."

Raask grimaced. The idea that their mother was still there in some way was a comforting thought for him. He would often go and sit by her stone, talking to her. He didn't like thinking that she couldn't hear him anymore. It was bad enough that he couldn't hear her. And with Aria gone, his mother's grave was the one place he could go to no longer feel alone.

Viggo of course noticed. He had practically raised Raask. He knew him better than anyone else. There would be no emotion, no thought, no idea, that Raask could have that Viggo wouldn't somehow know. "But if it will make you feel better, we will go after this."

"Right." Raask smiled, telling himself to not forget to order food to-go from Padge, so Viggo and Raask could have dinner with their mother. She would have liked that.

"Anyways, you mentioned needing to meet with me privately. It sounded serious."

Viggo cleared his throat. A deep and gnarly sound that always meant Viggo was about to deliver bad news. "I would like your permission to seek the sistros."

He had to be joking. The sistros were nothing but a bedtime story, and a scary one at that. "Yes and while you're at it, make sure to keep your reservation with Kel in the underworld." Raask retorted.

"I'm being serious."

"And why would the general of our army be sent to look for three imaginary sisters?"

Viggo looked back at the Morlok Palace. His gaze stuck on the renovations to the destroyed areas of Raask's tower. "Something is going on, Raask. Can't you feel it? You've unlocked your magic now. Don't you smell the blood and the rot?"

"So we will hire more cleaners. Now will you stay?"

"It's not the town. It's the air. I know you know what I'm talking about. I see it on your face. In your eyes."

Raask *did* know what he was talking about, but he assumed it had been a part of his own blood magic awakening. He didn't know things were supposed to be any different.

"You think this has to do with the Gods?" He asked, unconvinced. He had always known Viggo was a religious man. He would often catch him praying or visiting temples as a child. But he wasn't aware that Viggo believed the sistros were real sisters that he could visit. It seemed awfully silly to him. But he could see it plainly written across Viggo's face that it was anything but silly to him.

"I do." His tone didn't leave Raask much room to make fun of him. "Raask, I think they foretold some kind of prophecy about . . . about us." The words seemed ridiculous to Raask, but Viggo's tone was scaring him. Was this just a ploy to get out of the white palace?

"Vi . . . You just got back." Raask leaned against one of the tall pillars of the Spikes. He didn't want Viggo to leave. But he couldn't ask him to stay . . . Gods, he wished that he would stay without having to ask, but because he just wanted to, on his own.

"I know. But I think this is really important. I wouldn't leave if it wasn't. I've been hearing things about this prophecy, and I think we need to find out from the sistros themselves."

Raask tightened his lips. If Viggo believed it to be important, it must be. "Okay well, you don't need to ask for my permission. I would never stop you from doing anything like that," Raask said. He straightened off of the pillar and brushed past Viggo, heading back to the castle.

Viggo's massive arm grabbed onto Raask's bicep, pulling him back.

"Raask, I would like you to come with me."

CHAPTER 38
VIGGO

"I've checked with the king, and he says that it would be fine for you to travel with us. *If* your services are needed here at the palace, he will send word." Viggo kept a firm grasp onto Raask's arm. It took everything out of Viggo to hide the smirk that was aching to creep across his lips, when he pretended to have to leave him.

"With *us*?"

"Yes, the circle will also be coming. But you'll get used to them."

Viggo's heart warmed as he watched Raask attempt to stifle his excitement. If it weren't for the war, he would have taken Raask on a trip long before this. It wasn't that Raask hadn't traveled around the Arkts. He'd traveled far more than most of the military recruits had, that was for damned sure. But as a prince, Raask had gotten used to a certain way of living. And as the future King of Skierka, their father had ensured that Raask was only taught a certain way of thinking. Helk, Raask believed Viggo actually slaughtered all of the Surtrians he had helped to save.

Raask still thought their mother had died of an illness. And that the king was also Viggo's father. There was a lot that Viggo hadn't told Raask yet. Too much.

But it was past time for Raask to know the truth. He was a man now. It was time for Viggo to begin treating him like one.

He made sure to hold good on his promise to visit their mother's grave after their talk. Now wasn't the time to tell him the truth about their mother's death. It was always hard keeping the truth from him, but especially on the anniversary of her death. Especially at her supposed grave site.

It was odd. It was painful. And it was tough to put on a convincing face in front of Raask.

But it was over soon enough. Raask had to run off to the engineers for some sort of custom communication device. Viggo waited for him to walk all the way into the palace, and then a few more minutes, before leaving the grave and heading to the edge of the Gaulic, back towards the Spikes.

He continued along the edge of the Gaulic until the tips of the gargoyles on the palace, and even the dark carved columns of the Spikes, were out of sight. His heavy boots sunk into the mud with each step.

It was starting to get dark by the time Viggo came across the gnarled tree with four stones tucked under its roots. The silence of the sprites and toads told him enough to know that she was already waiting for him.

"Took you long enough." As usual, Silia's voice came from above. Viggo didn't flinch as she jumped down from her hiding spot directly in front of him.

"I got caught up with a few things." Viggo inspected Silia for a brief moment before looking up towards the skies. "Where is she?" He asked, not bothering to hide his anger.

"Where do you think?"

Of course she didn't bother to show up. Like most wraithkin, Silia and her sister were unbelievably proud. "Tell your sister that if she doesn't show up to another meeting that I've scheduled, I'll march myself to the West and drag her down here. For Kel's sake, she's lucky I haven't ordered her execution after her massive screw-up."

Silia closed the small distance between the two of them. Although she was significantly shorter than Viggo, she stared him down as if she was three feet taller. "She. Lost. Her. Wraith." She stabbed her finger into Viggo's chest with each word.

He swallowed his anger but didn't command his shadows to recede. Thick swirls of his death magic wrapped around Silia like a vine, tugging her back and keeping her arms tucked securely at her sides.

"She was supposed to get Raask out of here." His eyes darkened.

"Well we weren't exactly expecting him to be protected by some syren princess, were we? Especially not when you were the one to approve her stay in the palace." Silia spat back.

Viggo commanded his shadows to loosen their grip on Silia. It was the same thought he'd replayed in his head since he learned the truth of Aria. Had it truly been so easy for her to trick him? He constantly wondered if she had used her syren magic on him, to make him feel that she was no threat, or if he'd simply seen a small, bloodied woman and been unable to see her as anything more than someone who needed protection.

A few of his shadows instinctively cradled themselves against his feet, in a weird comforting sort of thing that they would often do. "Is she okay?" He finally asked the question he probably should have asked ages ago— he'd been too focused on finding a new way to get Raask away from the king and his war-hungry nobles.

"She will be." Silia answered, her voice wavering. Viggo knew enough about Silia to know that she considered her love for her sister, along with her wraithkin heritage, to be her greatest secret. As far as he knew, Viggo and the twins were the only non-wraithkin who were aware of her heritage and sister. He never knew if she had a wraith, or if she had one that was lost. It seemed too personal of a question to ask someone who went to great lengths to ensure that nobody knew anything about her past.

"I always thought wraithkins died when their bonded wraiths did."

Silia snorted. "A misunderstanding. When a wraithkin says that, we are referring to our souls. It's like losing the ability to laugh and to cry and to scream all at once. We don't die, and we eventually recover. But it's traumatizing."

Skullin's Scythe, Viggo knew that there was a unique connection between rider and wraith. But he didn't know that it went soul deep. He leaned back against the tree. Viggo was exhausted. He was past exhausted. For the past two decades of his life he'd been at war. His plans were constantly getting busted. And he kept failing them.

Oh Gods, he kept failing them. The Skierkans. The Surtrians. Emir. Skender. Silia. Silia's sister. Raask. He was failing and if it was just him that he was failing, it would be one thing. But he couldn't live with himself knowing that he was one of the only people in the Arkts with the power to overthrow the King of Morlok, and he hadn't yet.

He wasn't ready yet.

Nothing was ready yet.

He had to get Raask away from it all. He had to show Raask how the rest of the world lived. How other kingdoms took care of their subjects—and not just the wealthiest nobles—so Raask could create a better Skierka after Viggo wiped the curse of the Morloks off the map. He had to raise funds for his army. He had to find foreign support. He was so behind and getting stuck further behind, every day. He was failing them. He was failing them. He was failing them.

"It's not your fault, Viggo."

Silia, who was the least comforting person in the realm, awkwardly patted his shoulder. Viggo couldn't help but laugh at her attempt at support.

But then a twig snapped. Impulsively, his shadows pushed him and Silia back, effectively burying them into the darkness of the forest.

Eyes wide, Viggo relaxed into his shadows, bracing his magic in case things were about to become ugly. Loud, sloppy footsteps splashed across the forest floor. A reddish cloud of rank stench hit Viggo and Silia before they could even see their suspects. The thick combination of rotten eggs and bile made it nearly impossible to breathe. It took everything out of them to not start coughing and gagging. The heavy, red fog was moving quickly. It seemed to come from the direction of the palace and moved at a surprisingly fast pace.

The fog was getting denser as it moved its center closer to Viggo and Silia. Its stench grew with each passing second. Their eyes, watery from the combination of the rank and dense unnatural fog, almost missed the twisted leg of the man.

The twisted leg led to a gnarled body that seemed to barely hold onto the gashed skull of a man. Or a former man. Or a creature. Viggo couldn't quite tell just yet.

More came. They only became visible when they were close enough to feel their hot breath.

Some looked as if they had been skinned. Some of the bodies had obviously been torn apart and re-stitched together. They all stank. They all moved surprisingly fast for such obviously tortured creatures. And their eyes . . . Their eyes shone marbled red and black.

Something caught their attention, just a few feet from where Viggo and Silia hid. Viggo's shadows confirmed that one of them had caught a couple of sprites making love.

His shadows directed his gaze to the creature who managed to capture the sprites. Viggo watched as he clenched their tiny bodies into a tight fist and shoved their heads into his mouth. Their screams were replaced with the sounds of breaking bones. The ones surrounding him began to take more notice. They charged at him, fighting over the lifeless bodies of the sprites. They tore each other's arms off and bit huge patches of skin off of one another, while fighting for the sprites. When the last piece of sprite had vanished into their guts, they quit fighting and instantly resumed their stalk.

"What are they?" Silia asked, voice barely comprehensible.

"I don't know." Viggo admitted.

Viggo watched as another caught a rabbit, and they fought over the carcass like sickly dogs.

"Do you trust me?" Asked Viggo.

"Barely."

Viggo retrieved a dagger from his sleeve. He cut a line across his palm, drawing blood to the surface. He clenched his fist, allowing the blood to swell and drip.

The creatures halted. They twisted their heads in all sorts of directions in jittery movements. They began to tear apart the bark on the trees and the roots from the ground. The scent of his blood had sent them into a frenzy. And that alone told him everything he needed to know about the creatures.

"Let's have some fun." He smiled and removed the shelter of his shadows, unsheathing his sword, as he revealed himself and Silia to the creatures.

The creatures were on top of them in an instant. In mere seconds, a handful of the creatures had surrounded Silia and Viggo. After a few more seconds, dozens more creatures of meshed flesh trampled over to them.

Viggo felt the warmth of Silia at his back vanish, and in the recesses of his subconscious, he noted the sound of the leaves being disturbed and the whine of her arrows being unsheathed. Silia had always preferred to kill from afar when possible. She didn't like being close to the action, and she didn't like the spurts of blood that came from killing.

Viggo on the other hand, relished in it. He thrived in the bloodshed. He was a creature of death after all, and in battle he could feel a sensation that could only be described as his own blood gleefully welcoming death's presence. He cut through the creatures like a seamstress through soft cotton. He wielded his blades like a master painter, seeing the aftermath of his every move and anticipating the actions of the creatures, like it was all a book that he had read before. A slash here. A cut there. An elbow. A kick. A stomp. His death magic surged beneath his skin, amplifying his speed and strength until he was nothing but a blur of darkness.

Only a few of the creatures were left by the time the thrill of battle had peaked. The death in his veins begged to finish them off, but a warning shot from Silia zoomed just past his nose, alerting him to slow down. At least one, maybe two, should be left functional enough for questions.

Viggo unleashed his shadows onto the remaining handful of creatures. Although Silia was silent, he felt her presence approaching him from behind and knew she stood waiting just a few paces back. His shadows darted across the forest, crawling up the creatures' legs and into the mouths and noses until they were nothing but an empty husk. Two of his shadows came back, dragging creatures behind them. Once the shadows reached their master they halted, awaiting Viggo's orders. It was only then that Silia closed the space between them, announcing her presence with a purposeful crunch of leaves under her foot.

They both watched the creatures silently groan as they lay restrained by the shadows. One had an arrow still sticking out of its neck, just an inch off from the throat.

"Do you mind?" Silia asked.

Viggo shook his head. They had won enough battlefields to have a routine already in place. His shadows knew it, waiting only for Viggo's command.

Go ahead. He told them from his mind. Upon the order, the shadows of the forest began to retrieve Silia's arrows and piling the bodies of the departed.

"Who are you?" Viggo asked, although after observing the creatures, he had a fairly good idea that they wouldn't be able to respond. He doubted that they even understood his words.

"Where do you come from?" Viggo asked again.

No answer.

"Alright, you're up." He nudged Silia closer to the half-rotted creature.

"Hey, buddy," she kicked his leg. "I once killed a man with one of those tiny spoons for fancy tea. If you don't start talking I'll show ya exactly how I did it." When the creature still didn't respond beyond a moan, Silia stomped her boot against his ankle. The crack of his bones snapping echoed across the area, causing the shadows to halt momentarily.

"Alright, search him." Viggo ordered.

"Me?" She wrinkled her nose in disgust. "Why me?"

"Because I'm the general here and these things smell worse than a goblin's ass."

Unhappy, but surprisingly obedient to Viggo, Silia began to search the bodies. The leg she stomped on fell off the rest of the body like a roast and smelled like some shit-eating creature had been left to rot in the Surtrian sun for weeks.

The only thing that they found was a red brand on the back of their necks. A lovely and intricate M with loads of pretentious swirls. A slave's brand. The Morlok's own personal slave brand, more specifically. Viggo shuddered as he realized where exactly these twisted creatures had come from. And even he, the Skierkan Bruin and son of Death itself, felt goosebumps along his back as he wondered what other kinds of experiments were kept hidden far beneath the white palace.

It appeared that Viggo had a lot more work to do, and less time than ever to get it all done.

After his shadows confirmed that each body bore the mark of Morlok, he ordered them to dump the bodies into the Dahs and hide the evidence of an attack in the wood.

Viggo's mind raced as he and Silia walked back towards the palace. What would have happened if they hadn't been there to stop the creatures? What was the king planning on doing with the blood-thirsty creatures of mangled flesh he was creating? And the question that he hadn't dared to vocalize, even within his own mind, began to gnaw at him . . . If he were to take Raask away from the teachings of the king, in hopes of a better future for Skierka and the entirety of the Arkts, well then . . . who would be left in Etra to protect the Skierkans who were already here? The ones who are already suffering and the ones who would be the first to go unprotected?

For if Viggo and his loyal guard were to show Raask a kinder world, would there be anyone left in Etra who cared enough to protect those who couldn't afford gates and guards?

What if taking Raask away from the king saved himself and his brother and the family he had found in his guard, but also doomed the rest of his kingdom?

CHAPTER 39
MAYTA

Nobody ever questioned why Mayta offered to help. It never seemed out of place for her to provide assistance to anyone who may have needed it. No one would ever question why Mayta, a woman of assumed nobility, began to help in the kitchen and in the gardens. She was a sweet girl and that was what sweet girls were meant to do.

Therefore, nobody ever questioned what Mayta had been working on in the poisons area of the gardens. They all figured she was simply helping. She was simply being a good girl. Nobody ever considered that maybe she was capable of more than sweetness and kindness. They never, for even one second, considered that she intended to use the poisons.

Mayta was beautiful. She had long, golden red hair and evergreen eyes with eyelashes that could bat away even the wickedest of storms. She was naturally kind. Animals and babies instantly took a liking to her. Her voice was soft and gentle like a bumblebee's wings against a petal. Mayta had a kind heart. She would always have a kind heart. But that didn't undo what lay in her blood.

She thought it would be harder to get the prince to drink and eat her little gifts than it was. She didn't even have an excuse to give him the laced tawnies or breads most of the time. She would just hand it to him as if she was a silly girl looking to make the prince happy, and he didn't blink an eye at the idea.

It pissed her off of course. But it was an integral part of her getting away with it, for she was going to kill the Crown Prince of Skierka. And to kill a prince and get away with it, well, it wouldn't hurt to have the nobility be too naive to suspect a sweet girl like her.

Fools. Idiots. Monsters. Aria was right. The humans were cruel. They believed they were superior to not only all other species, but even to the other humans hailing from other regions. At least the different syren clans lived harmoniously among one another. Humans would slaughter each other without a second thought, citing irrelevant and stupid reasons like different facial structure or coloring, or the area of the Arkts they had come from. Nothing was too small for them to believe that it made them better than others.

Mayta couldn't rule over them. She wouldn't. They were not the sweet creatures she once believed them to be. To kill a creature you start with the head. The same goes for kingdoms. And without access to the king, the next best thing was Raask.

Mayta had been poisoning Raask in small dosages, gradually growing larger with each glass of tawny and plate of food. She became friendly with the kitchen workers, cooks, and Padge. She had become a kitchen regular with ease, securing access to the prince's meals. It had been so simple. So easy. The hard part would be getting away with it.

She still hadn't decided if she should take credit for her kill. The syrens wouldn't be able to survive a full-on war with Skierka. They had been enslaved for generations. Weakened. Hurt. Their numbers were low. And while they had been preparing a secret army, it wasn't ready and their fearless general who would be the only one able to possibly lead them into victory, was currently chained in the dungeons underneath the Morlok Palace. Maybe it would be best to simply kill off Raask and the Morloks and discreetly disappear back to the Dahs.

It wouldn't be long now.

His muscles would slowly weaken. He would confuse easily. His vision would blur. He would grow more trusting, easy to influence. And the tell-tale sign that death was near would be the cough and the paralysis. The scientists back home had spent ages developing a poison undetectable to humans. Untraceable. A combination of a warhic toad's sweat and syren blood. They said that once the paralysis set in, it would be mere minutes before the heart would finally give up.

She sat with the other women of the court, watching him sparring. She giggled and blushed at all the correct times. If she wasn't careful to remind herself of who these people were, and what they had done to her people, she would find herself accidentally liking the women of the court. They could be silly. They were often fussing about their outfits and hair and cosmetics. But she noticed that many of them simply relied on this to keep their high standing in the court, in other words, to keep their families' bellies full.

They made smart comments often too. It was from these women that Mayta learned that not everyone within the court necessarily agreed with the conquering of the Surtrian Islands. She learned that things as simple as a seating chart or a well-prepared menu could create great changes in policy. When the women wanted a deal to go well, they knew to serve warm, rich, and flavorful—but not spicy foods. For a deal they wanted to sour, they simply served cold foods made from the cheaper produce, with just a little too much salt. The men of the court never seemed to notice, but it often worked.

Mayta guessed that she *did* like the women. But she did also hate them.

They stood by as their men went to slaughter innocents. Hunt her people.

It was a confusing feeling, to like the women who ruled the nation responsible for so much grief. Mayta didn't like to think about it too often. It made her feel as if she had drunk too much of a soup that wasn't sitting right in her belly. Especially after she had started poisoning the prince.

Deep in her blood and her soul, she knew she was doing the right thing. Her ancestors would be so proud of her and Aria for killing a Morlok. Retribution at last. But sometimes, when she was with the women of the court, or the kitchen servants, she would wonder what would happen to them. The ones in Skierka who didn't have as much of a say in the slaughtering of the innocents. Did they deserve to die too? Because they stood by when their kingdom tortured her's? Who truly was innocent in all of this, and did innocence even really matter?

Maybe she did in fact eat too much soup that wasn't sitting right with her, now that she thought about it. Her belly rolled and grumbled, causing a few of the women to look at her strangely. Mayta excused herself, cheeks reddening from the embarrassment.

She rushed out of the training grounds and headed back towards the palace. The last of the fallen silver and gold leaves crunched beneath her incredibly impractical silk boots. She watched each step, careful to avoid any wet patches of soil amongst the decomposing leaves and branches. Winter was to begin any day now.

Her feet stamped delicately and quickly. She was almost at the door before she finally looked up to see a humongous flank of guards and the blonde, medical woman with a few of her students. This many guards and the leader of the medical chambers could only mean that the king was not far behind.

Her stomach flopped into a sinking sensation in her guts.

Without thinking, she took off to hide behind that awful tower. She couldn't face the king, not with a stomach of rolling vipers. She had only seen him a handful of times, and had always retched into the toilets after. He had this presence to him that made her sick. The air around him smelled of moths and dirt. Like an ancient power. And it always took her back to that awful flame he'd conjured on the night he came for the syren rebellions. No syren had ever seen that kind of flame before. It struck from above, like lightning without the rain, and it smelled of scorched hair. Syren bodies didn't typically float after death, they sank to the bottom of the waters and would eventually fade back into the seas from which they came.

The bodies floated on the day the Morlok King came.

She never figured out why. She never really asked why either.

Their mangled bodies burnt to the core. Their insides on their outsides.

She couldn't see the king. Not right now. She had to be brave for what she had been doing. And when she came into contact with the king, when she was simply in the same room as him, she became the little girl who saw too much.

As fast as her human legs could carry her, Mayta rushed to the tower. It had a similar scent and dark aura as the king, but at least it didn't come with the memories—and didn't require her to bow. In fact, it even made a decent place to hide. Or, it would have, if the king's eldest son hadn't already been using it for evidently the same thing.

Mayta ran straight into his torso. Her head collided with his chest, causing her to see stars. He felt like a thick tree or a stone wall . . . or a wall of muscle that smelled deliciously of smokey sandalwood, hot musk, and sweet amber.

"What are you doing here?" She whisper-yelled.

Viggo snorted. The ends of his mouth creeping up into a forbidden smile. "I bet the same thing that you're doing here."

"You're tending to the mushrooms?" Mayta asked. It was the only reason she could come up with for why she'd be by the Gods-awful tower of the Irridesci.

Viggo laughed. A sound slick of oil and honey. If her stomach wasn't already rolling, she might have noticed how his training leathers seemed to perfectly hug his massive arms and sculpted chest. Oh Freyite, even with her stomach doing spins she couldn't help but notice his legs were as thick as tree trunks.

He leaned against the tower, looking Mayta up and down. "No, I'm hiding from the king." After a beat he added, "among others."

Mayta smiled up at him between her thick lashes. "Well then you're wrong, because I'm only hiding from the king."

"I see. And why exactly are you hiding from the king?"

"I'm not feeling particularly social today."

His eyes narrowed in mock concern. "You? You are not feeling particularly social today? The girl who walked into the palace as a complete stranger and instantly made friends with every single person in the building? The girl who constantly has a trail of sprites or goblins or other little critters following her in adoration?"

She couldn't help but blush. "I don't think critters follow me around." She jokingly looked behind her, checking for a line of ants or mice. Unfortunately, there *was* a teeny air sprite hiding behind a mushroom that was carefully watching her.

"So, why are you hiding from your father? Trouble amongst the Morloks without any innocents to slaughter?"

She immediately wished she could swallow up her words like a hungry sea wraith. But it was too late. His smile had disappeared, and in its place was the sad look that she was all too familiar with. It settled on his face with ease.

"I . . . I don't know why I said that." She protectively crossed her arms against her chest, feeling ashamed. "I'm sorry." She added after another heavy moment of pause.

"It's fine." Viggo twisted his neck out from behind the tower, looking to see if the king had left. The sounds of carriage doors closing and horses stomping told her the same news. The coast was clear.

"I'll see you around, Mayta." Viggo called, not bothering to look back at her before going back towards the palace. She didn't bother saying goodbye, she doubted he would hear her anyways with how far he walked in those few seconds.

Viggo was undoubtedly upset by her comment. The Skierkan Bruin. Upset. About killing. It didn't add up to Mayta.

She had heard stories about his prowess at war, even when she was still under the Dahs. Ships of sailors and merchants all told stories of their fearless general. He was a living legend in Skierka. Maybe even the entirety of the Arkts.

Aria was a living legend among their kind. She was smart and ruthless. A born killer. She took pride in each and every one of her kills. She would never grow solemn over speak of her massacres, no, whenever they were brought up, she would straighten and even smile.

Viggo was definitely upset by her comment about his killings.

Mayta waited a few more minutes before running out of her hiding spot. The tuft of air at her ankles let her know that the little sprite followed her up until she entered the palace. She ran up to her room, took a long, hot bath, and crawled into her luxuriously soft bed, ready to indulge herself in an outrageously cozy nap.

Her blankets—some miracle combination of velvet and hot butter—curled around her entire body like a light cocoon. Her pillow, perfectly fluffed and cool, cradled her head like a baby. And her skin loved the decadent lotions almost as much as her nose did.

But she couldn't get Viggo's pained look out of her head. It just didn't add up. Why would a master of battle look so . . . ashamed?

It was dark by the time Mayta gave up on her nap. Her stomach growled, no longer hurting from her lunar cycles, and instead very focused on the idea of eating a rare steak with gravy and mashed potatoes.

After taking care of her bladder, she grabbed a pair of comfortable silk trousers with a black lace trim and a matching camisole. Over that, she threw on a dove-white robe with a long train that looked semi-presentable, in case anyone else was wandering the castle for a late night snack or romp or whatever the nobility did at such odd hours.

She didn't bother treading lightly as no one else stayed in this wing of the castle, anyways. By now, she knew the path to the kitchens like the scales of her tail. It didn't take too long before she made it there. Padge had already gone to sleep of course, but a bare bones crew worked at night in case anyone became peckish—or if they had traveled from afar. The usual late night spread of sweets and breads were all placed in crystal bowls. Many were decorated with images of fire or ravens, in homage to the Morloks. The sight of the cinnamon sweets tugged at her heart for a moment, bringing her mind to the sister who'd sacrificed everything.

She shook the thoughts off and requested the materials to cook her steak and mash on her own. The servants, as expected, insisted on making the meal for her. With a heavy sigh, she let them make the mash and gravy, but insisted on cooking her own steak. No one did it quite like her, that was for sure.

The only steak they had unthawed from the ice-lithed rooms, was massive. Easily enough to feed a family of four. Instead of cutting it up, she figured she would share with the staff, so more people than just herself could enjoy her cooking.

She lost herself in the trance of cutting up the garlic and onions. Under the sea she had always loved to cook. The syrens often would cook in the air caverns, alighting fires with the help of the syrens blessed with fire magic. A common magic among their kind. Another reason the Morlok King wished to obliterate them so thoroughly. How would his fire magic look so spectacular when it was so common among the syrens? His solution was to commit mass genocide against her kind. It did make sense in a twisted sort of way, why he would want to spread lies about her people, and drive a hatred against the syrens.

The onions and garlic hit the hot oil, immediately perfuming the air. She threw in a sprig of rosemary and heavily salted the steak while those flavors all meddled together in the pan. When Mayta finally placed the steak into the pan, it sizzled and smoked nicely. With a wooden spoon, she began to drip the flavored oil back onto the top of the steak while the bottom cooked. After only a few seconds, she flipped the steak. Another perfect sizzle, accompanied by the ideal crisp of a rare steak.

Mayta, like most syrens, liked her meat exceptionally rare. Most syrens would generally eat the meat raw, diced finely with a chip of seaweed or sea cucumber. She liked to crisp up the outside and keep the inside as raw as possible. A smile crept across her face at the satisfaction of making a perfect steak.

"That smells divine." She knew the voice immediately. A low rumble. A luxurious oil. A honeyed spoon. Viggo.

"It is." Mayta answered, placing the steak onto an ornate wooden cutting board with rivets to hold the juices.

She heard his footsteps, heavy with his training boots, approaching her. "Will you be eating that entire thing yourself?"

She walked over to the gravy pot and gave it a completely unnecessary stir, avoiding turning around to face him. "And if I am?"

"Well, I'd be quite impressed." She could hear the faint smile across his lips. After everything in the kitchen had been given a good stir, she finally turned around and looked at him.

He looked even better all mussed from bed than dressed up in his finery.

His black trousers hung low across his hips, revealing the deep v of his muscular torso. His long-sleeved shirt looked soft, and hugged his muscular arms in all the right places. And his eyes . . . well they were clearly amused by her not-so-subtle checking out of his body.

She blushed a shade not so far off from her hair and quickly turned back to the steak that she decided had rested enough and was ready to slice into.

"See something you like?" She heard from behind her.

Mayta's eyes widened at his comment. She'd never have thought he'd say something so brazen. From what she'd seen, he had always been the reserved and quiet type with a particularly brooding and angry face to go alongside his quietness. She had to think of something clever and quick to say back in this game. "Yes, a perfectly cooked steak." She smiled at her own ingenuity. Aria would have found that comment to be quite funny.

He came to stand next to her, and watched as she cut into the steak. "I think 'cooked' is a little bit of a generous word for what that is." He replied, brows furrowing while carefully inspecting the rare steaks.

She twisted to face him. "Don't tell me you're one of those psychos who like their meat cooked as gray and as hard as a boot!"

"If you had to eat mostly out of a war camp's kitchen your whole life, you'd want your meat cooked through, too." He accepted a warm glass of tea that smelled of cinnamon and cloves from one of the servants. She hadn't even recalled him asking for it in the first place.

Mayta twisted her face in disgust at the thought of the nasty food he must have eaten throughout the years. She thought the food at the palace itself wasn't quite appetizing, and couldn't imagine how it could taste even worse. "But you're the son of the king, the general, didn't you have a caravan of fancy cooks and servants following you around?"

Viggo nearly spat up his tea while laughing. "A caravan of servants at a war camp? Skullin's Scythe, you've got some imagination." He chuckled again, low and warm, evidently picturing the well-dressed and polished servants of the palace navigating a war camp. "No. I make it a point to eat with my men. Drink with my men. Listen to them. What I ask them to do... it wouldn't be right to act as if I was above them."

Mayta began plating her steak, potatoes, and gravy. She made enough plates for the servants, herself, and Viggo. The idea of the fearsome Skierkan General dining with his men on gnarly war camp food made her think of the syrenien picture books she had loved so much as a child. She wondered if the general was fighting for anyone in particular, when he was off at war. But in the books the armies had always fought for a noble cause, and when they won the maiden's heart at the end, they would live happily ever after. From what Mayta had seen, most men of nobility within Skierka kept many mistresses and treated their wives as little more than servants.

"Are you not though?" She meant the question, was he as she had been told.

"What?"

"Above them."

Once she was done plating, she handed the servants' plates to them and grabbed hers and Viggo's to eat outside the loud kitchens. He took the plates from her and followed her lead out to the stone tables in the gardens. Mayta couldn't help but notice that the swagger he had come in on had disappeared, and left in its place was a slow, purposeful walk instead. "You truly believe that the nobility are more important than their citizens?"

It was late enough into the night that only the light of the silver moon shone across the gardens. The indigo moon would be coming up soon.

"I assumed the Morloks believed that." She answered honestly.

"You don't think very highly of me, do you?" Viggo asked, watching her take a massive bite out of the bloody steak.

Warning bells rang in Mayta's head at the question. She'd gotten too comfortable with Viggo. She had to remember that not only did her and her sister's lives depend on their plan going well, but so did the lives of her people. The safety of their descendants. And the pride of their ancestors.

It didn't come naturally to her to plan and scheme. She had always acted on her heart's whims. She'd always been the light and loving princess, a beacon of hope. Once Aria had told her that she was glad Mayta was naturally gentle in demeanor, or else she would have to fake it. Aria had said it was important that one of them had a reputation for brutality, and that would always be her. But it was maybe even more important, that the syrens had a symbol of what their descendants *could* be. What a life without hardships would create within their lineage. A child of love and light.

But with Aria in shackles, Mayta didn't think that her people needed a symbol of hope. They needed a revolution. Mayta needed to be more like Aria—the strong one that her people needed—while her sister could not. And after all was said and done, she would have to find a way to live with herself, if there was anything left of her by then.

"You are the great Skierkan Bruin. Why would I think anything negative about you?" She batted her big lashes and allowed a sparkle of her syrenic abilities to shine through and create an allure, a desire.

She could feel Viggo's scrutinizing gaze. Feel his tension and confusion. Instantly, she became aware of the fact that Viggo knew her very well already. And if she were to start this game later than the rest, Viggo would not be an easy one to convince. He knew her heart already, and it would not be easy to convince him otherwise.

He took a bite out of the rare steak. "You don't have to eat that, I know you like it rubbery." Mayta muttered in between bites, feigning humility. She could be very humble, but not about her cooking.

He finished chewing his first bite and smiled. "It's really good, May."

"Yeah?" She smiled. She couldn't help it. Any compliment or kind word or verbal pat on the back, had always brought out an easy smile onto her face.

"Yeah, it is." They continued eating the rest of their meal in silence. It was only after they had both finished, and dropped off their clean plates into the kitchens, that they stood in the great hall of the palace just staring at each other.

Viggo was the first to break the silence. "Have you ever considered that there may be more to me than the stories they tell?"

She wasn't sure how to answer his question. If she was being truthful, with both him and herself, she would say that she couldn't handle thinking about the Morloks as more than the monsters that took everything from her and her people. It was too hard. Too complicated to see the monsters as the people they were beneath. Not since the final trial at least. But she couldn't admit any of that.

So instead, she asked the question that had bothered her since back on that rickety boat on the Dahs. "Why is it so important to you that I like you?"

She watched as his shoulders suddenly tensed at the question.

His knuckles turned white at his sides, and he quickly looked down to the cold stone floor. When he finally looked back up at her, he ran a hand through his chin length black hair. "Goodnight, May."

He gave her a nod and turned around, moving quickly up the stairs towards his chambers, leaving her standing alone in the frigid great hall of the palace. Her breath caught in her chest as she watched him ascend the stairs. An ache in her chest. A glimmer of something. A flash of not wanting him to leave so soon.

When he reached the top, she couldn't help herself from whispering a single demand. A question really. A test even. A single word.

"Wait." A begging question and angry demand all rolled into one quiet whisper in a far too cold room. Passion and confusion and an aching desire. Reams of anger and hatred. And last of all—hope. All said with that one word, that one plea not only to Viggo but to the belief in humanity, and goodness, for there *had* to be some kind of goodness even within the darkest of men.

The singular word, an arrow in the midst of a ceasefire, hit its target, and Viggo's body stilled on the last step.

Mayta's eyes, green as the first grasses of spring, frantically searched the back of his body for any clue as to what the formidable Skierkan Bruin was thinking.

CHAPTER 40
RAASK

Raask had developed the habit of silently walking down to the dungeons and listening to Aria. Tonight, he could tell that she was asleep by her slight snoring.

He came at random times at night, and he hardly ever heard her sleep. He was glad to know she was finally resting, but a part of him had ached to hear her songs. He rarely heard her singing, but on the nights she did sing, he could close his eyes and pretend that he was listening to her sing from the other room.

After a while, he forced himself up. He needed to get up early to continue training with the troops, and for a long day of meeting with the other nobility. His feet moved silently up the stairs, carefully avoiding the louder steps out of the dungeon, and he made his way to the kitchens.

The servants offered him a piece of a rather rare slab of beef that they seemed to be enjoying. But not in the mood for a hunk of meat, Raask opted for two thick slices of the fresh bread with a heavy spread of fresh butter, along with a hot cup of tea. He took his first bite of the hearty bread in the great room where the light of the indigo moon was just beginning to settle.

It was his favorite time of evening. As a boy, he would often sneak into the great hall to see how the paintings and tapestries with all the Morlok red would change into a radiant purple.

He took a long last look at the blue-filled great hall, before walking out the back door to the gardens. He was to meet with the Irridesci tonight in their tower and practice honing his blood magic. As he walked through the gardens towards the towers, his steps remained nearly silent thanks to his new wraith-skinned pointed boots. Silently, he looked down at them, appreciating the fine crafts-manship that went into creating such fine boots. They were pointed, as was the style of the younger Skierkans, but strong and durable. They said the wraith skin could deflect most blades while remaining light enough to jog in.

Perhaps, he thought, he should commission an outfit of wraith skin for Viggo. Viggo's would need to have a reinforced toe though, the man loved to deliver devastating kicks while sparring. He assumed he did the same in battle, although he couldn't be sure since he obviously had never been in an actual battle with the man.

Raask cocked his head up, looking back and deep into the gardens. He could have sworn he heard a giggle . . . He peered down into the direction of the roses, trying to place the source of a giggle so close to the Irridesci tower, so late into the evening.

There.

A flash of red, now slightly purple-tinted, hair.

Mayta.

And yes, next to her, the tall and brooding creature that was his brother. They looked physically close. They looked . . . happy even.

She giggled again.

Evidently, his brother was being quite funny.

Raask watched with a gentle smirk across his face, as his big brother attempted to woo the woman who had caught the attention of half the court already. Viggo had never really shown much interest in women, and to Raask's knowledge, Viggo had never chased after a girl before.

Suddenly feeling self-conscious about watching his older brother in a moment he was certain he wouldn't want him to see, Raask decided he would only watch one more minute before meeting with Balk and his team of torturers.

Yet, there was no way he could turn around now. It looked like Viggo was picking a flower for Mayta. A red rose! How classic.

And . . . she loved it. Of course she did. Raask silently chuckled to himself as he watched Viggo and Mayta together. She held so tightly to the rose that Viggo gave to her, as if it were a teddy bear. They seemed so sweet. He didn't know Viggo was capable of being so kind and doting.

Oh.

It looked like she may have held too tight to the rose and some drops of blood dropped to the ground beneath. Oh Gods . . . The blood somehow got onto that little sprite that had been following Mayta around, poor thing. Sprites' sense of smell were known to be very strong, the poor thing must feel like it's drowning in her blood with just those few drops.

Oh.

The sprite seemed to be in pain! It started to screech!

Eyes wide, Viggo stared at the sprite. Mayta was yelling, trying to catch the sprite and wipe the blood off of it. But why did her blood burn the poor sprite?

Without thinking, Raask walked forward a few steps. It was only when he got closer to the messy scene that he noticed that her blood didn't just appear purple from the light of the indigo moon. It was truly purple.

Mayta's blood was purple. Her blood killed a sprite.

Without any form of plan or sense of thoughts, Raask rushed down to where Mayta and Viggo stood over the lifeless body of the sprite.

"You . . ."

He couldn't get the words out.

Not again.

How foolish was he? How much of a fool could he be?

"You're a syren, too."

CHAPTER 41
VIGGO

Viggo Morlok, the general of the most feared army in the entire Arkts, for the first time in a long time, was scared.

Not for himself. No, he could handle himself. But for this delicate creature in front of him.

He'd known what she was, although he didn't admit it to himself. Not even in his own thoughts did he allow himself to put the words together that Raask just had.

Mayta was a syren.

A syren. A wicked creature that the king had encouraged the Skierkans to hunt. A sea creature who could inherently sense desire, who could create an irresistible allure. A killer. Perhaps.

And just as syrens could detect desire and lust, Viggo could sense dread. Fear. Darkness. Mayta didn't have any darkness in her soul. She was purehearted, he was certain of it. She represented everything good and kind, and everything that he fought for and would continue fighting for.

"I don't know what you're talking about!" Her voice, too high, too shrill.

It was too late. Raask saw the blood, saw it sizzle the skin and muscles off of the poor sprite. The smell of burnt flesh was still in the air when Raask tackled Mayta. She went down easily. Weren't syrens supposedly strong? Why was it so easy for Raask to take her down?

Her head fell, hitting a stone in the dirt. More purple blood began to slick the ground beneath. "Raask." The word came out so help-lessly. A mirror to Mayta's earlier plea.

Raask turned her over, her face in the dirt. Thorns, mud, and blood smudged across her sweet face. And tears.

Mayta looked up at Viggo, and she didn't beg him to make Raask stop. She just looked up at him with her big, green eyes. Bruised and swollen. Tears began to mix with the blood and mud that blurred her face. And Raask was yelling. He might have been yelling the whole time. Viggo wasn't sure.

He wasn't sure of anything, except that Mayta was trying to say something, but the dirt was in her mouth and Raask was hurting her. He was holding her hair and pushing her face into the dirt, and Viggo could tell that he was hurting her.

He saw her lips move. Couldn't hear anything. But he recognized the pattern of her lips.

"I'm sorry," she said.

Something in Viggo snapped.

Suddenly, he was not himself. Or at least not inside of his own body, but a spectator floating above the scene.

He tackled Raask. Raask, who hadn't expected his big brother to ever hurt him, fell easily. His sapphire eyes looked up at Viggo with confusion. They were both feeling too much all too fast. None of this was right.

Viggo watched from above as he began to beat his little brother. His precious little brother. The one creature he had sworn to protect above all others. The baby his mother had trusted him to hold, only after promising to always keep him safe.

Viggo screamed at himself to stop. From the top of his lungs he was screaming and pulling at his own hair. None of it mattered. He watched as his own fist kept connecting with Raask's face. Blood was everywhere. His hands were covered in Raask's blood.

He didn't know what he was doing.

Why was he attacking him? Why couldn't he stop?

It had been so long since he lost himself to his death magic, and when his unholy blood saw the look on Mayta's face, he succumbed to the nature of the Gods. His father's power now coursed through him, unable to stop—for he was not a God. He was not designed to harness the power that coursed through his veins.

But Raask had stopped.

He stopped moving.

Viggo fell to his spiritual knees, and with it back into his body. He looked at his brother's face. Dented. Bloody. Beaten.

By him.

Viggo threw up onto the roses. This couldn't be happening. He didn't understand what had happened. He just knew that when he saw Raask hurting Mayta, he fell headfirst into a rage.

He threw up again.

The taste of bile and the salt of his tears coated his mouth and all Viggo wanted to do was go back in time. "I don't understand." He cried.

"Why did I do this?" He asked.

Viggo beat his bloody fists against the dirt. "How could I have done this?" He sobbed, holding onto his baby brother's lifeless body. Raask was supposed to be king. He was going to save them all one day.

He had killed him.

How could he have killed him? He would never hurt Raask. Never ... Something wasn't right, it wasn't him. Something had taken over.

He had always been happy to not share a bloodline with the monster that was the King of Morloks, it had never occurred to him that having the bloodline of a dark God could be worse. He was a creature of death. It rolled in his veins, and begged to come out, every second of his life. He was a master of death, and his powers came with a price. They constantly ached to bring more death. They finally won. He was too tired. Too weak. Too focused on Mayta. And he lost control.

He had killed him.

He held his sweet brother's head in his hands. Kissing his forehead and ruffling his hair. He was still warm. Soon he would be cold. His sobs were loud and violent. "I'm so sorry." He kept repeating his apologies. They were not enough. They would never be enough.

He had killed him.

"I'm so sorry, Raask."

He looked into his brilliant blue eyes, their mother's eyes, and let out a howl of despair that he was sure could be heard by his true father down in the underrealm. "I love you. I'm so sorry."

He kissed his forehead again.

"I love you. I'm so sorry."

He ran his hand through his hair again. Feeling the softness. He grabbed his hair into a fist, and smelled it. It smelled of him.

"I love you. I'm so sorry."

There was no life without Raask. There was no future for Skierka without Raask. He was shaking, cradling his baby brother in his lap like he was a babe once again.

His head, a bloody mess, was slick in Viggo's hands. He lifted it up, and lowered himself down to his ear where he whispered his last promise to the baby brother that he loved more than anyone in the entire realm. In all of the realms.

"I'll find you in the underworld, Raask."

CHAPTER 42
MAYTA

Mayta could not see or hear what had happened after the general killed the crown prince. Viggo, wielding some strange magic, encompassed himself and his brother in a dark cocoon. It did not allow for any light or sound to pass.

It gave her a moment to sort through her options.

Except, that she didn't really need a moment. She had to run, book it to the Dahs where she could go back home.

It wasn't until she had made it to the edge of the gardens that she realized that they would torture Aria for this. She'd have to get her out of here, too. It shouldn't be too hard if she went now, before Viggo came out of his cloud of darkness and warned the guards of her.

Maybe this was for the better, at least she would have her sister back.

Her feet ached as she stomped through the gardens in her delicate slippers. Her dress, a bloody and muddied disaster, gained a significant amount of weight after soaking up all of the blood. There was so much of it.

She continued to push on, begging her legs to go faster. Faster. Faster. She had to beat Viggo if she were to save herself and Aria.

A long, echoing wail of despair cut through the silence of the night.

Viggo.

She turned her head as the wail began to fade, and saw that his cocoon of darkness had shattered. Even from this great distance, she could still see Viggo holding onto Raask as if he was a small child he was putting to sleep. She saw his shoulders shaking. Even distance couldn't dampen the despair written across his face.

She couldn't turn from him. She didn't know why, but she couldn't leave him. Not like this.

By the time she came back to Viggo, it didn't look like he had noticed that she'd left, nor that she came back.

She watched as he dried his face and gently laid his brother back down onto the ground that he would soon lay beneath. Maybe she shouldn't have come back, this felt all too personal. No . . . it felt so wrong to leave Viggo, especially in a state like this. It just wasn't right.

If she wanted to beat the monstrosity of humans, she couldn't become like them. She had to be better.

Careful not to slip on the purple and red blood, she kneeled next to Viggo and placed a hand on his back. A small comfort. A pull back into reality, and away from the emotional turmoil of his mind.

"I'm sorry that you had to see that." The words came out all mangled, his vocal chords obviously destroyed from whatever screaming he had done in the barrier of his cocoon.

"It's okay."

"It's not okay."

No, it really wasn't okay. But what do you say to someone who was living the consequences of their own actions?

She wanted to ask him why he did it. She would have, if she wasn't sure that he was wondering the exact same thing.

"We need to bury the body," she said after a long while. She doubted he wanted anyone to know what he had done. Certainly he would be put to death.

"I suppose we do." He answered.

Neither of them moved.

"We need to bury the body," Mayta repeated.

This time, Viggo began to move. Mayta grabbed the prince's shoulders as Viggo grabbed his legs, and they walked. She watched Viggo walking. The tremor in his shoulders caused him to shake every so often.

They walked towards the edge of the gardens and kept going. While she could easily see and hear everything around her, the smell of rot that accompanied Viggo's powers filled her nostrils so strongly that she assumed that they were under the protection of another one of Viggo's cocoons of darkness.

The prince was growing heavy in her arms. She tried holding him in different ways, before finally settling on resting her palms under his shoulder blades, with his neck held up with the tension of her elbows.

It was by holding him in this manner that Mayta was able to feel a slight pulse from the prince's neck.

A dark understanding of what was happening began to wash over her.

It was not Prince Viggo who could claim this kill. No. It was Mayta who was responsible for the assassination of the Crown Prince of Skierka, for her poison had worked.

The Prince was now paralyzed. He was close to death, but not dead yet. The prince was conscious and aware of what was happening right now.

He must have been in a lot of pain. He must have been really scared. The realizations didn't make Mayta feel good. Killing a man didn't make her feel proud. She didn't feel like a hero at all. She didn't want to kill anyone.

But this wasn't about what she wanted.

It was about leaving behind a better world for her people.

She would become a monster if it led to a better world. If she had to.

Her tears cascaded down her face and onto the prince's. She didn't wipe them away, but instead chose to let them fall and hit him like drops of rain. For if she was about to be buried alive, it would comfort her in some way to know that the people doing it were at least crying.

They finally reached the point that Viggo decided would be where they would bury the body. She held the prince's head in her lap, as Viggo dug into the dirt with nothing but his bare hands. Her fingers played with the prince's hair in the same loving way Aria used to do when Mayta couldn't sleep. Maybe he would fall asleep and not be awake when the dirt hit him.

When Mayta was certain that Viggo wasn't looking, and couldn't hear, she whispered softly into Raask's ear. "I'm sorry that it has to end this way for you, Prince."

She paused, allowing her salty tears to fall onto the prince's lips, to wet them one last time before they grew forever dry.

The tears of a syren princess, a last taste of his family's legacy.

With gentle fingers, she opened his eyelids so he could see her as she whispered, "I want you to know that I am not happy to kill you. I think it'll change me. But it's the only way to end the Morlok's reign of terror." After she closed his eyes, she kissed his cheek. And while playing with his golden hair she added, "You Morloks didn't expect to just get away with all of your cruelties, did you?"

They were the last words Raask would hear, before being buried alive in his family's forest.

CHAPTER 43
KEL

Kel heard the screams from across his castle. He rushed to her at once, as he always did, when she cried. Sapphire eyes that had long dimmed were now red. She had collapsed onto the floor, banging her fists repeatedly on the stone.

"My love, what is it?" He asked, kneeling on the floor next to hear. He brushed her hair to the side, her once golden locks now faded into platinum.

She didn't answer. She just kept wailing.

Kel was growing more and more concerned with each passing second. "My love, what is it?" He asked again.

"Can't you feel him?" Her voice, a broken husk.

Kel was growing irritated at his own lack of knowledge. "What do you mean? Feel who? Were you attacked?"

"My boy! Can't you feel him?"

"I haven't been in my brother's realm in quite a while, you know that."

She looked up at him, cheeks bloodied from scratching herself.

And suddenly Kel understood what had broken his beloved. "I will bring his soul here at once. He can come live with us."

His words only brought more wailing. He had never seen her so distraught. It broke a piece of his immortal heart to see his beloved crying with such pure despair written across her face. He was to protect her. To make sure she never felt this way. It was his duty as her husband. He would do anything to end the pain that she was feeling. He wrapped her in a protective cocoon of darkness. Playful and strong swirls of shadows wrapped themselves around her like a womb of love.

They weren't helping.

Kel, the God of Death and Darkness and Silence and Destruction, for the first time in his immortal life, felt helpless. His beloved was broken.

Suddenly he knew how to fix it. It would anger his brothers, but he would deal with that. He would do anything for her, even betray the laws of the Gods. So he silently commanded Skullin to escort his beloved's son back to the realm of the living, back to his body.

EPILOGUE
RAASK

F ar above even the highest points of the God of Death's castle, a prince, with eyes once sapphire and hair once golden, awoke six feet under the black soil of Etra. Blessed by the God of Death and gifted with unholy air in his lungs, the prince began to climb out of his grave and crawl.

Dive deeper into the world of The Songs of Beasts.

Scan to join Samantha Gonda's Substack for series news, bonus content, and more, including *an exclusive bonus chapter.*

ACKNOWLEDGMENTS

It's overwhelming, in a lovely sort of way, to have so many people to thank.

Firstly, none of this would be possible without my parents—Rohinton and Tamara Gonda. My father is the hardest working person that I know, and everyday I am inspired by his dedication to his family and his commitment to never being anything less than exceptional. Years ago, as a young man, he flew here from India by himself to receive a double masters from the University of Pennsylvania. Everything I am and everything I have done, is because of his bravery in doing so.

My mother, naturally, is the other half of the equation. It is because of her, that I am never afraid to fail. It just means you keep trying, bird by bird. She is a brilliant artist, who could craft the most compelling landscapes out of the seemingly thin air of a white canvas. And an even better mother, for her unwavering support. She has an endless pool of creativity and I'm so thankful everyday that she gave me a little piece of it to nurture as my own.

Without Peter Gonda, I reckon none of this would be possible either. He is my older brother, my north star. I don't think that he knows how much I have looked up to him, how much I have watched his path, and tried so hard to be like him. He's the smartest person I know and the first one to ever push me to write a book. And it looks like he was right, I could do it.

Valentino Gecaj, my partner. It would be hard to write a love story without ever experiencing one, luckily, I wouldn't know. For the year that the first draft took me to write, my life was mostly working, working on this book, and working out. It was difficult, but possible because of Tino. Whenever I get overwhelmed or stuck, we go on a ride, and listen to music with the windows down. Tino always seems to know just what I need to feel better, to make me laugh, to make me feel like something more than just a workaholic. To Tino — Thank you for always believing in me. Thank you for all of the break-fasts. And thank you for being you. I can't believe we were once strangers.

And to Tino's family, Violetta and Hugh Harris, who have given me another place to call home. I appreciate every meal. Every coffee. And every second that I get to spend with them. They are two of the best people to have in your corner.

To the RED PR team, Julia Labaton and Charity Guzofski, for taking a chance on me. I couldn't ask for two greater mentors. I feel blessed everyday to work at a job that I love with a team that truly inspires me.

To Merle Bennett and Fergus Edmondson of BeRead, who I would truly be lost without! Finding BeRead was one of the biggest strokes of luck that went into this book and I am so glad that our paths crossed.

Sydney Johnson, my cheerleader and betareader. Sydney has immaculate taste in literature, film, and even baking recipes. She is encouraging, a critical reader, and a great friend.

Kevin Wittenberg, a betareader and fellow author. This book is far better thanks to his input.

Wilhelmina Asaam, my dedicated editor, who has a gift for noting all of the little details.

Lydia Blagden, my cover designer, I was thrilled when Lydia was brought on to create the cover art. She is a legend in the industry and one of the most talented people I know.

And finally... Thank *you*, dear reader. Without you, there wouldn't be much of a point to any of this. I hope that you've enjoyed this story as much as I've enjoyed telling it. And I can't wait for you to see what's next.

ABOUT THE AUTHOR

Samantha Gonda is an award winning fashion and beauty publicist. After completing her degree in Communications and minors in Italian Studies and Economics at the University of Massachusetts Amherst, Samantha briefly worked as a certified personal trainer.

Originally a New Englander, Samantha now lives in New York City where she spends her free time meticulously planning her next trip, watching horror movies, and making a mess in the kitchen.

instagram.com/authorsamanthagonda

tiktok.com/@authorsamanthagonda